DAHLIA ALMOST DROWNING

AMANDA GALE

for the women of SEEN

ALSO BY AMANDA GALE

Meredith Out of the Darkness
Meredith Against the Wind
Meredith Into the Fire
Meredith With the Waves
Love in the Lavender
Strawberry and Sage
Sweet Lavvy
Catherine and the Wind
Gwyneth in the Garden
Maeve in the Morning
The Magic You Bring

We never know how high we are
Till we are called to rise;
And then, if we are true to plan,
Our statures touch the skies.

— EMILY DICKINSON

CONTENTS

PART I
THE OCEAN

CHAPTER ONE

THIRTY YEARS AGO

"Up, and down...up, and down...up, and down..."

Dahlia's voice undulated with the waves, reaching a high pinnacle before dropping, only to pick up once more. She was enjoying the physical sensation of moving between octaves; it reinforced the sense that she was being picked up and floating downward, that she was flying.

"Up, and down...up, and down...up, and down..."

She closed her eyes against the sun, and laughed, indulging in a good splash, and licking her lips to absorb the salt. She liked to twirl her arms in the constantly moving water; it made her more aware of the ocean's power. It was the vastness that impressed her, though she was perhaps too young to understand this. It was the heaviness of it, the infinity, and as she faced the horizon now she tried to imagine it, what it would feel like, what she would see if she were to drift out forever.

She pulled her head from the water, enjoying the softness of the water sliding from her hairline down to her shoulders. A flash of orange caught her eye: Tara, her oldest sister, stomping through the waves and back onto the shore.

"Come on!" Tara called to her, her hand waving in the air, her wet auburn hair fiery drapes that framed her face. "Dad says we're leaving!"

Dahlia nodded, then held her nose and sank back into the water. She'd delay leaving as long as she could.

She was six years old, and she had been to this quiet beach in southern New Jersey many times. It was their annual family vacation; they were staying, as always, at the Sandy Dollar Hotel. Her parents and sister April were maybe twenty yards up in the sand, her parents lounging in chairs they had carried all the way from the hotel themselves, their limbs sprawled and their faces turned toward the sun, absorbing the heat that hovered in the clear blue sky. It was a small beach, with a handful of shops and food stands, and the beloved familiar sights of the boardwalk were behind them. To the left was the pier with the big rocks around it, and the biggest one, that looked like a bear; to the right was the brightly colored Bubble's Ice Cream Dream. She imagined the strawberry cone she'd get later. It was a tradition, grabbing ice cream before they lugged their belongings back to the room. She could almost taste the sweetness as she'd lick along the sides, and her tongue tingled.

She turned toward the horizon again. It was funny how the waves were constantly moving, but out there, it was one straight line.

"Up, and down...up, and down, and up—"

She was startled to find that her feet did not touch sand. Her blood tensed: her face had gone under water, and she struggled to bring it fully back into the air. Her chin lifted, and her hands and feet moved frantically back and forth. She straightened her legs and tried to push upward, but this seemed only to make it harder to stay afloat.

Even in her terror she registered the contrast of the sun on her face and the cold, heavy dark just beneath her. A wave rolled in, and her face went under; it receded, and she sucked in a breath. The ocean was humming in her ears. She fought for the light even as she was swallowed by the dark.

Mommy...Daddy...

She attempted to turn her head in their direction. The tide came, and a wave pushed her toward the beach, and for a moment, relief flooded her chest. But when the tide pulled back, she was helplessly dragged out with it, and the tiny figures on the shoreline drifted farther and farther from reach.

Help me! Help!

She lifted her hand out of the water but was instantly sucked downward. Panic seized her. It was a great knot in her stomach, weighing her down to the bottom of the sea. She was dying, she was drowning; she was sinking to the darkness below. And no one could see her, no one knew—she would disappear, she would be nowhere, consumed by black infinity. The terror transformed her, even in these last moments before vanishing into the deep.

Her head was completely submerged. Her face rose toward the sun, just barely enough for her to gasp a final breath.

And then she was fully out of the water, two firm hands beneath her arms lifting her high up into the sky. Greater than relief was the surprise she felt as she registered the space between herself and the surface of the ocean growing greater and greater by the moment.

"Don't worry, I saw you."

It was happening so fast. Her legs were dangling beneath her. She was not being held, but rather carried. She was being saved, not comforted; it was someone who didn't know her, who knew not to touch her any more than was necessary.

"It sure is choppy out there today!"

She was deposited on dry shore, just beyond the wet line kissed by the oncoming waves. The heat of the sand beneath her was so welcoming after the chilly oblivion of the ocean. Dahlia moved her fingers in the sand, in the earth. She blinked the salt out of her eyes. In her periphery was the pier with the big rocks, still immovable.

"Have fun. And be careful."

She could barely brush the hair out of her face quickly enough to catch an incomplete, fleeting image of him. From behind a blur of saltwater-hazy eyes she saw two legs, and bright blue men's swim shorts; the legs were slim and strong-looking, and they were jogging, already, out of sight. In the distance, more legs—slimmer, and out of focus. She lifted her gaze higher: he had short brown hair, and he was shirtless. He was younger than her parents. He was nearly a silhouette against the high midday sun, his face obscured by a blinding halo of light.

She stood, the sand clinging to her like a blanket. She searched for him, but he was gone.

The world had stopped spinning around her. Something terrifying had occurred, but it was extraordinary, too. She was left in awe, singled out by an angel. She was by herself in the specter of his presence.

A figure was strolling toward her: her father. As he approached, she saw that he was smiling.

"There you are," he said brightly. "We're packing up, and you know what that means. Come on, your strawberry cone is waiting."

He patted her shoulder and walked beside her up the shore, where her mother was already standing. Dahlia said nothing. She was silent as they trudged over the dune toward the boardwalk, too stunned to reveal this strange thing that had happened to her, this secret she'd shared with a stranger and with the sea.

AFTER ICE CREAM they went to the playground. Everyone moved around her as normal. Tara, skinny and gangly in her bathing suit, ran from slide to slide and hung awkwardly from monkey bars.

Her middle sister April was walking unsteadily along a balance beam, her arms out and her feet following each other in a slow, straight line. Her parents chatted on the bench, looking relaxed and easy and very much in love. Dahlia sat on the swing, by herself, taking in the scene as if from a distance. It was a familiar scene, a safe one, but not familiar at all. Something in her had changed.

"Aren't you going to swing?" her father called to her, with a kind, happy smile. "Pump your legs, kiddo! Get some height!"

But Dahlia couldn't do it. She didn't want the feeling of her feet not touching the ground. She didn't want the feeling of her stomach overturning. She wanted her feet on the ground. She wanted them on the ground for the rest of her life.

CHAPTER TWO

PRESENT DAY

*"'Twas brillig, and the slithy toves
Did gyre and gimble in the wabe;
All mimsy were the borogoves,
And the mome raths outgrabe."*

A dozen children watched her, open-mouthed, as she quietly closed the book and rested it on her lap. Dahlia smiled as she gazed at them. A few of them had started to giggle. A few of them had furrowed brows. Still more of them were watching with faces of grave alertness, awaiting answers.

"What do you think?" she asked them. "Did you like that poem?"

A couple of them laughed. "It was silly," called a little girl. "All those silly words."

"I don't get it," said a little boy. "What does it even mean?"

Dahlia shrugged. "I don't know."

This made them laugh even louder.

"But you're *supposed* to know," sounded another child's voice from the center of the group.

"Yeah, you're a grownup."

Dahlia flinched, but covered it with a smile. As much as she enjoyed story time at the bookstore she managed, she tended to forget she wasn't one of them. That she was a source of power, of authority.

But am I?

She affected a look of thoughtfulness. "Do you think we *have* to know what it means?"

A couple of the children looked at each other.

A boy raised his hand. "Um...no?"

Dahlia shook her head. "No, I don't think so."

"Why not?"

"Well," said Dahlia, "why do we read books, anyway? Why do we read poems?"

The children were stunned. No one had ever asked them this question before.

One girl braved an answer.

"To imagine."

Dahlia nodded. "That's right."

"So if we don't know what the words mean...we can use our imaginations?"

"Yes."

"But then everyone is imagining something different."

Dahlia shrugged again. "So?"

This had not occurred to the children before. Curious, perplexed glances were passed around the room.

"I think the best books are the ones that ask questions," said Dahlia. "I think whatever you imagine gives you an answer about yourself."

A dozen pairs of eyes were set on her, enraptured.

"Whoa," said one child, and everyone laughed.

After the discussion, the children scattered with their parents into various nooks and crannies of the store. The four walls of the shop echoed with the chaotic but friendly sounds of children asking questions and of parents' calm responses, of the clattering of toys and the piling of books in arms. Dahlia meandered between them, answering questions, making recommendations, and plucking requested books off shelves. She then took her position behind the register and rang up sales, the long line diminishing until only a couple of stragglers remained to browse among the shelves.

By mid-afternoon the shop was quiet. As usual, there were a handful of customers at a time, and they quietly poked about in solitude, making serious decisions, studying back covers and absorbing first paragraphs to see if the worlds within could provide whatever their hearts and souls needed at that time. Dahlia reveled in the peace. She set up some displays and straightened end tables, periodically scurrying back to the register to help buyers. Occasionally she stole a glance toward the front of the store. Crisp September sunlight illuminated the elaborate displays she'd arranged in the windows; the first leaves of autumn drifted lazily onto the sidewalks or danced over the street, propelled by the breeze. Outside, it was bright and busy, but indoors it was cheerful and subdued. Dahlia liked days like today, when there was happiness everywhere, when she could witness the excitement of the street safe and cozy within these familiar walls.

Six o'clock was closing time. Sometimes customers lingered, and Dahlia patiently waited for them to finish. She hated to disturb them; they seemed so very much at peace. She always let them have the time they needed, as she never had anywhere urgent to go, and most times, the customers didn't even realize they were keeping her there after hours.

Today, though, the store was empty. She poked her head out to make sure no one else was coming. Then she locked the door and finished up her paperwork—she'd kept the store tidy all day, and did not have much to do by way of maintenance.

She stood for a moment by the register, frowning. She'd ordered new bookmarks and originally had placed them to the left, thinking customers' eyes would catch them as they stood to the right to pay. But now that she looked at it, she saw that it was possible customers would accidentally knock them over as they handed her their payments, and she wondered if she should move them six inches further. If she did that, however, they would look awkward and alone, as if they were an afterthought. She could move them to the right, but then they would be too far out of the way. She stood staring for two or three minutes, thinking, envisioning various scenarios; there were too many mistakes to be made, too many catastrophic possibilities, and she was trying to look into the future, to make a decision based on too many unknown events. Her heart raced a little as she imagined the ruined display, piecemeal on the floor, a customer apologizing and feeling guilty and walking away very sad. Her brain worked frantically, sorting through this problem, her eyes darting between spaces, choices swimming in her mind's eye. Ultimately she kept the bookmarks where they were, but snuggled the display in tighter, and role played a few times, stretching her arm this way and that in imitation of how a customer might pay. Pleased with herself for figuring out this problem, she stepped away, admiring her work.

Finally she shut down the systems and dimmed the lights, then looked about the shop, satisfied. She stood for a moment in the silence, admiring the shop in darkness. It took on new life in the evening, the bays now silhouettes, the air tense in its stillness.

She unlocked the door to exit, then locked it behind her. Cool evening air on her cheeks and in her hair, she walked a handful of steps to another door, one overlooked by most passersby, unlocked it, stepped inside, and locked it behind her. She climbed the steep staircase toward her apartment above the shop, flipping on the light and imbuing instant life into her few small rooms. As always, she left the curtains open for an hour or two so she could watch the sun set over Main Street, sinking slowly in a halo of gold until it was invisible behind the coffee shop on the other side of the road. In a building this old, there was no overhead lighting, but the lamps that rested on mantels and end tables cast a warm glow over the cream-colored walls and hardwood floors.

In her little sitting room, she took out her phone and casually scrolled through her favorite news sources, but she closed them quickly after reading a report about an earthquake in an overseas country that had claimed hundreds of lives, including those of many children. Instead, she streamed her favorite history program, and as its comforting sounds filled her tiny apartment, she pulled her laptop from the table and waited until precisely seven o'clock to order dinner to be delivered. She frequently ordered just this meal from just this restaurant—it was a delicious chicken curry she'd never been able to replicate—and she knew it would take twenty-five minutes to arrive; by then, the last of the pedestrian traffic would have died down, and she would likely encounter no one when she opened the door to retrieve it. She was careful to ask that the driver not ring the bell, but simply place it down, and leave; the bell startled her, and the anticipation of its ringing made her sweat, and she'd have her eye on the clock, as always. When her dinner arrived, she sat happily with the container on the couch, in the warmth and protection of her own little space, the power of the books below her ever present in her thoughts.

As she lay in bed that night visions of the earthquake appeared before her closed eyelids, and she stared out into the darkness, hoping they would fade. But the blank ceiling above her was like a screen on which they could dance, and before she knew it her heart was beating faster, and she was sweating under the blankets. She imagined the ground opening, the buildings falling and the children screaming, how fearful they must have been, how they must have cried for their parents. Their pain must have been unbearable; it was unbearable even to think about. She snatched her phone from the nightstand and made a donation to a charity that provided medicine to children around the world; she was glad to have done it, but she felt no calmer. The images kept coming to her long after, and she tried to stop them; they went away only when she'd exhausted herself with worry, and had fallen into the dark relief of sleep.

THE NEXT DAY after work Dahlia locked up and, rather than walk the handful of steps to the door of her upstairs apartment, turned in the other direction and headed toward her car, which sat in a residents' parking lot around the corner. It was a gray, cool day warmed by the remnants of the summer sun, which still radiated from the asphalt and from the stone buildings. She pulled slowly out of the parking lot and down the street, heading from her artsy, bohemian Philadelphia suburb toward Brentwick, a more reserved suburb closer to the city. As she pulled around corners and registered landmarks she had seen a thousand times, her mind drifted. When she came to a stop in front of a traditional colonial house on a tree-lined street, she sat for a moment, preparing herself.

She walked not straight up toward the front steps but rather around the side, to the entrance of the newly built wheelchair ramp that ran along the house. At the front door, she rang the bell, then stepped inside without waiting for a response.

"Mom? Dad?" she said, her voice clear enough for them to hear her, but soft enough to avoid waking her father if he was asleep. "Tara?"

A middle-aged woman poked her head from around the corner of the kitchen, her wavy red hair spilling over her shoulder. Her arms were working—she appeared to be drying something with a dishtowel. "Hey, you."

Dahlia smiled and, hands in the pockets of her jacket, walked in her direction. "Hey."

She joined her oldest sister Tara in the kitchen. It was clearly a scene of recovery from dinner—spaghetti and meatballs, from the look of it. Dirty dishes sat in a pile on the counter, and bowls of side dishes sat waiting to be put away. Tara had already returned to the sink and, in her efficient way, was scrubbing a pot, her elbow jerking as her hand rotated around the bottom with a sponge.

"Grab me another towel from the closet, will you?" she said over her shoulder.

Dahlia opened the pantry door and removed a neatly folded towel from a shelf. She handed it to her sister, who brusquely dried the pot and hung it on a hook over the stove.

"Thanks," she said, now dumping the remains of the pasta into a container. "Have you eaten?"

"No, but it's fine."

"Nonsense. Sit your ass down."

Tara scooped pasta onto a fresh plate and set the plate on the table. She pulled a chair out and gestured toward it with her hand as she stepped back toward the sink.

"Sit. I command you."

"I was going to help you clean up. I feel bad that I didn't help with dinner."

"Don't feel bad. You were working."

"You've probably been on your feet all day."

"I'm used to it. Sit down."

Dahlia sighed in resignation. She knew better than to argue with Tara.

Tara faced her and leaned against the counter as she continued drying the dishes.

"He's asleep right now," she told her. "I'm sorry."

"It's fine." Dahlia closed her mouth around a forkful of pasta and chewed gratefully. She hadn't realized how hungry she was. Swallowing, she dove in for another bite. "I'm off tomorrow. I can stay late, if you need me."

"No need, but of course you're welcome to if you want to. Tom's got the girls at home. I'm here until Mom's in bed, at least."

"Does she know that?"

"Does it matter?"

Dahlia grinned over a bite of meatball.

Tara put down the serving plate she was holding and relaxed, crossing her arms. "How are you?"

"I'm fine." She reconsidered. "I'm okay." Her brow furrowed. "How are you?"

"I'm fine." Evidently deciding to take a break, Tara took a seat across from Dahlia. She closed her eyes a moment. "I'm tired."

"How about a glass of wine?"

Without waiting for a response, Dahlia stood and pulled a bottle of wine from the cabinet. She poured a generous glass of red for her sister, then held it out for her outstretched hand.

"You're an angel." Tara took a greedy sip, smacked her lips together, and smiled at her sister, a rosy flush in her cheeks. "So how are you, really?"

"I don't know." Dahlia paused to think about it. "I mean, I never know." She braced herself. "How is he?"

"Mmm." Tara took a deep breath. "He seems better today. But it's always an illusion."

"That's the worst part."

Tara took another sip of wine. "I think Mom's starting to falter a little. Like she's starting to lose it."

"What makes you say that?"

"It's just a lot on her, you know? The nurses are great, but it's hard to have strangers in your house, in your life and in your things. And she's trying to cope with her grief, and it's hard. Her patience is a little shorter today. She looks a little harried. I don't blame her."

"It must be hard for you to see Mom like that."

Tara shrugged, hiding behind a deep draw of wine. "No worries. Crisis management is my cardio. Mom and I run on crisis management the way other people run on caffeine."

Dahlia watched her sister with awe and intimidation, and also a touch of sympathy. While Dahlia and their father had a special connection, Tara had always been closest with their mother. The sharp, capable oldest sister, Tara would never outwardly acknowledge her exhaustion or her stress.

"Did April email you?" she asked, interrupting Dahlia's thoughts.

"No." In her mind Dahlia saw a flash of her middle sister's pretty face; she hadn't seen it in person in quite some time. "Why, did you hear from her?"

"Yeah, she had some info about a new drug trial. It actually sounds pretty good. She's already looked into it. She's been doing a lot of research."

"Oh." Dahlia was surprised. April lived in Connecticut with her husband, a university professor well known in his academic niche. She hadn't been around much in recent years. Her absence had been a source of contention with Tara and their mother. "Does it seem promising?"

"Honestly, it really does. Mom's already talked to the doctor. They're hoping he'll be approved."

"It certainly would be great." A simmering of worry seemed to light deep inside Dahlia. Their father had been diagnosed with ALS about two years ago. Subtle symptoms had gradually morphed into more severe impact; Edward could no longer walk independently, and on his worst days he struggled with speaking and eating. He now required full-time care, which was split between family and hired nurses. Wouldn't it be wonderful if he really could get better. Wouldn't it be good for things to go back to normal, without all this sickness, without all this fear.

She felt her heart beat faster, and swallowed the bile down.

"How are the girls?" she asked, changing the subject.

"They're fine." Tara drew a sip from her wine. "No thanks to the district."

Dahlia's eyebrows rose, and the hand she was raising to her

lips for another bite of dinner paused abruptly. "What do you mean?"

"I mean the whooping cough outbreak."

"What whooping cough outbreak?"

"Oh, you didn't hear about that? Sorry, that's why I thought you were asking."

Dahlia's heart had begun racing with alarm. "No, I didn't. What happened? Are the girls sick?"

"No, they're fine." Tara sighed. She was clearly very tired. Dahlia was sorry for making her tell the story, but she had to know if her three nieces were okay. "There was a whooping cough outbreak among some kids at school. The district let us know, but days later. It's a really long story, not super important. It was handled badly, and we were scared for a minute, but it's fine."

"Oh. Good." Dahlia frowned. Her stomach was clenching as it always did any time there was a threat to her nieces' wellbeing, even a hypothetical one. She had already begun imagining them seizing and gasping for breath, their frightened faces, their poor little bodies wasting away. Before she knew it it was already happening in her mind, and she had to deliberately focus on the room around her—the sink, the cupboard, her sister casually sipping wine—to remind herself that her mind was not reality.

"So you're sure?" she asked, grateful for once to be able to push these images aside. "The girls are okay? There's no chance they're not okay?"

"They're fine."

Motion in the doorway drew Dahlia's attention upward; Tara, noticing, turned to look. An older woman had appeared, her clothing as washed out and dark as her expression. Dahlia started: her mother had aged, even in the two days since she'd seen her last.

"By the way, Mom," said Tara, rising and clearing the table. "I forgot to mention, I brought some more of that tea you like."

"Thank you, sweetheart," said Vera, stepping forward and tucking Tara's hair behind her ear. "You're the best."

"I got you the mint this time. It's my favorite, so I thought you'd enjoy it too."

"I'm sure I will. Thank you."

"What tea?" asked Dahlia, standing to help Tara.

"That tea I bought Mom from the little shop downtown. You know what I'm talking about."

Dahlia didn't, but she didn't say so.

"Hi, Mom," she said brightly, sticking her hands in her front pockets for lack of anything else to do.

"Hi, baby," Vera said, distractedly. "Good that you're here. Late night at the store again?"

"No, I was out on time."

"He was asking for you."

"I'm sorry."

Vera nodded toward the hallway from which she'd just come. "He's up, if you want to see him."

Dahlia and Tara stood and followed her mother down the hall. When they arrived at a closed door, Dahlia turned to Vera.

"You know, Imani was thinking of bringing in some food items to the store," she said. "Maybe we can stock your tea."

"That's sweet of you. But Tara gets it for me when she's downtown. No need for you to go to any trouble."

Dahlia blushed. Should she not have intruded on this special thing between Tara and their mother? Should she stock the tea anyway, as a surprise?

"Okay," she said, unsettled. "No worries."

Tara gingerly pushed open the door. Their father was in bed, half sitting and half lying down, a comfortable smattering of pillows behind him.

"Hey," he said, taking stock of who was entering the room. His face brightened. "Look who it is!"

"Hi, Dad." Dahlia leaned down and kissed her father's head.

18

He had lost most of the thick hair that had been his signature physical attribute—people had often commented on how a man of his age was lucky to have retained such a thick head of hair. His skin looked paler, and his skin sallow—but his blue eyes were sharp, as always, his smile warm and sincere. Dahlia's heart enveloped in warmth at the sight. "How are you feeling?"

"Amazing."

Dahlia somehow doubted that, but she kept that feeling to herself. "I'm so glad. What can I get for you?" She fussed a little with his pillows and brought a blanket up from the bottom of the bed. "I'm sure Mom and Tara have been taking good care of you."

"I don't need anything, just your smiling face. You know, I was reading today that Paul Higgins has a new book coming out. Have you heard anything about it?"

"Yes, we have a box in the back. We can put it out on release day next Thursday."

"Reserve me a copy, will you, kiddo?"

"Of course." She settled into her seat at the foot of the bed, and patted her father's leg. "So what else is going on with you, Dad? Have you read anything else good lately? Any news from the shop?"

"Well, as a matter of fact," said Edward, a sly grin creeping onto his face, "I do have a little shop news. I was waiting for you to get here to mention it."

"Oh?" Tara was sitting in an armchair in the corner—their mother was opening the curtains to let in the day's last light. "Mom, are you keeping secrets?"

"It's not my secret to tell." She glanced at her husband and smiled. "Go ahead, dear."

Edward took a deep breath. "I sold the green chandelier."

Tara and Dahlia cried out in unison. Dahlia's hands were at her mouth; Tara's were in the air.

"Dad," Dahlia said, her eyes tearing. She was nearly breathless.

"That's such a big deal. The biggest. I'm so, so very happy for you."

"Thanks, kiddo," said Edward, his eyes soft and his smile kind. Dahlia listened as he launched into a story of the buyer who had purchased the chandelier. Edward was a master glassblower; he had a gallery just outside the city. He was known for his colorful, ornate pieces, for his whimsical lines and colors. The green chandelier was his pièce de résistance. He had said it was his work of greatest inspiration, and it had taken him over a year to make. The materials, complexity, and time it had entailed put it well out of most people's budget, and it had sat in the gallery for years. The sale of this piece meant not only the relaxing of financial struggles brought on by medical bills but also, a much-needed boost to Edward's confidence.

"That chandelier is my favorite of all your works," said Dahlia. "It just says so much about who you are. So much of your personality is evident in that piece." She smiled, a bit sadly. She'd sometimes dreamed of having a house big enough to display this beautiful work of art, this representation of her father. But she hadn't really expected it; she'd never come between her father and a buyer. "I'm so proud of you, but I have to admit, I'll miss it."

"That means a lot to me, kiddo, and I'll miss it, too. You're right, I put a lot of myself in to that piece. But thankfully, I'm still right here."

Dahlia stayed a couple of hours, until well after sunset. After her father fell into a fitful sleep, she sat by his bedside reading quietly while Tara and Vera engaged in quiet conversation in the living room. Eventually she rose and kissed her sleeping father's cheek, watched his face for a moment or two while indulging in a warm rush of nostalgia, and crept from the room, shutting the door behind.

As she gave her mother a kiss and prepared to leave, Tara rose. "I'll walk you out."

By the front door the sisters stopped and faced each other. Each let out a sigh, relieving stress.

"How are you?" asked Dahlia. "I mean really."

Tara crossed her arms and leaned against the doorway. "I'm fine. I mean..." A shadow seemed to cross her face, and her expression crumpled subtly, as if from behind. "I'm sad. I'm angry." Her eyes flooded with tears, but she firmed her face and helped them back. "I don't know why."

"I understand." Dahlia wanted to pat her sister's arm, in reassurance, but she refrained. "It makes sense."

"I mean I know this is life. Shitty things happen to people all the time, I get it."

"But it's never happened to our dad."

Tara frowned, and the tears she'd kept at bay spilled over. She inhaled shakily in a last desperate attempt to keep it under control. But it escaped in a blubbery burst, rather suddenly, and her older sister's uncharacteristic faltering frightened Dahlia. Without thinking, Dahlia took on the role Tara had abandoned. She leaned in and extended her arms toward her sister, who fell into them, burying her head in Dahlia's shoulder and wetting her sweater with her tears.

Dahlia stood completely still, save for the motion of her hand as she rubbed her sister's back. As Tara's shaking subsided, Dahlia rested her cheek on her head. She neatened her sister's long auburn hair, a softer, silkier version of her own. Finally, Tara calmed. She sighed, kissed Dahlia's cheek, and ran her fingers through her hair, then rubbed her face in her hands and laughed.

"Whew," she said, feigning confusion. "Not sure what that was about."

Dahlia smiled in silence as she watched her sister reclaim her usual tenaciousness.

"Anyway," said Tara. She took a breath. "What do you have going on at work?"

"Nothing." That wasn't exactly true. They had a winter kids' craft tomorrow, book club on Wednesday, and classical music night on Thursday, not to mention the local author fair that was going on all weekend. The author fair was a big deal that required days of setting up, shopping, and coordinating; the event itself was popular, so they would juggle not only an increase in the number of customers but also questions and demands of the sometimes persnickety writers. As manager, Dahlia would handle most of it. It was a busy, chaotic time, but it gave her purpose. "I mean, just the usual bookstore stuff."

"That's not nothing. Anything fun? Anything the girls would like?"

"There's a winter craft." Dahlia didn't really want to talk about it—it seemed petty after the drama of the evening. "But the girls are too old. Maybe not Celeste."

"Ginger would like it too. I'll bring them."

"Okay." Dahlia perked up a little. "It'll be good to see them."

"Okay." Tara pulled her in for a hug, and squeezed tight. She rubbed her back firmly, and Dahlia reveled in her sister's comforting touch. "You take care of yourself."

Without warning, Dahlia grew very sad, for reasons she could not explain. She and Tara pulled each other into a tight embrace, then pulled away, waved, and bid goodbye. As she walked to her car and fell into the driver's seat Dahlia had the sense that when they had comforted each other, they had physically held each other up and that if one had moved, the other would fall.

"So why don't you tell me a little bit about yourself."

"Well, I'm thirty-six." Dahlia thought it was interesting that this was the first fact about herself that came to mind, the first she apparently thought Gita should know. "I work in a bookstore. I live in a little apartment above the shop."

"Oh? That sounds charming. How do you like that?"

"I love it." Dahlia uncrossed and crossed her legs. "It's very peaceful, and quiet."

"Do you like quiet?"

"Yes."

Gita nodded and smiled. "What is it about quiet that you like?"

Dahlia thought about it. It was the kind of thing one didn't generally explain.

"I like that I can think."

Gita nodded again. "I can understand that."

"It isn't that I can't think under normal circumstances," Dahlia added; she didn't want to give Gita the wrong idea. "I don't suffer from anxiety, or anything like that."

"Hmm," said Gita. "Do you think I'd think you were suffering from anxiety?"

"That's usually what therapists like to tell people. At least, that's what I'm told."

Dahlia shifted in her seat. She'd already slipped up. This was her first therapy session; she'd never done this before. How would she know what therapists usually tell people? Why did she even think that? She had no idea what therapists liked to say. Where had she even come up with this?

"I could be wrong, though," she said, hoping it tempered her undeserved confidence. "I mean you'd know better than I would."

She had placed her purse on the couch beside her; she moved her arm toward the arm of the couch, but it was in the way. She heaved it up and placed it on her other side, but now it was between her and Gita, a barrier of sorts. It was in her line of vision, a distraction, but also, she didn't want Gita to think she was imposing a wall on purpose. She moved the purse to the floor and leaned back against the couch. But now the strap was sprawled out before her, and she didn't want anyone to trip. Granted, it was just her and Gita in the room, but someone could come in at any time. Besides, her session was an hour, and she couldn't be sure she wouldn't forget that it was there. She imagined herself standing to leave, taking a step toward the door, her foot catching in the strap, and falling forward, perhaps onto Gita's chair, perhaps onto Gita herself. Her worry went from a low simmering to a full on flame, and it was clouding her ability to think clearly. With decision, she lifted the purse from the floor and put it back on her right side—but it was in her line of vision again, and she wouldn't be able to think. Slowly, and with painful self-consciousness, she replaced it on her left, where it was originally, and folded her hands in her lap.

Gita was watching her in silence.

When Dahlia was finished, she continued.

"How is your thinking different when it's quiet and when it's loud?"

Dahlia stared at her. She didn't know how to answer that question.

"This got really philosophical really fast."

Gita laughed, and Dahlia chuckled a little, too.

"It's okay," said Gita. "You don't have to answer that, if you don't want to. I have another question, if that's okay."

"It's okay."

"What brings you into therapy?"

That was an easy one.

"My father is very sick. Maybe dying. I don't know."

Gita's face crumpled with sympathy; kindness softened her eyes. "I'm so sorry, Dahlia."

Dahlia attempted a smile to suggest it was just life, that she had accepted it, but she knew it was pathetic and weak. Besides, she clearly hadn't accepted it—she'd just told Gita that was why she was here. Her heart, which had been slumbering, seemed to awaken with a start; it did a quick, sudden turn, a dull ache left in its wake. Tears sprang to her eyes, but it wasn't an emergency—one trickled down her cheek, but she was able to contain the rest.

Gita was giving her a few moments to compose herself. Dahlia was grateful. She rubbed her lips together and sighed.

"I don't think I'm handling it any differently than I should be," she said. "This is almost preemptive, in a way. I'm sad, really sad. And scared. But that's probably normal. I'm really here because my sister thought it would be a good idea."

"I think it is normal, yes," said Gita, "though we all process grief differently. I agree with your sister, though. It's good that you're here. You admire your sister? You seem to take her advice seriously."

"Yes, Tara's amazing." A quick vision of Tara fluttered through Dahlia's head—her flowing red hair, her wide green eyes. But what stood out most was her fortitude. It was evident in her stance, in her expression. It was evident in the way she walked across the room. "I admire her a lot."

"Is Tara your older sister?"

"Yes. Well, my oldest. I have a middle sister, too, named April."

"And how is your relationship with her?"

"A little different. She lives in Connecticut with her husband and rarely comes to visit. Tara's the dependable one, the rock. She's the one who's been helping with my father."

"That must be a tough job. She must carry a lot of weight on her shoulders."

"She does. And she's got three daughters of her own, and a husband. She used to work for a pharmaceutical company, but she quit when she got pregnant. It was her choice, what she wanted. But she's smart. She's always been. Now that she's home with the kids she still makes money. She's really good at selling things on consignment. She's very...determined, you know? And all the little things add up. She's been known to flip some furniture, too. Whatever she can do from home, on social media, that kind of thing."

Gita was watching her, nodding with attention, her eyes wide.

"She sounds like a pretty special person. I don't blame you for looking up to her."

"I wouldn't want her life," said Dahlia, not really knowing why. "I just respect her for doing such a good job with it. Not that there's anything wrong with what she does," she added quickly. "It's just not for me."

Gita smiled again. Dahlia returned her smile. She didn't have anything else to say, currently, about Tara.

Gita changed the subject.

"Tell me about your job."

Dahlia shrugged. "My job is great."

"I'm glad to hear it. What do you like about it?"

"It's just so cozy in the store, and I'm in charge, so it feels like home. I manage the store for the owner, an older woman named Imani. It's her passion project, and she's wonderful. Actually, she has four stores now; they all kind of blossomed from this one. I've been there since the beginning, so she trusts me. She lets me have a lot of discretion as far as events, displays, and all that. I love books, always have. I'm a really voracious reader. I love being around books all the time. It's like..."

Gita raised her eyebrows, waiting.

Dahlia shifted in her seat again. "It's like a thousand little secrets, all around me." She flushed. "That sounds pretty stupid."

"No, not at all." Gita's face had brightened; Dahlia was encouraged. "Tell me more about that. What kinds of secrets, do you think? And why does that feel cozy?"

"Well, it's like...You know that feeling you get when you drive by someone's house at night, and the lights are on inside, and you can see all the rooms and people?"

Gita was nodding along. "Yes, I do."

"I mean no one wants to admit they look, but everybody does. There's something...voyeuristic about it. It's pretty harmless, usually—I mean if the curtains are open, clearly no one's doing anything they don't want anyone to see. But you realize, there are lives going on, and thoughts, so many individual minds working, so many needs, so many wishes and dreams. And you can't ever really know them, but you get a glimpse of them, for a second." She paused and swallowed. "That's how I feel about books. A bookshelf is a house with many windows. It's an apartment building. It's a treasure box of secrets, of other people's dreams."

Gita was wide-eyed and attentive. "That's beautiful."

Dahlia was silent. It wasn't beautiful, it was just the truth.

Gita turned serious. "Why do you think this appeals to you so much?"

Dahlia shrugged again. "I don't know. I guess I just like a good story, and I'm interested in people. But people are also exhausting. Plus, no matter what happens in books, you're safe on the outside. It's a way for you to experience things without bearing any of the consequences."

"That's interesting," said Gita. "I've heard that about horror movies. They're a way for people to cope with anxiety in a safe, controlled space."

"Right. I get that. Though I hate horror movies. They scare me."

"Me too." Gita smiled, then furrowed her brow with thought. "What kinds of things in books resonate with you?"

"Everything." Dahlia thought about her favorite books, too many to count. She had favorites for every mood, every genre; there were books she returned to time and time again, and others she cherished deeply having read only once. "It's a way to absorb trauma without the trauma. I guess there are lessons in that. But I can also experience good things, things I don't have in my life."

"Like what?"

Dahlia let a beat pass. "Like love, I guess. Like normalcy."

"Normalcy." Gita studied her. "What do you think that looks like?"

"I mean, you know. Romance, adventure. Kids, a decent job."

"But you love your job."

"Yes, my job is decent, certainly. It could be more, though."

Gita's eyebrows rose. "More how?"

"I don't know." A vague pulling in her gut. "It's a good job. Sometimes I feel..."

Gita was watching her. "Yes?"

Dahlia sighed silently. "Sometimes people see it as a crappy job, though. You know. Because it's retail."

"People like who? Anyone you know?"

"My mom, sometimes. My mom is great, and she doesn't say anything directly. It's just a sense I get, I guess. Tara's closer to her than I am."

"Why is that, do you think?"

Dahlia shrugged. "I don't know. Maybe they can relate to each other more, or something. I'm closer to my dad."

"So Tara is more like your mom, and you're more like your dad."

Inexplicably, Dahlia grew very sad. She didn't respond. Gita waited, but nothing came. Tactfully, she moved on.

"What kind of trauma?"

Dahlia's eyes turned sharp. "What do you mean?"

"You said that in books you can experience trauma without the trauma. Can you point to any examples? What kind of trauma do you take lessons from in books?"

"I don't know. Anything." She thought about it. "It can be emotional trauma, or personal demons. But I'll read anything. I've read thrillers, too, and that's fun."

"Is there anything in your own history, anything you think makes this control, this safety, more appealing?"

"Well, my dad is dying. So there's that."

"Of course." Gita's voice had quieted, and she offered a rueful smile. "I mean anything from earlier in your life."

No, was her first instinct, and she opened her mouth to say it. But she stopped.

Gita's eyebrows rose. "Dahlia?"

Out of nowhere her senses were full of the musk of the ocean, her eyes recalling the sharp sunshine of the beach. Dahlia straightened. She didn't know why she was thinking of this now.

"I almost drowned, once. I don't know if that counts."

Her heart was beating faster. She hadn't wanted to say it, but the words had been pulled with thread from her throat.

"Oh." Gita's eyes widened. "When did that happen?"

"I was six."

"That definitely counts. It must have been terrifying. I'm so sorry."

"It wasn't really that big a deal. At the time, obviously, it was scary, but I'm here, so it's okay."

"Sure." Gita took a deep breath, crossed her arms. "Where were you when it happened? Who saved you?"

"I was down at Seashell Cove Beach, with my family. I was playing in the ocean, and the riptide started to take me. It was really scary because nobody saw it happen. I legitimately thought I was going to die. I started sinking, and I remember thinking that it was my last view of the sky, that I was being pulled into forever darkness. That's when a stranger pulled me out."

"A stranger." Gita leaned back in her chair and folded her arms over her chest. "How amazing. What happened after? Were you able to talk to the person, find out their name?"

"No, I never knew who he was. He kind of plopped me onto the sand and ran away. He was nice, though. He noted how choppy the water was, like he didn't want me to feel bad. He said, 'Don't worry. I saw you.'" Dahlia paused at the memory, which always brought a tumult of warmth in her chest. "That was it."

"Oh, my God." Gita was silent for a few moments. "What did your parents say?"

"I never even told them." Dahlia laughed—she hadn't realized until that moment how strange that was. "I don't know why."

"Hmm." Another few moments of silence passed. "I wonder

how keeping this experience private all these years has affected you." She paused again. "What do you think?"

Dahlia shrugged. "I don't know. I never really thought about it." She narrowed her eyes, considering. "I mean...it was genuinely scary. It's like one minute I was safe and innocent, and the next, I was seeing the vastness of the universe. Or something." She laughed nervously. "But I hate to psychoanalyze myself."

"I understand that." Gita was watching her. "Strange question," she said, swiveling in her chair a little. "What would you say your life is like? How would you characterize it?"

Dahlia blinked. "I mean, I guess it's good. It's quiet."

"I know you like quiet." Gita smiled. "It's a pretty safe life, would you say?"

"Safe?" Dahlia didn't know where this was going. The air in the room had become a little more tense. She didn't know why, but she didn't like it. "I guess it's safe. As safe as life can be." Her eyes sharpened. "Why do you ask?"

"No reason. I'm really just musing. But I do think it's interesting because an experience like that will change you, quite a bit. It's traumatizing."

"I don't know about that. I have an amazing life. I love my job and my apartment. I have great relationships with my family." Why did she feel like she was defending herself? When did this turn into an accusation? "I'm a completely competent and capable adult. I mean," she added, realizing that she'd sounded confrontational, and not wanting to offend, "I'm not saying you're saying I'm not. I didn't mean for it to come out like that."

"Absolutely, I get it." Gita gestured warmly with her hands, perhaps in something of apology. "I certainly didn't mean to suggest you weren't competent and capable. It's just that experiences such as yours can cause long-lasting effects, even if we don't realize it. How can they not? They open our eyes to our mortality, to our smallness. I'd think that would be really tough on a kid."

"Sure. Okay."

Gita raised her eyebrows. "Do you disagree?"

"Not in theory."

Gita studied her but said nothing. In the silence, Dahlia lost control of the forces that usually suppressed the constant suspense that lived in her chest. They were like hands that grasped it tight, hands that she shoved under the surface. She was actively wrestling to submerge them once again and hoped her efforts were not visible on her face. The simmering tension inside her rose a little once more.

"Do you ever think about him?" asked Gita then. "About the man who saved you?"

A soft flutter in her chest. "Of course."

"What do you think about?"

Dahlia thought about him right now, as she had a thousand times over the last thirty years. It was always the same vision: a young man in a halo of light, with a tousle of hair, and strong, warm hands. An enchanting smile, a comforting voice. A man who was her secret—a man who was her savior.

"I think about how good a person he is," she said, "and how I hope he's had a good life."

Up, and down...up, and down...up, and down...

Dahlia was at the beach, swimming in the ocean like she used to when she was six, only she was all grown up. As she bopped up and down, her toes just touching the soft sand beneath, it occurred to her that she hadn't set up the Terry Yang display yet, and people would be expecting it tomorrow. A tumult of panic overtook her. Then she laughed. No, they would not be expecting it tomorrow—the book did not come out until next week. It was the delivery she had to prepare for, not the release. She couldn't wait to read Yang's new book—it was very highly anticipated, and her first book was marvelous.

Maybe she'd run a book club about it. She'd have to talk to Imani.

All at once, the sky turned black; without warning, she was overwhelmed by a wave that curved over her head and engulfed her. She was one with the sea. However, she had revisited this scene many times and, despite an initial, reflexive rush of adrenaline, she did not panic. She knew the sea would expel her, in its way. She didn't see him, but she knew he was there; his hands protected her, his soft voice resonated in her soul. Now that he was there, the air changed around her. She let the tide push her forward, arching her back with its force.

Thank you, she told him in her mind. *Thank you.*

She was on the beach, but the darkness had not left her. She was alive, but she had given herself to the water. She looked down at herself and marveled at her own appearance: her skin was inky like the water, and seaweed was growing from her hair. Far away, her family was watching. They saw her, but they didn't see how she had changed.

CHAPTER THREE

Brilliant, thought Dahlia, staring at the final page for a moment before closing the book. She held the book in her hands for a moment or two, not yet ready to unburden herself of its weight. Once she did, it would be over. *Unbelievable.*

She looked at the book in silence, immune to the ruckus of the shop around her. The text on the cover seemed to rise into the air, burning its impression into her eyes. *The Night Flower. Terry Yang.* She wanted to savor it, to remember the moment, just as she remembered the moment when she'd first opened the box. The sound of the blade slicing through the seam, the smell of cardboard and paper that had wafted toward her nostrils—the brief anticipation as she pulled away the paper, and then, there it was, the treasure itself. She'd pulled it with care from its wrapping, aware that hers were the first hands to hold it. She'd brushed the cover with her fingers. It was flawless as an infant's skin, and as soft. It was a swirl of purples and blues; the text was orange, bold and unapologetic. She lifted the cover; despite her tenderness, the spine creaked in its newness. She flipped the pages reverently with her fingers. Though the pages were freshly printed, the scent was ancient, familiar, sage.

She hugged the book to her chest, acknowledging its heft and all the secrets inside. Then she set it aside for later. It hadn't officially been released, but she could start reading and pay for it when it was. Imani had already approved it; it had almost been understood. She knew how Dahlia looked forward to it, and she was kind.

Dahlia had taken it home that night and read more than half of it. She'd stayed up way too late and had had to force herself to put it aside until tomorrow. She'd read a few pages here and there during work—on her lunch break, in between customers, after finishing tasks. About an hour before closing, she'd finished it. Usually she preferred to read special books in the privacy of her little upstairs apartment. But this one wouldn't wait.

She sighed, a mixture of satisfaction and sadness. That was the thing about a special book, it was always so painful to wrench yourself back toward real life. It was another dimension in which anything was possible; even in its tragedies, it was unlimited and interesting. It was often far preferable to the world that actually was. It hurt to know it was temporary, that despite the visions the words brought forth one could never really be there, could never really stay. All you could do was take the lessons with you, and bring them into the next world.

The bell over the door tinkled, pulling her from her thoughts. A burst of cool autumn air swept in with a customer. Dahlia turned her head, catching a glimpse of twirling leaves thrown into a tumult by the movement of the door. She placed the book on the little shelf beside her, leaving her hand on the cover for a second longer than necessary. Then she made herself smile and stepped out from behind the counter, forcing reality, forcing normalcy.

~

"You've outdone yourself this time, Dahlia."

"Thank you so much. I'm so glad you like it."

"It's so original and creative. How did you come up with the idea for this?"

"Oh, I don't know. It just came to me, I guess."

Imani crossed her arms and walked slowly around the display table, nodding, assessing. She pointed. "This is particularly good."

She was referring to the rainbow that arched from one side to the other, the one Dahlia had made herself using copper wire and tissue paper flowers she'd been fashioning in her apartment for weeks. With the variously sized stacks of books and the lavender table cloths layered unevenly so as to achieve a rippled effect, it all came together to give the appearance of a magical city on a cloud.

Imani stared for a moment in reverential silence, then looked at her. "It's incredible."

Dahlia smiled. "Thank you."

"The kids are going to love it," said Imani. "So is the Association."

"I hope so." It was a table of books with unicorn themes. It also held stationery, diaries, stickers, and cases of glittery pens. Dahlia had spent a little extra time constructing it because it wasn't only for customers—it was meant to impress members of the Morlin County Independent Bookstore Association, who were gathering at the store that evening for a soiree of sorts. Imani had asked her to be there. "I really liked putting this one together."

"What is your inspiration, Dahlia? I never would have known this was possible."

"I don't know." She wasn't being modest: the ideas entered her brain like waves slid onto the sand during low tide—smoothly, calmly, quietly, inevitably. "I just enjoy it. Honestly, it's nothing."

"It's outstanding."

"That's really nice of you, Imani. Really, though, it's fun for me."

The doorbell tinkled, and they looked over: it was a couple of mothers with young children. They looked around upon entering. One of the children spotted the table, then another, then another. Instantly, their eyes widened, and they glided toward the display as if involuntarily.

"Mommy, look!"

"Look at the rainbow! It's so pretty!"

"So many sparkles!"

Dahlia and Imani smiled as the children oohed and aahed. Imani welcomed the customers and chatted a moment with the awestruck children, then stepped aside to give them room to wander. Imani motioned for Dahlia to follow her to the register. She leaned against the countertop, arms crossed, her weight on one hip.

"So," she said, her voice warm, and leaning in intimately. "I have a little opportunity for you."

Dahlia's heartbeat picked up speed. She loved these little side chats with Imani. She loved the conferring and the whispers. They were like little secrets, and a bookstore should have secrets. Dahlia had been working here for almost fifteen years, ever since she graduated college, and she'd moved her way all the way up to manager. She knew all the store's secrets. The only one who new them as well was Imani herself, and sometimes, Dahlia even thought she herself knew them more. Imani was something of a local hero. She was involved in all the committees, she was on all the boards; she was active in all the charities, and had even dabbled in local politics. She could do all this because she could trust Dahlia, and Dahlia knew this. She was proud that she could support such a power force as Imani.

"That sounds interesting," she said, eager to hear about the next display table or event idea. "What did you have in mind?"

"There's a conference for independent bookstores, specifically related to the children's book industry. I've long thought I'd like to step up our children's programming. All the leaders of the industry will be there, and there are going to be workshops and discussions, all sorts of things. I think it would be good for us. I'd like you to attend with me."

Dahlia raised her eyebrows. "That sounds amazing. Sure, I'd love to go. Where is it?"

"Los Angeles."

Dahlia's eyes widened. "Oh. Los Angeles? Oh, okay. Los Angeles."

"I'll pay all your expenses, of course. Airfare, everything. So don't worry about any of that."

"Oh, okay. Thank you. Okay." She swallowed, and tried to silently take a deep breath. Her heart had begun pounding, and heat had crept up her neck into her cheeks. The low simmering had turned up to a scorching blue flame. "I don't know, though. Los Angeles."

"Is that a problem?"

Dahlia frowned. She had never pushed back against Imani, had never told her no. She was the perfect employee, dependable and hard-working and compliant. She took pride in her work, in her dedication, in the fact that Imani could trust her. In an instant, everything had changed.

Her throat was dry. "Los Angeles," she croaked, and swallowed. She was trying to remain calm, to allow herself time to absorb, but she was sure her hesitation was clear on her face. "It's just a little far."

"I know," said Imani—there was kindness in her face, but also staunchness. It was the combination that had served her so well, that had helped elevate her to the success that she was. "It is far. But you can do it."

"Who would manage the store?"

"Marilyn's already agreed to sub in," she said promptly, referring to her long-time, retired friend who loved the store and sometimes came in to help out. "She's looking forward to it. You know how she is. And George and Alana will pick up some shifts."

Dahlia attempted a weak smile. Inside, a sinking sensation was pulling her gut to the floor. Her heart raced as she imagined it—finding her way in a city she didn't know, mingling with strangers, keeping a hold on her wits in what was sure to be a big crowd. And the flight! Dahlia had never been on an airplane before. She had never even driven out of state.

"We can talk about it," said Imani, with a squeeze of Dahlia's arm. "It's not until the spring. Plenty of time to prepare."

Dahlia saw for the first time how superficially Imani seemed to know her; she felt suddenly alone and isolated, but she was too frazzled to care. All she knew was that she was suddenly in an impossible situation, with an impossible choice.

"Okay," she whispered. She smiled more earnestly. "Okay, that sounds good. Thanks."

Imani stepped away to answer her phone. Dahlia stood frozen, the sinking in her stomach dissipating, leaving behind the sick heaviness of dread. And it wasn't just that she had a choice to make, to retain her impeccable work record or put herself in the path of this excruciating task. It was that regardless of which decision she made, she would have to reveal herself—that the real Dahlia would be forced from the shadows, the one who was always afraid, the one who was always drowning.

DAHLIA STOOD SMILING at the periphery of a large group of well-dressed, laughing bookstore owners. Everyone was holding a glass of wine, Dahlia included. She didn't drink often. She didn't dislike it, but she didn't particularly enjoy it, either. Nor did she often have a need. Usually at the end of a day she retreated to the safe familiarity of her tiny upstairs apartment. Tonight she found herself mingling with brash, confident entrepreneurs, mustering her energy to pretend to be confident, too—it was masking, of a sort, hiding the fact that she wasn't outgoing, that she wasn't comfortable, that she wasn't them.

She sipped her wine, not ungrateful for the dull numbing sensation that followed. She nodded and laughed when they did, playing the game, and not particularly badly. The jokes were funny, but not so funny to require this much laughter. She wondered what it was about her that made her see things so differently.

"And you're the beating heart here," said Trixie, a tall woman with a tightly pulled ponytail and round, bold glasses. She held out her hand in invitation for Dahlia respond—a long-fingered, well manicured hand, slender and fine in a perfectly pressed beige sleeve.

Dahlia straightened and refreshed her smile, in an instant shifting into the center of attention. She contrasted the owners' slick, sophisticated clothing with her own dingy cardigan and slacks, and wished she'd thought more about what to wear tonight.

"That's so kind of you, but no." She smiled more widely and turned to Imani, who was standing by her side. Imani must have talked about her earlier. She knew Imani had meant what she had said, but Imani always overestimated what it took to run the store. "I just work here. Imani is the heart of this place, the inspiration."

"I told you she was way too modest," said Imani, with her buoyant, hearty laugh. Everyone laughed with her, and smiled all around. Imani slinked her arm around Dahlia's back and hugged her in close. "This store could not survive without Dahlia. She's a master. She came up with every display you see."

"That's so nice of you." Dahlia wondered why she couldn't come up with something better to say than that. She'd repeated almost exactly the same comment she'd just made. She was worried they'd think she was feeding them lines, that she didn't actually appreciate the nice sentiments, which she did. She tried to compensate by adding more. "Imani is absolutely the best boss I could ask for. I mean I do the physical work, but she inspires me to do it. She gives this place its energy. She creates a space where creativity flows. She has a magnetic personality, as you can see." She'd meant it all, of course. But now she'd overdone it. It was true, but it sounded like flattery. Now she worried they'd think she was insincere, and that it would reflect poorly on Imani. In trying to praise her, she'd insulted her.

A cold sweat broke through her pores, and her heartbeat picked up speed. She really liked Imani. Why couldn't she get her words right? Why couldn't she show admiration without getting it all twisted? Why couldn't she engage in conversation? Why couldn't she be normal?

"Dahlia," said Allan, an owner of a store in Philadelphia, "you should join us at the conference in Los Angeles. You wouldn't believe the brainpower in that room. You always learn something. And I know they'd appreciate your insights."

An enthusiastic uproar of agreement followed. Dahlia's stomach contracted, rendering her breathless.

"Oh, she's going." Imani gripped her tighter. "We talked about it just this afternoon, didn't we, Dahlia? It's going to be a blast. I'm psyched."

"You could even run a seminar," Gretchen, another owner, chimed in. "They get dozens, sometimes hundreds of attendees."

"Great idea," said Allan. "What you do is, you go on the website and you submit your idea. They'll ask you to put a pitch together, and you'll do the interview virtually. If they accept you, you get a whole hour. They'll put you in the program, and people will sign up."

"You'd be amazing." This from Patrice, who'd traveled nearly an hour to be there. "It's usually stuffy owners, like us," she added with a chuckle, and everyone laughed around her. "It would be nice to get another perspective. It would liven it up, don't you think?"

Dahlia didn't know these people. It was nice that they had this faith in her. But also, they were wrong. She didn't know why they felt they could predict how she'd perform. She opened her mouth, but no sound came out. She couldn't think quickly enough, couldn't meet them in their excitement. She felt small and exposed, and she swallowed against the familiar rush of an oncoming episode of panic.

"Dahlia, what is your email?" Patrice was pulling her phone from her purse. "I'm going to send you the information. I'll give you my number, too. I want to be in touch about this. We need to discuss your pitch."

"Email her at the store." Imani took a sip of wine and smiled brilliantly. "Better yet, come by tomorrow."

"I'm heading home at noon. Dahlia, how about coffee at eleven?"

"Done," said Imani. "I'll make sure Dahlia is free."

"Oh." Dahlia nervously brushed some hair out of her face as Patrice took out her phone to record her email address, as given to her by Imani. She noticed her hand was shaking, and promptly returned it to her side, but then didn't know what to do with it and so brushed some nonexistent hair away again. She was sweating profusely now, and the rapidness of her heartbeat was making it hard to breathe. She looked around, trying to take note of whether the party was winding down. Abruptly, she had met her threshold, and all she wanted to do was hurry next door to her apartment and retreat into some blankets.

"Let's go to Fila's," cried John, the owner of a store the next town over. He was referring to a bar with a happening social scene; late-night stragglers awaiting ride shares often woke Dahlia at midnight when the bar closed its doors. "It's only a couple of blocks."

"I shouldn't, but I will," said Trixie, and everyone laughed.

"I'm having too nice a time with all of you. You're my people. Who needs sleep, anyway?"

The group enthusiastically agreed. As they prepared to move the party to the bar, Dahlia found herself beginning to float above her own body. There was danger, but she didn't know what it was; it was a kind of vacuum, a vague sense of breaking rules and of being vulnerable that triggered an almost animalistic urgency to flee.

They were talking all around her, their smiles in ominous juxtaposition with her own oncoming terror. Something was sitting on her chest. She inhaled, but the air wouldn't fill her lungs.

"Dahlia," said Imani, shrugging into her coat, "don't worry about the mess. The cleaners are coming tomorrow."

Dahlia nodded, distracted, and falling even deeper into the vortex of despair. The cleaner wouldn't know how to arrange things. There would be books misshelved, items out of place. She'd have to fix it before customers came in or everything would be wrong.

Imani was tugging at her sleeve. Dahlia was rooted to her spot. In addition to being afraid she was also now angry, pressed under the necessity of thinking quickly, of adjusting to the change of plans, of having to come up with an excuse to avoid it.

"No," she said, because it was happening and she had to say something, and it was the one word she knew that would stop these developments in their tracks. "No," she said again, managing a smile, and more calmly. "Imani, you go. Everyone go. I should get home."

"But why, honey? Come on and have some fun."

"I'd like to come in early tomorrow with the cleaners to make sure everything gets done."

"No need. They'll be fine, and if they aren't, it'll still be fine."

"No, Imani, really. I should go home. I'm not an owner." This flash of inspiration struck her, and her heart lightened somewhat now that she had something tangible to cling to. "You should spend time with fellow owners." Dahlia smiled more sweetly, hoping to affect the appearance of nonchalance. But even she could feel the desperation in the wideness of her eyes, the crumpled rise of her brow.

Imani studied her a moment. The two locked gazes, and in that moment Dahlia feared Imani was seeing something in her, something she hadn't seen before, something that would make her feel differently about her tomorrow.

But Imani simply returned her smile. She patted her arm and leaned in to kiss her cheek.

"If you're sure," she said, and briefly Dahlia worried she was going to offer to walk her home. Before she could stop it, she imagined her graceful, elegant boss in her shabby upstairs apartment. Imani picked up her purse and looked at Dahlia from underneath the rims of her glasses. "Do you mind locking up after us?"

"Not at all."

"Take whatever leftover food you want. There's not much left, just leave it."

"Great. Thank you."

"You threw a good party. I appreciate you, Dahlia."

Imani kissed her again and headed out in a blur of well-dressed academics. The room emptied, the boisterous laughter and chatter growing fainter as it drifted through the open door into the wind, and Dahlia allowed herself to exhale. Her heart was still racing, but not aching; the cool breeze soothed her where sweat was shining on her skin. The door closed, and she was alone. She stood for a moment, quite still, listening to the silence, watching the emptiness like it was a lover finally returned. She rubbed her face in her hands, pulled her hair back from her misty forehead. Then she glanced about the store, slowly reentering the world outside her own mind.

The owners had left it nearly as neat as they had found it.

They'd diligently placed their plates and napkins in the trash, had stacked empty trays for easier cleanup, had even intuited which stacks of books Dahlia had moved for their convenience and replaced them where they belonged. A grin pursed her lips and slowly curled up the corners of her mouth. They'd been very tidy, of course they had. They knew where things went. They knew how important it was for every treasure to be in its place.

As Dahlia assessed the remaining food she recognized the familiar tug of encroaching guilt. She didn't know why she had been so angry. Nobody had done anything wrong. They were nice people; they were just trying to help. They'd looked after her, inviting her out and complimenting her and insisting people wanted to hear what she had to say. They'd helped her clean the shop, without being asked, had taken it upon themselves to anticipate what she'd need to do herself.

There was some crudite left, some cookies, a couple of sandwiches. Dahlia wrapped most of the cookies in plastic, saving one for herself; she left these in the breakroom for Imani the next day. The sandwiches and crudite she dropped into a freezer bag to bring home. It was silly to leave the sandwiches, barely enough for a meal. And no one would want the crudite.

Dahlia straightened up as best she could, taking out the trash and moving the tables back to where they were. The cleaners wouldn't have much to do. She'd leave for them the vacuuming, the dusting, the wiping surfaces down. But she could go to sleep knowing her books were okay.

She turned out the lights and took a final look, then walked outside into the chilly air, locking the door behind her.

It was darker than when she usually left, and quieter. The streetlights cast cones of light across the sidewalk; she watched as her feet stepped in and out of shadows. She unlocked her door quickly and shuffled up the stairs, the pressure leaving her chest as she climbed higher and higher into the darkness. Toward the top she registered the comforting scent of her apartment—the wood floors, the books, the candles she left open to release the fragrances of rose and ginger and jasmine.

Once inside, she shut the door and fell onto her couch, pulled a blanket over her knees and sat there, gazing out into the night.

It hurt her because she felt warmly toward good people. She was afraid of them, but she didn't dislike them. She respected them, she admired them—she appreciated that they made the world a better place. Tears sprang to her eyes as she imagined them, straightening her piles, reading her mind—doing little things, unnoticed and unacknowledged, just because they wanted to, just because they could. Dahlia wished she had been more thorough in her conversation, just to show them that she cared. She feared she would die one day without their knowing, without understanding that she'd seen them and that they'd touched her in some way.

She knew she wasn't a bad person. Then why did she never, ever feel free? It was a cycle, and she knew it, and she knew she'd regret it for days. It would haunt her, keep her up at night, the way she could have given something back, and didn't.

Every time this happened, Dahlia swore she wouldn't let it happen again. But it would be one more thing she'd fall asleep thinking about, one more weakness, one more failure, one more display of selfishness.

Dahlia made herself a cup of tea within the safe confines of her kitchen, then sat for a while in the living room, reading. The artificial light reflected on the cream-colored walls was brazen and bright, and it cheered her. Warmed by the tea, the tension in her belly unloosened, she escaped for a bit into a magical world of fantasy, with fairies and queens and cottages built into mountains. Later, in her pajamas, she lay in bed reliving the events of the evening, which filtered through her mind like leaves drifting downward in a stream. She fell asleep beneath the stars twinkling from the other side of the open curtain, and dreamed of fairy worlds, far from parties and stress and conversation.

"WONDERFUL." Dahlia's father reached for the package she held to him; she'd wrapped it in tasteful plaid paper, but she knew he knew what it was. He chuckled as he quickly pulled back his arm to allow for Dahlia's niece Celeste, age six, to run by: she was fleeing Ginger, age eleven, who was chasing her in an attempt to help her tie her shoe.

Tara looked up from the laundry she was folding and gave them a stern look as they ran out the door. "Girls, girls, be careful, my God."

"They're fine," said Dahlia. "Dad likes it."

"I do," confirmed Edward. "Who wouldn't?"

Ginger reappeared in the doorway, frowning.

"I can't catch her," she complained to her mother. "She's too quick."

"She's going to hurt herself," said Tara. "Celeste," she called, "come here."

"Ginger," whispered Dahlia, gesturing with her finger for Ginger to approach. A grin touched Ginger's face as she met her aunt's gaze. She took stealthy steps into the room while Tara was distracted calling her little sister.

Dahlia leaned down to whisper into her ear. "Tell Celeste I have a surprise. That'll make her come."

Ginger nodded and rushed from the room. Moments later, Celeste reappeared in the doorway. Her eyes were wide with expectation. Dahlia smiled wryly and crooked her finger, prompting the little girl to step inside.

"Celeste," she said, her voice low and deep, suggesting a secret. "Guess what. I got you a present."

"What is it?"

Dahlia's eyes darted to Ginger, who immediately understood. The perceptive middle sister sidled into the room and was almost immediately at her little sister's side, then crouching on the floor to tie her shoe, completely unnoticed by Celeste, who was enraptured by the knowledge that a present was coming imminently.

Dahlia reached for her purse, which was resting on the floor in the corner of the room, her mind frantically going over the contents. She dug inside for a few moments, until her fingers grasped a pen. Dahlia with effort hid her relief. She'd swiped this pen by accident earlier in the day—she'd just ordered them for the shop, and it was a sample she'd meant to leave on the counter but had dropped with her keys into her bag instead.

With a burst of triumph, she pulled the pen from her purse and held it for Celeste to see.

Celeste's brown eyes grew even rounder, and her jaw dropped.

"Wow," she whispered, fingers extended. Her gaze met Dahlia's. "I can have this?"

"You certainly can," said Dahlia, and released the pen into her niece's tiny hand. "It's for you."

Celeste held the pen before her with awe. It was gold, with a working miniature snow globe on top. Inside the snow globe was a tiny replica of the Philadelphia Museum of Art. Celeste gave the pen a little shake. Snow whirled inside the enclosed little universe, falling in dancing circles and drifting toward the ground.

Celeste stared at it, entranced. She blinked a few times, and she smiled.

"It was nice of Aunt Dahlia to bring you a present," said Tara. "What do you say?"

"Thank you." Celeste lifted her gaze and met her aunt's eyes. "It's so pretty."

Dahlia leaned down and kissed the little girl's nose. "Just like you."

Ginger rose from the floor, a wicked grin spread over her lips. Celeste looked at her. Her face straightened, and she shrugged.

"I'll have to bring presents now for the two of you," Dahlia told her older two nieces, as Celeste wandered from the room, calmer now, presumably to use her new pen. "It was lucky I had that with me." She paused, and turned to Ginger. "It just occurred to me she doesn't have any paper. Someone may want to make sure she doesn't…"

"I'll go after her." Ginger sighed the sigh of the older sibling who was used to being responsible. She turned to leave.

"Hey, Ginger," said Dahlia, and Ginger turned back around. "I'll make it up to you. Maybe we'll go for ice cream? Maybe this weekend?"

"Okay." Ginger's face brightened. "But I don't mind."

She walked from the room. Tara's eyes followed her, momentarily distracted from her exhaustion, and warm with affection.

Dahlia handed her father the package once more. He took it in his hand, but his fingers weren't strong enough to hold it. He dropped it, and it fell to the floor.

"Oh," he said, trying to reach down, but it was clear he was having trouble moving. "I'm sorry."

"It's okay." Dahlia bent to pick up the book, grateful for a moment to recompose her face. This was new. Did it mean he was getting worse? Were they moving into the next stage? She smiled upon rising, trying to hide her unease. "It happens."

She removed the wrapping paper and placed it on his lap. He opened the cover, but his thumb couldn't grip the pages quite enough to flip them.

"Just as well," he said, in a clear attempt to be lighthearted. "I know once I open it, I won't stop until I finish it."

"I guess you're right." He was making a joke of it, but she wasn't ready to joke. Now that she looked at him she saw his cheeks looked a little hollow, his complexion a little pale. Was he not eating? She'd have to ask Tara.

She attempted another smile. "Technically it isn't even out yet. It comes out tomorrow. But I won't be here at midnight, so…"

"So I've got an early peek." He brushed the cover lightly with his fingertips. He closed his eyes a moment, almost imperceptibly —it was the same look Dahlia herself had when taking in a new book in through her senses. He opened his eyes and looked at her. The corner of his mouth turned upward with a sly, mischievous grin. "So are we breaking the law?"

"Maybe a little," said Dahlia, folding the wrapping paper and placing it gently in the wastepaper basket. "Don't tell Imani."

"You two and your books," said Tara. "And this one. She's from your side."

She stepped to the side to reveal a chair. In the chair was Evelyn, age fourteen. Quiet-looking and bespectacled, she was curled up in a little ball, and in her hands was a thick, well-used paperback. She'd been holding the book in front of her face; upon sensing that people were looking at her, she lowered the book and smiled sheepishly.

Tara fell into an armchair in the corner, crossing her legs and leaning back with her head resting in her hand. "I used to read. I should start to read again. What's that one about, anyway? Do you think I would like it?"

"It's a thriller." Dahlia took a chair on the opposite side of the bed and sat watching her father flip through. A pile of clothes had fallen out of the laundry basket Tara had placed on the floor; Dahlia reached over and put it back on top, tidying a couple of items that had come unfolded. "Higgins started out with straight mysteries. But he's gone between genres a number of times."

"So what is it, then? Drug deals? High speed chases?"

"More like political secrets, assassinations."

"Oh. Well, no thanks. I've got enough drama as is."

Vera stepped inside, carrying a tray table with a bowl of soup and a glass of water. "Drama?" she asked, gingerly placing the tray over Edward's lap. "What now? The good kind or the bad kind?"

"No kind. I was just telling Dad and Dahlia that I'll stay away from that book she brought him. Not that I have time to read anyway. A shame, really, as I used to read all the time."

"There's always time to read." Edward lay the book down beside him and lifted his chin to accept a kiss from his wife, who stepped to the side; Dahlia rose to give up her seat, but Vera patted her shoulder, insisting she sit. "Reading is thinking. And thinking should be a priority, especially these days."

"I thought reading was supposed to be an escape."

"That, too."

"Your father will have that read by morning." Vera leaned against the dresser at the front of the room, her arms crossed and her weight on one hip. "Have you read it, dear? I'm sure he'll want to talk about it."

"I haven't read it, no." Dahlia thought of the fantasy novel with the bookmark stuck halfway through; it was sitting on her nightstand, waiting for her. "Thrillers aren't really my thing."

"We should do a book swap," said Edward, lifting the handle of the spoon from the bowl, then laying it back down. "You read one of mine, I read one of yours. We can discuss each other's genres. You come, too," he added, turning to Evelyn. "Wouldn't that be fun?"

Evelyn lowered the book and looked at her grandfather over the rims of her glasses. "Should we rotate? One person chooses each month?"

"Month," protested Dahlia, scrunching her brow with horror. "How about *week*?"

"Okay." Evelyn smiled, her eyes widening with hope and innocence. She appeared lit with sunshine. Dahlia's heart squeezed with warmth.

"Dad," she said gently. "Eat your soup."

He looked at the soup with a grimace, and leaned back against his pillow. "Honestly, kiddo, I'm not that hungry."

"Can I help you with the spoon?"

"That's not it. I'm just not hungry."

His words had become more slurred. Dahlia removed the tray from his lap and placed it on a nearby table. She was suddenly very stressed. She supposed his decrease in appetite was something that had happened gradually, something she hadn't noticed. It was one more sign that things were growing more dire, that they were headed, like it or not, into the unknown.

At one point Edward sent Vera from the room to fetch something.

"Thanks, my love," he said to her as she reentered the room. She reached over Dahlia's head to hand something to Edward—looking closely, Dahlia saw that it was a little green bowl. He examined it a moment, then held it out to Dahlia. "Look what I found. It's for you."

"Really?" Dahlia reached out and took it, and held it in the palm of her hand. It was green, with her father's trademark gray swirls. The edges, though, were curved, almost scalloped, which was unusual for him. She looked at him. "It's gorgeous. What is this for?"

"I know that green chandelier was special to you," he said. "You liked it, always have. This green bowl was going to be part of it. I've been going through my inventory, and I thought you might like to have it."

"Oh my gosh, thank you. I love it." A lump materialized in her throat, and her voice caught. The cozy warmth of affection encased her: he really knew her so well. And though it hadn't been said, she knew why he'd been organizing his old work, and why he was giving it away. She knew it, but wouldn't think it, wouldn't let herself go down that path. Everything today had so much meaning. She was exhausted. She was ready for some simplicity, ready for the comfort of her room.

The conversation drifted here and there for some time longer. When Dahlia stood to leave, her father called her and Tara over.

They stood on either side of his bed, flanking him, protecting him.

He took one of their hands in each of his, and squeezed.

"My daughters," he said, and his lips shut tight—his eyes grew misty and red, and he shook his head, overwhelmed. "And my granddaughters." Evelyn rose, resting her book on the chair, and joined them. "I just love you so much."

"And we love you." Tara leaned down and kissed his forehead, her auburn hair brushing his face. She had an air of authority, as always, but she paused a moment before rising, her expression pained. She smiled, then, though, and she was her fortified self again.

"Thank you for taking such good care of me. And my dear Vera. I'm a very lucky man."

"We're lucky to have you."

Hugs were shared, hands were held, and breaths were expelled. Dahlia, green glass bowl nuzzled carefully into her chest, waved her family goodbye; Vera and Tara made to follow her, but she insisted they remain to care for her father, assuring them she could see herself out.

"You have a lot of respect for Imani, don't you."

"Yes, I do."

"What is it about her you respect?"

"She's the strongest woman I know, other than Tara."

Gita was watching her studiously, nodding, her eyes narrowed a little with thought.

"How do you define 'strong'?"

"What do you mean?"

"Well, strong could mean a lot of things. It could mean she's persistent, that she doesn't give up, or that she's faced adversity and somehow pushed through. It could mean she's intelligent, she's accomplished, she's principled. It could mean she's fearless, or courageous, or steadfast, or even kind."

Dahlia rubbed her lips together. Imani was all those things.

"What do you think?"

Dahlia sighed and shifted in her seat. "Well, she did all this herself. The bookstores, I mean. She's also brilliant. She had a corporate job, and she left it to follow her passions. She does a little of everything."

"How so?"

"Well, she's been a commissioner, she's been on the school board. Things like that. She's an incredibly active volunteer, mentoring children and getting involved in all sorts of important causes. And now the bookstore is almost an establishment in town. It's amazing that she's done all this, like she just puts her mind to it, and it happens."

"She's independent, then."

"Well, yes. She's married, though, to a man as strong and accomplished as she is. They have three kids, though they're all grown now. I know he supported her through it. The bookstore, I mean. Obviously it was a huge risk, leaving a high-powered job and opening her own business."

"And what about Tara?"

"What about her?"

Gita shrugged. "You said Imani was the strongest person you know, other than Tara. Is Tara strong in the same ways?"

"More or less, though it's different." Dahlia didn't really know where this was going, and she was wary of saying something that would open a door she didn't want to walk through. But the question seemed innocuous enough. "Tara left a career, too. It could have been a shit job, I mean you know how medical companies are, but she did a lot of good there. She had compassion, and she made other people have compassion, too. She wasn't there to screw anybody. She was there to make sure people were heard."

"She sounds incredible." It could have been an empty statement, the kind one is obligated to make after an impassioned speech about a beloved sister, but Gita's voice was full of sincerity. "Why did she leave?"

"She had Evelyn. But she wanted to stay home with her kids.

She always knew she would do that, it wasn't like Tom forced her. Does that make any sense?"

"It makes perfect sense. Tom is her husband, I presume."

"Yes. They've been married almost twenty years."

"Do you like Tom? Her husband?"

"Tom's a good guy. I like him a lot."

"What do you like about him?"

"He's just a nice guy. He treats my sister well."

"How so?"

"He respects her. Defers to her, you know. He's romantic with her. He takes care of the kids, without calling it 'babysitting.'"

Gita laughed. "I hear you."

"He's also a good dad. He really loves the girls, and he does a lot for them. I appreciate that."

"That's understandable."

Dahlia smiled politely and nodded, not knowing what else to say.

"How about your other sister's husband? April?"

The smile on Dahlia's face straightened. "He's okay."

Gita was watching her carefully. "Really?"

Dahlia cleared her throat and shrugged. "He's just...not as warm a person. I don't know. She's been different since she's been with him. I feel like maybe he's part of the reason we don't see her."

Gita raised her eyebrows. "Oh? That sounds like it could be serious, actually."

"No, it's nothing like that," Dahlia said instinctively.

She blinked a few times. Was it, though? Was it like that?

Gita asked, "Have you talked to her about it?"

"I haven't. But my mom has, and Tara."

"And what happened?"

"It blew up. They don't talk about it anymore. We see her when we see her."

Neither said anything more, and some heavy moments passed.

Dahlia's eyes widened with panic as it occurred to her that Gita might be getting ready to ask her about her father. His decline was the reason she was there, but ironically, it was the one thing she couldn't bring herself to talk about.

Thankfully, it appeared that Gita was not going to ask her about Edward; she adjusted her position in her chair, somehow indicating the subject was about to change, too. Dahlia's relief was short-lived, however, as Gita broached the only subject she was less inclined to discuss than her father.

"How about your own romantic life, Dahlia?" Gita had softened her voice, no doubt on purpose. "You've never said anything about it. Is it something you're open to talking about?"

Dahlia's face had hardened; she attempted to smile. The simmering in her stomach, which usually hovered low enough for her to ignore, turned up a degree or two. "I mean," she said, and cleared her throat. "I mean, I guess."

Gita was staring at her, as if in expectation that she would say more. When she didn't, she smiled in encouragement. "So tell me about it."

"There's really not much to say." Dahlia's stomach turned in the same way it always did when someone asked her about her love life. Usually, it did so because she knew she was about to be judged. She knew she was an outlier, that she didn't really fit in. She had to remember she was talking to her therapist. Surely she wouldn't be judged here. That was, allegedly, the point.

She took a breath, and brushed an imaginary speck off the thigh of her pants. Immediately concerned Gita would see it for what it was—a weak attempt at false nonchalance—she furrowed her brow and looked at the couch beside her, as if seeing the speck she'd just flicked off herself. She then pretended to flick it onto the floor, but she had now gotten herself into a quandary, because she did not want Gita to think she'd throw garbage onto her floor. She leaned back in her seat as if nothing had happened, but she had a feeling her face appeared troubled.

Gita watched all this but said nothing.

"I'm not currently with anyone," said Dahlia.

"Mmm." Gita nodded, indicating, Dahlia guessed, that this was fine. "When was your last relationship?"

"Relationship?" Dahlia stared at her. "It depends how you define 'relationship.'"

"How would *you* define a relationship?"

"How would *I* define it? I guess I'd define it as two people who care about each other, or think they do, seeing each other exclusively, or maybe not. I don't judge." She swallowed. "I don't know. It's people hanging out together, wanting to be together. Being dedicated to each other."

"Fair enough. So when was your last relationship?"

"It's been a while."

"Is that by choice?"

"Choice?" Was a therapist supposed to push like this? Shouldn't she be warming her up first, or doing things on her terms? What did "choice" even mean? She supposed it was by choice. Men just didn't impress her. They were complications, distractions; they expected too much, and not enough. She was attracted to men, physically, but somehow with every man who passed out of her life she felt less and less inclined to try a new one. Maybe it was because she knew it wasn't worth it. Maybe she'd choose differently if she didn't know all this to be true.

She said, "I don't know how to answer that."

"You don't have to answer it, if you don't want to." Gita was smiling softly now, and leaning forward a little, her body language intimate and unthreatening. "It's just that you mentioned Imani's husband, and Tara's. You seem to have great respect for men who respect their partners."

Dahlia supposed that was true.

"Your father, too," Gita went on.

Dahlia nodded. "Yes."

Gita waited. Dahlia rubbed her lips together. She was thinking of him again, the one other man she respected. The mental image made his presence almost tangible. She carried him with her, faceless but beautiful, she knew. But she kept it all to herself.

"I was just curious about your own experience with men."

"I don't really have that much experience. If I'm honest."

"Have you dated?"

"Ever? I mean, yes, of course."

"How many dates do you typically go on?"

"A couple. A few. Maybe over a few weeks."

"What happens?"

"It just doesn't work out. I don't know." Dahlia was surprised by how defensive she was feeling. Her heartbeat had picked up speed, and her skin was prickling with alarm. "I haven't liked any of them enough to continue."

"That's completely fair."

Gita paused, giving Dahlia a break, or preparing her next question, or perhaps assessing where to go from here.

Dahlia threw her a bone.

"I don't enjoy my time with them."

Gita nodded. "I understand."

"It's fun at first, I guess, but they don't seem to get me. I don't get them, either. It also just gets dull."

"Dull how?"

"It just isn't stimulating." She realized how that sounded. "Intellectually. Or emotionally."

"I see."

An awkward few moments passed.

"Or physically, I guess, if that's what you were wondering."

"I wasn't wondering," said Gita, gently, "though I'm happy to talk about that, too."

"I don't necessarily want to talk about it." Dahlia could feel heat rising to her face, and scolded herself; it wasn't something that was even on her mind, and she didn't know why she had said it. Now she was blushing furiously, for no reason, and Gita would surely conclude that there was more to this than there was. "It isn't that I want to talk about it. But I also don't *not* want to talk about it. I didn't mean to suggest I was looking to talk about it. I probably phrased that all wrong."

"We don't have to talk about it, Dahlia," said Gita. "We don't have to talk about anything you don't want to talk about. I'm here for whatever you need, for whatever reason you want to be here. I'll ask probing questions when I think there's a path that might be useful to you, especially in these early stages, so I can get to know you. But you're always welcome to put the brakes on something if you don't like the direction in which we're headed." She raised her eyebrows in conciliation. "Okay?"

Dahlia exhaled and nodded.

"Now, *if* you were willing—and as I said, if you're uncomfortable, by all means, let me know"—Gita held out her hands, and put them up, in a gesture that represented, *Stop*—"I'd be interested to hear more about your encounters, where you meet people you date, and why it ends."

"I'm not uncomfortable, it's fine. And as I already said, it gets dull."

"Why do you think that is?"

"We have nothing in common, no common interests. I mean I guess we do, like I might meet a guy at the library or something, so we both like to read. But they're always so distant. It's like..." She hesitated, rubbed her lips together.

Gita smiled sweetly. "Take your time."

Dahlia's heart squeezed. When she thought about it, it really wasn't that they had no common interests. She narrowed her eyes: memories flitted through her mind like a film reel, vague and airy and random. It was something more than that, something more elusive, something more personal. She didn't know how to explain it; she didn't even understand it.

"I don't remember."

Gita paused for an almost imperceptible moment. "Okay," she

said then, her smile brightening. "We can save it for next time." She glanced at the clock. "We've got about five minutes left. Was there anything you wanted to talk about before our time is up?"

Dahlia shrugged. "Not really. It was a pretty quiet week."

"Quiet is good. How's work? Did any good books come out this week?"

"Lots. But that's normal." A subtle twinge pulled in her stomach. She hesitated, breathing more heavily; she thought about letting it go, but she was here, she should make a good faith effort —and this was something she truly needed help with. "There is something, actually."

"Oh? What's that?"

"Imani." She swallowed, and shrugged again, affecting calm. "She wants me to go to a conference in LA."

"Oh." Gita's eyebrows rose high. "That must mean she trusts you a great deal."

"She does. But I'm stressing over it. Like why couldn't things just stay the way they were?"

"Have they changed?"

"Yeah, they've changed a lot. I don't travel. I like being home. I've never been on a plane before, and I've got no desire to go on one now. I don't feel like mingling with hundreds of people, being put on the spot like that, having to make small talk. I mean I do it all the time at the shop, but it's different somehow. It feels like a really big ask. But I can't say no."

"Why not?"

"Because this is my job." She was surprised by the vehemence in her voice. She took a breath—this wasn't Gita's fault. She made an effort to quiet herself. "It's just that...my work is my identity. It's who I am. I'm good at it. It's like the one thing I'm good at."

"Well, I don't think it's the *one* thing you're good at, but I understand what you're saying."

"No, it isn't just that. It's like...who am I going to be now? What am I going to do? It's like it's not just about the trip, or my job, it's about everything being different from what I thought it was, it's like I'd even be different *from myself.*"

Gita was watching her, and the sympathy in her eyes triggered a feeling in Dahlia that was very like panic. That was interesting, in and of itself, thought Dahlia, even as she consciously tempered her breathing, in a desperate effort to calm herself down.

"I just don't like it," she said, with an attempt at casualness, though her voice was shaking. "It's like I almost resent her for putting me in this situation."

"What situation is that?"

"It's like I'm in this no-win position now, like disappoint a woman I respect or do something I'm profoundly uncomfortable with."

"I don't blame you for being uncomfortable," said Gita, "and I think your feelings are very normal."

"So what should I do about it? Like I can't say no, but I can't say yes."

"Well, I think the first thing to do is to give yourself some grace. All these feelings are valid."

"But what should I do?"

"I can't tell you what to do." Gita rubbed her lips together, thinking. "I think you should go. I hope you go. But if you don't go, I'd understand, and it wouldn't make you a bad person."

"I don't think it would make me a bad person." For the first time, she saw the nuance. "But there's a difference between what I know of myself, and what other people see."

"And it matters to you what other people see."

Dahlia said nothing. That wasn't what she meant; it wasn't true. But somehow, it seemed true.

"Never mind," she said at last. "I'm having trouble verbalizing. This has somehow gotten off path."

"Okay." Gita turned to her laptop. "I'd like you to think about it a little more so we can pick it up next week. I think there's more here." She clicked on her calendar. "Same time next week?"

DAHLIA SAT in her car for a minute or two before leaving Gita's office. It was true, what she'd said about LA being a no-win situation. She'd felt the same way at the party in the shop that night, and she'd felt the same way at her parents' house after noticing her father's weakening condition. She had a simmering in her stomach, the sense of a burner always running, always keeping her on edge. Her father's health was the only thing she cared about. But these new added stressors certainly weren't helping.

She turned on her car and pulled out of the parking lot, driving toward home in a haze. Too much was happening; she'd been thrown too much at once. Simply living in the world was already hard enough. Things had begun spinning very quickly, and she didn't know how to make it stop, or at least, how to handle the fact that it might not.

CHAPTER FOUR

"Do me a favor," said Tara. "Bring this tea in to Dad while I finish cleaning up in here."

"That's not a favor." Dahlia took the mug in her hand and began walking carefully toward her parents' bedroom. She turned back momentarily to retrieve a small dish from the cabinet—he'd want to remove the tea bag after the tea had steeped.

She found her father being pampered by her mother. Vera was straightening the blankets around him, fussily, whispering anxiously about the cold, the heat, the pilling of the sheets. Her father was quietly shushing her, pushing her hand away with gentle affection, assuring her the blanket was enough and that he was fine.

Dahlia smiled.

"There she is," said Edward, between Vera's concerned castigations peeking his head to the side, over his wife's shoulder. "I was hoping I'd see you today."

"Honey," Vera said to Dahlia, "he was just getting ready to rest. He just told me he was tired."

Edward waved the thought away. "Nonsense. For Dahlia, I'll always make time."

"Okay," said Vera, clearly with hesitation, as Dahlia handed her father his tea. "But don't let him overdo it."

"Of course I won't. I'll take good care of him."

"Dahlia always does," said Edward. "Sit down, sit down." He took a sip of tea and allowed Vera to straighten his pillow, enabling him to lean back; Vera then withdrew toward the kitchen to help Tara with the cleaning. "Do you have work at the bookstore today?"

"No, it's my day off." Dahlia took a seat in the armchair to the side, and relaxed, stretching her legs out and folding her hands lazily in her lap. "That's why I'm here early today."

"Tara made soup. Do you want some soup?"

"Maybe later." She paused. "Did you have any?"

"A little."

Dahlia tried to smile, but couldn't. "A little" meant a bite or two.

"I started Higgins." Her father took a sip of tea and glanced around. Dahlia handed him the dish; he pulled the tea bag from the mug, and thanked her. "It isn't what I was expecting."

"Oh, really? How so?"

"It's not like anything he's done before. It feels rather experimental."

"Experimental can be good."

"It can be, yes. If it's done right."

"And how's Higgins doing?"

"Remains to be seen."

She and her father chatted for a while. He grew tired, but it came on gradually, and he seemed to drift into sleep without hardly even knowing. Dahlia was used to his sudden exhaustion and normally would step quietly from the room, letting him have his peace. But today she felt compelled to watch over him. She dimmed the lights and adjusted his blanket. Then she sank back into her chair, pulled her paperback from her bag, and read quietly by the meager halo of the lamp.

Tara burst in, not realizing he was asleep.

"Oh," she whispered, stopping short. "I'm sorry."

"It's fine." Dahlia stood and stretched, then drifted to the doorway toward her sister. "He's been asleep for a while. Where's Mom?"

"She went out to pick up prescriptions." Tara glanced at her father; her face, so firm nowadays, much firmer than Dahlia remembered, softened as she gazed at him. She sighed and returned her attention to her sister. "How are you doing?"

"I'm fine, Tara. You keep asking me that, but you're the one here, doing all the work, with Mom."

"It's nothing." Tara's voice was terse, maybe even impatient. She seemed to catch herself. "I'm sorry, I'm just tired. But it's nothing. I'm home, and the girls are at school. I don't know where else I would be."

Dahlia looked at her sister's face. She always thought Tara was so beautiful. She had a sharp jawline, a sharpness that matched her eyebrows; she could cock one of those eyebrows in humor or sarcasm, or as if to ask, *Are you sure?* It was a sharpness that demonstrated her competence, but it was tempered by the depth of her emerald green eyes, the soft curving of her lips, the dimpling on her cheeks, so soft as to be barely visible, only if one were close. The two shared the same thick auburn hair, but somehow Tara's had bounce Dahlia's seemed to lack—she could pull it up in a playful ponytail, or make it silky for a romantic evening out. And it was all done so naturally, with such ease; Dahlia doubted Tara even realized any of this at all.

She noticed now the signs of aging, the wrinkles around her eyes that were a little deeper, the way the corners of her mouth turned downward just so. She seemed thinner, which Dahlia guessed made sense—she'd been taking care of everyone else, and not herself. Her voice, too, was often brusquer; likely she didn't have time to slow down. Likely she had to remain so busy, lest she become derailed by emotions ever simmering down beneath.

Dahlia wished she could take away some of this burden. She should be doing so much more. What kind of sister was she, anyway?

"You're doing a great job," said Dahlia. "I don't know if you know that."

The effect was immediate, and unexpected: Tara sniffled, then crumpled in tears. Her hands at her eyes, she allowed Dahlia to wrap her arm around her and draw her just outside the room. Dahlia enfolded her in a hug, breathing in the warm fragrance that seemed to follow her sister wherever she went.

"Jesus," gasped Tara. She wiped her eyes, then opened them wide and made an exaggerated show of shaking it off. Then she was herself again, the redness of her eyes the only evidence of her faltering. "Jesus, sorry."

"Don't be sorry."

"I guess between this and the school stuff, I'm just off."

"School stuff? What school stuff."

"You didn't hear about that? There was some threat made over social media, some stupid trend that's going around." Tara rolled her eyes. "You know. It's been happening. All the schools in the county were involved."

Dahlia's heart was on the floor, and it had left a gaping vacuum in her chest. The simmering seemed to consume her, burning her from the inside out. "So is there a threat?"

"No, it's just some bullshit. Copycat nonsense, you know. They assured us there's nothing to worry about."

Dahlia was horrified. "Did you send the girls to school?"

"Yeah. I kept them home last time, and it was nothing. They investigated thoroughly. It was nothing this time, too."

Dahlia stared at her. "Last time."

"That's our world."

Tara rubbed her face in her hands and muttered a few

choice expletives. Dahlia worked on getting control of her breath. Her blood was roiling. She imagined her nieces' faces, their wide eyes and freckles. She wanted to gather them up, sit with them in a safe, quiet room, read them stories and give them presents and keep them there forever. She wanted to hide them inside so they would never be in danger again. There were so many things that could hurt them, so many things that could go wrong. It seemed so normal, so everyday. Even Tara was desensitized.

Seriously. What kind of world was this?

Recovered, Tara rolled her eyes, clearly at herself. She peeked backward into the room; their father was still asleep. She faced her sister. "Anyway, thanks."

Dahlia took a breath. "You okay?"

"Of course." But Dahlia could see in the lines around her eyes the toll this was taking. She started: the longer she studied her sister the more she saw her mother. It was in the jawline, now more acute, and the downturn of the eyes, now a little more pronounced. Her eyes drifted to her sister's hair, which was weaved with strands of gray. When had that happened?

As her sister dried her eyes on her sleeves, Dahlia stole a quick glance at the mirror on the wall. Had this happened to her, too?

"You know, it's funny." Tara's voice, more sturdy now, broke Dahlia from her reverie. "I'm usually fine. It's when people ask me if I'm fine that I'm not fine."

Dahlia returned her gaze to her sister's pretty, serious face. "I'm sorry."

"No, it's not your fault." Tara slapped her arm. "It's like I'm swimming, swimming, swimming, and then someone calls to me, and I realize the bottom's drifted out from beneath my feet." She furrowed her brow. "You know what I mean."

Dahlia stared at her. "What did you just say?"

Tara appeared startled by the sharpness of Dahlia's voice. "I said it was like the bottom drifted out from beneath my feet."

"No, after that." Dahlia tried to swallow, but her mouth was dry. "Did you tell me I know what you mean?"

"Yeah." Tara narrowed her eyes. "You okay?"

"So you knew. You knew?"

"What are you talking about? I knew what?"

"You knew, that day?" It didn't make any sense. "You knew that I was drowning."

Tara bowed her head and gripped her sister's arm, pulling her roughly until they were just outside the door.

"What are you talking about, Dahlia? What do you mean, you were drowning?"

Dahlia felt frozen, and confused. Her eyes darted toward their father, who was sound asleep in his bed. He looked so fragile, so old. When did everyone get so old?

Tara tugged her arm; her face was now firm.

"Just tell me what you mean. Okay? I'm so tired."

The familiar authority in her sister's voice brought Dahlia to attention.

"That time I almost drowned." But her own voice was weak with hesitation. Her sister's words had seemed to suggest she had seen Dahlia almost drowning that day, but now she wasn't so sure. "At the beach, that time."

"Dahlia." Tara put her hands to the sides of her face and closed her eyes. She rubbed her lips together, gathering strength, then regarded her sister with an expression Dahlia recognized from when Tara was frustrated with her children. "I have no idea what you're talking about. Can you take it back, like twenty five steps?"

Dahlia's heart was hammering, and the rush of blood made her dizzy. "It was years ago, when we were kids." The shaking of her voice surprised her; as she went to run her fingers through her hair, she realized it wasn't her voice but her entire body.

Tara seemed to sense something was wrong. She placed her hand gently on her sister's arm.

"Dahlia?"

Dahlia made herself look her sister in the eye. She didn't know why this was so hard for her to say.

"I was six," she began in a whisper; she cleared her throat and continued. "Everyone was up on the sand, by the chairs. I was in the water. It sounds strange to say that now, like what kind of parents leave their six-year-old in the water, right?" She laughed, awkwardly. "But they knew I could swim. And it was a different time, back then."

Tara was watching her, her eyes wide with expectation.

Dahlia swallowed and took a deep breath. "I was just playing. Like I'd done a thousand times before. But the current must have taken me. I realized I was in too deep. I started drowning." She had never said these words before, and she was not prepared for the force of her own response. She would have thought there would be something freeing in the confession. Instead, she felt like she was losing something. She hesitated, afraid to give up the secret completely.

But the door had been opened; Tara wouldn't let her go back now.

"So what happened?" Her expression was now almost manic. "Dahlia, I need you to understand that I'm at my wit's end. You need to either tell me the story, or not tell me, and walk away. But I just can't stand here and get it in dribs and drabs. Just tell me, what happened? *What happened?*"

"A man saved me." The words burst from her, a bit too loudly. "A stranger. I didn't know who he was. He just pulled me out of the ocean. He told me not to worry, he saw me. He said the water was choppy. He told me to have fun, and be safe."

"What's this about drowning?"

Tara and Dahlia turned their heads with surprise. Their father was now sitting straight up in the bed. In the sharpness of his expression he looked more like himself than he had in months.

"Dahlia." His expression softened as his two daughters

stepped back into the room. He held his hand out; Dahlia took it, and he squeezed. "Kiddo, you almost drowned?"

"It was years ago." The words sounded ridiculous as soon as she said them. As if that made it better, that she'd been only a child at the time. "It wasn't a big deal."

"You almost drowned." He was staring at her in disbelief, his eyes wide. "I'd say that's a pretty damn big deal."

"She's been holding this secret for thirty years." Tara was shaking her head as she folded some laundry in the corner. "And here I thought we knew everything about each other."

"Stop." Dahlia clucked her tongue and shifted her weight, in an attempt at casualness. "It isn't like it matters now."

"So you never knew who saved you." Her father watched as Dahlia sat down in the armchair, her hands in the pockets of her sweatshirt. "You didn't know who he was."

"I only barely got a glimpse." Dahlia's gaze had rested on a spot of nothing on the floor. She recalled the stranger in her mind's eye, the way he glowed in a halo of light, the echo of protection he'd left in her and the bodily memory of being held in his hands. Conjuring the vision of him here, in the presence of her family, had somehow changed it, like a garment stowed away in a chest in the attic, then unfolded decades later, when it was dusty and out of date. Seeing it in the sunlight was a strange sensation.

Her father was regarding her with soft, mournful eyes. "Where was I? I didn't see you."

"You and Mom and the girls were on the beach." Dahlia felt a strange, sudden squeezing in her chest as her father's hand tightened around hers. She hadn't meant for him to feel guilty; she hadn't meant for him to hear the story at all. "It was a fluke thing. It was fine."

"But I didn't see you." Edward's eyes had sharpened, despite the tears that had gathered at the corners of his eyes. "You could have died, and I didn't even see you."

"It isn't your fault, Dad. There was no way for you to know."

"I should have been there. I should have been watching. What kind of father lets his daughter almost drown?"

"You didn't 'let' me drown, or almost. I don't want to make you upset. Please, let's not talk about it."

"I agree." Tara had stepped further into the room and was now opening drawers to put away neat piles of laundry. "Maybe this is a story for another time."

"I wish I had known, so I could thank him." Her father was shaking his head, and frowning, distressed. "The man who saved my daughter's life. You wouldn't be here if it weren't for him. You wouldn't be here." He looked at her. "You should see if you can find him."

Dahlia's eyes widened. "What? No, Dad. No."

"Why not?"

"Because it's over. It's in the past. It doesn't even matter."

"It isn't over, because you're here. It's never over, every day. Every day, it matters."

Dahlia swallowed, rubbing her lips together against the pounding of her heart.

Her father's voice was quiet, now, and somber. "Every day you visit me. Every time you talk to me about books. Every time I ever pushed you on the swing, or tucked you into bed, every time I wiped your tears or scooped you ice cream or picked you up from school." A tear slipped abruptly down his cheek. "None of that would have happened had it not been for this man."

Dahlia felt sick. It hadn't even been her choice to talk about it; now it was not only wafting through the room, but in the spotlight, suddenly holding meaning she had never considered and never wanted. With its release, a part of her was missing, something intimate and personal. In its place was something shared and communal, and she mourned it, without knowing why.

"Dad," said Tara, her hand gently rubbing his shoulder. "I can see why this would make you upset right now." She paused—the rest didn't need to be said. "But I think we should focus on what we have, and what's here. Not what was almost lost."

"I wonder if you could find him," said Edward, ignoring Tara's soft plea. He was looking up at Dahlia, and even as her heart contracted in resistance to the enormity of what he was suggesting Dahlia knew she had no choice. "Wouldn't that be amazing? To find out who he is?"

Dahlia studied her father. His face was gaunt and harrowed. The illness had taken from him more than she'd allowed herself to see. He looked older now, yes, but his skin was thin and sallow, his eyes haunted. He seemed to her like a scared, lost child. She pitied him, and hated herself for it.

"I don't think I can," she whispered, and swallowed, clearing her throat. "I mean how would I even do it? I don't know who he is. I don't even know when it was."

"I know. It's not really a reasonable wish. It would probably take a miracle." He shrugged. "It would just be so nice to thank him."

Edward smiled, but there was latent urgency in his expression. They both knew why this was so important, and why it was so important now. Dahlia understood what it was he wasn't saying, and it tore at her insides like a rip in fabric already worn thin.

Dahlia braved a glance up at her sister. Tara was frozen, exhaustion clouding her face. She shook her head at Dahlia, almost imperceptibly, but Dahlia couldn't tell if she was telling her to refuse or lamenting the fact that she couldn't.

She looked back to her father, and forced herself to smile.

"I'll see, Dad," she told him. "I'll see what I can do."

"Sounds like a quiet week," said Gita, smiling. "Just the way you like them."

Dahlia nodded. "Yes."

"Nothing of interest, no news? Nothing about Los Angeles?"

She hesitated a split second too long. "Nothing to report, no. Same old, same old."

Gita blinked. "Nothing at all?"

Dahlia sighed. She hadn't mentioned the party at her last session. She wasn't sure if that meant it was unimportant, or so important as to be overwhelming. "The store hosted a party the other night, for local store owners. They were trying to convince me to go."

"They? You mean the other owners?"

"Yes. They were telling me it would be nice to hear my perspective, that I could do a presentation." Dahlia scrunched her face as if it were ridiculous. "But obviously I'm not doing that."

"Why not?"

Dahlia laughed. "It's so not my thing."

"What is your thing?"

Dahlia stared at her. *I don't know.*

"I mean," she began, "I like to be in the store. I work behind the scenes, setting up the tables, running the register. Talking to customers. You know. I'm good at that kind of thing."

"That's definitely true," said Gita. "I wonder, do you think maybe they're right, though? Maybe you might have something to teach others? Maybe you'd even have a good time."

"It's too much. It's all too much. It's just not something I can do." Dahlia's voice sounded cross even in her own ears. Her chest flooded with the familiar ache of guilt. "I'm sorry," she murmured, tucking her hair behind her ear. "It isn't you. It's just..."

"I know." Gita smiled reassuringly. "And I certainly don't want to push you."

"You aren't. I know that's why I'm here." Dahlia frowned as she recalled the way she'd shut down with the owners, the way she'd rejected their offer to join them at the bar and the way she'd wished she'd told them how she appreciated being around them. "I do that sometimes," she ventured, her hands fidgeting with themselves. "I get defensive, I think, and I regret it. I did that at the party. With the owners."

"What did you do?"

"They were being really nice to me, including me and talking to me like I was one of them. I wanted to tell them how nice they were. Like it would have been really nice for me to let them know I appreciated it. But I just couldn't get out of my own head. It was almost like I was inside myself, trying to speak, but I couldn't. I feel bad after, like why can't I just be nice back?" She frowned further. "I don't know if that makes any sense."

"It makes perfect sense. Your anxiety voice overpowers your own voice."

Dahlia raised her eyebrows. "What do you mean?"

"It's the anxiety talking. You can't respond the way you would like to respond, because the anxiety takes over. Anxiety about change, about performance, about the unexpected." A kind smile curled at Gita's lips. "You are nice, Dahlia. That's why you feel guilt after, when you've had time to absorb everything. You're all the things you want to be. But anxiety gets in the way. It makes it difficult for you to accept things happening quickly. It speaks for you first." She furrowed her brow as if to ask if Dahlia understood. "You just need to grow confident enough so your own, true voice shines through."

Dahlia stared at her. She didn't think that was anxiety, but she didn't say anything. It was just her social awkwardness, like it was with everything else.

"How is your father?" asked Gita, gently. "Were you able to see him this week?"

"I saw him, yes. I see him often."

"How did this week's visits go?"

"Same as always, he sleeps a lot, sometimes wakes up, and we talk. I talk to Tara. I talk to my mother."

"How are things with Tara?"

"Things?" Dahlia looked at her. "What kind of things?"

"I mean how have you been getting along. She's bearing the brunt of your father's illness, you said."

"Well, she and my mother, but Tara's also got her own family."

"Did you see her this week, too?"

"Of course. She's always there."

"Where are her kids during this time?"

"They're at school, or they're home with Tom. Tom's been great. He picks them up, gives them dinner, makes them do their homework. I mean he's their dad, he should do that, but a lot of dads don't."

Gita smiled. "Yours did."

"Yes."

A minute or so passed in silence.

Dahlia didn't know what she was doing here. She'd come on recommendation from her sister, but every week she was more convinced it was a waste of time. Gita was nice enough, but Dahlia couldn't see how she was helping. She didn't even know what she needed help with. Her father was ailing, but this was hardly new to the human experience. People had been dealing with ailing parents since literally the beginning of time. The weekly hour she was here talking about her family, she could be spending helping her father, or reading. She was about to politely thank Gita and end things once and for all when Gita abruptly changed the conversation.

"I'd like to hear more about the drowning."

Dahlia sucked in her breath. "What?"

"If you don't have anything else more pressing, of course, and if you don't mind."

Dahlia's eyes narrowed. "I don't mind, because it was nothing."

"I don't think it was."

"I was there. It was nothing."

Gita watched her, her face soft with sympathy that made Dahlia uncomfortable. "You're a little defensive about it."

"I don't think I'm defensive. It's just that I'm uncomfortable when people make a big deal out of it." Dahlia flushed. "I'm sorry."

"No need." Gita regarded her with interest. "Someone else made a big deal of it?"

Dahlia stifled her exasperation, with effort. "It came up the other day, with Tara and my dad."

"Would you like to tell me about it?"

Not really, Dahlia thought, reflexively, but she knew it would be rude to say it, and she already regretted the shortness with which she'd spoken to Gita, who certainly meant well. Also, part of her thought it wouldn't hurt to talk about it, to get validation that everyone was making too much of something so insignificant, and so far in the past.

"It just came up, by accident. Tara said something about drowning, metaphorically. I thought she was referring to that time, you know, on the beach, and was surprised she knew. But she didn't know. And then of course I had to tell her what on Earth I was talking about."

"So you told her the story?"

"I told her, yes, and my father overheard, and then I had to tell *him*, and everyone was acting like it was super important and horrible."

"And it wasn't?"

"Of course not. These things happen. But my dad, it was like he felt guilty, he damn near almost cried. He couldn't believe he didn't know this, sort of blamed himself for not knowing it went on. He wished he could thank the man who saved me. He wants me to find him. I mean he didn't say so flat out, but he wouldn't." Dahlia laughed wildly, and stopped abruptly, surprised.

Gita said nothing for a moment or two. Dahlia's laughter was still echoing through the room. She didn't know what Gita was waiting for. She glanced to the side, just to break their gaze.

"So this was the first time you'd told anyone," she said finally. "Why hadn't you told anyone before?"

"Like I said. It was nothing."

"Is it hard for you to think about it?"

"No, I don't think about it at all." She wondered if Gita could tell that she was lying. She made eye contact, hoping to appear confident and calm, but she had a feeling it only made her dishonesty more obvious.

If Gita thought anything of it, she didn't say so.

"How do you feel when you think about that time in your life? Your childhood?"

Dahlia blinked. "I'm fine thinking about my childhood."

"Did you have a happy childhood?"

"Yes, it was happy. I loved my family. I still do."

"Is it hard to think about those times? The times that are over?"

A beat passed. "Why would it be hard to think about?"

"Maybe it isn't. Just a question." Gita smiled. "So why did you tell Tara now?"

"Like I said. It came up. I had to explain what I was talking about."

"I think it's possible it's more than that."

Dahlia frowned. "It's not."

"Okay."

Another few moments of silence.

Gita said, "What was Tara's reaction?"

Dahlia took a deep breath. "She demanded I go into detail. She was upset, but she didn't want to upset my father."

"She demanded it? Is that why you told her?"

"She made me nervous." Dahlia straightened; she hadn't intended to say that and didn't know where those words had come from. She sank back again, and qualified it. "Not nervous, exactly. But Tara's six years older than I am. She's always had a certain firmness. I don't know why it still does that to me."

"Do you see her as a figure of authority?"

"I guess so, a little. I mean, she was my playmate, too. I loved her growing up, and I love her now, as a sister. But, you know."

She didn't know if Gita knew, and didn't even fully know herself. She said nothing more, letting Gita interpret this how she would.

"Do you often fill those roles, you and Tara?" Gita asked then. "Of youngest and oldest, I mean."

"Well, of course." She paused. She felt like there was something important in that answer, but she wasn't sure what it was. "That's literally our relationship."

"Yes, but you're adults now."

"Does that matter?"

"Not necessarily. I just think it's interesting that she still has that power over you."

"I wouldn't say it's power." Was it power? Or was this some kind of mind game, some psychology nonsense about childhood and past lives and some kind of Freudian-inspired complex? It was becoming hard to tell. Dahlia was confused. "I don't think there's anything down this path, honestly. It's probably pretty normal, you know, to have a relationship with someone as kids and see remnants of that relationship as adults. I don't think there's any meaning there."

"Totally fair point."

But Dahlia was thinking about it; something had resonated. "I mean maybe there's something to it. But not as much as you seem to think. I'm saying that maybe there's something in the fact that in situations like this, it's like we're little girls again, like we've always had those roles and for some reason we slip back into it? I don't know." Her heart was fluttering; she was muttering whatever came out of her mouth, and she made herself slow down. "But it's weird because if we're going back to when we were kids, how can it be like we're the older generation?"

Gita's brow creased. "How do you mean?"

"I mean when we were standing there, I was looking at her, and it was like I could see how old she was, all of a sudden. She's always been closer with my mother than I've been, you know? But...I realized, she looks like her. More so than ever. It's like... when did we become our parents' age? Like I don't have kids, myself, but Tara does, and I think to myself, they must see Tara the way we saw our parents, you know? And it's like...my father is dying..."

Her voice trailed off. She watched Gita watching her. What had she just said? Where on Earth had that come from?

"I don't know if any of that makes sense," she said.

Gita watched her for a moment or two.

"I've noticed you do that a lot," she said then. "Ask if something you're saying makes sense."

Dahlia shrugged noncommittally. "I don't think it's a lot."

"Everything you say makes sense, Dahlia. You're a lot clearer than you think you are."

Dahlia flushed. "Good to know. Thanks."

"It's okay for you to take up space, to take as long as you need to explain something."

"Thanks."

Gita waited, but Dahlia said nothing more.

"I think that makes a lot of sense," said Gita finally, shifting in her seat. "You're witnessing the generations shift, maybe for the first time. It sparks thoughts of mortality. It makes time look very different." She raised her eyebrows. "Is that it?"

Quite out of nowhere, Dahlia was sick with nausea, as if someone had reached inside her and turned her stomach upside down. The simmering, that damn low, constant simmering, was once again rising in her stomach, in her heart. She sat for a few moments in a panic, feeling unable to breathe. Then, the anger came—anger at Gita, for telling lies that made her feel this way; anger at her Tara, for making her come here; anger at April, for never being around, and escaping all this; anger at her parents, for reasons she couldn't identify.

"You know," she said, her chest pounding—she wasn't used to confronting people like this, preferring instead to absorb unpleasantness until it came to its natural end, "this isn't working for me. It's making me really stressed out, which is the opposite of the intended effect."

"Oh, I'm sorry to hear that," said Gita, and her lack of reaction angered Dahlia even further. "Can I try to convince you to keep trying? Can I ask what isn't working?"

"It's everything, it's just everything. It's that...no offense, but I feel like you just listen, you ask me questions and nod and say you get it, but you never actually come to any conclusions. You don't give me anything to help me. I've had a totally normal, uneventful life. I just don't need to analyze my relationships with everyone in my entire family. I just don't need to share all this personal information only to move on without any *meaning*. I'm supposed to be here to feel better about my father. I mean I'm sad about my father, but none of this is going to change that. If there's something that can help me, fine, but I still don't know what that is. It just feels like...like a waste of everyone's time."

She had started regretting her words very shortly after she'd begun saying them, but she'd been propelled by the momentum of her emotion, and as she'd gone on it had been as if the only way to recover was to become more and more firm. Her face had flushed with heat that seemed to cast a cloud over her vision. It was being pumped through her veins and out of her pores by the frantic pounding of her heart, and the ache of its unnaturally violent movement made her incapable of speaking, once she'd stopped.

She swallowed against the lump in her throat. She wanted to apologize to Gita, to tell her it was possible everything had built up to the point of explosion and that she was taking it out on her. But she couldn't find her voice, and she didn't trust herself to keep talking.

Gita's face was neutral, unreadable. If she'd been offended, or shocked, by Dahlia's uncharacteristic outburst, she wasn't showing it.

"Okay." Gita swiveled on her chair to replace her pen and notebook on her desk, then turned back to Dahlia, folding her hands neatly in her lap. "This isn't usually how I do this, but it's your money and your time. If you'd like conclusions, I can give you some conclusions. Would you like them?"

Dahlia actually did want conclusions, whether because deep down she knew she needed help or because she was merely curious, she didn't fully know. She swallowed and nodded, her eyes wide, in the recesses of her mind understanding the magnitude of what was happening.

Gita nodded in return. "Great. Here they are."

Dahlia inhaled and braced herself.

Gita looked her in the eye. "I think, Dahlia, that you are an incredibly kind, intelligent, and loving woman who brings nothing but good to those around her. You excel at your job, not only because you're great at it and because you have genuine love and passion for what you do but because you have an exceptional work ethic, because you take pride in what you do and because you find higher purpose in doing it. You're also a generous and giving daughter and sister, often contributing behind the scenes in ways that feel less obvious and so tend to be less noticed, but are no less meaningful or important. In fact I think that very much encapsulates who you are, in the sense that you don't like to be in the spotlight, you prefer to be a supporting character—and you're good at it, because you see little details that other people miss. You pick up after people. Your scope may be smaller, but it sparks the flame that contributes on a scale that's larger than you probably realize. You also have true, selfless respect for the people you know who deserve it. You don't feel threatened by it; you acknowledge it, you revere it, and you aspire to embody it."

Dahlia was lightheaded. Whatever she'd been expecting Gita

to say, this was not it. She'd never been complimented so, and with such honesty; she'd never been *seen* like she'd been seen in this vision. She'd never even considered she was worthy of such careful analysis. It took a few moments for her to rest with the implications; it turned her whole world upside down. It was only now that she was seeing herself as a whole person, and what was more—it was only now that she saw that she hadn't done so before.

Gita went on.

"The problem," she said, "is that you don't think you embody it yourself. You don't realize you don't think this; I don't even believe you've ever thought about it. It's your role in life, it's who you are. You live a very quiet life, by design, without a lot of new experiences. It isn't that you don't like to meet new people, it's that you want to know that an end is in sight. You're perfectly fine in conversation—here, and at the bookstore, for instance—as long as it's limited, as long as you can go home. You like your little apartment above the bookstore; you don't have to go very far for the various corners of your life. Your apartment is small, cozy, manageable. You can watch the street from high above, without participating. You can be an observer, you can spark your imagination, without having to take part in it yourself. Your experiences are in books, and you're happy that way. You live vicariously through the people you read about, because it's safe, and everything always works out. I'm not quite sure yet if this is totally by design, meaning I don't yet know you well enough to have a clear vision of whether you'd prefer it this way, or whether you're afraid of the alternative. But I have a theory, and that's that it started when you almost drowned."

Dahlia said nothing. These were vulnerabilities it had never occurred to her to think about, because they were simply who she was, and had always been—they'd never been framed as a problem, never as something there had to be a reason for. Dahlia felt she should be offended by them—through Gita's eyes, she seemed to appear docile, fragile—a shadow of a person, a shadow of what she could be. It could be more psychological nonsense, but somehow Dahlia knew they weren't. She was breathless because it made sense; she was breathless because it was true. Dahlia had always figured she was a homebody, an introvert, a bookworm, and she was, but she was beginning to recognize the nuance. She didn't know what to do with it. Too often lately, it seemed, she'd been thrust into existential crisis, fingers digging in the innermost crevices of her heart and pulling her forward, without her approval or her consent.

"I feel like this fits a narrative," she told Gita, calmer now, but still riding waves of the adrenaline charge that had driven her earlier diatribe, "like it's low-hanging fruit, and that you're putting words in my mouth. You ask a lot of probing questions, and I feel like they're all getting at the same predetermined point."

"Well, Dahlia, everyone comes to therapy differently, and from a different place. Some people talk and talk and talk, and that's fine, that's why they're here, to unload and to be heard, often because they aren't heard in their own lives. But you're not a talker. You don't give me a lot, if I'm honest, so it's up to me to put the pieces together when you do. And you're free at any time to tell me if I'm off base, which is what you seem to be doing right now." Gita crossed her legs and her arms. "So," she said, raising one eyebrow, in challenge, "am I off base?"

Dahlia was smart enough to understand that Gita knew Dahlia knew she wasn't. She remained silent, boldly meeting Gita's gaze, intending defiance, but inside her burst of confidence was losing momentum, and she saw that Gita knew this, too.

"Dahlia," said Gita, gently. "Why are you here?"

Dahlia straightened. She blinked a few times, taken aback.

"I'm here because my father is dying. My sister said I should come."

"I mean why are you really here."

Dahlia stared at her. She rubbed her lips together, thinking.

The truth was that she'd come because Tara had told her to. She'd done it to appease her, to make her feel good, and, if she was honest, to get her off her back. For the first time she felt that she had learned something from it, that talking about herself had led her somewhere unfamiliar, somewhere with windows and doors of unlimited entrance, a universe of revelations and nightmares, all needing to be faced, all needed to be sorted. The discovery was upending in and of itself.

"Can I change the subject for a second?"

"Of course."

"I mean as long as I'm here, I might as well say it."

"Go on."

Dahlia hesitated, but pushed forward. "I feel like I lost something. When I told them about almost drowning. I don't know what, exactly. And I don't know why."

"Thank you for sharing that." Gita smiled, as she always did, but somehow now, it seemed to Dahlia even more sincere. "I think that's something for us to discuss."

One more entrance, one more nightmare. One more dark corner, with so much to go wrong and so scary possibilities unknown.

THE AUTUMN AIR was becoming crisper, more sharp; soon, it would be winter. With the golden glow of the leaves that flushed the trees and lay like an iridescent cloak across the ground, impossible beauty was everywhere, but it portended bleak days ahead.

That night Dahlia didn't dream of drowning; in fact, she didn't dream at all. She couldn't stop thinking about what Tara had told her earlier, about the threats to her nieces' schools, about the danger they were in every day. She was still shaken by the images, and still at their mercy—the fear on the little girls' faces, their tears, their yearning for Tom and Tara and the pits in their stomachs as they realized what would happen next. Dahlia stared into the darkness, the visions relentless, and as they moved over her consciousness like phantoms before her eyes she felt as if it were really happening, and she grieved, her eyes misting and her stomach squeezing, the ache in her heart stealing her breath and making her feel empty, a gaping black hole. It didn't matter that the threat had not been real—the suggestion was enough for Dahlia's soul to feel it, even if her mind knew it wasn't true, and Dahlia knew in those moments the fear would never go away, that it would be merely one more worry for the pile, for the rest of her life.

She wrestled with herself in this fashion, lying still in body but grappling in her mind. She drifted in and out of sleep in a kind of mindless torment, a cycle of pushing and pulling against her own body that mimicked waves on a storm-chilled shore. Exhaustion would waft through her, and rest would take her; she'd then awaken in a sweat, seeing Tara's and Tom's faces, hearing their wails, feeling their misery. The sleep she found was tumultuous, an interlude between bouts of illness. She was trying to submerge herself in the darkness, but the waves kept spitting her out. The rejection felt brusque, deliberate. She would dive in until it absorbed her.

Eventually Dahlia gave up. She sat straight, her hands on the bed beside her, her hair disheveled, the strap of her nightgown falling from her shoulder. She then picked her phone from the nightstand and made a small donation to a gun violence prevention charity, and rubbed her face in her hands, trying to stop the simmering.

She exhaled with exasperation and glanced out the window. The moon was high above the building across the street; the chimneys vomited pillowy spirals of smoke, which rose in a burst and disintegrated into the night. Dahlia rose, folding her arms over her chest and approaching the window with silent steps. She stood for a minute or two, watching the slumbering street. It was deepest night, after the night owls had finally relented, wearily setting their alarms and cursing themselves for the pain they'd feel at sunrise, and before long the earliest risers would yawn and stretch their limbs so they could stumble into their day. The stillness carried its own weight, as vast as an endless sea. Watching the totality of nothing, her eyes darting from window to dark window, Dahlia was conscious of her aloneness, the isolation and the power of being alert while the world around her slept.

If something happened to Tara and Tom the situation would be reversed; it would be the girls wailing and miserable, lost and fearful children, innocent souls bereft. Their pain was too much for Dahlia to bear. Tom's family were in Colorado, and while the girls knew them, they didn't see them often enough to be close. Dahlia imagined them moving to an unfamiliar place, in addition to losing their parents. Tom's family would be good to them. But Dahlia considered that it was likely she herself would be in charge of them. With her father ailing and her mother getting older, she was the only logical next in line. Dahlia's life would change quite a bit. She'd have to give up her apartment, her quiet—but she wouldn't hesitate to do it, and it wasn't even what scared her. It was that they'd really have no one left, that if something happened to her there was nowhere else they could go, and what then? Dahlia was sick with the thought of it, and she wondered if it was possible she'd avoided having children herself to avoid the very pain she was suffering right now.

She turned back toward her bedroom. Moonlight bathed her modest possessions in a soft wash of silver—her dresser, her rug, her bed with its tangled sheets. A vintage red velvet armchair, scuffed and worn and rubbed down with time, sat in the corner, out of the moon's all-knowing reach. She took a few steps and sat in the chair, folding her legs beneath her bottom, encasing herself in darkness. From this angle, she observed her room like she'd observed the street outside, out of the light, out of view. It was a lived-in room, books askew on the nightstand, an empty teacup on the desk. Her sweater was askance on the desk chair, where she'd thrown it upon coming home; a basket of neatly folded laundry rested against the wall, waiting to be filed into her closet and drawers.

The familiarity of this room calmed her, and her vision grew heavy and blurred. She was swept by a tide of drowsiness, and she stumbled toward the bed, where she wrapped her body in her blankets and welcomed the current that pulled her out toward the sea.

PART II
THE SEARCH

CHAPTER FIVE

*D*ahlia's fingers mindlessly tapped a pen on the register. The sound mimicked the pitter pattering of raindrops outside. It had been raining steadily since early that morning; the clouds had gathered shortly after Dahlia had managed to fall into a restless sleep. She'd overslept, then awoken suddenly to a rhythmic tapping outside her window. She'd scurried to the shop with her hood up over unwashed hair and had made a cup of tea in the breakroom microwave. Somewhat warmed against the chill of the relentlessly gray day, she'd set to work, putting the final touches on displays and readying the register for what was sure to be a quiet shift. She'd unlocked the door at nine o'clock, as always, but it had been almost eleven before the first soaked customers had wandered inside, shaking their umbrellas out before carefully leaning them against the foyer wall, then nodding hello and drifting off toward their desired sections.

Now Dahlia stood behind the register, scrutinizing the scene before her. She tended to enjoy rainy days, which made the book-store a cozy hideaway, muting the sounds of conversation and somehow drawing out with more distinction the smoky scent of new books. On a day like today, it was easy to imagine the breadth of undiscovered knowledge contained within their pages. Today Dahlia registered these things absentmindedly, her mind diverting onto new and daring paths.

Her eyes caught sight of a box of playing cards she'd ordered on a whim in the hopes of bringing in impulse buys. She picked up a deck, its tightly stretched plastic wrapping crinkling in her hand. She turned it over and looked at the back. The cards were decorated with a painting that hung in a New York City art museum—it was a contemporary landscape oil painting depiction of a girl standing on a mountain, in swirling colors, which imparted to the work a playful, magical feel. Dahlia had never seen the painting in person, despite living only a couple of short hours from New York. She'd recognized it only from reproductions, and had been drawn to the figure on the mountain, who stood tall and straight, her hand on her back, her hair whipped by the wind as birds soared beneath her.

Dahlia had never climbed a mountain, had never known the feeling of standing among the clouds.

She replaced the deck in the box and stepped out from behind the register, then glided to the left into the fiction section. Here were tales of adventure, of finding treasure, finding love, finding purpose. Many were tales of finding trouble, of making mistakes and of unbearable heartache and loss. There was evil in these books, and redemption, and people coming to justice, or hurting people without consequence. But regardless of the people inside them, these books all held lessons—and if not for the people enduring the trials within, for the people reading about them, far removed.

It was amazing, Dahlia thought, how a small action taken by someone so far away—as far away as another dimension, like the people in these books—could have such long-reaching, impactful effects.

Dahlia stood for a moment, her vision absorbing the sight of so many stories. These aisles were like apartment buildings, teeming with life one could never fully know. They contained individual pains and sorrows, joys and accomplishments, so important in their respective stories but meaningless beyond the scope of the pages between the covers. Characters in one book knew nothing of characters in another. But they'd all experienced something, anything—in that, they were all alike.

Dahlia thought about how many times she had shelved books into these aisles. She'd had all these stories in her hands; these pages had passed through her fingers. And what of her own stories, her own pages? Was she destined to be the guardian of other people's lives?

A mystery display caught her attention; she drifted toward the table and picked up the first book she saw. It was a detective novel of the usual type, the gathering of evidence, the locating of a suspect. Dahlia had read many mystery novels and like many mystery readers liked to make a game of getting ahead of the sleuth. She wondered, not for the first time, how the writers planned their story, the complex maps and timelines they constructed to ensure the efficient laying of clues. And there were always clues, weren't there? No matter how impossible it seemed, there was always an answer; there were always just enough signs.

Mysteries didn't occur in a vacuum. There was always someone who knew, someone who had seen...someone who had noticed something they didn't even deem important at the time.

Dahlia sighed and moved on. There was a table of romance novels, featuring the new bestseller by a well-known author. Dahlia had put the table together herself, as always. There was the stack of new hardcovers, but there were paperbacks of the writer's other books. And there were complementing books, on a similar theme, all of them containing sweeping tales of falling in love and starting new lives, of people embarking on journeys together, learning together, experiencing the heights of passion together. They were hopeful tales of growth and redemption, of friends and forgiveness and the myriad emotions of interpersonal relationships. Dahlia flipped through the pages of the book nearest her fingers; the cover bore an illustrated vision of a couple holding hands.

And when was the last time Dahlia had held someone's hand? The last time she'd felt passion, of any kind—her last growth, her last redemption?

Dahlia closed the book and sighed, moving forward. There was the travel section, to her right; to her left, scores of blank notebooks, just waiting to be filled with new ideas. Further toward the front were the self-help books, the art books, the biographies—people building, creating, developing systems and philosophies to absorb the most out of life they can. People expressing themselves, contributing—making connections, making beauty, making change.

Dahlia looked around at the carefully laid tables and displays. She'd designed all of them, and it had seemed so meaningful at the time. She'd placed the books so deliberately, had decorated with so much thought and care. It had meant so much to her, and it still did. She loved the store, and her role in it; it was her little corner of the world. Here, she puttered around as she pleased, setting things up and taking things down, laying out things of interest for other people's eyes. She always thought she was making small differences, that when someone picked up a book she'd set out to be seen, she was indirectly responsible for that someone gaining knowledge. But at the end of the day, it was other people's knowledge. And everything she did, she was making money for somebody else.

As her eyes took in this beloved labyrinth of tomes Dahlia thought about all her displays, how lovingly she'd arranged books that held depictions of things she'd never done. The irony hit her quite suddenly, and it twisted like a dagger in her heart. She should do something. She needed to do something. The urge to act was immediate, and alarming. She didn't know if it was Gita's assessment of her life, or her father's failing health, or a combination of both that had stoked this fire from the dormant ashes it had been. But she saw her familiar world differently now, and she silently cursed them both.

Dahlia returned to the register and stood waiting—for what, she didn't know, as her customers had left empty-handed. She was alone in the store, as she very often was. Sometimes she felt so insignificant, invisible even, and she supposed this was where she felt safest. But for the first time she saw that it was a kind of self-fulfilling prophecy, that as she closed further and further in on herself she'd made it harder and harder to return. What happened in her mind was automatic, now; it was a shortcut that circumvented the hard things in between. And for the first time she was wondering if the hard things were where life actually was.

She could continue to display people who had conquered the unknown, or she could actually do something herself. She didn't know what that meant for her. But for the first time she saw that it didn't have to matter, that being a tiny person in a tiny universe didn't preclude her from trying. Her father's haunted face filled the vision of her mind's eye. He had given her an unknown, a glimmer; he had given her a reason to try. It didn't have to matter to anyone else, as long as it mattered to her. And as long as it mattered to him.

THAT EVENING DAHLIA was snuggled on her couch in her living room, a cup of tea in hand. She'd closed the curtains against the view of the buildings across the street, against the endless sky. Typically she enjoyed it, watching the tops of the buildings, being at eye level with the horizon and above the hustle and bustle. Tonight she was feeling closed in, even more closed in than usual. She was more keenly aware of the simmering that was always in her, containable, but waiting. On the television screen before her, characters on one of her favorite shows repeated lines Dahlia knew by heart; she did not watch a lot of shows, but what she did watch, she watched over and over. She found it comforting, knowing what to expect. And plowing through the seasons every few weeks helped her see things she'd never seen before—the comic timing of an almost imperceptible pause, an eyebrow lift suggesting subtle sarcasm, a lilt in a spoken word, which turned it unexpectedly into a term of endearment.

The curtains were simple white linen, freshly pressed by Dahlia last week. They helped brighten an already bright room. The walls were a warm cream; the rug was soft and boasted an understated pattern of forget-me-nots. The furniture was unremarkable but tidy looking, and uncluttered, practical, in a standard oak shade. Her father's green bowl rested on the window sill, where it was in her line of vision as she enjoyed the view outside. A plant stand rested in the corner, another beside the TV. From the top of each, a pothos bloomed happily, its rich green tendrils spilling with plenty over the legs and onto the hardwood floor. During the day, the windows allowed copious amounts of light, which bathed Dahlia's plants with nutrients. They flourished here, in her cozy little apartment, brightening their little corners of the world.

Dahlia had seen this episode countless times, and her mind was drifting. She took a breath over her tea, inhaling the comforting scents of chamomile and lavender, and let her eyes graze over the sights in her apartment. It really was quite charming. It was small, but the smallness was containing; it was a hideaway, a secret compartment, an oasis. Dahlia understood why cats preferred to sit in boxes, why babies slept in cribs. There was something safe about an enclosure. Her apartment was a pleasure to return home to. She was grateful for its warmth, grateful for this retreat.

It was strange, though, the way something had changed. It was only a couple of weeks ago that her life had seemed permanent and safe. But she'd been doing so much thinking, had been put into so many new situations that had forced her to consider, *What if it's not?* She didn't like these changes, these demands on her safety and her routine. Even worse was that part of her—a very small part of her, a specter of a sliver of an idea—wondered if it wasn't safety that she had, but stagnancy.

Was it possible she could be climbing mountains? Was it possible she could be the main character in her own story? Was it possible that Gita and Imani knew this? There was so very much that could go wrong—but was it possible that something could go right?

Dahlia was frustrated, but she wasn't sure with what, or with whom. She didn't want to go to Los Angeles. She should want to go. Why didn't she?

Was she treading water? And was there really, when you thought about it, anything wrong with that?

Her eyes caught sight of her computer, which rested on her childhood desk. She stared at it a moment, then pushed the blanket from her lap. Before she knew what she was doing, she was sitting in her desk chair, punching her password into her keyboard and pulling up her browser, preparing for a search.

She had to do something, anything. At least dip her toe in the water.

She thought a moment, then paused against a light flutter in her chest.

She typed,

Near drownings in Harbortown, NJ

She knew this would return no useful information. A near drowning that nobody witnessed would not have been recorded, much less immortalized online. Nevertheless, it was a start, and she watched, heart pattering, as the results filled the screen.

Tragedy in Harbortown After Man Dies While...

Lethal Weekend: Harbortown Swimmer Drowns...

Body Found in Harbortown Identified as Missing...

Harbortown Beach Access Restricted After...

Dahlia scanned the headlines, then added the year. These results were closer but no more helpful.

Drownings in the United States Between the Years...

A Nostalgic Vision of the Jersey Shore During...

Smithville Man Identified in Past Drowning That...

Dahlia inhaled deeply. None of these incidents had anything to do with her. But seeing these thoughts written so explicitly brought on a physical, aching stress. The very word—*drowning*—on the screen in front of her, in her cozy, familiar apartment, was frightening in ways she wasn't expecting. She took another shaky breath, from a distance recognizing the quickening tightness of her chest, of her entire being. It was a visceral reaction, a chemical response; her fingers having typed that word, letter by letter, with deliberation, so it sat blinking in black before her, charged the air around her. The words were brought to life, a new presence in her house that was once completely secure. She felt a little less safe now, the words physically existing within these very walls; it left a crack in her shell of protection, contaminating what was once a place of purity.

She had started with a vague search she knew would not yield results, something far away from the information she actually needed. She wasn't ready to circle closer, just yet.

Her fingers were shaking; her nails were making tapping noises on the keys. She made herself type,

The Sandy Dollar Hotel

She pressed return and was overcome with a wave of nausea as the photos instantly filled her screen. She had spent some of her happiest days there, with her family; they were so young, then, and things were so much simpler. No one had been hurt, no one was ill; their entire futures lay before them, invincible, with limitless possibility. So much lay ahead that it would never have occurred to any of them that limits could exist—it was a carefree and innocent time, before heartbreak, before responsibility, before mortality dispelled the illusion.

Dahlia had not been prepared for the force of emotion that would accompany going back in time. She stared at the photos for many moments, transfixed, simultaneously breathless with nostalgia and sick with longing. It was over, now, forever; they were adults, living apart, no longer the center of each other's lives. They would never be that family again.

She stood suddenly and ran into the kitchen, where she leaned over the sink and vomited. Her stomach revolted in rhythmic, angry clenches, and she heaved, hunched over, for many minutes before the fit passed through her. Shuddering, she rinsed her mouth out with water, then wiped it, exhausted, with a towel.

The simmering had become a hammering. Her skin throbbed with a clammy sweat, and she was shaking. She didn't know if she should wait it out by sitting down or standing up. Her knees were weak, but she was stable leaning against the counter. She was afraid to risk movement, but she longed to relieve her unsteady legs. She stood like this for a minute or two, bent forward, head resting in her hands with her elbows on the cold laminate, in indecision. Frustrated with herself for overthinking, she resolved quickly to sit on the floor, but the suddenness of her movement made her more dizzy, and she rested her head between her legs until the room stopped spinning, chastising herself for never getting it right.

She turned back to her computer. It illuminated the apart-ment with cold, sickly glare.

Warily, she rose and stepped toward it, and sat gingerly back in her chair. She stared at the photos for a moment or two, and breathed, calm but unnerved. The words had existed tangibly; the idea was now in her apartment. And having looked up the hotel right after the drowning connected them somehow, in the universe. It was as if she had actually drowned, as if she were nothing now but a ghost.

With quick fingers she deleted her search history, turned off her computer, and stood. Out of the corner of her eye she spotted a sweatshirt she'd slung over the side of the couch; she reached over and grabbed it, and threw it over the monitor. Somewhat satisfied, she went to the window, where she opened the curtains wide, to air out the words she'd summoned and to send them back out into the darkness.

Maybe stagnancy was safer after all. When the water was quiet, it couldn't pull you in. You wouldn't be overwhelmed by it. You could still swim back to shore.

CHAPTER SIX

The next day was Monday. The store was closed Mondays and Tuesdays, and Dahlia enjoyed a much-needed day of rest. She slept in until the sun was high in the sky and her bedroom was softly lit by golden rays that mellowed as they sifted through the curtains. Then she rose, enjoyed a leisurely cup of coffee and bowl of oatmeal, and prepared to visit her father.

The weather was cheerful today, brisk, bright, and clear. Dahlia felt hopeful as she navigated the suburban streets toward her parents' house, the still perky October sunshine glimmering off her car and windshield and allowing her to forget that they were on the cusp of winter. When she arrived, she was surprised to find her father up and about, and wearing a wide smile, evidently cheered, as she was, by the crispness of the weather, as he didn't even seem disheartened by his need for his walker, as he usually was. Emboldened by his own regained strength, and eager to enjoy the nice weather, he'd enlisted his wife's help to go for a walk around the neighborhood. When Dahlia knocked and let herself inside, she found her mother easing her father into his wheelchair. Both their faces brightened at her arrival. They greeted her with boisterousness and a warm invitation, telling her she'd made her entrance at just the perfect time.

Dahlia was delighted. She held the door for her mother as she gently maneuvered the wheelchair outside; then Dahlia followed her parents down the ramp, over the driveway and to the side-walk. Hands in the pockets of her jacket, she breathed in the earthy October air. She could almost taste the season in her nostrils and in her throat. It gave a sensation of sap and soil, roots and herbs and fast fading flowers. Beneath her feet, the first fallen leaves of autumn crinkled and cracked. Dahlia's steps fell into a slow, easy rhythm. She grew lulled by the sound of it, by the motion of her mother's footsteps in front of her.

They walked around the block twice, then returned to the house. Dahlia helped her mother ease her father back into bed. While he rested, Dahlia assisted Vera with some cleaning—folding laundry, sweeping the floors, going through paperwork. These were jobs often left to Tara who, while her daughters were in school, had made this housework part of her routine. However, even Tara needed a day off now and again. She was taking time to herself today, meeting a friend for lunch.

Dahlia enjoyed a quiet cup of tea with her mother, then a light lunch with her mother and father on the back patio. She left them mid afternoon, before her father once again grew tired, casting them a final glance and smile as she left them sitting at the table outside and walked around the side of her house toward her car. A twinge of guilt pulled at her as she turned the corner, putting them out of view; her conscience told her to stay another hour, to help her mother with the second half of the day. But her mother had insisted, assuring her she could handle it, was used to handling it, and in fact didn't mind the quiet. Dahlia happily would have stayed but was not unhappy to believe her. So often her final view of her father was of him sleeping, or receiving medi-cine or treatment. It was nice to leave him looking lively, to have that image in her mind to take with her.

Back at home, Dahlia still had much of the day before her. She spent it reading in the chair by her bedroom window, curtains pulled wide, windows flooded with sunlight that pooled onto the floor and over her hands as she turned the pages of her book. It was fourth in a series of eight, and Dahlia had bought it together with the fifth and sixth once she'd felt certain that she'd read until the end. She passed a peaceful few hours flying through the pages, then read the last lines and closed the back cover, sighing with satisfaction and with the knowledge she could continue the saga immediately.

She stretched and yawned, feeling relaxed and calm. Evening was falling now, and Dahlia decided she'd fix herself a quick dinner and shower before slipping into comfortable pajamas and picking up the next book. Before she did so, she sat gazing out the window at the scene outside. The sun had begun to set, and the horizon beyond the buildings was a glistening ombre of gold that faded into indigo. A few early stars were beginning to faintly spot the sky. Below, on the sidewalks, people were smattered about, meandering from the ice cream shop, cones in hand, or chatting as they swaggered into restaurants, their laughter billowing up into the sky. Many storefronts were dark, as the bookshop would be. Cars lined the curb, partly hidden by trees. From this height, the imminentness of winter was clear: in a few short weeks, the branches would be bare.

As she observed the treetops, she was lulled by the motion of the oncoming twilight, which shifted the shadows on the street and elongated them along the buildings. Suddenly the street became the water, and she was watching from above as two arms reached outward, grabbing into the air. By their thinness, Dahlia could see it was a child—her hands were reaching, stretching, as if in a dance, but it was no dance. She was drowning, sinking beneath the surface, as Dahlia sat frozen and helpless in the sky.

A man approached, his footsteps splashing in the sea. He bent at the waist to reach into the water before him, and reemerged with the child in his hands. She was dripping wet, she was gasping, her arms hanging limply at her sides. He turned to rush her toward the shore, and she saw he was her father; she watched in shock as Edward stomped through the water and deposited her safely on the shore. He took the first steps up the beach, his feet leaving footprints in the sand, until he dissipated into a million pieces, vanishing into the air.

Dahlia jerked in her chair, awakening with a start. Her heart was pounding; waves of heat rippled through her veins and beads of sweat through her pores. She sat for a moment in terror, feeling unable to breathe; sucking in deeply, her lungs struggling to be filled, she turned toward the window and gripped the ledge with her hands. It was her street, her buildings, her neighborhood, bathed in oncoming moonlight. She stared, eyes wide open, only gradually accepting that she was home, safe and dry. But she did not feel safe at all, for she now saw shadows lurking in the corners, the darkness obscuring their forms; the people's rushing now felt ominous, and she wondered, where were they running to, who were they running from?

Her book had fallen to the floor. Dahlia reached over and retrieved it. Just hours before, she had found comfort in this book. Now it seemed a falsehood, a fairytale, the naive idealism of a little lost child.

She rose and stepped away from the window, crossing the threshold into the living room. Her heart was still hammering, and the rush of blood was blurring her vision. She stood for a moment in stillness, waiting for it to pass. She looked around her apartment. It was familiar but changed, cast in shadows, full of hidden corners and secrets. Silhouettes of furniture she used every day seemed alive, almost moving. She stood for a minute or two, observing. She flicked on the light, and it was her cozy apartment once more.

For inexplicable reasons she wanted to talk to her nieces. She glanced backward into her bedroom, where her cell phone sat on the window sill. She took a few steps back and retrieved it, and then dialed Tara; after a half a dozen rings, she was transferred to voicemail, and she hung up before the message was over.

She put her phone back on the table and stared absentmindedly outside. She wanted to call someone, but she didn't know who. She was safe up here, above the noise and chaos of the street, but it also meant she was alone. Every so often, when she looked at the town just right, she wondered if she wasn't just alone, but lonely. She was safe, yes, but at what cost? Because aside from Tara and her nieces, there was no one. She wouldn't disturb her parents. The only other person she was close to was Imani, and despite her respect for her boss, and their mutual fondness for each other, she was forced to acknowledge, with an unexpected pain to the chest, that she wasn't Imani's friend.

Dahlia sank back into the chair she'd just vacated, and slumped a little, hands folded in her lap. The sky outside was big, a kind of silvery blue with the streetlights outside. She watched it, curious, without any expectation that something would happen. Even on the clearest night, there were not a lot of stars. There were too many lights here, too many people. Further into the suburbs there were too many trees. The only time she'd seen a sky full of stars was at the shore, above the ocean, where the darkness swallowed you and you were trapped between heaven and the inscrutable pull of the sea.

"So you've never missed a day of work?" asked Gita, nodding, in her usual way, a smile on her already friendly face. "Wow. That's impressive."

Dahlia shrugged. "I guess."

"You don't think so?"

"Not really. I've just been lucky. I don't really get sick. And I don't really have much else to do."

"I think you have more than you think you do. But no matter. Imani must be grateful for your dedication and work ethic."

Dahlia paused for an imperceptible moment. The thought had occurred to her that it wasn't dedication so much as aimlessness, but she brushed the thought aside.

She shrugged again. "She's grateful, She's so busy, though, and I think she sees things holistically, like she knows I do a good job but she doesn't really think about it."

"Well, you must have sick days available. Vacation days, too."

"I do. I don't take them. Imani sometimes tells me I should."

"Maybe she's right."

They looked at each other, neither saying anything more. Dahlia submitted first, and smiled, just to break the tension.

"I never missed a day of school, either. But nobody noticed that."

Gita raised her eyebrows. "You never missed a day of school? Ever?"

"Yeah. My mother never said anything about it. My father, either. I guess it was just one of those things that was understood."

Gita was silent. "And did that bother you?" she asked finally.

Dahlia shrugged, yet again. "It occurred to me that the school could say something. But it didn't really bother me that they didn't."

"I see." Gita watched her curiously. "You were quiet about it. You didn't say anything to anybody else."

"I just didn't need that kind of praise. I never have. And I really don't like attention. Tara was the overachiever, and she needed it. She'd tell you she didn't, but she did. She was used to it, I think, so she didn't see how much it motivated her. Tara missed a lot of school, actually, but it was for things like field trips, volunteering, and college tours."

"And how about you, Dahlia? Did you go on any college tours?"

"I knew I was going to go locally. It didn't matter where it was, so much, so long as I got an education."

"And you wanted to stay safe."

Dahlia stared at her. Her eyes turned hard. "What?"

"I said you wanted to stay safe."

"No."

Gita blinked a few times, and let it slide.

"Do you do anything for yourself?" she asked then. "Self-care, I mean. Massages? Vacations? Retail therapy, anything?"

"No." It never occurred to Dahlia to do any of those things. She never even felt tempted by them. She paid her bills and helped her parents; she bought gas and food and the occasional fluffy sweatshirt. She never spent any real money on herself. She couldn't think of anything she really wanted to do. And besides, what if she one day needed it? What if she'd wasted it, and then something urgent occurred? Better to save it for a rainy day than spend it needlessly, on things that didn't matter.

"What was college like for you?" Gita asked her, uncrossing and recrossing her legs. "Did you have friends, relationships? Did you go to social events?"

"I had friends."

The words were clipped, her voice weak. Dahlia lifted her chin to compensate.

The two women looked at each other across space.

"Were they fulfilling? Is there anyone you keep in touch with?"

"I don't really remember."

"Did you get involved in things, in activities? With other people? Were you active?"

Dahlia turned red. "Are you trying to ask me if I'm a virgin?"

Gita looked surprised. Her back straightened, and her lips parted.

"No," she said, gently, clearly taken aback. "Dahlia, I'd never ask you that. That's the kind of thing you bring up yourself, if you want to." Gita's eyes narrowed with thought. "I can nudge you, if you want nudging. But I won't make you talk about it."

Dahlia didn't say anything. She worked her jaw a little, her mind awhirl.

"What would you like to talk about?" Gita swiveled in her chair a little. "I'm more than happy to continue prompting you." She chuckled, a bit humorlessly. "But this often works best if it's client led. So feel free to interject at any time."

Dahlia cleared her throat.

"I'm not a virgin," she said, with more confidence than she felt. "Just in case you were wondering."

"Okay." Gita wore her warmest expression; she seemed to be inviting her to say more, that there would be no judgment. Dahlia didn't know how she did it or whether it was sincere, but it worked. "And has it been a positive experience for you?"

"I guess."

Gita blinked and nodded, waiting for her to say more.

Dahlia cleared her throat.

"Sex is fine," she said, throwing Gita a crumb, but a small one. "I don't hate it. I don't actively seek it, though."

"That sounds like a healthy attitude."

Dahlia was inclined, inexplicably, to say more.

"It isn't that I don't think about it," she murmured, blushing despite her best efforts. "It's just that..."

She braved a glance at Gita. Her eyes were wide and kind.

Dahlia sighed. "It's just that, I've never been all that attracted to anyone. Not enough for it to...compel me forward." She'd never said these words to anyone. There was an odd thrill in acknowledging it out loud. The thought was a train crossing a bridge, and there was one more compartment. "I don't know what's wrong with me," she made herself say, half relieved, half horrified to let the backend of the train scuttle to the other side.

Gita's face wore a soft smile. "Can you tell me a little about the men you've dated?"

Dahlia wasn't even sure she could. They were all so average, so nondescript. It had gotten to the point where she couldn't even tell them apart. A series of blurred, faded memories filtered through her mind's eye—men who couldn't make conversation, men who were bored, who were bored by her—men who all looked the same, even when they didn't.

"They were pretty unimpressive," she said, and was embarrassed by this description of her own life. "I mean they didn't have a lot of personality. I thought they did, at first. But they all became the same."

"The same how?"

Dahlia's brow furrowed as she thought about it. "Just...the same. Uninteresting. Emotionless." *Passionless*, she thought, but she didn't say it. "Like they didn't care."

Gita raised her eyebrows at this. "Like they didn't care about what?"

Dahlia blinked a couple of times. "Anything."

"That's interesting." Gita leaned back in her chair. "So, did you stop caring, too? About relationships, I mean."

"I guess. Yeah. I mean it just seems like all men are the same."

"Tom isn't. Neither is your father."

"April's husband is."

"I think maybe you're deflecting. Is that unfair to say?"

Dahlia was taken aback. "I mean," she muttered, and cleared her throat, "it just shows how crappy a relationship can be."

"But you have plenty of examples in your life of when they aren't crappy at all."

A knot in Dahlia's stomach tightened, and she frowned.

Gita looked up to the ceiling for a moment, in thought. "I'm wondering," she mused. "How long did your relationships last?"

"Not very long." Dahlia didn't know what "very long" meant, but instinctively she knew hers hadn't mattered. "A few weeks. A month. A couple of months, tops."

"And did you feel like you ever got close to them?"

Dahlia's eyes sharpened. The simmering had swelled into a low but painful boil. She said nothing.

Gita lowered her gaze and looked at her. "Dahlia?"

Something in Dahlia's consciousness had shifted, but she didn't know what, or where.

Passionless. Am I passionless?

She squinted a little, studying the woman before her, at the same time, directing her gaze inward in a way she never had before.

"No," she said, folding her arms over her chest, and rubbing them with the opposite hands, absentmindedly. "It was like...I couldn't."

"Why not?"

"They were like...workaholics, some of them. Or they just had other interests. They just didn't seem to want to be in long-term relationships, like it...like it cut too much from their own lives? It was fine, for a while, but it's like it always came to a standstill. Like they wouldn't want to commit to any plans, they wouldn't want to talk about anything even a little serious. They were..."

"They were emotionally unavailable," said Gita. "Detached, commitmentphobic, nonconfrontational, mentally distant."

"Yes." Dahlia was surprised by the force with which she'd said it. It was, to her surprise, refreshing to talk about it, and with someone who understood—it felt good to get confirmation, that it wasn't in her head, that she hadn't been imagining it.

Gita settled in her seat. "You have to be attracted to his personality in order to be attracted to him physically. It's not all that uncommon. It's also why you've never been truly attracted to anyone you've dated. You never get close enough. And you pick the wrong men."

Dahlia raised her eyebrows. *I don't*, she insisted in her mind, but deep down she knew that she did. And even deeper, in a place so hidden even she couldn't fully pierce its shadows, was the reminder that she at least had *him*—her secret stranger, the one who was perfect and strong, the one who was always there. Even as the familiar tenderness overtook her at the thought of him she recognized how it sounded, this irrational intimacy she felt with a person whose face she'd never seen.

"Did you ever go in the ocean again?" asked Gita.

Dahlia straightened. "What?"

"Sorry," said Gita, with a hand gesture of apology. "I was just wondering if, after almost drowning, you ever went in the ocean again."

Dahlia blinked. "What does that have to do with anything?"

"Dahlia," said Gita. "I think you have generalized anxiety disorder."

Instantly, Dahlia's blood rose into her face. "No, I don't." She laughed. "That's a bit of a stretch."

"I don't think it is." Gita sat patiently, waiting for Dahlia to recover. "I think your experience changed you. I think you're still recovering. I think that's why you're here."

"I'm here because my father is dying."

"Maybe. But you're also here because you're depressed."

Dahlia's vision was clouded by a dark wave of anger, which leaked from her heart and resonated through her veins and out of the pores in her skin. Her stomach revolted at what Gita had said. She worked her jaw a little, suppressing a frown, and forcing herself not to speak.

"Does that bother you?" asked Gita, with what Dahlia saw as almost absurd lack of awareness. "The change in your demeanor was almost instant."

"I'm not really depressed." Dahlia had croaked the words out. She cleared her throat and shifted in her seat, the dark haze clearing. "I like my life. I don't mind my life."

She stopped.

I stay safe, but I'm not passionless. I have passions. Right?

Gita waited for her to say more, but she was silent.

"I think you should consider it," said Gita. "I think your anxiety is real but that there's a whole lot more to resolve."

Dahlia watched her with wary interest. She didn't really believe what Gita had told her. But part of her, in the deepest, most secret corners of her mind, held up a finger at her, imploring her not to dismiss it out of hand.

"How about friendships, Dahlia?" Gita's voice was quiet, tentative, and the sympathy in her voice only heightened Dahlia's discomfort. "Do you have any close friendships?" Gita went on, and Dahlia squirmed in her seat, looking frantically about the room, as if she'd find escape there. She felt cornered, all of a sudden, and her chest squeezed and tightened. She spotted the clock on the desk, and grasped her purse strap with her sweaty palm.

"Actually, it looks like our time is up," she said, slinging the purse over her shoulder. "I guess we'll have to finish this next week."

"We have a few more minutes," said Gita, rising, turning toward the door, but not intercepting Dahlia as she took wide steps across the room.

"No, really, it's fine. I'm fine," Dahlia said, amazed at the unchecked movement in her legs. She put her hand to her forehead, hiding her vision of Gita, of herself. "Thank you so much. I'll see you next week," she called over her shoulder, and strode from the office, down the flight of stairs and into the parking lot, where the dingy but familiar comfort of her car awaited.

THAT NIGHT DAHLIA was particularly tired and fell asleep early, reading on her bed, still in her clothes. It was a dark, heavy sleep, interrupted only by a dream in which she was drowning, in the winter, and in the nighttime—an adult who had only been trying to go home, who'd left the bookstore after her shift and had found an ocean between her and her apartment. Having been tumbled by the waves, she didn't know which way was the sky, and she threw her arms about wildly, looking for the surface, looking for freedom.

Her hand grasped another, and she gripped it tight, with desperation; the hand pulled, and as she emerged from the frozen darkness of the deep she heard the rumblings of a storm, though it was still very far away. She looked at the face of her savior—it was a stranger, young, and with short brown hair.

He's here, she assured herself, relieved and uplifted. She couldn't see his face, but she knew that he was beautiful.

She blinked, and now it was her father; she tried to call for him, but her throat constricted around her voice. She watched in horror as the face morphed upon itself, transforming before her eyes between the stranger and her father, until the man himself disappeared, running toward the moonlight over the hills, and then dissipating into dust before rising up into the heavens.

She awoke with a start, confused and bereaved. She blinked, her eyes adjusting to the softer, translucent darkness of her bedroom, with the curtains wide open, the moon and stars silver beacons over the city. She stared at the night sky, which like every night grew brighter closer to the horizon, where streetlamps and illuminated windows cast artificial light into the blue infinity. Dahlia waited as her heartbeat slowed, willfully suppressing waves of nausea, wondering if this was how it would be now, as she dug deeper and deeper into the blue infinity of herself.

She sighed and stood, and stretched: she'd fallen asleep in an uncomfortable position, something that never bothered her when she was younger. Sore and tired, and troubled from her dream, she stumbled into her living room, where she flicked on the light and gazed absently about. Her stomach pulled: she realized she'd fallen asleep before she'd eaten dinner. Mechanically, she stepped toward her kitchen and fixed herself a plate of leftovers, leaning against the counter and staring at nothing until the brash beeps of the microwave jolted her from her thoughts.

She ate at her little table, reflecting on this evening's dream. When she was through, she laid her fork down on her plate with a clank, and leaned back in her chair, deep in thought.

She should call the hotel. They wouldn't be able to provide her any information about what had happened, but something they said might jolt her memory, might inspire her with a lead. Her father was counting on her, and she didn't want to make him have to ask her twice. Even as she began the process of formulating a plan she recognized the tingling of dread in her blood. She had no idea where to begin, and she didn't like to talk to new people. She worried about what she would say, how she would sound, whether they'd find her awkward, whether they'd think her stupid. And worse, if it was futile, she'd have to start again. It was almost easier never to start, when the possibility was out there; once the task began, she'd encounter roadblocks, and the enormity of having to workshop solutions made her stomach revolt and her heart squeeze.

She picked her phone from the table and opened her browser, and typed in the name of the hotel. The phone number came up instantly, but Dahlia didn't call. Instead, she placed the phone down and leaned back in her seat once more, eyes closed, arms folded across her chest. She could already envision it, her fumbling for words, her rapidly dwindling confidence—her hanging up in shame, no closer to her goal than she'd been the minute before.

For the first time, she was aware of the train of thought that prevented her from acting—that kept her at the base of the mountain, that kept her from climbing. She cleaned her dishes and crawled back into bed, burying herself in the covers, and as she drifted back off into a restless sleep she wondered if she was still almost drowning, what it meant that she'd thought it was normal, and that it had never occurred to her that it didn't have to be.

~

ON HER DAY off Dahlia slept in, awakening when the sun was already high over the skyline and the street beneath was bustling. She went to the window for her usual assessment of what the day looked like. It was windy, with crisp fallen leaves drifting from their branches and landing in russet pools along the sidewalk and on street corners. Dahlia yawned, stretched, and made coffee in the kitchen, then put on one of her favorite shows while she enjoyed a light breakfast with the curtains open.

She found her mind drifting like the leaves. She turned toward the window, where the buildings across the street sat stoic, as always, despite the breeze that rustled the trees below. The shapes of the buildings against the sky remained the same in all weather, all seasons, all times of day, and she'd come to see them almost as friends. She knew every inch of the brick of the old bank, every turn of the fire escape pouring from the upper floor and every dent in its metal, every notch where paint had been scraped away.

Her eyes then dipped to the window sill, where they fell upon the green bowl her father had given her, the one he'd saved for her because it was part of the work she loved. Her smile widened at the image of her father's face, then faded, haunting images of illness and pain intercepting her view, demanding her attention.

Dahlia stood and picked up her phone from the table, then opened her browser. She still had a tab open with the Sandy Dollar's website. She scrolled to the bottom and pressed the number quickly, heart pounding, before she had time for worry to take control.

The phone rang three times. On the fourth, someone picked up.

"Sandy Dollar Hotel, where memories are made, this is Tamsen. How can I help you?"

Dahlia's face flushed and sweated. She held the phone to her ear and her hand over the other, and began pacing, working off nervous energy.

"Hi," she said, in an unusually high voice. She cleared her throat. "I have kind of a strange question I was hoping you could help me with."

"Of course."

She was encouraged. Tamsen sounded friendly. Dahlia imagined people called with strange questions all the time, that Tamsen was professional enough to think nothing of it—or at least, if she did, not to say anything about it.

"So I stayed there with my family a really long time ago. Like, decades ago. We used to stay there every year."

"How nice."

Dahlia took a deep breath. "It's a long shot, I know. But I was wondering if there was ever a report of a near drowning. You know, where someone saved the person? It was a child, someone staying in your hotel, which is why I'm calling. It's a really long story, but it's related to my family." She paused a moment, impressed with her ability to come up with this vague explanation on the spot. "Like I said, I know it's a long shot. I don't think it was reported." Why would something like that be reported? The words sounded ridiculous to her even as she was saying them. Within seconds, her confidence began dwindling. "But I wasn't sure if, you know, like maybe somebody saw it, and talked? I mean you probably wouldn't have been working there back then." She laughed; she closed her eyes and cringed at the maniacal nature of the sound. "But I didn't know if, you know, like if maybe it was a story that was, kind of, passed down?"

Dahlia stopped talking, mortified, but mostly satisfied with what she had said. Though her question was absurd, and though she'd been rambling a little, she'd sounded, she thought, mostly lucid. It was a long shot, but it wasn't impossible to believe; it was a sentimental question, one a nice person like Tamsen surely wouldn't criticize, or mock.

"Hmm," said Tamsen, and relief flowed through Dahlia like an arctic river. "I don't recall hearing anything about that, honestly. Can I put you on a brief hold?"

"Sure. Thank you so much."

Dahlia exhaled and tucked her hair behind her ear as tinny classical music piped through the line. She waited a minute or more before the music abruptly stopped. She stiffened with alertness, picking up the mantle of courage she'd hesitantly dropped during this brief pause.

"I'm sorry," said Tamsen, "but nobody's heard of anything like that. Was the person who saved the child staying here, too?"

Dahlia straightened, and her eyes widened. She'd never thought about that before. "I don't know."

"Well, I truly am sorry," said Tamsen, and Dahlia was so grateful for her kindness at such an unusual request. "I hope you find what you're looking for."

"Thank you, me too. Thanks. I really appreciate your help."

"You're welcome. Enjoy the rest of your day."

"You too."

Dahlia hung up the phone and ran her fingers through her hair, a flood of adrenaline tingling in her blood. Accomplishing this first task, small as it was, made her feel like she was in the process, like she was no longer starting from scratch—like she had taken the first step up a mountain. She certainly wasn't far, but for once in her life, she was climbing. She was no longer at the base. She was proud of herself for managing it about as well as could be expected. And despite the fact that she was no closer to finding her savior than she was before, the phone call had opened up a new path of thought: he could have been staying in any hotel. The shore was also resplendent with bed and breakfasts. And maybe he wasn't even staying overnight at the beach at all.

Wheedling the possibilities down until she pinpointed the information she was looking for seemed an impossible task, but so had making that phone call just minutes before. *Who knows?* she thought to herself, continuing to pace a few more minutes in an absentminded attempt to purge her excess energy. Maybe her next inquiry would also yield another path, another question, in a continuous process that would ultimately bring her results.

Regardless, she was satisfied. She had taken the first step, a single step. She was in it now. It was like staring at a blank page, she imagined, as she had imagined her favorite authors doing many times. Before you start, the task seems infinite. It's that first sentence that's hardest. After that...you're simply adding pages to a book that already exists.

CHAPTER SEVEN

"*E*velyn. Ginger." Dahlia crooked her finger discreetly. "Come here for a sec."

Intrigued, Tara's two elder daughters followed Dahlia into the dining room of their house. Tara and Tom were in the kitchen making dinner. Little Celeste was watching a movie in the living room, sitting on the floor and coloring with crayons.

Out of sight of the youngest Spangler daughter, Dahlia pulled two small gifts from her bag.

"This is for you," she told Ginger, handing her a roll of vintage floral stickers. "And this is for you." For Evelyn, she held out a slim packet of stationery with an elegant Florentine design.

"Ooh," cooed Ginger, admiring her present. She looked at her aunt with wide, pretty eyes. "Thank you, Aunt Dahlia! What's this for?"

"It's for you. To do whatever you want with it."

"She means, why do we get presents?" Evelyn had opened the packet and brushing her finger along the gilded design. "It's so pretty. Thank you so much."

"You're very welcome. And it's for no reason. I guess it's really because you were so good with Celeste the other day, and because she got a present and you didn't. But really it's because I love you."

"Aw." Ginger, the most effusive of the sisters, flushed and smiled. "We love you, Aunt Dahlia."

"Yes, this was so kind of you." Mature Evelyn dutifully hugged her aunt. "You didn't have to do this."

"Well, I wanted to."

A little crash from the direction of the living room interrupted their conversation.

"What happened?" called Ginger to Celeste.

There was a pause. "Nothing."

Ginger and Evelyn exchanged a look, then turned and ran into the living room to check on their little sister.

Dahlia waited a few moments to make sure there was no emergency. Once she'd gathered the crash had been the result of fallen crayons, not fallen child, she chuckled to herself and drifted toward the kitchen to help her sister and brother-in-law.

After a raucous, lively dinner, Dahlia stepped in to clean up, relieving Tara and Tom, who used the time to attempt to get the girls ready for bed early, or "at least on time for once," in Tara's words. After the house was quiet, the girls spending some time reading books or playing with puzzles upstairs, Tara and Dahlia sat at the dining room table with a cup of tea and some chocolate —which Tara had hidden in "her secret stash," feeding the girls cookies for dessert, instead.

"I just feel like I deserve something for myself," Tara said, blowing daintily into her tea. "It isn't that I don't want to share." She raised her brow. "Actually, it is, a little."

Dahlia wondered what Tara's day had looked like, the way she'd absorbed so much responsibility to the detriment of her own interests, the way she took care of her kids, the way she took care of her parents.

She eyed her sister over her mug. "I think that's fine."

The two sat and chatted for a time, this in-between stage

of the day, not quite day, not quite night. Tara updated Dahlia on their father's health and treatments. He'd been approved for the drug trial April had found for him, and everyone was cautiously optimistic. Dahlia tried not to become too excited that it would make everything better, that he'd be cured and that their lives could go back to normal. But it was hard.

"That sounds promising," she said, eyes a little wider.

"We'll see."

The two sipped their tea.

"He mentioned it again today," said Tara. "The guy who saved you when you were almost drowning."

Dahlia froze. "He did?"

"Yes."

Neither said anything for a moment or two.

"What do you mean 'again'?"

"He mentions it pretty much every day."

Dahlia stared at her.

"I'm there pretty often," she said finally. "He hasn't said it again to me."

"Well, he has to me."

Dahlia shrank back in her seat a little.

Tara looked up. "What's wrong?"

Dahlia frowned. *I've disappointed him. I've disappointed you.*

Tara took a sip of tea. "Have you found out anything yet?"

Dahlia rubbed her lips together and directed her gaze downward, toward her tea. She spun the mug by the handle, gently, in a show of nonchalance.

"I've made a little progress," she murmured, and lifted her mug to her lips. "I've made some calls."

"And nothing yet?"

She shook her head. "Not yet."

"You should go on social media," said Tara. "I'll bet you'd find something that way. People love mysteries and investigations.

119

They also love a good story. I'll bet they'd help you. I'll bet you'd go viral."

Dahlia couldn't think of anything she'd like less. "I don't think so," she said, shaking her head. "I wouldn't know where to begin."

"No one ever knows where to begin when they try something."

An uncomfortable feeling began settling inside Dahlia; it knotted in her stomach and opened outward into her blood. Why did it feel lately like the ground was shifting beneath her? Nothing would stay still; nothing would remain the same. It was bad enough that her father's future was so uncertain, that this illness had descended upon their family and shaken everything into chaos. Now she was supposed to talk to people on social media. She was supposed to fly to Los Angeles. Why couldn't she take care of her father, why couldn't she grieve for him, without all this extra—whatever it was that it was? Why couldn't she invert in on herself, in her pain—why did she have to stretch outward, when all she wanted to do was retract?

"I don't know." Dahlia shifted in her seat. "It would probably just be easier to keep calling hotels. Maybe someone heard something."

"The problem is," said Tara, "that nothing actually happened. There wasn't a drowning. I mean obviously I'm glad there wasn't." She smiled slyly. "But my point is, it's not going to be in any papers. It's not the kind of thing that would have been talked about."

"Maybe he told someone."

"Maybe he's on social media."

Dahlia huffed inside, but she begrudgingly acknowledged that Tara had a point. It was possible she could find him right online, and talk to him herself.

And talk to him. A wave of heat rushed her. All this time she'd worried she'd never find him. Until this moment it hadn't occurred to her to worry about if she did.

"Dahlia?" Tara's voice was soft, inquiring. Her brow was lifted; her hand was reaching across the table to pat her own. "Are you okay?"

The color had drained from Dahlia's face. She smiled meekly. "Of course."

"Here," said Tara, leaning backward toward a side table, where her hand grasped the edge of her laptop. She lifted it from the table and placed it between herself and Dahlia, and scooted her chair closer. "Let's open your account right now."

"Wait, Tara..."

"It's really not that big a deal. You'll see." She quickly punched in a website address and logged out of her own account, then typed in Dahlia's email. "You can be on as much or as little as you want. Also I won't have to text you all the news anymore."

"So that's your ulterior motive."

"It's not the reason, but it helps."

Dahlia sighed, her stomach fluttering nervously. Tara had been trying to get her on social media for years, but Dahlia had always resisted. It felt like an entire universe, and she'd just learned to navigate her own. She didn't even want to talk to strangers in the real world—why would she want to talk to them online, from her apartment, which was supposed to be safe and comforting?

She watched Tara type her name into her new account. "I don't want people to be able to look me up," she told her. Not that she had much of an online presence to begin with; not that she had ever done anything. "Will people be able to look me up?"

"Theoretically, they always could," said Tara. "You could use a fake name, if you want."

"Okay, let's do that, then," said Dahlia, cool relief tempering somewhat the anxiety that was fizzing in her veins. What sounded like Dahlia Polinski? "How about Dolly? Dolly..."

"Dolly Polly."

They both laughed. Dahlia felt a little lighter.

"Hmm," said Tara. "How about a different flower? Something with a 'D'? Daisy?"

"Ooh, I like that." The cloak of anonymity made her feel better. "Daisy...Daisy Pol? Daisy Polin?"

"Daisy Pollen. That's funny."

They laughed again. Dahlia sat and thought for a minute.

"Daisy Polinski," she said, noting the sound of it, hoping inspiration would strike. "Daisy Polinski...Daisy..."

"Planski," interjected Tara, abruptly. "Polinski fast is Planski. It's your plan."

"I love it." Dahlia smiled, even a bit giddily. She didn't really want to do this, but as long as she was, it might be interesting to exist for a time as an alias. Maybe it would give her a little freedom. Maybe it would even be fun.

"Okay, Daisy Planski it is." Tara's fingers clicked away, and with a final dramatic click, Daisy Planski existed. "Just that easy."

I wish, thought Dahlia, but she looked on curiously as Tara showed her around the site.

"Here's where you see your own profile," she told her, "and here's where you read your friends' updates."

What if I don't have any friends? Dahlia ignored this objection, and watched on.

Tara showed her how to do searches, find business pages, and, most importantly, join groups. Tara was convinced that was where the answers would be—local groups, groups about the shore, groups sharing vintage photos of hotels.

"Sometimes they make you answer questions to join," said Tara, clicking away. "Just answer them all, and they'll usually let you in."

"Okay." If she joined groups, she'd definitely have to talk to people. On the other hand, it would be a confined space, with similarly minded people, people with a common thread. Maybe it wouldn't feel so public; maybe it wouldn't be so bad. "What kind of group should I look for?"

"I'd look for anything about Seashell Cove Beach. Just do a search and see what comes up. There have got to be a hundred groups full of people who love it there. They're like fan groups. People just share stories and pictures and whatnot. I'm in a few Disney groups," said Tara—her daughters loved Disney World, and the family tried to go at least once a year. "And one for Brentwick." She shrugged. "There are groups for just about anything you like. And if you don't find a group, there will probably be pages."

"Pages?"

"Yeah, like profiles but for businesses, places, and that kind of thing. Literally everything is on here. Play around with it. Follow some stuff."

Dahlia stayed a little while longer. Before leaving, she went quickly upstairs to kiss the girls goodnight and tell them she'd see them soon. Then she climbed into her car, noting with surprise how quickly the weather had turned from brisk to cold. Huddling into her scarf, she pulled out of the driveway and drove home, scurrying up to the warmth of her little apartment, where she promptly dropped her clothes into her laundry basket and slid into her most comfortable pajamas.

As she brushed her teeth and washed her face she stared at herself in the mirror, seeing the features she'd seen a million times, studying the subtle new wrinkles around her eyes and the extra gray or two in her hair. She looked the same, but somehow different; she looked like a person with the world moving around her. She preferred to stand still and move with it, aging quietly and silently without anybody noticing. She didn't really care about the changes in her appearance. What concerned her more was the expansion of her borders. Like it or not, she was in a whole new world now. She didn't want it, but she couldn't stop it; people's expectations, it seemed, were finally catching up. She hated expanding, but she hated disappointing more. She couldn't live with herself knowing she'd lost the respect of her father, of Tara, of Imani. She'd put off making these decisions as long as she could. Now she was out of time.

She didn't know why everyone couldn't just leave her alone, why living in the world required such specific, insistent demands. It was all too much. Why couldn't she just be who she was? Why couldn't she live in her apartment, with her books and her things, work her job, love her family—why wasn't what she was capable of, enough?

IT TOOK a few days for Dahlia to return to the website herself. It was in the back of her mind as she built displays, checked out customers, visited her parents—and she was prepared to relate the new development to her father, should he ask. But he never did. He greeted her with a smile, as always, and talked to her about common books they'd read, or books they hadn't read, but should. He did not push her or pressure her about the search for the unknown savior in any way. His kindness and patience made Dahlia feel all the more guilty for continuing to put it off.

On the third night Dahlia pulled her laptop from the table and perused the site as she watched a history documentary. As Tara had suggested, she searched for various things she liked, or thought she might like—art museums, authors, restaurants. She smiled as she accepted Tara's friend request: she was her only friend, which seemed appropriate.

She procrastinated a bit by perusing Tara's profile. It was more or less what she'd expected, pictures of the girls and witty, sometimes self-deprecatory remarks about parenting; commentary about her favorite (and least favorite) movies and shows; recipe successes and failures; videos of quirky art, impressive dancing, or satirical presentations of teenagers' behavior; and the infrequent, but characteristically bold, statements about current events, usually accompanied by a news article. All in all it was very familiar, very Tara. Dahlia took a moment to appreciate the feeling of Tara being in the room with her. A warm feeling overtook her. She read some comments from Taras' friends, comments on pictures of her nieces—she recognized some family members, too, talking to each other, making common observations and joking around just as they did at the Thanksgiving table. Dahlia looked at it all but did not comment herself. It was as if she were late to the game, as if she'd obtained a vision of a party she'd been invited to, but had declined to attend.

Finally she sucked in her breath and typed "Seashell Cove Beach New Jersey" into the search bar up top. It yielded about a dozen results, some more professional-looking than others. She joined three groups: "Seashell Cove NJ Beach Lovers," "Vintage Seashell Cove," and "Seashell Cove, NJ: Then and Now." The third was the only one that asked her questions to be approved, and they were easy. She simply had to agree to standard rules of conduct, and offer one reason she loved Seashell Cove.

I spent time there with my family, she responded. Twenty minutes later, she was in.

Dahlia spent a little time scrolling down the page, skimming other people's posts. It was largely people sharing vintage photos or family snapshots over the years, or asking if such and such business was still open. Most of the posts had inspired enthusiastic conversation. Not all of it was nice. Largely, people joined in with pleasant reminiscing. But some people had chosen to respond in a rude, snarky fashion—"Of course that place closed, where have you been?" or, "Who's that loser in the background?" Dahlia couldn't imagine inserting herself into this, inviting people to read *her* words, to comment on *her* family memories. Once again she was overwhelmed with the fear of being exposed, of talking to strangers, who would feel entitled to come to conclusions about her life and her family. She put her hand on top of the laptop, intending to close it for the night—she'd taken more steps than she normally would in one day, and it was enough for right now. She could come back to it all tomorrow.

But then her eyes lighted on the green bowl that rested on the window sill.

I'm there pretty often. He hasn't said it again to me.

Well, he has to me.

The hurt that had seeped through her when she found out her father had been waiting for her to take action—had been waiting for her to do this thing, this one thing, that he wanted her to do —reemerged from the darkest depths of her. She inhaled against the fear—of disappointing him, or failing him, of pretending she had time until suddenly, it was too late.

She opened her laptop and pulled up the group.

I was wondering if someone could help me.

She bit her lip, thought about it.

My family and I used to vacation here every year when I was younger.

Dahlia swallowed: it felt so personal, even this.

One year, when I was six, I almost drowned.

Just do it, she told herself. Just keep going.

A man pulled me from the ocean. He was

Dahlia paused. Her eyes widened: she didn't even know what to say about him.

She sat for some time, thinking. She closed her eyes and thought about the objective details she knew.

He had floppy brown hair. He was wearing navy swim trunks.

What else?

Dahlia didn't know. So much of her recollection of him was a feeling, nothing quantifiable in words. She couldn't talk about how he'd made her feel chosen even in her terror, about the unspoken tenderness between them that she fully acknowledged possibly existed only in her mind.

It felt like a fool's errand; she had so little to go by, such fragmented memories of something that was a mere blip in someone else's life. How on Earth was anyone supposed to remember this? He probably didn't even tell anyone about it. No one else likely saw it—even her family hadn't seen it.

But, as Tara had said—maybe he himself was on social media. Maybe something in the story would ring true. Maybe she could assuage the guilt of having brought this trouble on her already ailing father; maybe she could, at least, tell him that she'd tried. And maybe she could tell herself she'd taken one more step up the mountain.

He was a young white man, maybe in his twenties, and he had brown hair. He was wearing blue swim trunks. I apologize that this is all I can remember. But this is important to my family, and I thought it was possible that he'd see this, or that it would be seen by somebody that he knew.

Dahlia hit "post" and closed her laptop in an instant. It was really all she could bring herself to do, for now. To make herself safe again, she turned up the volume of her show and made herself a cup of tea; later, she climbed into bed with a book, the halo of light from her bedside lamp casting a soft glow over her bed and pillow, encasing her in light and erasing the memories of the day.

～

SHE FORGOT about it until the following afternoon, when she arrived home from work and checked her email, only to find several dozen notifications alerting her that people had commented on her post.

She immediately texted Tara.

Why am I getting emails? Do I have to get the emails?

You can turn off the emails, Dahlia. Just go into your settings and opt out.

But how will I know that people are commenting?

You'll see a little flag on the corner of your page.

Dahlia signed on, reluctantly, and checked the right corner. Sure enough, a little flag with the number "57" leapt out from the icon of a person talking—her notifications, she gathered. She clicked on the flag, only to be bombarded with a list of names, each followed by the phrase "has commented on your thread."

She clicked the first notification, which led her to her original post.

Immediately she was sucked into a conversation that had happened without her knowledge and without her presence— unfamiliar, unrelated people who all had opinions about what she had said and how she had handled it, some of whom were helpful and others, less so.

Aw that's so sweet I can't help but I hope you find him

I think my uncle was there about that time and he also had brownish hair, I'll ask him if it was him.

Sounds like this is a job for the police, not random people online.

How about a little more info? Age of said person? Area of said beach?

How the hell do you expect anyone to know this?

This has got to be the dumbest fucking post I've seen all day.

You sound pathetic, too bad he didn't let you drown

Dahlia had the sensation of falling, of turning in on herself; she felt vulnerable and small, no more than a child drowning in an ocean of hate and criticism. Her stomach churning, blood rushing to her face, she tried to recognize what she was feeling and was surprised to find not just hurt and embarrassment, but also shame. She felt she was in the spotlight and marked for ridicule, and she once again wondered why it was she never quite seemed able to keep up.

The prickling of tears began behind her eyes, but she was too stunned and traumatized for crying. She stared at the screen, dumbfounded, and deeply bothered by this snippet of cruelty in this tiny corner of the universe. She wished she'd never exposed herself to this. She'd put out her hand hoping it wouldn't be slapped; it was really no great surprise that it was.

She shut her laptop and made herself a cup of chamomile tea. She drank it in the armchair by the window, staring at nothing.

She spent the evening in this fashion, making herself dinner and forcing herself to eat it in a kind of mindless blur, mechanically dressing and washing for bed as if in a nightmare, where everything suddenly had changed. She tried to take comfort in the familiar things around her, but she was floating above it, separated. Even her blankets, the silhouettes of her furniture, all her old friends that sustained her every day and every night, were not enough to erase the knowledge of what she had seen. The world wasn't safe, and the intensity of her reaction to it told her she wasn't strong enough to take it. She couldn't climb the mountain after all. She found herself feeling anger at herself, and at Tara; she'd been better off not knowing about this meanness, and about her softness and vulnerability—at least, then, she hadn't had validation.

This is why, she said to herself, *I never do anything.*

～

"HONESTLY I CAN'T EVEN REMEMBER. Some of them, anyway. It isn't that there were so many. It's that they were all the same, they didn't matter."

Dahlia shifted in her seat, played with the hem of her shirt. She really didn't want to talk about her love life, or lack thereof. But she'd known continuing the conversation was inevitable, that the point when she couldn't avoid it would arrive sooner or later. No matter how many times Gita told her she could talk about it on her terms, she knew that its dysfunction was obvious. She acknowledged that in fact, it might be something worth talking about—still, that didn't mean she wanted to do it.

"Can you tell me about your most recent relationship? When was it? What was his name?"

Dahlia crossed and uncrossed her arms. "It was about a year ago," she said, and crossed her arms again. "His name was George."

"How old was he?"

"Forty."

"How did you meet?"

Visions of sterile aisles and worn carpets, fluorescent lighting and plastic business card holders filtered through her mind's eye.

"It was at an office supply store," she murmured, embarrassed without really knowing why. "I was there picking up ink for the bookshop printer."

"And what happened?"

"He was looking at desk chairs. You know, the kind that swivel. I was walking by him with the ink trying to get to the register when he asked me for my opinion."

"And what did you think about that?"

"I thought it was a little weird, but not weird enough to raise any red flags. People are different. To each their own."

"So you stopped what you were doing and helped him?"

"I honestly didn't think they were all that different, like it's just an office chair, they're all kind of the same. I just told him I liked the one on the left better. It wasn't as clunky. Didn't look as much like it came from a big box office store."

"And then what happened?"

"He told me a little about the struggle it had been to find the right chair. It wasn't for him, it was for his boss. We laughed a little, I guess. Then he walked up with me to the register. He paid for the chair but couldn't leave with it because they didn't have it in stock. He had to order it."

"And you left the store together?"

"He waited for me to pay for the ink and then asked if I wanted to have coffee."

"So you had coffee?"

"No, I had to get back to the store. I mentioned where I worked, by accident. I wasn't intending for him to find me there, but he did."

"Oh, he went to the store? When was that?"

"A couple of days later. He was polite about it, seemed to understand that I might think it was strange. He just said I seemed friendly and that he'd enjoyed our conversation and that he'd love to take me for coffee or lunch if I wanted to. If I didn't want to, no worries."

"So you went."

"It was fifteen minutes until my lunch break anyway. He looked around the shop for a bit. When the other employee got there, we left together."

"Where did you go?"

"Just this little place up the road. Like a little sandwich place. Super casual."

"And did you like him?"

Dahlia blinked, then shrugged. "I liked him well enough."

"I find it interesting that he said he enjoyed your conversation, because from what you're telling me, the conversation was all about him."

Dahlia didn't say anything. It wasn't untrue.

Gita went on. "What's missing in your story is any evidence that you actually wanted to see him again."

Dahlia chewed her lip. "I guess."

Gita was studying her. "What do you make of that?"

Dahlia stared at her. "I don't know."

Gita waited a few moments, then continued. "So go on," she said, gesturing with her hand. "What happened next? How did the relationship develop?"

"We exchanged numbers and went out a few more times. We became friends, I guess, like we did things together, like going to the movies, going out to dinner, etcetera. We hung out at his place a few times, or at mine."

"Did you enjoy seeing him?"

"I mean it was kind of nice to have someone to do things with." It had been. Despite her willingness, even eagerness, to spend time by herself and to keep to her own space, the company had been a not unwelcome diversion, a break in the monotony of her routine. Dahlia liked her routine, even thrived on it. But she'd had to admit it was good to have someone to talk to, even if the conversation had been superficial—which it was.

"How long did it last? How did it end?"

And this was where it always got messy. She wasn't even sure what had happened, this time, or all the other times before. It was like they were spending time together, until they weren't—like they plateaued well before they became close and never really crossed into dependence, or even real friendship. It started with the texts that weren't returned; then came the cold shoulders and tangible tension across the dinner table or in the bed. Dahlia would press for a time, asking what was wrong, trying to hold his hand or make a nice dinner to bring him back around. But he never did, and she'd never been in it enough to really care. She backed off as they did, cutting her losses and building the defenses just a little bit higher. Sometimes they had a final text of closure; sometimes, whatever they had just vanished, as if it had never even happened at all.

"It just kind of fizzled," she said to Gita, because it did, and because there was nothing much more to say. "We just kind of fell out of it. He got really distant all of a sudden. He didn't seem to want to be there, and I just kind of let him go."

"Why do you think he didn't want to be there? Why was he so closed off?"

"I don't know, I mean I guess he had a lot going on at work. He had some family stuff. He didn't really tell me."

"Did it bother you? Did you miss him?"

Dahlia shrugged again. "Not really. I mean if he doesn't want to be there, I'm not going to force him to stay. I mean why would I do that?"

Gita nodded. "And this is a pattern, would you say?"

"I mean I guess it's a pattern. Yeah, I guess it is."

Gita took a deep breath.

"Are you interested in hearing my thoughts?"

"Okay."

"Listen, Dahlia." Gita leaned forward, her elbows resting on her thighs. "I really think the fact that you almost drowned has had more of an effect on you than you think. It's stood out to you as a trauma, enough so that you mentioned it early on."

Dahlia firmed her jaw and rubbed her lips together. She'd had a feeling Gita was going to say this and was prepared to hear her out before telling her she was wrong.

Gita went on. "I think your past experience of feeling unseen and unsafe during a critical moment in your life has led you to seek out partners who replicate that feeling. Your fear of vulnerability has led to a fear of deep emotional connections, and this has made you subconsciously choose partners who are unlikely to demand more from you than you're capable of giving. It helps you maintain control." She paused. "Should I go on?"

Dahlia watched her stoically. It was a lot. She felt she should be feeling something, but she was slow to absorb Gita's words. "Sure."

"In other words," said Gita, "your avoidance of risk has led you to choose partners who mirror your avoidance. Relationships, therefore, have been shallow, but safe. That's because you're with men who are non-committal, who keep a safe emotional distance. The result is short-term flings that prevent you from having to worry about truly caring for someone, which would mean you'd have to risk loss or abandonment. I think this reflects unresolved feelings about your family's inattention when you almost drowned."

"That's not true," inserted Dahlia, almost involuntarily. "My family just didn't see me. It wasn't their fault. My parents are great, it wasn't like they were neglectful. It was a long time ago, times were different, parents didn't keep such a close eye on their kids. And besides," she added, a little fire in her belly as she defended her family, "I have deep emotional connections. I have them with my family. And I mean my father is dying, it isn't like I'm not facing risk or fear."

"Right, well, it's apples and oranges, though, isn't it? Your family is your family. They're already safe."

"You just told me they weren't."

"You know what I mean, Dahlia. I think now we're splitting hairs."

Dahlia didn't say anything—she was frustrated, and she didn't want to speak too soon. Gita's theory was, of course, utter nonsense, but she felt it was better to hold off saying so.

"To sum up," said Gita, leaning back in her chair, "the trauma of nearly drowning has left you with a fear of losing control. This affects your choice of partners and impacts the dynamics with those who make it past the first defense. The fact that your family didn't notice might have led to trust issues, the realization that you can't rely on others—even when they have the best intentions, when they're the people who love you the most."

She paused again, awaiting a reply. When none came, she continued.

"Keeping the incident a secret I think has prevented you from processing it fully. It's led to unresolved fears and anxiety. It might have even led to low self-esteem."

Out of nowhere Dahlia's eyes warmed with the beginnings of tears. The confusion over their origin only made them come faster. She didn't have low self-esteem, so what was happening? Sure, she would have liked to be better at some things, but who didn't? She lowered her brow, crossly, and blinked a few times, then cleared her throat and straightened in her seat. Mercifully the physical movement was a distraction, and the tears retreated. Dahlia pushed the interruption aside.

"Furthermore," said Gita, "I think it's possible that the mysterious rescuer who disappeared might have created a romanticized idea of the 'perfect' savior. Now no one can measure up. So you don't even try. Then it's easy for you to find a reason to end the relationship, before it becomes too serious."

Dahlia smirked without intending to. Gita raised her eyebrows.

"What do you think of all this? Am I way off base?"

Dahlia took another breath and ran her fingers through her hair. "I just..."

Gita smiled. "Go on."

Dahlia let her hand fall back into her lap, and sighed. "Honestly, I feel like this is a lot of meaningless psychology jargon."

"I see. You think it's too by-the-book, maybe?"

"Sort of. I think you're reading too much into it."

"Fair enough." Gita shrugged, but not the way Dahlia had been shrugging; she lifted both hands and moved her shoulders up in a dramatic fashion, her lips turned into a lopsided, lazy grin, as if to say, *Who knows?* "I'd like you to think about it, though, regardless. I think it's something worth exploring."

Dahlia glanced at the clock. They had a little over ten minutes left. Not quite enough time left to get into a new topic, too much time left to smoothly begin picking up her belongings to leave.

Gita noticed, and smiled. "Was there anything else you wanted to talk about today?"

"Not really." A thought occurred to her. "Actually, there is. I was wondering if you had any suggestions, I mean about my boss wanting me to go to LA."

"Sure, why don't we make a list of pros and cons."

"No, I mean suggestions for how to tell her I'm not going."

Gita nodded slowly. "I see."

"I've been thinking a lot about it," said Dahlia, trying to attempt a tone of confidence. "I just don't think it's right for me, right now."

"What brought you to that conclusion?"

"I mean the first thing obviously is my father. I just can't leave when his health is so unpredictable."

Gita nodded again. "That's certainly a legitimate concern."

"But then there's the fact that I really don't want to be away from the store. I just like to be able to keep up with it. I mean it's Imani's store, obviously, it would be fine. And her friend Marilyn can come in to help. Marilyn's always looking for a reason to help. But I have too much responsibility. I just feel like it would be wrong for me to leave."

"Well," said Gita, "Imani clearly thinks it wouldn't be."

Dahlia blinked. "I know. But I mean…"

She stopped. She and Gita looked at each other in silence.

"If you're not ready to go," said Gita finally, "I think that's okay."

"It's not that. I just don't think it's a good idea."

"Well." Gita watched her for a moment or two. "Then I'd say you should just tell Imani the truth."

It wasn't a helpful answer. Dahlia smiled politely. "Okay. Thanks."

"Okay." Gita placed her hands on her knees and swiveled to her computer. "Same time next week?"

CHAPTER EIGHT

By mid November the weather had fully turned to winter. It was a cozy time of year for a bookshop—and for Dahlia, who worked with new energy to the view of snow flurries and people rushing by in their coats and scarves, paper cups of coffee in their gloves hands. Like many people, Dahlia objected to the early encroachment of the Christmas season, staunchly believing in November's entitlement to exist in its own right and preferring to enjoy the anticipation of her favorite holiday—Thanksgiving—before diving into the chaos of December. Imani seemed to agree, and while she could not ignore the necessity of accommodating those who liked to shop for their loved ones early, she astutely identified the balance, and one noticed signs of the December holidays in her store—an endcap here, a table display there. Dahlia appreciated that she, like autumn, had been given license to take her time, and to enjoy what was happening presently, rather than merely looking ahead.

The new season was a fresh start and a reset, and Dahlia allowed herself to put her troubled thoughts on the table for another day. She spent her free time visiting with her family and planning for Thanksgiving with Tara and Vera, who were hosting for the first time in many years. Traditionally, the family traveled down to northern Virginia for the holiday, to visit Vera's sister and her husband, Grace and Frank. But with Edward's health being what it was, everyone agreed it was better to stay at home. It would be quiet this year, quieter than usual. Grace and Frank, for their part, would be with their own daughter in Ohio.

Thanksgiving was as joyful as it could be. It was nice to have a smaller, more intimate gathering, and it was certainly nice not to travel. Dahlia was more inclined than ever to be surrounded only by immediate family, the people she loved most in the world. She enjoyed the boisterous dynamic among Tara and her family, and she and her father indulged in long book discussions that soothed her soul and allowed her to forget, for a time, that anything was changing. She helped Vera, Tom, and Tara in the kitchen, and made a point of helping Evelyn prepare a few dishes, as her oldest niece had expressed an interest in learning how to cook herself.

As they sat around the table with coffee and pie she noticed that her father looked quite tired, and he excused himself early to rest a little in bed. Dahlia kissed him and embraced him, alarmed to realize that he had lost quite a bit of weight. As Vera helped him to bed Dahlia took a moment to herself in the bathroom, unnerved. Her father had not mentioned her search, but she knew he was thinking about it. She knew they were running out of time. This made her wonder how many more Thanksgivings they would have with him, and the simmering inside her burned hot with leaping flames. She looked outside to the falling leaves, her heart pulling downward with dread.

As November drifted into December Dahlia allowed herself to create the illusion that he had forgotten all about the search for the mysterious stranger. She put the search out of her mind. She rested at the base of the mountain, choosing instead to focus on the now very real inevitability of the winter holidays, setting up holiday displays and getting ready for special events in the store, and of building her to-read list for the following year. She organized her tea cabinet, taking stock of what she was almost out of so she could reorder before the rush of holiday shopping.

Running low on the lavender rose, she noticed with a frown. This was the tea she drank on Sunday evenings, and she had only three bags left. That meant only a three-week supply, and she ordered it from England, which of course took some time. She sat promptly down to place her order, adding some loose-leaf mint, as well. She still had a fair amount of the mint—which she sipped in bed in the evenings—but this way she wouldn't have to order from the teashop twice.

When she wasn't working Dahlia enjoyed the excuse to remain in her little apartment, snuggled under a blanket with a cup of tea and a book. She anticipated with excitement the gradually encroaching heaviness of winter. It was a time of introspection and of meaningful darkness, a time when people hurried indoors and night fell early, when you fell asleep that night knowing those around you were safe and cozy in their homes, as well. It was a time that gave permission for passivity, and Dahlia basked in its reticence.

She did enjoy the lights. After Thanksgiving the holiday lights truly came alive, wrapped around fir trees and lined diligently along rooftops and front porches, strung along between street lamps and hanging lazily from storefront entrances. Dahlia herself hung the lights in the bookshop, and it made going to work even that much more delightful. The bright, cheery light inside the shop contrasted with the ever-darkening sky, and she was grateful for her job, her home, her town. She was grateful for the season, which relieved her ever-present feeling that she loved too much remaining indoors.

The one exception was her nieces. She took them ice-skating, and she took them out for chocolate chip pancakes; she drove them around town to see the lights, and she joined them on a wagon ride in an orchard during the first snow. Being with her nieces was a privilege and a treat, one she did not take for granted, and it drew her outside, drew her to life. She hugged her sister among the swirling snowflakes, smiling into her hot cocoa and forgetting, for a time, the world and all its cares.

DAHLIA SOMETIMES LAY in bed with her eyes wide open, thinking of her nieces. If she were to become their guardian, it would mean she'd have to find a new job, something that paid more, that could support three growing children. Unless Tara and Tom had insurance money, which Dahlia was sure they did. Plus her job was only one door down—she'd be close to home all the time, in case they needed her. Maybe she wouldn't have to quit. She'd have to put some more thought into that.

If she did have to quit, she didn't know what she would do. She didn't really have the skills to do anything else. She wondered if she could get a job at a big box bookstore, and rise in the ranks to manager? Surely managers of those big stores made more than she did at the shop. It was something to think about. It wouldn't be too bad a transition.

She would have to do things she was afraid of. Like talking to teachers, taking them to the doctor. Dealing with other parents. Looking into colleges. She'd have to mask it for their sake. She didn't want them to grow up afraid, too. It would be the hardest thing of all. It made her stomach feel as if it were turning inside out.

She had to remind herself that all this was unlikely to happen. But it never hurt to plan. And part of her believed—or hoped—that worrying and preparing could keep something from actually happening. She'd finally started seeing Gita because her greatest fear was coming true. And with Edward's health declining, she was learning that the worst thing could actually happen. She'd spent so much time consoling herself thinking the worst was unlikely to occur. But now it was certain, inevitable. It was something she couldn't control. Bad things came whether you deserved them or not. And how could she cope with that knowledge? How could anyone?

In the second week of December Vera called Dahlia very late. The drug trial had fallen through, and Edward would not be receiving the exciting new treatment after all. Dahlia went into a tailspin. She looked at the green bowl on the mantel and grew dizzy and sick to her stomach. Every nerve in her body seemed to thrum and shriek with warning. She paced aimlessly around her apartment, her mind rushing to the worst case scenarios. She lay in bed awake for hours that night and overslept the next morning, and called in sick for the very first time in her life.

SHE FINALLY AWOKE AGAIN at noon and squinted in confusion at the aggression of the sunlight stinging her eyes and coating the room in a hostile glare. It seemed to flood every corner, leaving her nowhere to hide and forcing her into a day she had no desire to face. She lay beneath the covers for a time, blinking into the light. The familiar noises of the day drifted up from the street, but she felt an outsider. Her world had been flipped, inverted; it was hard to reconcile that it went on as normal for everybody else.

She remained in bed for a half hour or so. Her blood was restless, but her mind was numb; it was as if her body was grieving the devastating news while her mind still struggled to accept it. After a time her limbs began to itch, and she tossed among the blankets with frustration, trying to get comfortable. She wanted to spend the day in bed, to float in ignorant oblivion until darkness filled the room, and her mind. But grief turned to anger, which turned to energy, and she sat upright in bed, looking around, knowing she had to do something but not yet knowing quite what.

She rubbed her face in her hands and opened her eyes wide against the haze. She stared from her bedroom into the living room. And then her eyes fell on the green glass bowl.

Dahlia frowned and firmed her jaw. *Fuck disease. Fuck death. Fuck life.*

And suddenly she knew what she had to do. She swung her legs over the side of the bed and pounded across the apartment to the bathroom, where she took a quick shower, threw on some clothes, grabbed her coat and bag, and scuttled down the stairs toward her car, shoving an apple in her mouth on the way out.

Outside, she was met by a crisp breeze that hardened her skin and shocked her lungs. She pushed forward against the resistance of the wind and sank into her car, then pulled out her phone and punched the location into her GPS.

Sandy Dollar Hotel Seashell Cove NJ.

Dahlia sat in tense disbelief as the wheel on her screen spun, finding the best route. She had never made this trip by herself; she had not driven this distance on her own since she'd traveled back and forth in college. She had not been to Seashell Cove or even seen the ocean since she was a teenager. She did not stop to think about why she was going or what she intended to do there. She was compelled by a force larger than she was; it was greater than her will, greater even than her anxiety.

She looked at her phone as it finished calculating. The Sandy Dollar Hotel was eighty-nine miles away; it would take her just shy of two hours to get there. She stuck her phone to the charger on the dash and pulled out of her spot, and drove into the sunshine.

∾

STRANGELY ENOUGH, Dahlia did not mind driving. Whereas it had the potential to be frightening, the rushing of cars around her and the necessity for quick decisions, she found it freeing, a chance to spend time with herself and, once she pushed through the traffic of Philadelphia and achieved the open highway, to experience the sensation of going somewhere, all within the familiar comfort of her own car. As the skyscrapers of Philadelphia receded behind her into the distance Dahlia rolled down the window and inhaled the early winter wind, which cleared her lungs and brushed through her hair, and filled her ears with its rushing rumble, drowning out the sound of her own thoughts.

She barreled down the tree-lined expressway for some time, numbed by the noise and the monotony of the scenery. As the expressway slowed into a more local road with traffic lights and convenience stores the hum faded, and awareness slowly crept back, filling the spaces left by the open drive. She found herself slipping bit by bit back into the moment, and with the return to reality came questions about what she was doing there. She'd had no plan and no real motive for driving all this distance, to the beach, in the first weeks of winter; she'd been pushed by a force outside her understanding and out of her control, and now that she was here, the voice that had coerced her into doing it had abandoned her, leaving her lost and well outside her boundaries. She inhaled against a familiar tightening in her chest and an overturning of her stomach. Veering right onto the two-lane road that hugged the water she realized with a start how far she was from home. Her heart squeezed, and the view became blurry; abruptly, she swung into an empty parking lot by a small ramshackle building, and sat with the motor running, her eyes closed tight and her face in her hands.

She waited for the hammering of her heart to subside. As she focused on the inner workings of her own body she became aware of the rhythm of her breathing, the sound of her own inhalations and of her thumbs massaging her own temples; looking downward, her fingers in her hair, she cracked her eyes open, and saw the blue of her jeans, the curves of her own hips. She exhaled. She directed her gaze upward, saw the gray of the steering wheel, the dust that had settled on the dash. Further up still, she saw the black of the windshield wipers and spots of dried moisture on the glass.

And there was something else.

Slowly she removed her fingers from her hairline and let her arms fall to her sides. She sat straight and leaned back in her seat, now feeling the clothes against her back and against her head. Before her was a dock, beyond that a few meager boats bobbing in the gentle lapping of the bay. Beyond that, she knew, was the ocean, its vast endlessness just visible on the horizon.

Dahlia gazed forward. From this distance, the ocean seemed a flat, still thing. She knew it was changing by the second, waves rolling forward and being pulled back by the tide. It was teeming with life, and with death, an entire universe beyond people's knowledge and beyond their scope.

A seagull flew into her line of vision and soared over the sky, along the sea. Dahlia followed it with her eyes, then inhaled and pulled out of the parking lot, back onto the road and toward the edge of the world.

IT WAS A FRIGID DECEMBER DAY; at the edge of the cape, hers was the only car. Dahlia had her pick of parking. She swerved off the road and easily into a spot beside the concrete barrier separating the road from the sandy dunes beyond. She swung open her door and was met by a cold sea wind that chilled her neck and made her eyes water. She pulled her scarf tighter around her throat and shut the door, the sound muffled by the roar of the waves.

Dahlia walked up the bank and onto the path toward the

ocean. She stood for a moment looking back and forth, from the inn-lined road to the distant horizon. There was not a soul to be seen. Somewhere, birds called to each other. The feeling of being completely alone in so open a space was jarring, comforting, confusing. There was a quiet peace inherent in it, despite the sounds; but the peace was watchful and unsettling, like the world was holding its breath.

Hands in her coat pockets, scarf up over her chin, Dahlia looked out toward the ocean, then turned her attention to the beach. She wasn't sure what she'd expected, whether she'd recognize a memory, whether ghosts would appear over the sand. She dug deep within herself, trying to resurrect some long-forgotten part of her soul, but the landscape was emotionless, without recognition.

She stared at the horizon, then let her gaze drift toward the left. She blinked: something stirred in her, like a ribbon of seaweed rippling at the edges of her mind.

Dahlia tramped over the sand, fighting the wind. As she approached, the memory revealed itself: the pier with the big rocks around it.

She walked a few minutes, watching as the pier came further into view. Was it always this small—was the wood always this battered and worn? She wondered if her memory had betrayed her. But then, recognition hit her. A dark lump by the water's edge: the rock that looks like a bear.

Dahlia slowed as she approached the pier, her eyes watchful, almost wary. Her feet seemed to carry her of their own accord, just a few feet further, until she was on the other side. She inched closer to the water's edge, the soft sand fading into a flat slab where the ocean swept above it, then pulled back out into the waves. She continued until it kissed the tips of her boots, until she could feel its spray on her face and until the musky scent of the deep filled her nostrils.

She turned and faced the beach, the horizon at her back.

The scene was lifeless and indifferent, its colors faded in the frigid winter light as if washed out by the ocean itself. Directly beyond, over the dunes, where the ice cream shop should be was a burger joint of some kind—quiet and closed for the season. Dahlia squinted into the light. Her eyes moved over the dunes, stopping just before a patch of grass. Something about the shape of the weeds stirred a rustling in the corner of her mind. She blinked; she let her eyes glide a few feet forward, over the sand. She strained her eyes, trying to imagine the beach chairs, the sandcastles, the wispy fire of her sisters' red hair.

The scent of salt and seaweed was a presence in the air. Dahlia closed her eyes, concentrating. She took the musk of the ocean into her lungs, conjuring images, inviting the past to rise.

She opened her eyes, but the scene remained unchanged. Where there should have been laughter and life, there was only a hollow stillness—the pale, sterile quiet of something long abandoned. Dahlia gazed at it with a certain heaviness. Something shivered in her, a sense of loss too vague to name, slipping away as quickly as it had come.

It was too far away, too long gone; she saw it, but from a distance. A sadness settled above her like fog over the sea.

The crush of the waves grew louder, and in came the tide, slipping around her boots and sliding up the shore. Instinctively, Dahlia hopped forward out of the water. The toes of her boots were dark with wet, and sand had collected around the soles. She faced the horizon and stared at the ocean. She had the odd sensation that it knew her, that it knew why she was there. She took a step backward, then another. It would not reclaim her today.

The sadness inside her had been replaced by fear. Step by step she retreated, looking back only when she'd reached the safety of the boardwalk, when she could stomp the sand from off her feet.

ON THE WAY back toward her car she stopped abruptly on a street corner. Her body knew this spot, and a long-dormant response activated somewhere deep within her mind.

She eyed the ocean on her left, then turned warily to the side street on her right, letting instinct guide the way. Her feet seemed to move of their own accord, remembering breaks in the concrete sidewalk, the places where in busier times one would do well to watch for children running down the stairs. It was a cozy street lined with colorful bed and breakfasts. Dahlia and her sisters had made friends on this street—they'd made pinky promises and shared bags of candy, then returned to their homes at the end of the week, never to see each other again.

Soon the cluster of Victorian houses made way for a row of motels, set back from the road, empty pools in front. In the cold winter light they looked pale and faded; Dahlia could imagine the musty smells of the interiors, the threadbare auburn rugs and peeling wallpaper. She passed the first two and slowed before the third. She stood still and silent on the pavement, watching.

She felt that she should be moved more than she was. This was the place, the structure that housed her and her family during the best times of their lives. They were times of greatest inno-cence, and of greatest joy; they were days full of laughter, and playing, and indulgence, and love. She and her family had yet to disperse—they were a unit, solid and indestructible as the concrete building that protected them from outside forces. Dahlia had thought those days would never end. Growing up had been a vague, nebulous concept, something that would happen but something that wouldn't *be*. She couldn't imagine, in those days, being anything different; she couldn't imagine the paths they would take, the ways they'd separate, the ways they'd fall apart.

The building looked duller and less glamorous than it had all those years before. Dahlia studied it, examining the memories in her mind like pages in a photo album. Had her memories faded, had she idealized it in her mind? Or had the building changed, had it aged like she had? She certainly wasn't the same person she'd been when she was six. She wasn't sure if the changes she was seeing meant that it was different, or that she was.

She stared at it for some time, letting her eyes drift over the neat rows of rooms, the pillars in the doorway, the sign that read The Sandy Dollar Hotel. Dahlia had to smile. This, at least, she was certain was the same. The letters were script, and blue, and surrounded by red and orange lights. At night the lights would chase each other around the lettering, calling from afar as she and her family returned from a twilight stroll along the beach, ice cream cones in hand.

A car sped by, startling her from her reveries. She retraced her steps until she faced the ocean one last time.

Time. There was just so little time. The thought was a gut-punch that made her feel helpless, a feeling she remembered, a feeling she deplored. The fear of imminent loss had turned her back into a little girl. But she wasn't a little girl anymore. Why had she come here today, anyway? Was it just to run away? Or to take action? Was she fleeing her grief, and if so, why do so here? *If I don't help him now*, she thought, *I will never have the chance. That's why I'm here. That's what this is about.*

But also, the ocean. It was where it all began. Maybe that mattered more than she'd realized.

I don't know, she thought sadly. *I just don't know why I'm here.*

She turned and walked away, back toward her car, and home.

DAHLIA RETURNED HOME JUST as daylight was growing dimmer, and placed a dinner order to be delivered before discarding her coat and clothes and slipping with relief into warm pajamas and chunky socks. She sat on the couch with her hair in a ponytail and a blanket wrapped snugly up to her chin, watching the familiar images of a favorite show flash across the screen. The comfort of this familiarity was indescribable. It had been a day full of newness, and oldness, and heavy things that pulled at her and drew her from herself. Now she was in her own apartment, with her own possessions and sights. She could almost pretend the day had been a dream; she could almost pretend it hadn't even happened at all.

After dinner Dahlia read with the television on, then moved into her bedroom when her eyelids began to droop. The apartment was dark except for the little lamp on her bedside table, and the shining of the moon outside her window. She read for a time, then grew weary; with a satisfied sigh, she lay the book on the table and flipped off the light, and set to sleep.

All of a sudden, she was out of the bed, gliding almost involuntarily back into the living room and at her desk, by her computer. Her fingers moved almost of their own accord as they signed onto her only social media account, and clicked the icon to check the notifications for her thread.

Thankfully the conversation had settled; most of the passionate commenters had moved on to other subjects. She had a few stray comments, nothing overly helpful—people tossing out impossible ideas, or simply wishing her the best.

And then, at the bottom, she saw it:

try hypnotherapy

Dahlia paused with her fingers on the keyboard. She rolled her eyes. *Well, I'm not doing that*, she thought with a smirk. hypnotherapy was quackery, woowoo nonsense for desperate and gullible people. Images of swinging stopwatches and prostrate, vapid women shuffled across her mind. Was this a joke? It just wasn't a serious response.

Thanks, she wrote under the comment. *For nothing*, she added in her mind.

She shut down her computer and went to the living room

window, staring at the sky for a time until she grew weary and chilly, and bored with the view. Then she climbed back into bed, surprised to find herself drifting into blackness without her usual parade of unwanted images. But she wasn't as safe as she'd thought, for they occupied her dreams, as vague, monstrous shadows, as empty buildings and black oceans and mysterious strangers, reaching to her from the deep.

CHAPTER NINE

*D*ecisions about the conference in the spring were looming. Imani wanted to reserve places for herself and Dahlia and to book their rooms and flights. Dahlia was already feeling somewhat hungover from the vaguely jarring events of the day before. She was hoping for a quiet day at the store, a day when she could fall back into her routines and pretend everything was easy and fine. But no such luck.

"One of the panelists is holding a dinner the first night," said Imani as the two removed books from a dolly and arranged them on a winter-themed table. "It's a reservation for twenty. I put our names down. Now we don't have to worry about what to do the first night."

If Dahlia had any intention of going, which she didn't, she'd elect to order room service and spend the night reading and by herself.

"That's great," she muttered noncommittally, her nose in a stack of paperbacks.

"I'm thinking of sending you a day before me," Imani went on. "There's a workshop on children's marketing, but I can't get away for that long."

Dahlia smiled blandly but inside was wracked with torment. She never had told Imani her feelings about going to LA, and she'd figured she'd had time. It was at least a small comfort, that of all the things she worried about, it was something she could push off for the future. But she hadn't accounted for Imani's compulsion to organize, to plan in advance. The time when it would be too late to confront her was approaching much more quickly than she'd hoped.

"You know what else," Imani went on, "you should plan to take your vacation. You could just stay in LA, you know, see the sights after the conference."

Dahlia looked at her with surprise. "My vacation?"

"Yes, you know, those days that employees are entitled to, when they have time off from work? You might not know what it is because you literally never take it." She looked at her slyly. "Don't think I haven't noticed."

A tumult of emotions swept inside Dahlia. So people did see it, or at least, Imani did. The truth was, the thought of disrupting her routine with vacation filled her with strange existential dread. But a very small part of her, in the recesses of her heart, appreciated that she'd been seen.

In the meantime, Edward had started a recently approved drug that was part of ongoing studies to determine long-term effects. Research suggested it might slow progression but not reverse symptoms, which was frustrating, as his loved ones had hoped for more. However, it was something. And it gave them hope, a reminder that new possibilities could exist just around the corner.

Dahlia spoke with Gita about her quick visit to the beach, and she mentioned, offhandedly, that someone online had suggested she try hypnotherapy. To her surprise and frustration, Gita did not validate her immediate dismissal of the idea as mere quackery or fluff. To the contrary, she seemed to think it might be helpful, calling it "legitimate and safe psychological treatment" and arguing that if nothing else, it might help her with her "anxiety." To make matters worse, she seemed to believe that Dahlia's subconscious objection was in fact based in fear that if it worked, she would be one step closer, that what was preventing her from trying it was not necessarily her wariness of the treatment itself but the possibility that it would propel her further outside her boundaries.

The conversation—though Gita had made every effort to be gentle in her discourse—had put Dahlia in a foul, tense mood. That night she ate dinner in front of a favorite show, but she found herself unable to follow or to pay it any attention. She was preoccupied by her irritation with Gita for being so contrary, for never believing her about her very own thoughts. But after the anger wore off Dahlia grew sad. She was so defensive; she was so quick to be up in arms. Why was she like this? Why was her first instinct to be frustrated, and not kind? Though she didn't really think hypnotherapy would help her, she knew that Gita meant well. Dahlia chastised herself for her ungenerous thoughts. She relived the session in her mind, over and over, trying to assess whether she'd done an adequate job hiding her negative feelings.

She would be brave this time, for her father. He put his faith in new medicines and new treatments; he was a veritable pincushion of trials and of hope. She would follow in his footsteps, honor his action with her own. If he was trying new solutions, so must she.

She would try to meet regression with progress: it was time to take the next step up the mountain. She rose and went to her computer. She took a deep breath and brought up her social media page.

She had a few stray notifications from her thread, a few more "likes" and a couple of unrelated comments—nothing of great consequence. She clicked on a random one and soon was looking at her question, with its dozens of comments, its inane controversy. She scrolled toward the bottom until she came across the comment about hypnotherapy. It was left by someone named Noel Bar.

She clicked on Noel's name, which took her to his profile page. In the corner was a button that said "message." She clicked on that, and it took her to an empty text box, and a blinking cursor waiting for her words. Dahlia began typing quickly, before she could think too hard about it. She didn't know this person, she reminded herself—she'd never have to talk to him again.

Hi, she typed. *I don't know if you remember, but a few weeks ago you commented on my thread about almost drowning. You suggested I try hypnotherapy. Was this a serious suggestion? Have you tried hypnotherapy yourself?*

She read it over once; it wasn't perfect, but it would do. She clicked "send," then clicked off her browser. She went to the kitchen for a bowl of ice cream, and ate it in her chair by the window, reading her book.

About fifteen minutes later, her phone pinged from the table. Dahlia rose and looked at it. It was a notification: Noel Bar had responded.

Dahlia placed her bowl on the table and, heart thumping, hurried to her computer. She went to her page and her message box, and clicked on the little red icon.

Yeah I've done it

Dahlia blinked and furrowed her brow.

Can you tell me about it? I guess it helped?

Her foot tapped a quick staccato on the floor as she waited.

Lots of relaxation stuff just a relaxed state and it helps you remember

She figured out quickly that Noel was not instinctively forth-coming with details, and resigned herself to pushing.

What is it like? How do they make you remember?

The back and forth came evenly now, if not a little coldly.

They played music

And that helped?

It helps clear your mind so you can fill in the blanks

So what's their role in this, exactly?

They make you pick a mantra

What do you mean?

Like a focus, whatever you want to remember

Dahlia wanted to ask Noel what it was he'd been trying to remember, and why, but she refrained.

But how does the remembering happen? Like how do they get you to do it?

It's like a dream state

Dahlia still didn't really understand. She wanted to know what to expect, but everything was so superficial; it was clear he wasn't willing, or capable, of going any further than that. She stared at the screen, a little frustrated.

Noel surprised her by going on.

She asked me some questions kind of helped me put myself back in time

Dahlia frowned. Wouldn't that put thoughts in a person's head —wouldn't it inspire false memories, lead you astray?

So it's like they're guiding you? You don't remember on your own? I don't want to be coerced.

Its not like that I cant explain it you just kind of have to do it

Dahlia nodded and firmed her jaw. This was about as much as she was going to get from this person on the other end of the screen. She didn't really know any more than she had before this... well, she guessed she'd call it a "conversation," though it had felt, in fact, quite one sided. She didn't know what she'd been expecting from a faceless being whose words blinked across her screen. Still, part of her was intrigued. And in its own way, she supposed, that was something.

Okay, she typed. *Thank you.*

Np, he responded, and was gone.

IT TOOK HER A FEW DAYS, and a few books, to clear her head. And every time she thought about it, she grimaced, as if she were going to be sick. But eventually she'd gathered enough courage, and sat down at her computer again, determined.

She'd struck up what she'd hoped had seemed like a casual conversation with one of the cashiers at work. If she needed help with something, or if she needed to find a service provider—hypothetically—and she didn't know who to ask—what was the best way to find a recommendation, for someone in her area, someone people could vouch for?

Betsy had told her to ask in "a recommendations group." Oh, Dahlia had responded. Yeah, sure. Like, a group of friends? No. Betsy had laughed, making Dahlia bristle, but she let it go. On social media. You're not a member of those local rec groups? No, said Dahlia. And I would find one how? Betsy shrugged. Just do a search.

That was what Dahlia was doing right now, right after work, while her momentum was still high. She'd come immediately home and thrown her bag on the couch, then sat in her chair with a *thump* and logged right onto her account.

Local recommendation group near Brentwick, PA

A number of groups came up, some of them relevant, some of them not. There was a group called "Brentwick Twp PA Recommendations Group." It had 576 members. Dahlia clicked to join, then answered the questions and waited.

The acceptance came within minutes. With a leap in her chest Dahlia clicked on the group and then to the post box, where she began typing her second question ever on social media.

Then her eyes fell on a magnifying glass in the corner. Brow crinkled, she deleted her question and instead, brought her cursor to the little box beside it.

Hypnotherapist, she typed.

Immediately she was greeted with about a dozen posts from as far back as a few years before. Pen in hand, and relieved she could get her answers without having to interact with anyone, she took note of the names mentioned in the comments, for once overwhelmed by the volume of information. When she had written down all the names, she clicked out of her account and turned to the list. She immediately crossed off all the men. There were three women left. She turned back to her laptop and proceeded to look them up.

The first had a professional website with lush scripts and soothing colors. Stock images depicted beautiful people looking skyward, or basking in the light of the morning sun. Dahlia clicked the "about" section and frowned. Staring back at her was a quite ordinary-looking woman, about fifty years old, with short curly hair and rosy cheeks. She was smiling widely and dressed well, in a blue cardigan sweater with a paisley scarf around her neck. But there was something about her eyes Dahlia did not like. The smile didn't quite reach them; they were sharp but not kind, seeming to pierce rather than see.

The second person on the list appeared to no longer be practicing—the website produced an error message, and there was no phone number listed as far as she could tell. But the third one held promise.

Dahlia clicked onto the website for Amelia Prue, licensed hypnotherapist.

Welcome to a space where transformation begins. As a certified hypnotherapist, I help clients safely unlock their subconscious to overcome challenges, reclaim memories, and enhance confidence. Whether you're managing stress, breaking habits, or seeking clarity, your journey starts here in a supportive and empowering environment.

It all sounded good, if not a little contrived. Dahlia read over the practitioner's biography and credentials, and the inevitable series of reviews at the bottom of the page. It seemed as legitimate a place as any other. She clicked on the "contact" link at the top and was faced with an empty text box, awaiting her inquiry. Dahlia stared at it a moment, then leaned back. She put her computer to sleep, and stood, but she didn't close the tab.

It took her three days to log back on. She did so after a quiet day at work, when she'd had time for introspection and for courage gathering. By the time she'd hurried up the stairs to her little apartment and sat heavily in her desk chair the adrenaline of anticipation had made getting the task over with more appealing than prolonging the delay.

She pulled up the tab and punched in her name, her email address and, reluctantly, her phone number, then rattled off a quick sentence explaining the "purpose" of her inquiry.

I am trying to flesh out details of a memory so I can find someone from my past.

Satisfied, she shut down her computer and migrated to her living room chair, where she sat for an hour reading until it was time to heat up some leftover soup for dinner.

While she was eating, she checked her email on her phone. She dropped her spoon into her bowl with a clatter: Amelia had responded.

Hi Dahlia, the email said. *Thank you so much for getting in touch with me. I'd love to offer you a free phone consultation so I can get to know you a little and so you can hear a little about what I do. Please let me know what times work best for you. Yours sincerely, Amelia*

Dahlia put her elbows on the table and punched out a response right away.

Hi Amelia, she said. *Thank you for the offer for the free consultation. To be honest, I'd rather just come in for a session. I'm free Mondays and Tuesdays, and the other days after work. Thank you. —Dahlia*

Dahlia finished her dinner quickly, barely tasting it. After, she fluttered around the apartment in a kind of manic rush, simultaneously anxious to check her email, and afraid to. When the counters had been wiped clean and her dishes put away, when her rooms were as she left them that morning and the space seemed restful and waiting, she returned to her desk chair and straightened her back, clicking on her email and readying her calendar.

She was disappointed to find that Amelia had not written back. She'd already prepared herself for this interaction, and having to turn off her computer without having resolved it felt anticlimactic and frustrating. She climbed into bed that night ill at ease, with the weight of this responsibility still over her head.

By the time Dahlia had sat down in the breakroom for lunch the next day, Amelia had returned her email and suggested the very next Monday at ten o'clock for their first session. She told her she would be emailing her a questionnaire about her health history, sleep patterns, and other lifestyle habits. Dahlia was queasy as she responded, with shaking fingers, that Monday at ten o'clock worked fine, that she'd answer the questions as soon as possible, and that she appreciated Amelia's fitting her in so quickly. She placed her phone back on the table and stared into the nothingness before her, her stomach a jittery knot.

The remainder of the week passed without incident. Dahlia received Amelia's questionnaire and wrote long, thorough answers; she was sure she wrote too much, but she was nervous, and she wanted Amelia to have all the information she needed to ensure that she was safe. She spent most of the weekend with her family, joining Tara and Tom at the elementary school for the younger girls' chorus concert and then back at her parents' house for a late dinner and conversation. Sunday after work she joined her mother, Tom, and her nieces at a local Christmas tree farm while Tara stayed back with Edward. After wrangling the fragrant tree into the house they passed a couple of joyful hours decorating and hanging up ornaments as Christmas carols bellowed from Tara's phone. Dahlia was in charge of hot chocolate, and she passed steaming mugs around the room, having placed a few extra marshmallows in the mugs she gave the girls. She warned them to sip carefully so as to avoid burning their mouths—she'd burned her mouth on hot tea earlier that week, and she hadn't stopped imagining little Celeste smarting and crying if it had been her.

Finally Monday arrived. Dahlia rose early that morning and sat reading for a few minutes to calm her nerves. After she'd dressed and eaten breakfast she supposed there was nothing else to do but go. She marched resolutely down the steps and into the relentless cold, shivering as the wind slipped under her collar and down her spine. The almost breathtaking cold inside her car felt fitting—unyielding, indifferent to her fear, propelling her forward whether she was ready or not.

After just short of fifteen minutes she arrived at a nondescript office building with a smattering of cars parked in neat rows in the parking lot. The structure itself gave nothing away; it was the kind of place that housed nothing and everything, doctors and insurance offices, interior designers and financial consultants. Dahlia pulled open the heavy glass door and stepped inside. She was promptly greeted by an almost uncomfortable warmth that vastly overcompensated for the cold outside. Shaking off her nerves, she checked the business listing on the wall, then turned to the elevator, which she took to the third floor.

Amelia's office was the first on her right. She pushed open the door and found herself in a room with dim lighting and candles, lush furniture and curtains in cool, muted colors. There was a desk in the back, but no one was sitting there. Dahlia looked around: there were two closed doors, and one that was open. What she was expected to do now was unclear. She was just starting to suffer the familiar pull of indecision in her stomach when a woman appeared in the open doorway.

"Hi, are you Dahlia?" the woman asked, approaching with an outstretched hand. Dahlia took quick stock of her. She was a tiny woman, about her age, with long blond hair and a casual but tidy air. Her gait was quick, and the comfort with which she moved in her office made Dahlia feel a little more confident and secure. Dahlia smiled and shook her hand.

"Yes. Nice to meet you. Thanks again for fitting me in."

"Oh, it's my pleasure. Come on back," said Amelia, gesturing with her hand and already turning back to the other room, "and have a seat so we can chat for a minute."

Dahlia followed her into the room, which was clearly made to feel like a living room, and it had succeeded. There was a loveseat with oversized pillows, an end table with a lamp and some subtle knickknacks; a bookcase loomed against the opposite wall, a shaggy rug between them, and the effect was that the space felt warm, intimate, like a den in someone's home. Dahlia sat on the far end of the couch, placing her bag beside her and immediately feeling like it served as a barrier between her and the other woman in the room. Amelia was closing the door; Dahlia quickly moved the purse to the floor while her back was turned.

"So, Dahlia," said Amelia. She took her seat in an armchair next to the bookshelf. Dahlia shifted her body to face her, wishing she'd sat on the other side of the couch. "Why don't you tell me a little about why you're here today."

"Okay." Dahlia rested her hand on her knee in an attempt to appear relaxed; out of the corner of her eye, she noticed the strap of the purse a little too far from the couch, and she kicked it away casually. "Well, long story short, when I was six years old, I was at the beach with my family and almost drowned in the ocean. But I was saved by a random stranger who pulled me out. No one else saw it—no one I know of, anyway. After he saved me, he ran away." She smiled. "I'm trying to find him now, so I need to remember everything I can."

"Oh wow, that's some story." Amelia was sitting with her legs crossed, her elbow on the arm of her chair. Her eyebrows were high, her expression sympathetic. "Can I ask why you're trying to find him now, after all this time?"

"My father is dying. He might be dying." An almost imperceptible catch in her voice. "He wants me to find him. So I really have no choice."

Amelia's eyes turned soft. "I'm so sorry about your father, Dahlia."

Dahlia blinked and smiled. "Thanks."

"Would you want to find him, if it were up to you?"

Dahlia's eyes widened. She sat for a moment in silence.

"I don't know."

"What I mean is are you curious about him, or are you doing this purely out of love for your father?"

"I..." Dahlia tried to think about this, but she couldn't hear her thoughts over the beating of her heart. "I...don't think so. Well, maybe." A smattering of words had collected, seemingly on their own. "I think what it is, is that before, I didn't want to, but now, I'm like invested, or something." She furrowed her brow. "Like...maybe I was afraid before? Or something?"

Amelia was watching her astutely. "Okay. That's fine. That's great." She smiled gently. "That might be something to explore. If you want to."

Dahlia blinked again; the corners of her lips turned upward just slightly.

"So let me tell you a little about how this works," said Amelia, uncrossing and recrossing her legs. "In hypnotherapy, you have to be really careful not to guide people. I don't want to pull anything out of you. I'm just here to bring you to a state of heightened focus. I'm going to help you relax so you can clear your head, and fixate on the things that are deep inside your memory. I'd like to help you go back to the scene, almost like age regression. We're going to achieve this by doing some visualizing exercises. But you're going to be in full control."

Dahlia swallowed and rubbed her lips together.

"Does that sound scary?" Amelia smiled and continued, without giving her time to respond. "It's okay if it does, I get it. A lot of people come in here not really knowing what to expect. But I promise, it's super casual and low key. You can stop at any time."

"Okay," said Dahlia, taking a breath. "Thanks."

"Sometimes people feel emotional when they go back to an earlier time," Amelia went on. "When they go back to the past. You're remembering something that was traumatic for you, something that was scary. And you're remembering a time of innocence and of joy. It's understandable that you may have some big feelings during, or after. Just remember, I'm here for you."

Inexplicably, tears had sprung to Dahlia's eyes. She blinked them away quickly, alarmed and unnerved. "Okay," she said, more loudly than necessary. "Thanks."

"Okay, Dahlia." Amelia reached for a small music player on her desk, and pushed a button. "I'm going to put on some soft music for you. And what I'd like you to do is close your eyes and take a breath, and just focus on my words. Does that sound good?"

"Yes." Dahlia closed her eyes and inhaled. *This is it. Here we go.*

From behind her closed eyelids she sensed the lights dim. The music was quiet, with a mild, slow melody and a repeating refrain. Her stomach twisted with unease—yet there was an undeniable pull, a quiet thrill beneath the fear.

"Now, Dahlia," Amelia said. "I'd like you to feel grounded in your senses and in your body. What I'd like you to do is think about the top of your head. Feel your scalp, your hair. Think about your ears. Relax the muscles of your forehead, of your cheekbones. Let your jawline slack, the corners of your mouth drop."

Dahlia did as she said, with surprise. She had not been aware of how taut her muscles had been. As she thought about these physical aspects of herself she began to see them not from afar but from the inside, as they were hers, to do with as she wanted.

She told them to loosen; she envisioned them and then was one with them. She inhaled again, and realized her shoulders had been raised. She lowered those, too, and exhaled, feeling the tightness leave through her nostrils and through her pores.

"Now feel your neck and your shoulders. Let the tension leave your throat; let your shoulders sag and soften. Feel your chest loosen. Feel your stomach unwind and unfurl."

Dahlia had never really thought about the control she had over her own body, in this micro, nuanced way. It was startling, how the discovery aided in slowing her breath, in quieting the static in her mind. She'd never noticed how much power she had over the physical forces that hitherto had moved on their own.

"Now feel your hips, your thighs against the cushion, your knees and your calves and your feet. Feel your feet upon the ground. The ground is solid beneath you. You can feel it on your soles. Your entire body is here, it is present, it is alive. You are breathing the air around you, taking it in, easing it out. Your body is living, feeling, existing. Your senses are awake, alert, aware."

Dahlia hadn't noticed that the room smelled vaguely of jasmine, that the cushion was supple under her weight. The air was warm but not oppressive, the kind that contrasts with the cold outside, wrapping around you like a blanket.

"Now, Dahlia, I'd like you to think about the beach. Think about when you were six years old. Picture yourself there, in the water. Can you see it?"

Dahlia nodded. "Yes."

"Can you feel the water around you? How does it feel against your skin?"

"It's cold," said Dahlia, dreamily. "And on my lips it's salty."

"What are you feeling? What is your body doing?"

"My body is going up and down." Dahlia's head swayed a little, and she let it. "The water lifts me up and down."

"What are your arms doing? What are your legs doing?"

"My arms are going up and down. I'm pushing myself up and

down. My legs are lifting in the water. My feet are touching the sand, and then they're only in the water."

"What else are you feeling, Dahlia? What are your eyes seeing?"

My feet don't touch the sand, and my face is in the water, Dahlia said, but only to herself. *It was light because my eyes were in the light; now it's dark, because I'm under water.*

"Think about what you're feeling on your skin, what sensations are all around you."

Around me there is cold and darkness, and I know it doesn't end but I can't see it. I'm in a different world, I'm leaving the world I know. The sunshine is gone, I can sense that it's above me but I can't break free.

Mommy. Daddy. Help me. Help.

"What do you hear, Dahlia? What is filling your ears, filling your nose, filling your senses?"

I hear the ocean, I hear the waves and the crushing of the deep. I feel it in my bones. I am going, I am falling. I am gone.

"Now think about what happens next. Think about what you feel, what you can see. What you can hear."

Dahlia inhaled shakily.

Two firm hands beneath my arms, she said. *I'm in the sunshine. The ocean is below me. I'm in the warmth, I'm in the air. I'm back with my family, though they're all the way up the beach.*

Dahlia's eyes were closed, but her mind was opened wide. In her chest, her heart was pounding; around her, the salty air was hot, evaporating the droplets that fell from her bathing suit and from her hair. She was now still, she was sitting on the sand; her hair was a wet slab in front of her face, and through the strands she blinked away the harsh light of the mid-summer sunshine, stunned by her fear and by being lifted and released, by the sea and by unknown hands.

"Tell me what you see. Tell me what you hear."

Don't worry. I saw you.

It was happening so fast. The heat of the sand beneath her bottom, legs, and hands.

It sure is choppy out there today!

Dahlia moved her fingers in the sand, in the earth. She blinked the salt out of her eyes; in her periphery was the pier with the big rocks, still immovable.

Have fun. And be careful.

"Can you picture yourself? Can you see what happens next?"

From behind saltwater-hazy eyes, two legs, bright blue swim shorts, jogging out of sight. In the distance, slimmer legs. Short brown hair, shirtless. A silhouette against the sun.

And something that bloomed inside her, something tender, soft, and strange. A feeling without a name, a gentleness she didn't understand. It stayed for a breath, then drifted, like a mist fading into the sky.

"Take in your surroundings. Look around. What do you see out of the corner of your eye?"

Bubble's Ice Cream. Red hair. And the rock that looks like a bear.

The legs and blue bathing suit running out of sight. Joining the slimmer legs—she had never noticed before.

And then.

"Look at the colors around you, Dahlia. See the details. Use your sense of touch, of sound, of taste. Notice how the colors contrast with each other, how they distinguish objects and occupy their own space."

Dahlia was noticing. And as the legs ran away—four legs, two strong and two slender—she looked up for the very first time.

He was wearing a hat.

How had she not remembered that?

Dahlia scrunched up her face with confusion. Was he wearing the hat before?

She took a closer look. It was a blue hat, a baseball cap, but the symbol wasn't anything she knew.

"It's a..."

Her eyes seemed to widen beneath their lids as she concentrated. It was an animal of some sort, in some kind of multi-sided shape.

What the...

It was two-legged, but bulky on top, with horns... something mythical, even a little frightening. It was Bigfoot, or a Yeti... standing on a mountain, holding a spear.

What?

Dahlia opened her eyes.

She'd just been outside, in the sun, and the lighting now felt sterile, unnatural. Dahlia blinked a few times, getting ahold of where she was. At her feet was not sand, but subtle, tasteful carpeting; all around her, the openness of the shore had confined in on itself, and she was contained now between four white, stifling walls. Before her was not her cherished rescuer but rather Amelia, sitting in her chair, whose legs were crossed professionally, her beige high heels dangling just above the floor.

She sat for a moment, stunned.

"Okay, Dahlia." Amelia's voice was soft; she was easing her back in. "Can you tell me a little about what you're feeling right now?"

Dahlia couldn't. As she drifted out of the haze the warmth of the scene still clung to her, like sunlight on her skin hours after it was gone. For a fleeting moment, a long ago innocence had been untouched by time. Her senses sharpened, and the present settled around her; a hollow ache crept in. The face on the beach was distant now, his smile faded back into the recesses of her memory; the light of his presence receded, and for a moment, she scrambled to retrieve it. But reality came, relentlessly, and with it the sobering weight of knowing the innocence would not last. The little girl inside her—the one who had been tucked away like a forgotten keepsake, folded neatly into the layers of the woman she had become—could not have known that.

"Are you okay, Dahlia?"

Her throat constricted. "Yes, I'm okay."

"Would you like to talk about it?"

Dahlia said nothing. The truth was, she wanted to close her eyes again and feel the last lingering remnants before the memory turned the corner and was out of sight again. It was a frightening memory, but a longing one too. There was comfort in holding onto the innocence of that time, when the world was simpler and the future uncertain.

And there was pleasure in the pull of her quiet, startling awe, a shared moment of trust with a stranger that had flickered, and was gone. He'd left a heavier mark than she'd let herself believe.

"I feel like..." Dahlia let the visions in her mind's eye resurface, blurring the image of the woman before her. "I feel like there's something about...time."

Amelia raised her eyebrows with interest. "And what do you think that is?"

Dahlia's gaze drifted over the sand, to the red-haired family playing beyond. "It's like...like we can't go back in time. But time can meet us here." The image faded, and the white walls of the office came back into view. She looked at Amelia and blinked. "I don't know if that makes any sense."

"It makes perfect sense." Amelia smiled widely. "The past is always with us. Time is a back and forth. It always impacts us. It never dies."

"Never dies." Dahlia understood, but that wasn't quite it. She inhaled deeply. "I saw something. When I was dreaming."

"Oh? What did you see?"

"I saw an emblem of some sort. On his hat. Oh! He was wearing a hat."

"Did you not remember a hat?"

"No, I didn't think there was a hat. Why would there be a hat?"

"Well, memory isn't a perfect recording. It's a selective reconstruction that over time, can fade or be altered by subconscious biases. High levels of stress hormones impair our ability to absorb memories clearly. When you're in survival mode, your memory is going to suffer. Also, dissociation is a common response to trauma. It can create gaps in memory as you distance yourself from the experience."

Dahlia nodded, overwhelmed.

"You might not have remembered the hat because you were focused on survival. You were prioritizing other details. There's actually a name for this—selective attention. Your brain filters out less relevant information. That's why hypnotherapy can help. When you're in a more relaxed state, you can retrieve details by bypassing these filters and reaching more effectively into the subconscious."

Dahlia frowned. "So if memory is impacted over time by bias, can't the hat be wrong? Isn't it possible something in my mind put the hat there?"

"Yes, that is possible. Hypnotherapy helps, but it's not infallible. There's always a possibility that new details are influenced by recent experiences or biases. Our brains are constantly reconstructing memory. Under hypnotherapy, they can incorporate elements from our current thoughts or emotions. That's why it's important to approach it with curiosity but also caution, because they may be altered by recent influences."

Dahlia felt herself growing frustrated by the thought that this was all just a big waste of her time. "But then how can I trust anything we've just done?"

"I hear you, Dahlia. It's a fair question. It's totally natural to be skeptical. It's healthy, even." Amelia leaned forward and folded her fingers together thoughtfully. "Let me put it this way. Rather than seeing memories as absolute truths, think of them as pieces of a larger puzzle. Truth isn't about assuming they're perfect, but about being open to what emerges while grounding them in what you already know. Together, we can explore what feels consistent and meaningful. Then you can decide how much weight to give your recollections."

Dahlia sat and thought about what she said. Her mind was a chaotic jumble of conflicting thoughts and emotions. Though a strange part of her had been drawn by her return to the past, she somehow knew it was not something she'd be returning to do ever again. Maybe it was that the draw was too strong, that she'd be lost in the allure of its safety and familiarity; vaguely she recognized that returning too often could throw off her balance and her sense of self, like some kind of emotional butterfly effect. Amelia was talking like they had work still be done. However, despite her recent crisis of identity, Dahlia knew herself well enough to know that once she went down that path, she might never fully return.

Regardless, and even given everything Amelia had said about bias and the fallibility of the process, Dahlia's instinct told her that the hat was not a mistake. She couldn't think of any reason why it would have appeared just now, out of nowhere. She had no emotional connection to any hat. No one she knew or cared about had a proclivity for one, and there was no hat she could think of that had ever had any meaning to her whatsoever. Not even in her beloved books was there a hat of any significance, much less a baseball cap. Through the tumult of confusion resulting from her dalliance with the past Dahlia at least had this —she had made, however small, some progress.

Dahlia talked with Amelia for the remainder of the hour, mostly as a formality and because she didn't want to be rude. When Amelia took out her laptop to schedule another session, Dahlia demurred, suggesting she had a lot to think about, her schedule was pretty full, she'd rather look at her calendar when she was calm and not so distracted. After she'd risen and waved goodbye she scuttled quickly to her car, then drove off without looking back, toward the familiar streets of her own safe neighborhood.

After dinner that night she bundled up in her most comfortable pajamas and bathrobe, and sat at her computer without hesitation: any apprehension she'd normally be feeling about edging closer to the mysterious stranger was overshadowed by her curiosity and bewilderment over what she had seen that afternoon.

She started by looking up "mythological symbols" and was unsurprised to find that this was too broad. Seemingly thousands of images assaulted her, pages of esoteric icons listed in rows and columns, and divided by time period, religion, and geographic location. She attempted to narrow the search by punching in "creature symbols," but the results appeared mostly geared toward educational purposes. "Creature symbols in mythology" did not narrow the results very much further. Dahlia searched for "folklore symbols," "monster symbols," "animals in folklore," "monsters in folklore," and "monstrous animals in folklore"; when none of that yielded success, she grew more desperate, searching with increasingly unlikely terms such as "Aesops fable imagery," "horror film costume designs," and "horror film symbols and imagery"—the last of which pulling up photos of blood and gore that made her turn away with a shudder.

Dahlia turned off her computer, cleaned up her few things, and washed for bed. She attempted to read for a while but couldn't concentrate, and she tossed the book aside, resigned to a night of stress and worries and unwanted images. She was truly trying her best to push through a journey she herself had no interest in taking; her sanity, it seemed, depended on her completing it, and on her not completing it. Regardless, she had hit another roadblock. She was left once again in limbo, without closure, neither safely absolved of responsibility nor safely having put it behind her. She was so tired of feeling stressed; she was so tired of feeling tired. She was beginning to feel that she was treading water, way out to sea, that she was managing to keep her nose about the surface but that she was really, truly drowning, and there was no one around to save her.

CHAPTER TEN

*W*inter came harshly and quickly, with frigid cold and gusts of swirling wind. For Dahlia, who lived only steps away from work and only a few short miles from her family, it was welcome in its beauty and its quiet. She loved to sit by her window and watch the snow fall; from her apartment above the town, she had a wide view of the sky, and her eyes would follow a single snowflake from its first appearance, all the way down past the buildings and onto the ground, never to be seen again. There was something calming about the purity of the snow, the way it covered the cars and sidewalks and every nook and cranny in the trees. After, it was a sparkling field of white, until the snow plows came and turned it into slush-topped mountains, or children bent low to dig pockets, reemerging with snowballs in their hands.

She was devastated to learn from Tara that Ginger was being teased at school and that she was coming home crying every day. Tara and Tom had had endless conferences and phone calls, and Dahlia admired their tenaciousness. But her heart broke at the thought of her sweet niece crying, and sad; she imagined her falling asleep frightened about what would befall her the next day, the way her eyes would water, the way her rosy lips would turn into a dejected, pitiful frown. She imagined the way her chest would tighten the next morning, the way she'd feel lonely, like she didn't belong. She wondered if she would be traumatized, if she would take new insecurities to college; she pictured her walking through campus alone, her head down, sitting by herself on benches and forcing herself through solitary meals. These images became physical feelings in Dahlia, and the pain of it almost killed her.

She attempted to stave off these feelings by taking action and occupying herself with her search for the mysterious stranger, and in a burst of motivation one day looked up Seashell Cove Beach lifeguards online. She found the website for the beach patrol, and promptly called them—having written herself a short script first.

Dahlia presented a similar story that she had to Tamsen at the hotel. She told them that she knew it was unlikely but that she was curious if anyone remembered a story about a man pulling a child from the ocean, and that she wasn't sure if it was even possible to find out who was working back then. The kind duty officer who'd answered the phone told her that their records did not go that far back but that they did have a long-serving sergeant who might be able to provide some information. Dahlia waited on the line while the officer put her through. The sergeant didn't remember anything like what Dahlia had described, and asked her for the exact location. Dahlia explained as best she could. Her description sufficed: the sergeant knew the spot as well as the lieutenant who had been responsible for that zone of the beach. The lieutenant was now retired, but he and the sergeant were friends. The lieutenant took down her number and promised to make some inquiries.

Dahlia thanked him and hung up, unsure where to go from here. She was pretty certain this would be another dead end. But at least she was trying. At least she could tell her father that she was doing all she could.

On Christmas the family reconvened again. They were surprised when April made a last-minute appearance, without her husband.

She was warm and loving with them, but damage had been done, and it was clear from the subtle stiltedness in the conversation that she was trying too hard, that she was attempting to pretend there was no tension between them. She fussed over Edward like the most dedicated caretaker. Dahlia had the sense that she was trying to undo the years of absence.

Vera was not amused. "How nice of her to grace us with her presence."

"At least she's here," said Tara, sliding cookies onto a plate, with a mildly dismissive tone Dahlia understood as desire to avoid pointless drama.

Vera let it go, but not without a parting remark. "I guess caring is back in style this season," she said, picked a cookie from the tray, and moved on.

Dahlia understood her mother's frustration but felt sorry for April, too. She had made her choices; she'd gone away, built a new life, and now was a mere secondary figure in their family. She could see that April was very much stuck between two lives; it was painfully clear that she'd missed them, but that barriers existed where they hadn't existed before. And it seemed to reinforce to her that too much change held too high a cost. As busy as Tara was, and as independent, she'd stayed close to home, close to what she knew. It was, thought Dahlia, painfully clear which path was the more desirable.

The family sat down for a warm dinner and gathered around the tree to open presents. Dahlia thoroughly enjoyed spoiling her nieces. Her heart swelled with joy at the vision of their smiling faces as they opened what she had brought them. They were three pictures of perfection; she hoped they were always this happy. She was struck briefly by a moment of grief as she considered that their innocence wouldn't last. Ginger's troubles in school were only the beginning: adulthood brought so many trials and hurts. She rubbed her face in her hands, shoving these thoughts away. They were here now, and they were happy. There was nothing she could do about the future.

That evening she and her father sat talking. It was subtle, but his speech was slowed, and Dahlia ached with the urgency of time. At a moment of pause in the conversation, she sucked in her breath, and braced herself.

"I haven't had any luck with my search," she admitted. "I've made a few calls, but I haven't found anything so far. I'm sorry."

Her father smiled. He looked so tired. "Don't apologize, kiddo. I know it's a lot to ask."

"It isn't." She swallowed against the tightness in her throat. "I want to do it for you. And I will. I'm just—"

"You don't have to explain," he said gently. "I haven't brought it up because I don't want you to feel pressured."

"I know. I noticed." She hesitated. "And I appreciate it. But still...I'm sorry."

"You don't have to be." His voice was steady and kind. "Go easy on yourself."

Something about his tone made her pause. What was that in his voice—pity? Sympathy?

He was watching her carefully, his expression softening, the corners of his mouth pulling downward in thought.

"I say that because I know that you don't," he said.

Dahlia frowned, caught off guard. "What? I don't—"

"I've always seen it," he murmured, keeping his voice low. The room around them hummed with quiet conversation, family scattered in the background. "I didn't notice it at first—you were always quieter. Always lost in a book. And I loved that about you. I still do." He exhaled, studying her. "I tried to meet you there, to talk about the things you love. I thought that maybe, with all your knowledge and the way you see the world, you'd grow into your confidence. But..." He hesitated, blinking as his expression grew troubled. "It pains me to see you so tense all the time."

She swallowed hard, unsure what to say.

"There's nothing wrong with being quiet," he said. "Or keeping to yourself. If that's what makes you happy, do what makes you happy, by all means. But I don't want you to do it because you're afraid."

"Dad," she said, a bit urgently, over a wave of sudden nausea, "even if that were true, one thing has nothing to do with the other. I'm doing this for you. I promised I would, and I will."

"Oh, Dahlia, I love you so much." Tears filled his eyes; the simmering inside her burned and scorched. "I don't want to add to your burden."

To *her* burden. All this time, she'd been adding to the weight of his worries; all this time, when she should have been helping. Dahlia was speechless. At that moment, she was called away by Celeste, and she rose stunned, and in a daze.

That night she dreamed that her nieces were swimming in the ocean, and she herself was standing on the shore. The waves were wild and crashing, but the girls didn't see the danger. They were playing and splashing, enjoying the undulations of the tide.

They were pulled out too far, and they called to her, but she was rooted firmly to her spot. She tried to lift her feet, haunted by their screaming; she saw the fear in their faces, the way their arms reached up for help. But her legs wouldn't move. She was incapable of action.

Why couldn't she do what was needed? She herself had been rescued, long ago, and for what?

They began sinking into the deep. Dahlia screamed and screamed.

She woke up sweating and panting, and kicking at the sheets in the dark. She was wide awake now, her heart pounding and her head spinning with visions. Rather than attempt to fall back to sleep, she rose and dressed, and made herself breakfast; then she walked outside in the early morning shadows, and went to work, the company of her books providing comfort against the monsters inside her head.

AFTER THE NEW year Imani insisted on booking the rooms for the conference in Los Angeles, and Dahlia did not object. Vaguely, and for reasons she couldn't pinpoint or explain, she sensed she would not be going regardless. In her clearest moments, she recognized that the belief she could avoid the inevitable was a defense mechanism, a way to delay the anxiety of facing the unknown. But a deeper part of her couldn't shake the feeling that even having been asked to step so far outside her norm signaled a shift, as if her life had entered a new, uncharted phase and that things were changing in ways she couldn't yet comprehend.

When the hotel rooms were reserved, Imani, in contrast to Dahlia, who entered a heightened stage of stress, seemed more able to relax, and she sent Dahlia email after email suggesting she check out this link or that, look at the rooms, look at the bar, read over this list of shops and restaurants they'd have easy access to the week that they were there. Dahlia skimmed over these emails without much reaction. Either she was going to the conference, or she wasn't, and each possibility held so much question and uncertainty that she felt at an impasse with herself, almost as if there were so many conflicting threats that they canceled each other out.

It was a bleak, slushy Thursday afternoon when she was shelving books in the travel section of the store. There had been snow the night before, but the temperature had risen above freezing, and now it was drizzling, the kind of cold, bitter January drizzle that makes icicles drip off houses. The sidewalks were heavy with the grimy remains of the boot-stomped snowfall, and there had been only a handful of customers that day. Dahlia had more than once taken a dry mop to the floor, trying to stay ahead of the wet brought in from underfoot.

She was in a kind of mindless trance as she picked books off the cart and slipped them into their appropriate alphabetical locations on the shelves. She was nearing the bottom and had just picked up a guidebook on Paris when she stopped suddenly, and straightened.

"Hang on a second," she said out loud.

She placed the Paris book haphazardly back on the cart and retraced her steps to the section on Appalachia. She let her fingers trail over the books on the top shelf of the bay, until she found what she was looking for. It was a book she'd put away a couple of minutes before. She plucked it from the shelf and turned it over, searching the back cover.

Her eyes opened wide. She hadn't been mistaken: in the bottom corner by the barcode was the symbol she'd seen in her dream in Amelia's office. Above the logo read the words, "Endorsed by the Northern Horizons Alliance."

It wasn't a monster after all. It was a man with a backpack, in silhouette, his arms raised.

The room seemed to tilt, and the ground felt precarious beneath her feet. Heat flushed her cheeks, followed by a chill that prickled her arms. This was it; it was the key to the door through which she'd find the answers. The inevitability sent a shiver down her spine— part excitement, part dread. She felt weightless, incredulous; the end was within her reach. Finding the stranger was no longer a question of if, but when. The certainty was both exhilarating and terrifying.

She stood staring for a few moments, the logo blurring in her vision. Quite unknowingly, she'd loosened her grasp, and the book fell to the floor with a *thud*; the sound startled her out of her reveries, and she bent to retrieve it.

There was nobody in the store, no customers in need of any

help. Dahlia placed the book on the shelf and pulled her phone from her pocket. Huddled over her hands, she quickly punched in a search for "northern horizons alliance" and waited a tumultuous couple of seconds while the page populated.

The first link appeared to be the official site. With a galloping heart Dahlia clicked through without barely seeing a thing—registering only vaguely further links to information on the history of the club, the club's mission, and the club's current board of administration. This last link she clicked on without much anticipation, and the results were as unhelpful as she'd expected. Of the five board members, four of them were white, two were young, and the others looked about as nondescript as any other post-middle aged white man she'd known.

No matter, she thought, putting away her phone and getting back to work as the bell over the door tinkled, indicating a new customer. She'd spend the rest of the day in quiet contemplation, thinking about what this meant, thinking about what steps to take from here. From a dearth of promise now came an overabundance of possible paths. The difficulty now would be to wheedle them away, until she found the one that would lead to the answer she was looking for.

"SO ABOUT YOUR EMAIL," said Gita, settling her body into her chair and folding her hands in her lap, preparing for serious conversation. "It sounded pretty urgent."

Dahlia swallowed and nodded. She was waiting to speak; she feared that if she opened her mouth, if she released her voice, her control would be released with it. Even now, sitting here in silence letting Gita take the lead, she felt on the cusp of a breakdown—as if she were standing on a cliff, and the slightest whisper of wind would cause her to free fall to unknown depths.

"So what's going on?" Gita's voice was intimate, inviting. Dahlia shrugged.

"I just felt like I couldn't take it anymore."

"Couldn't take what?"

Dahlia took a breath and steeled herself.

"It's the Torrent."

Gita cocked her head, her brow crumpling. "The Torrent?"

"It's from a book. *Germinal*, by Zola. Have you read it?"

"I can't say that I have."

Dahlia took another, more deliberate breath, and went on. "It's a lot to explain. But the book, it takes place at the quarry. I mean it's about the quarry workers, how they're exploited by their bosses and how they end up revolting in response. But that's not why I bring it up."

Gita was silent, waiting for her to go on.

Dahlia said, "Beside the mine, there's an underwater sea. Water trapped deep below the surface, so enormous that it has its own tide and its own storms." Her hands fidgeted at the hem of her shirt. "It crashes against the walls. It's always there, just on the other side."

Gita listened intently. At these words, a quiet warmth settled in her eyes. "Go on."

"They're always afraid of it. The miners. It's like it's not there, but it's there. They can hear it. Sometimes it leaks. Sometimes the pressure causes accidents that hurt people." She paused. "In the end, a discontented worker meddles with the wall, and the Torrent rushes in and floods the mine. A lot of people are killed, including the heroine."

"I see." Gita watched thoughtfully. "Is there a reason you're thinking of this now?"

"I feel like my mind is the Torrent. Or my thoughts are. It's like...it's like somebody else is living in my head, like I can't push the person aside and I'm hiding inside myself while someone horrible takes over my thoughts. I'm not hearing voices," she added quickly, alarmed by how she sounded. "It isn't like that at all."

"I understand." Gita was nodding along, and Dahlia was encouraged.

"It's like...it's like I have all these horrible thoughts, like all the time. Literally all the time. I constantly think about the worst case scenario. I feel like...like my mind is a thermostat that's broken, you know? Like I get a thought and my mind just runs with it. And it's not just that." The words were pouring from her now, like the Torrent itself. "It's that I *feel* them. I feel the thoughts. So for instance if I imagine my nieces drowning, it's like my mind thinks it's happening, you know? Like I'm imagining it from the inside, like I'm inside their minds and their bodies, I'm feeling the suffering and the fear. I'm..." A lump gathered in her throat, and tears sprang to her eyes. "I'm feeling the water take me. I'm seeing the darkness." Her voice shook, and she swallowed, calming herself. "And I'm not just saying that because I almost drowned. I'm just using that as an example."

"I understand." Gita waited a moment for Dahlia to settle herself. "So you're having intrusive thoughts."

"Yes." So there was a word for it. "Yes, they just come, and they don't stop."

"And how do the thoughts make you feel?"

Dahlia thought about it. It seemed like such a simple, easy question, but it was more complex than she'd realized. "I mean they make me sad and scared, obviously. Like I feel like I'm constantly living a tragedy. It's like I'm always in grief." Dahlia stopped—that had never occurred to her before. Her eyes widened with the discovery. "Like I'm not just thinking it, I'm living it."

"Well, that makes sense," said Gita. "The chemicals in our bodies that respond to anxiety are the very same chemicals that respond to danger. So when you feel anxious, your body thinks you're in danger."

Dahlia's lips parted with the impact of what Gita had said.

"You're also an empath." Gita smiled kindly. "You're very attuned to how people are feeling, and you feel it yourself. It can be very overwhelming because you absorb all the emotion around you."

"It's exhausting."

"Yes." Gita leaned back in her chair and relaxed a bit. "So now that I know this, we can really focus on it. We can help you manage your intrusive thoughts. We're going to try to increase your tolerance to them because engaging in them further ingrains them. Does that make sense? The more you engage them, the deeper the pathways becomes. It gives them validity."

Dahlia's chest was tight, making it hard to breathe. "So I can make them go away?"

"Well, look, Dahlia, you are who you are. You're always going to have anxiety. The only question is how you handle it, how you channel it. You can channel it into something positive. It's a burden, but it can also be a gift. It makes you who you are. As long as that's true, you learn to manage it and to do something with it."

"I don't understand."

Gita lifted her chin toward the ceiling, thinking. "Let me put it this way." She looked at her. "May I use an ocean metaphor?"

Dahlia stared at her and nodded.

Gita said, "Intrusive thoughts are like a riptide. If you try to fight it, you're only going to exhaust yourself further. The best thing you can do is ride it out and then swim parallel to the shore until you're safe. In other words—let it have its space. Then let it float away." She paused. "We can do some exercises to help you with all this. But if I may say..."

Dahlia waited.

Gita shifted in her seat and leaned on the arm of her chair. "The reasons you're here. Your grief over your father, for instance. These are things we need to work through. But you can't do it properly with all this other stuff in the forefront. It has to be cleared first. So let's make a commitment, together, to do this. And Dahlia."

Dahlia straightened. "Yes?" she whispered.

"Just remember, water is also cleansing." She smiled. "What happens at the end of the book? Of *Germinal?*"

"Oh." Dahlia crossed and uncrossed her legs, and took a breath, grateful for the change of subject. "Well, I mean, people die, and the mine is destroyed, but the hero escapes, and he promises to keep fighting."

Gita nodded, her eyes saying more than any words. Dahlia was skeptical, but she got Gita's point.

"Correct me if I'm wrong," said Gita. "But would *Germinal* come from the root 'germ'? As in, to germinate, or to grow?"

Dahlia didn't say anything. She supposed she understood, and she supposed there was a lesson in it, but fiction was fiction, after all. And besides, she'd still have to endure it. Before the growing comes the drowning. And the overwhelming difficulty of pushing oneself above water could feel like a drowning all its own.

CHAPTER ELEVEN

*D*ahlia had been thinking a lot about the Northern Horizons Alliance. She'd done about as much research as she could without actually reaching out to anyone; she'd read every word of the website and had looked at images of hikes and events from every decade since the organization began. She felt she had a path, but the direction was unclear, as if she were standing in a thick fog and the road could be anywhere, on any side. She couldn't recognize her stranger in any pictures: no one had struck her as familiar, and anyway, she'd seen him for only seconds, with eyes full of saltwater, and thirty years before.

Sending a message through the website's contact form was at the top of her list of things to do, but she'd been putting it off because she was conflicted as to how to word her request. She was on her lunch break one day when she received a text from her father inquiring after an upcoming release. She responded to his text immediately. Then she opened her browser and pulled up the Alliance's page, almost desperate to have this off her shoulders.

Good afternoon. I was wondering if you might be able to provide

me with a list of people who were members thirty years ago. I am
trying to find someone I knew back then.
Thank you so much,
Dahlia Polinski

Dahlia sent the message and got back to work. She checked her email during a slow period when the only customer had exited the store.

They had responded,

Hi Dahlia,
Thank you for reaching out. Unfortunately, for privacy reasons, I can't give you a list of members; also, though, thirty years later that information would be archived, and I can't access it for casual requests.
However, if you have any specific questions, or if you can tell me a little more about who you're looking for, I might be able to help you. We have thousands of members at any given time.
Baila Smith, Outreach Coordinator, Northern Horizons Alliance

Dahlia's fingers flew over the keypad.

Hi Baila,
Thank you for the quick reply. In short, someone saved me from drowning when I was a little girl, and a complex series of events has led me to believe he was a member of your organization.
I don't have a lot of information to go on right now, but I'll continue to investigate and get back to you if I have questions.
Thank you again.
Dahlia

Dahlia put her phone away for the rest of the day. It was enough excitement for one afternoon, and she did not want the anticipation of another response weighing on her as she tried to get back to work. That evening as she locked up the store and climbed the staircase to her apartment, however, her stomach was twisting like a tense coil, and she plucked her phone from her purse as soon as she'd dropped her bag on the floor.

Hi Dahlia,

That's an amazing and beautiful story! It wouldn't surprise me at all to find that he was a Horizoner.

I can ask around a little, and I'll get back to you if I learn anything. Good luck with your search. I do hope you find him.

All the best,

Baila

It was a few days later that she got the call.

Dahlia was already home, but she didn't answer it when it rang; it was an unknown number, and she didn't generally like to talk even to people she knew. She waited as the person left a voicemail. When it was finished, she picked up her phone.

"Hi Dahlia," the man said. *"It's Bill Richards, the sergeant with the Seashell Cove beach patrol. Remember me? We spoke a while back, you'd called about a near drowning? Anyway, my friend Monty finally got back to me, you know, the lieutenant I was telling you about. He said he doesn't remember anything about a drowning, but he does know there was some hiking organization staying at the beach that week, some outdoors club of some sort. He remembers specifically because it was his thirtieth birthday and they took him out for a beer. He doesn't keep in touch with any of the guys, so he can't help you with any names. But I don't know, I thought maybe this might help you. Give me a call if you need anything else, and take care."*

Dahlia's hands were shaking as her fingers pulled up her email app, seemingly of their own volition. She'd just assumed whoever it was, was there on his own, on vacation—that he'd actually be there *with* the organization had not occurred to her. She found Baila's email and hit "reply," and typed quickly without reading what she had written.

Hi Baila. I've just been informed that a hiking group was staying at Seashell Cove Beach that week for an event. Could it be Northern Horizons Alliance? This would be the second week of July, exactly thirty years ago—that's the week we went every year. Please let me know if this is information you can share with me and if so, if it would be possible to get any further information about where they were staying or who was there. Thank you so much. Dahlia

Dahlia checked her email dozens of times that evening but did not receive a response. She went to bed with nervous jitters, and tossed and turned for an hour or more, unable to concentrate on her book, unable to concentrate on anything.

The next morning she rose and prepared for work, checking her email every few minutes. She was putting on her coat when she checked once more. She jolted upright when an email from Baila came through. And what's more, it had an attachment.

Hi Dahlia,

I checked our records, and as a matter of fact, about a hundred Horizoners were at Seashell Cove Beach that week for their annual retreat. The retreat is at a different location every year. I spoke with our archivist, and I can send you some photos. These were all taken by a local reporter who covered the gathering; I'm attaching the photos and also a link to the article, which has been archived online. Maybe he'd remember something?

I'm so glad I was able to give you this information. I hope it helps.

Baila

Dahlia felt as if her heart had stopped beating. She touched the link to the article, which brought her to a scanned copy of *The Seashell Cove Weekly*. She zoomed in to read:

National Outdoors Club Makes Waves In Seashell Cove
by David C. Wells

Upon a quick scan the article appeared to be a low-stakes reporting of Northern Horizons Alliance's yearly retreat at the Old Victorian. It involved about a hundred members who engaged in a few planned outings but largely enjoyed the beach and fancy dinners, including a banquet with speeches and awards. A few members were interviewed; there was speculation as to the location of next year's retreat. Dahlia held her phone close as she examined the photos, then clicked on the photos Baila had attached. They were mostly the same, unremarkable candids, save for a full-group shot that did not appear in the article. She hurried to her computer and sat down in her coat, eager to see the photos on a larger screen.

She downloaded the photos to her computer and looked at them carefully for any flicker of recognition. She paid special attention to the group shot. There were three haphazardly formed rows of men—two in the back, with the shorter men generally in front, and one row of men crouching.

Dahlia swallowed hard. She looked at each face. He was somewhere in this photo—she was looking at him, for the first time in thirty years. Was this photo taken before he saved her, or after? Was their meeting yet to come, or was the salt of the ocean dried on his hands?

A shiver rippled over her skin, and her palms turned clammy. A flush rushed to her face, and her mouth grew dry. The shock of what she was looking at was too much to process. It was here, it was in front of her—an almost surreal connection between the present and the past. As she looked over the faces wondering at what moment she was connecting with him once again she was hit with the weight of it. It was possible, she acknowledged, that she'd been willfully denying it, the fact that it had changed her, the fact that it mattered.

Emotions tumbled and intertwined in her like seaweed tossed in the waves. Her breath hitched, and she was six years old again, cold and dying and reaching into the sky. The trembling of her body seemed to shake her in two, the little girl drowning and the grown-up at her desk; it was a visceral thing, the terror, but in the trembling was gratitude, too. The two Dahlias gasped, and shuddered, and inhaled, struggling for air.

Dahlia opened her eyes wide, shaking the memory away. *Which one was he?* she wondered with frustration, suddenly desperate to see him, and desperate to know. She wanted to look into his eyes, to touch his face; she wanted to hold his hand, to feel it gripping hers once again. And suddenly, another terror: who was he now? What was his life like? What if he didn't remember? What if he was dead?

Something heavy settled over her, a kind of shocked resolve when a dream plays out in reality. She was on the cusp of solving this mystery. Dahlia had spent months simultaneously awaiting this moment, and dreading it. But even as she stared at the photograph knowing her eyes were looking at her savior without even seeing Dahlia understood that this was not about her father anymore. She had to know, and she had to find him, not for Edward but for herself. She still didn't fully know why, and she couldn't predict what was at the end of this journey. But she was determined to see it through to its end, no matter. *Why not*, she told herself as she turned off her computer. *Everything is messed up anyway*.

~

It was the beginning of February. Dahlia waited until Monday, her first day off, to drive to Seashell Cove and visit the *Weekly*. The things that worried her as she was swept deeper into this quest were so numerous as to blend together ambiguously in her mind. But the sight of her father's glass bowl prompted her forward. If she couldn't climb the mountain for herself, she had to do it for him. And as ridiculous as it was, making a phone call was somehow more frightening than walking into the building itself.

The drive was gray and foggy, the damp of February visible in the air. When she arrived at the location of the newspaper office, she pulled into a small square parking lot with half a dozen spots and looked at the building before her. It was a squat structure, content-looking despite its obvious age and disrepair, and painted yellow. A sign reading *Seashell Cove Weekly* stuck out from the doorway. Dahlia emerged from her car and inhaled the briny sea air, then walked up the three steps to the front door. It was wooden, painted white, and the doorknob stuck when she turned it. She stepped inside and was hit by the odors of paper, ink, and coffee. There was a receptionist desk, but no one was sitting there. Dahlia looked around. It clearly used to be somebody's house; now it was carpeted in beige, and overrun with books and newspapers and vintage maps hanging on the wall, askew. It possessed a certain small-town urgency that Dahlia found charming.

There was a hallway to the left of the desk, and a staircase; to her right were a few chairs arranged in a makeshift seating area. A door was open beyond, but she didn't hear any movement or sound. Unsure what to do, she stood for a few moments before the desk; she pretended to be interested in the brochures and magazines on the window sill, on the pretext of not looking inconvenienced. When a few minutes passed she decided to sit in one of the chairs, making a point of stepping heavily so as to alert someone she was here. She was just beginning to panic, wondering if she should peek through the open doorway to gently ask for help when a woman emerged from the room, looking right at her.

"I'm sorry, I didn't know anyone was here. Hi, I'm Erin, can I help you?"

"Hi, I'm Dahlia. And thank you, I hope so." Dahlia had risen to shake the woman's outstretched hand. She now reached into her coat pocket and pulled a paper folded into four. She unfolded it and held out it to show her. "So, long story short, I was interested in this article and was hoping you had more information. I'm trying to track down someone who was in this organization. I wasn't sure if maybe it would be possible to talk with David C. Wells, the writer? I mean it was thirty years ago, of course I don't expect he'll remember much, and I know it's unlikely he still works here, but maybe someone knows where he is?"

"Well, he doesn't still work here, but I know where he is." Erin offered a lopsided smile. "He's my grandfather."

"Oh. Oh, really? Oh, wow." Dahlia was already a little breathless with nerves. She hadn't expected it to be this easy. "I know it's so weird, and I really don't want to be a burden or to intrude. But, if you think he—"

"I'm sure he'd be happy to talk to you." Erin leaned against her desk and hugged her papers to her chest. She smiled genially. "He loves to talk. And he loves to talk about his work."

"Oh, that's great. Um." Somehow the questions seemed more invasive, now that she was asking about someone's grandfather. "What would be the best way to talk with him? Should I give you my number, or..."

"Yeah, why don't we do that, I'll take your number and I'll pass it along to him, and he can let you know when he's back in town."

Dahlia's heart sank. "Back in town? Oh, he's not in town."

"He's on one of his birding trips. He does this a couple of times a year." Erin straightened and leaned back to pull a framed photograph from the desk. "Here he is at Chincoteague last year. He has a few friends he goes with. This time he went up north, way up in Nova Scotia." She placed the photo on the desk and faced Dahlia once more. "His itinerary is always kind of tentative. He was supposed to be back yesterday, but I guess they made some unexpected stops, as always. So it should be any day."

"Okay." Dahlia was thinking quickly, something she didn't like to do. She pushed through the mind freeze that always accompanied the necessity of coming up with something to say on the spot. "Well...if you think it's really going to be any day, maybe what I'll do is just get a room and stay. Or maybe I'll go back for now. I don't know."

"Are you from out of town?"

"Outside Philadelphia, yes."

"Yeah, not too bad, but still a hike. Well, it's up to you. In the meantime why don't you give me your number."

Dahlia took the pen and paper offered and wrote down her name and phone number. She was distracted, already working out the options—staying in town and waiting, on the chance he came back tomorrow, or going home and driving all the way back when she knew he'd already returned. She was weighing the risks, trying to determine which had the greatest chance of being the right choice, and which would result in the greatest inconvenience. It would require a good deal of thought; it was too big a decision to make right now, in this stuffy little room, with a stranger waiting.

She thanked Erin and stepped back outside into the pungent sea air, and stood for a moment in the parking lot. She'd never been to the newspaper office before, but she must have passed it many times as her family drove down this road going to the hotel, the beach, some restaurant. She looked around. It all had the low, salt-deteriorated wood look of a small seaside town, off season; what had been charming and exotic back then appeared tired and rundown now. But there was love suggested in the way the chipped, eroded wooden siding had been freshly painted, in the well-manicured flowers that poked their heads from the mulch around the buildings.

Dahlia walked to her car and fell inside, and pulled away without another glance, toward the boardwalk.

Once there she parked on the street and once again stepped onto an empty beach, the rolling dunes unblemished by footsteps. She let her mind empty, focusing on the sudsy waves and the curling patterns of clouds above the horizon. Above her, seagulls circled and cawed. Being at the beach always felt like being at the edge of the earth. And without the hoards of summer beachgoers there was a quiet, deserted peace...tinged with loneliness but soothing nonetheless.

She decided to stay. She still had one more day off tomorrow; she could stay one night, at least, before she had to get back to work.

But what if he still wasn't back tomorrow?

Well. That could be decided tomorrow.

A weight lifted from her chest. There was legitimately nothing she could do about that possibility right now. It was a decision she truly could delay, without consequence. And in the meantime, she could enjoy the quiet. There was nobody here. The streets would be empty, the view outside her window silent and still. She could venture to a restaurant, even, and not have to sit among crowds of chattering people. She could do things she declined to do at home, simply because they required too much social interaction.

She turned and hiked back up the beach toward the boardwalk, content and satisfied.

Of course she didn't have fresh clothes, or anything else for an overnight stay. Well, that wasn't such a big deal. She'd check in at the hotel and then treat herself to an outfit, and hit up a pharmacy for anything else she needed.

She was simultaneously leery of returning to the past and curious about the future, and therefore did not consider even for a moment staying in the Sandy Dollar. Instead, she climbed into her car and drove straight to the Old Victorian. She knew just where it was. It sat on the best corner of town, a grand, almost monstrous structure with turrets, dormers, and towers, as well as an alluring wraparound porch. As a little girl Dahlia had always wanted to stay here, or at least go inside and explore. It would be a good place to play hide and seek, a good place to get lost with a book.

She checked in and, on the way up to her third-floor room, took a good look around. It offered classic Victorian interiors, with ornate furniture and books and knickknacks on every surface, and wallpaper in complex, elegant patterns. It was heavy and dark, but made cheerful by the generous windows opening out onto the sea. Her spirits lifted. As she exited the downstairs parlor Dahlia could tell it would be a good place to read that night; it would possess a kind of enveloping coziness that was tinged with tension and mystery, as only a Victorian parlor could. It was the kind of place where ghosts would linger, where you passed between worlds as easily as between rooms.

Dahlia dropped her bag in her quaint Victorian room, with its asymmetrical shape and its floral drapes and bedspread. Then she stood by the window looking at the ocean. In all this time she had not seen a single other person on the shore. She considered reading in the armchair but decided she would take a walk outside: she was almost as unlikely to encounter anyone on the beach than she was in her room. There was freedom in this expansion of her boundaries; she was safe for a wider perimeter here, and she breathed in deeply, relieved.

She walked along the beach until her lungs were bitter with cold and her boots were crunchy with sand. She turned right and walked through town, poking in the shops that were open and mindlessly examining window displays of those that weren't. She ate lunch in an unpretentious quick-serve dive with hearty soups and sandwiches, then sat for a minute or two, weighed down and satisfied, before making her way back to the hotel.

The hotel restaurant was still closed for the season. For dinner, Dahlia treated herself to takeout, which she ate alone in her room, watching her favorite show on her phone. It was the only comfort she had now that night had fallen and she had begun to feel homesick, imagining her rooms and her things and the emptiness of her apartment, which was waiting for her return. She was out of her element, displaced. She focused on what she knew, the familiar routines she could bring with her anywhere.

She thought about taking a nighttime stroll along the beach but decided against it; there were so many places dangerous men could hide under the boardwalk and in the reeds, preying on women just like her. She'd be on her own, in the dark and defenseless. She imagined her family weeping and wringing their hands; unless the man left her on the open dunes, which was unlikely, she would simply go missing, and no one would even know where to look for her, because no one even knew she was here.

THE NEXT DAY Dahlia awoke early with the sunrise pelting her from the other side of the open curtains. She ate a quick breakfast in a pancake house around the corner and then returned to her room to await a call from Erin.

She was waiting long enough to finish her book and to grow hungry for lunch. She sat for a while in the silence, staring at the waves beyond the dunes. Finally she gathered her courage and picked up her phone, and called Erin at the newspaper office.

Her heart sank when she learned that Mr. Wells would not return until Wednesday. Erin wanted to know if Dahlia would still be there and whether she should have her grandfather call her. Dahlia surprised herself when she answered "yes" to both questions, without hesitation.

She thanked Erin and hung up the phone to think.

After a time, she called Imani.

"Hi Imani," she said, her heart banging from inside her rib

cage. "I've been held up with something and was wondering how inconvenient it would be for me to take tomorrow off."

Imani let a beat pass. "Sure, Dahlia, if you need the day off, we can figure it out."

"I'd be happy to call George or Alana, if that would help."

"No worries, honey, I've got it." Another pause. "Is everything all right?"

"Yes," said Dahlia, a little flutter in her belly. She'd anticipated the question but still wasn't sure how to answer it. "It's kind of a long story, but the short version is I need to do something for my father. If it's really a problem, I can do it another time, seriously. I just thought that—"

"It's no problem, Dahlia, I've already told you to take it. You ask for so little, and you never take your days, so I know it must be important."

"Thank you," said Dahlia, a swell of relief rushing her lungs. This was so unlike her, so unfamiliar, and it had been easier to do than she'd anticipated. Imani really was so kind, and for a second, Dahlia considered telling her the whole story—but it was too big a decision to make on the spot, and also, she couldn't guarantee she could avoid breaking down in the process. "Thank you so much," she concluded instead, and she hoped her voice held the weight of everything left unsaid.

After she hung up she immediately picked up her purse and her room key, to grab some lunch and a new book and to walk off some of her nervous energy. She took the long way back to the hotel to enjoy the fresh air and the exercise: she planned to remain in her room for the rest of the day, reading and preparing for her phone call tomorrow. She bought a salad and a slice of cake from a café, and put it in her room's refrigerator until she was ready for dinner.

Dahlia awoke early again on Wednesday and returned to the café for coffee and a croissant. She was just finishing breakfast in her room when her phone rang on the table.

It was the right area code to be David C. Wells. She picked it up with a shaking hand.

"Hello?" she said, making her best attempt to sound relaxed and confident.

"Hi, I'm looking for Dahlia?"

"Hi, yes." The man's voice was gruff but upbeat. She let her guard down somewhat. "This is Dahlia."

"Hello, Dahlia. This is David Wells calling. My granddaughter told me you were interested in speaking with me about an article I wrote some years ago."

"Yes, thank you so very much for calling." She cleared her throat. "I know you just returned from a really long trip. I don't want to be an imposition."

"No imposition at all, I promise. But thank you. You're in town, I assume?"

"Yes, yes. I'm in town."

"Good, that's great. Why don't you come by this afternoon, then, around noon? Join me for lunch?"

"Oh," said Dahlia. "Oh, that's so nice of you. I don't want you to go to any trouble."

"It's no trouble, I'll be eating lunch anyway. Do you have pen and paper? I'll give you my address."

Dahlia snatched a pen and the hotel stationery pad and took down the address. She listened as he informed her of landmarks she doubted she'd need, and smiled at his insistence he call her if she got lost.

"Thank you so much, Mr. Wells. I really, truly appreciate this."

"It's my pleasure, Dahlia, and you can thank me by calling me David."

"Okay. Great, thank you." She smiled. "I hope you enjoyed your trip."

"Yes, my trip was extraordinary. Do you like birds, Dahlia?"

"Birds? Oh, yes. I like birds. I mean, I don't know birds. I mean I know birds, but I can't identify them, as I suspect you can."

"Ah, well. I'm an amateur! But I spotted a Eurasian teal, it was gorgeous. Just gorgeous! My buddies didn't believe me, and I guess I don't blame them, it hasn't been seen up in those woods in ages. But I don't want to bore you, so I'll keep my trap shut about the birds."

Dahlia laughed, smiling genuinely. "Oh, it's no problem, Mr. Wells—I mean David. I'm happy to listen."

"Well, see you soon. So long now."

Dahlia thanked him again and hung up, her chest a tumble. She cleaned up her room and then, to distract herself, walked about town, spending some time in the bookstore browsing displays and taking mental notes for her own displays back home.

Finally it was time. She made her way to her car and then punched David's address into her GPS app. It was only a few minutes away, with a handful of turns. Dahlia enjoyed the sunshine of the day and the pastel colors of the houses in David's neighborhood. It was a couple of miles from the beach, on a street lined with small Victorian homes and shaded by a canopy of mature and stately trees. Dahlia slowed as she approached, and parked along the curb just before a yellow-painted home with a wide front porch boasting wooden rocking chairs and cascading plants. She walked up the steps toward the front door, charmed, but in nervous torment.

She rang the bell and waited, and saw him approach from the other side of the glass. When he swung it open she saw that he looked exactly as she'd expected.

"Dahlia, I presume?" he asked, in the same warmly booming voice as over the phone. He was wearing camel-colored corduroys, worn at the knee, and a navy blue sweater with a plaid shirt collar peeking up around his neck. He was a tall, solid man with a gristly gray beard and thinning hair. Dahlia smiled and answered in the affirmative. As he invited her in and waved her inside, she saw his hands were large and thick-fingered.

He made light chitchat about the mess as he led her down the hall to a formal dining room, but Dahlia didn't see a mess at all. She looked around in awe and respect at the gallery walls displaying antique botanical prints and paintings of some landscape or other, and of the piles of books and papers appearing dropped haphazardly on every surface. The interior of the house was grand but approachable, with high ceilings and chandeliers but a kind of frenetic untidiness that spoke to down-to-earth authenticity, intellectual curiosity, and a creative mind.

"Forgive the hodgepodge nature of this lunch," he said, sitting at the head of the table and gesturing toward one to his side. "It didn't occur to me I've been gone for two months and wouldn't be well stocked. I just picked up a few things."

"It's lovely." Dahlia took the chair he'd indicated and browsed the collection of ceramic plates and bowls gathered before them. They contained sliced meats, cubes of cheese, fruits and vegetable and crackers and olives. "I really appreciate your having me so soon after your return home."

"Bah, I like the company. Might be why I travel with a dozen old geezers like myself." He laughed heartily and began digging in. "I'm happily retired now, as I guess you know. But I have to stay busy. I've never been one to sit at home, as suited my home is to my needs."

David regaled her with some stories of his exploits and adventures since retiring, and at her prodding told her about his start in journalism, how he'd been a teacher for decades until deciding to scale back—which is how he ended up writing for this small local paper. He'd left the paper five years before, after his wife's passing; he'd needed a change of routine and a change of scenery, and he'd begun traveling the country and the world, "to examine the flora and fauna," as he put it. He asked her a little bit about herself, if she'd been to this place or that, what she did for a living and what she did in her free time.

"Oh," she said, shrugging and waving it off. "I like to read, you know, I like to take walks. Just a little of this and a little of that."

Eventually David steered the conversation around to the reason for her visit.

"So, Dahlia," he said, leaning back in his chair and folding his arms. "You're interested in the article about the hikers' club. The Horizons something or other. Northern Horizons Club? It was something to that effect, anyway."

"Yes, the Northern Horizons Alliance." Dahlia smiled and nodded, firming herself. "You wrote an article about their stay here."

"Yes, it was at the Old Victorian." He lifted his chin slightly so that his gaze was directed not at her but through her, at some invisible point in the distance, or in the past. "A lot of events were held there in those days. Not so much anymore, now that the Oceantide Resort opened at the end of the boulevard. Management changed, too, and they're not keeping up with the place as much as they used to. Rooms are nice, don't get me wrong, and the staff is friendly, but you know how it is with these old buildings. Upkeep and whatnot. But they seem to be getting along, still, as far as I can see, the place is fully booked from day one to the end of the season."

"Yes." Dahlia shifted in her seat. "The hiking group stayed there for a week, as I understand it."

"Yes, a full week, and a rowdy week it was. All youngish men, you understand, away from their spouses and families. They kept the tavern hopping, oh you bet they did. Invited me along one night, they did, but I didn't go. I had my own family back here, you see. I was youngish too, back then, but not *that* young, and I was never a partier like those fellas."

Dahlia smiled.

"So what did you want to know? I've got to be honest with

you, Dahlia, it was thirty years ago, and it wasn't all that exciting a story. It was filler, really, nothing of any import, at least none that I knew about at the time. Anyway, I'm curious to know your interest in that story."

"Well," Dahlia began, rubbing her lips together, "you see, I have reason to believe that one of the men who was here with the group that week saved me from drowning. I was six." She swallowed and tried to smile. "It's a long story. Really long story, actually. But my father has asked me to try to find him. My father is... very ill. So I'd like to keep my promise if I can."

David had been watching her intently. By the end of her little speech his expression had softened to the point where Dahlia considered, and almost hoped, that he would stand and embrace her.

"Oh, sweet darling, I'm sorry." He watched her in silence a moment; Dahlia was grateful for the time to recover. "I understand, of course. His need, and yours." He sighed ruefully, and frowned. "Honestly, though, dear, I'm not sure how much help I can be. No one ever said anything to me about a drowning. I never had any idea." He continued studying her. Then he rose and gestured with his hand. "Let's take a look, though, shall we? It certainly can't hurt."

Dahlia stood and followed him through the doorway into a room lined with built-in bookcases. They covered three full walls, the fourth of which was composed nearly entirely of windows overlooking a colorful garden. Dahlia gasped, then melted a little with jealousy.

"Over here," said David, stopping at the far wall. "This is where I keep my personal archives. Every article I ever wrote, cut out and filed into these books."

Dahlia glided absentmindedly in his direction, her eyes absorbing every object they could before moving on to the next. She joined David at the far wall and watched as his fingers trailed over the tops of the scrapbooks, which were dated by month and year.

"You remember the date, by any chance?"

"It would have been the week of July 17, exact thirty years ago."

"July 17...March, April, May, June, here we go." He opened the book and began turning pages as he meandered toward an armchair and sat down. Dahlia took the one opposite and crossed her legs, leaning forward expectantly, as he searched.

"Here it is. Here we go." David took a pair of reading glasses from the end table and began to scan the article. "Northern Horizons Alliance, the Old Victorian, dinner in the banquet hall..." He continued reading, and shook his head. "There really isn't anything of interest in here." He read a moment more, and held it out for her to see. "You can see it, if you'd like, but I assume you've already read it."

"I have," she said, but she took the book anyway. It was the same article she'd read online, with the same photographs, and the separate group photo beneath. Dahlia skimmed it mindlessly, trying to think of something she could say, or ask. She held the book back. "Do you remember anything about any of the men there that week? Or maybe there are photos that aren't in the article?"

"Unfortunately no, and if there are, the photographer's long gone. Please understand, this was not a very important article. I'm sorry to put it that way, but it's true. This was a fluff piece, a feel-good little story to please the organization, and the hotel. I was in and I was out. Didn't really talk to anyone about anything of import."

"And you didn't see anything yourself? Nothing anybody said in passing that maybe didn't seem to mean anything out of context?"

He must have heard the desperation in her voice. The look on his face was sympathetic, but it made Dahlia feel pitiful, perhaps a little unhinged.

He shook his head sadly. "I covered so many stories back then. I barely remember this one—just a group of hikers staying at the beach." He blinked. "I'm sorry."

"Okay." She hesitated a moment, in case either of them thought of anything else. Then she placed her hands on the arms of her chair, and rose to leave. "I really appreciate your seeing me anyway. I guess it was a long shot. I understand."

He rose to walk her out. "It's no problem at all. I really do hope you find him. Maybe there's another angle you can take, someone else who might know something. I'm sure there'll be a way."

Dahlia nodded. She didn't think so, but she was disheartened, and she wanted to leave. It was another dead end. She didn't know where to go from here.

She sighed and walked beside him toward the door. "Maybe I should look for the woman," she said, offhandedly.

David stopped short. "The woman?"

Dahlia turned and looked at him. "Yes, the woman. I can't be sure, but I think there was a woman there, too." She was leery of revealing too much of her recollection; it seemed ridiculous, her coming all the way out here, with as little information as she had. She shrugged, brushing it off. "I don't remember a lot. But there were women's legs in the background of my memory."

David was staring at her. His eyes had widened, and his face blanched.

"Wait a second." He held up his index finger, and began shaking it, as if in thought. "There was a guy there with a woman, a wife or girlfriend. I remember because they were the only couple there. I thought it was unusual, for such a rugged, rowdy group. And sure enough, they gave him hell about it." He turned on his heel back toward the library. "Hang on a second. Just hang on one second."

Dahlia's throat had turned dry, and her heart had begun hammering. She retreated back into the room, and stood by his side as he turned to the article again.

"I don't know his name," he said, "but I remember he was in the group photo. He stood on the end because she was off to the side. That's how attached they were." He found the group photo, and pointed—a finger tap planted firmly to the spot. "That was him. Right there."

Dahlia leaned in; she could smell David's cologne and musty sweater. He lifted his finger, and she stared at the faded black and white photo. It was thirty years ago, and such a vague recollection—Dahlia furrowed her brow and concentrated. He was of average height, with an athletic build. He was shirtless, in a dark bathing suit. Dark hair pushed from under a dark baseball cap.

And that was when she knew.

"Oh my God, it's him. It's him." She was holding the book close, her finger pressed to his torso and her face frozen in disbelief. *He's here, oh God, I'm looking at him. I'm looking right at him, there he is right now.*

"Honey, are you sure now?" David had his hand on her back and was talking gently, as if to a child. "I can imagine how much you want this. I'd feel terrible if I led you in the wrong direction."

"No, it's him. I'm sure of it." She laughed once, loudly, with nervousness. She felt like jumping up and down. "I remember the bathing suit, and the hat. I remember him. I remember." Details of her memory floated upward, emerging out of the fog. It was like the full vision had always been in her mind, and she'd had to shoo away the haze that had clouded its full truth.

"Okay." David was not convinced. As Dahlia calmed down, he scratched his head and frowned. "It's certainly worth investigating."

Dahlia was barely hearing him: she was floating in the ocean, being carried by the waves, then being lifted into the sky by firm hands, a kind voice. She was six years old, and the world had just changed. She was cold and wet and sandy, her family far, far away.

"Listen," said David, rubbing her back in a grandfatherly way, and pulling her back into the present. "I hope it's the fellow you're looking for, and I hope you find out who he is. Just promise me you'll take care of yourself, that you won't be too disappointed if you don't."

"I promise," said Dahlia, though she knew she couldn't and that if she was wrong, she'd be destroyed. She looked at him. "So you definitely can't tell me who he is? There's no, like, master list of members in the photo, or anything like that?"

"I'm afraid not, no."

"Okay." It was still a tall order, but it was something. Her fingers trembled as they traced along the man's figure. She took one last look at the photo and handed the book back to David. "Thank you so much, David. Really, you've helped so much."

"Well, I certainly hope so." As they made their way back to the door, he raised his eyebrows at her imploringly. "Will you keep me posted, Dahlia? Let me know if you find him?"

"I will." She smiled at him, with earnestness, and extended her hand in his direction. "Thank you again."

"You're very welcome." He took her hand and shook it, then covered it with his other hand in a gesture that warmed her heart. "Good luck."

Dahlia waved and headed out the door; he waited a few moments, then shut it behind her. She walked to her car light with hope, and terrified: for so long, every clue had been hard-won, trickling in like drops. Now they were rushing at her like a tidal wave, and it left her breathless, scrambling to keep up. She had no time to worry about ramifications; she was compelled forward, now, and surging ahead whether she feared the results, or not.

~

DAHLIA DROVE BACK to the hotel, where she scrambled up to her room and shut the door in a rush, then sat down on her bed with her laptop and pulled up the group photo once more. She enlarged it as much as she could without blurring it, until his face was in the center of the screen.

For the very first time, she really looked at him.

He was ordinary enough, but handsome, with well-set eyes and a straight, strong nose, a full, easy smile and a square, angular jaw. Dahlia guessed he was in his mid to late twenties—he was well into adulthood, but younger than her parents. He looked like a hiker, slender but strongly built, with muscular shoulders and calves. He had his arm around the man next to him, as they all did; the other arm, as he was at the end of the row, hung by his side. She took a closer look at his eyes. His smile was in every line of his face, deepening the creases around his mouth and eyes. The smile had pulled up and accentuated his cheekbones. One corner of his mouth was slightly higher, giving him a playful, knowing appearance.

It was so strange, she thought, to see him as he was—as a real, mortal human, as opposed to the saintlike figure of her memory. It was simultaneously unsettling and enlivening. This mundane image of him centered him back down on Earth. But it brought depth to her trust and her tenderness. It channeled her sense of wonder into something she could see.

She smiled as she studied him, breath quickening. He was as beautiful as he'd been in her mind. As the features of his face became familiar heat inexplicably rushed to her cheeks, and the air was suddenly still. She inhaled against a tightening in her chest, the quiet trilling of her heart.

Dahlia looked into his eyes. She imagined the scene from behind those eyes, the sand at his feet, the ocean to his right, movement from the sea that didn't appear quite right.

Don't worry, I saw you.

She saw herself as he saw her, red hair a sunken fire spreading above her submerged face. She saw his arms reach out, but they were her arms, and saw her own hands reach under the little girl's armpits, felt her weight in his elbows and biceps as he lifted her out of the sea.

It sure is choppy out there today!

She saw herself on the sand, a mangy mermaid, staring blankly back with stunned, wide eyes. She saw herself fade from view as he turned and held out his hand, and a woman joining his side as they continued up the dune, out of sight.

Have fun. And be careful.

Dahlia wasn't having fun, but she'd been careful. That promise, certainly, she'd kept. She looked at the man, frozen in time—frozen in an ordinary moment that had been more consequential than either of them could know. He didn't even know they were connected in any way. If they passed each other on the street they would never even realize they carried this bond between them.

Dahlia felt as if the air had been sucked from her lungs and inhaled to refill them, but they remained terribly, frighteningly empty. She knew she wasn't suffocating because she continued to breathe, but she felt like her chest was hollow, and the deeper she breathed the more hollow it became. Surely she was having a heart attack, surely she was dying; her heart was leaking, somehow, unable to keep up. Now she truly couldn't breathe. Her vision was blurred, her heart racing. She was shaking, she needed to lie down.

Dahlia hung her head between her legs until the excess of blood left her chest, which helped the dizziness but did nothing to fill her lungs. Eventually she sensed that the deeper breaths were doing more harm than good, and instinctively slowed it, counting five in and five out, training her body to remember what breathing was like. After a few minutes of doing this she felt she was over the worst, and realized she was sweating; she was suddenly cold, and shivering, but she was afraid to move lest she disturb this tenuous stability. Finally she was lulled by the rhythm of her own movements, and drifted into a kind of blank, formless trance. The haze lifted in time, and she rose, a little unsteady on her feet but back in her mind again, and in her body.

She closed her laptop and ran her fingers through her hair, still damp with sweat. She fell onto her bed and into a restless sleep, rising when it was already dark and confused about where she was, and what on Earth she was doing there.

As EXPECTED, asking at the front desk about the man in the photo yielded no results whatsoever. Dahlia checked out of the Old Victorian and thanked the staff once again, then walked to her car with her bag over her shoulder. She would have preferred to stay one more night but had already pushed it by taking today off from work. She'd go home, get some real sleep, go to work tomorrow and then call Northern Horizons Alliance to see what she could find out.

She spent a harrowing two hours driving home and trying to tamp down the overwhelm that she could only attribute to the resurfacing of her memories. Her increasingly frequent dalliances with the past were not unpleasant, but disorienting nonetheless. Her breathing hadn't fully recovered; every so often she'd open her mouth wide and gulp the air like water in a desert, only to be left with a pain in her chest and a sense that she was vanishing.

When she'd climbed the steps to her apartment and unpacked, starting a load of laundry and heating up a frozen dinner, she found that a strange thing was happening to her mind. She felt she should be thinking about what to do next, or at least trying to process the events of the day and their place in her task and in her life. But she was somehow stunted, as if she had reached such a peak of emotion and worry as to be above the clouds of her own mind. Though the thoughts eluded her, the physical reactions did not, and she struggled to breathe and to calm her racing heart even as she stared into nothingness, of her mind and of her room. Later, she lay in bed suffocating, and considered going for a walk outside until she worried she would pass out on the stairs. Her train of thought led her from the stranger to her parents to her nieces, whom she imagined sleeping peacefully in their beds, and for a moment, she was calm, and she smiled—but the joy reached a pinnacle and fell off the other side, and she thought of all the ways they'd be hurt in their lives, wondered if any of them had inherited her own fears and insecurities. She wept heavily and loudly, and pulled at her own hair, and the weeping forced such breaths as she was able to fill her lungs, and she fell asleep with wet, tear-stained cheeks, dreaming of oceans and storms and little girls swept out to sea.

CHAPTER TWELVE

*I*t was Monday, four days later and her day off, before Dahlia could make herself contact Northern Horizons Alliance about the man in the photo, and even then it was by email rather than by phone.

She woke up to cheerless gray light barely brightening her bedroom. She put up water for tea and sent the message while it was boiling.

Hi Baila,

It's me again, hope you've been well. By any chance can anyone identify the man all the way on the righthand side, second row?

Thank you.

Dahlia

She walked away from her computer and sat with her tea and breakfast by the window, figuring it would be hours, at least, before she received a response. But she checked her email on a whim before rising to put away her mug, and found Baila's response already waiting.

Hi Dahlia, good to hear from you.

Unfortunately we don't have any way of identifying anyone in the photo, as it was an informal shot and names were not taken. However, I will send the photo around to my boss and a few others in the org who might be able to give you some more info.

Hang tight if you can! I'll get back to you when I hear something.

Baila

Dahlia was simultaneously disappointed by the waiting and relieved by the reprieve. She punched out a quick note of thanks to Baila and abandoned her computer, and spent the day tidying up her apartment and deciding on the next book she'd read.

Her relief turned to frustration as the days went by without any further updates. She passed a normal week, working full hours at the store and visiting her parents and Tara, tending to her few home responsibilities and continuing to drive through her books at night. But always, in the back of her mind, was the knowledge that more was coming, that eventually, she'd be required to stand up and take some kind of action. She'd been using Baila's radio silence as an excuse to forget about it for a while. But she couldn't relax while she was still so far from the conclusion. And every time she saw her father she was stabbed by urgency and regret.

Finally by Sunday she couldn't take it anymore. Baila likely wouldn't be on her work email, but she could email her now and await a response tomorrow.

Hi Baila,

I'm so sorry to email you again but I was just wondering if you'd found out anything. No worries if not, I just figured I'd touch base.

Thank you again for all of your help.

Dahlia

She spent the evening at Tara's house and tried to distract herself by playing with her nieces, but somehow the girls' sweetness and beauty made it even harder to get through the day. She couldn't stop worrying about them; they were getting older, and there were so many things that could happen to them now. Dahlia had worried when they were little, but it was different, then: most of the things she imagined—kidnappings, falls involving broken teeth, something happening to Tara and the girls being alone in the house, and frightened—were possible, but highly unlikely. Now they were teenagers and preteens, with more independence, less supervision; their hurts were bigger hurts, bigger than scraped knees and paper cuts. If it was hard to protect them before, now it seemed virtually impossible, for how could she control mean kids at school? How could she control intoxicated drivers? How could she control partners who would break their hearts or exploit them—how could she prevent the deep insecurities that came with growing up?

She left earlier than she normally would and checked her email with a kind of morbid resignation. When she saw that Baila had responded she didn't know if the flip in her stomach was curiosity or dread.

Hi Dahlia,

I'm sorry for the delay. I sent the photo and the question around, and people have been forwarding it to others. No one is able to identify the man in question. He doesn't appear in photos from any other event, as far as anybody can tell.

I really can't send you a list of members, but if you find out what his name is, let me know, and I can try to confirm for you that he was there.

Baila

Dahlia was in a tumult of emotions. Disappointment and frustration competed with the sweetness of relief. She stood from her computer and went to the chair in her bedroom, where she sat in the dimming light for some time, staring out the window and letting the dust settle a little in her mind.

When she emerged the apartment was dark; the sun had fully set. But the air was rife with energy. Now that she'd come so far, failure to achieve closure was a sort of torturous limbo. The only thing more frightening than climbing was holding herself halfway up, of living in a state of relentless anticipation. Her fingers now itched for action, if only to put the suspense to rest.

She flipped on the lights and sent Baila a quick response. Then she pulled up the number for the Old Victorian.

"Hi," she said, when a cheerful staff member named Toni had picked up. "I was hoping to book a room for tomorrow night, if you have one."

"Sure, I can do that for you," Toni said. "How many nights will you be staying?"

"So here's the thing, probably just one, but it's possible I'll be staying longer. Is that going to be a problem, if I let you know at the last minute?"

"Let me see..." Dahlia heard the clicking of the keyboard as Toni looked up availability. "No, that shouldn't be a problem at all. So should I put you down for the one night, then?"

"Yes, excellent, thank you." A thought occurred to her. "Actually...do you have any rooms tonight? Can I book for tonight and tomorrow?"

"Yes, I think we can do that...yes, we have a few rooms available. What time should we expect you?"

Dahlia finalized her plans and hung up with renewed determination. She was glad she decided to go tonight, despite having to drive in the dark. It would mean she'd wake up there tomorrow, that she could dedicate the entire day to searching and the entire next day, too.

With spring in her step and resolve in her heart, she went to her closet for her overnight bag. A little voice was asking her what she thought she was doing leaving for the beach at eight o'clock on a Sunday night, without a word and without a plan. But there were so many voices in her head of late, it was a cacophony of ideas and doubts and "what ifs" that might never come true. None of them seemed to know what they were doing, and they all seemed to disagree. She barely knew where her own voice was in all of it. She'd might as well follow the loudest one.

IT WAS ACTUALLY A RATHER peaceful drive, with few people on the road and no traffic whatsoever. Most of the cars she did see were going in the other direction, toward the city. People were coming back from their little weekend getaways, ready to get back to work. Dahlia drove on into the night, away from them, clinging to faith that she'd know her purpose when she arrived.

The room she was given this time was on the second floor, and a little larger than her first room, but it was overlooking the parking lot. The familiar tug of uneasiness was pulling at her stomach, but she had done this before, and despite the apprehension she now knew she could do it again. And through the nervous static of longing Dahlia also felt something else, something that if she didn't know better she might identify as a whisper of excitement.

She unpacked a few things and washed for bed and then watched a few shows on her phone before falling into a quick, surprisingly easy sleep. She woke up early the next morning refreshed and ready to continue her search, which she'd decided would start with a long, thoughtful walk along the beach.

She made coffee in her room and then put on her jacket and scarf, and headed outside and across the street. She sipped her coffee as she walked along the boardwalk, then ditched it in the trash and made her way down to the shoreline. The tide was out, and she could walk far out down the dune where the sand was hard and cold and the water slid lazily, bubbling at the edges like delicate white lace. A smattering of clouds glowed with sunshine against the periwinkle sky. It was hard to believe it was the same ocean that crashed and raged and pulled you out in its currents, that dared surfers to conquer it.

Truth be told, she didn't know why she had come here; she could have done her research from home. But like the tide itself the pull was unassailable, and deep. For lack of answers she could only recreate the past, in the hopes something would rise to the surface.

After a time she stopped and faced the water. She was out of ideas. She could call the organization and attempt to speak with someone other than Baila, but she was wary of going over Baila's head and besides, Baila had already asked around. She could not reasonably expect anyone here to remember him. No one had heard anything about an almost drowning, and even if they did, the chances of their having exchanged information with the stranger were slim to none. Dahlia considered talking to Beach Patrol again but decided it was a waste of time. She wanted to explore all avenues, but there came a point where she was taking action just to take it, which didn't help anyone and only delayed real progress.

She sighed and turned back toward the hotel. Today would be a thinking day. Sometimes all you could do was wait.

By late afternoon the next day she was out of faith and out of patience. In the absence of anything else to do, she'd walked around town with the group photo and asked after him in random hotels and shops, expecting, and receiving, nothing. She was in a foul, irritable mood, having thrown her hopes to the wind; she'd tried to manifest the best outcome, for once, instead of the worst, and she'd only been validated that things just didn't work out.

Maybe she just hadn't wanted it enough; maybe she'd stood in her own way. It wouldn't be the first time she'd sabotaged herself. It wouldn't be the first time she'd taken a fruitless path.

She was tired from walking, and hungry. Seeking a quick lunch, she turned into the first place she passed, which was a pizza shop just outside the main shopping area. It was a small place, a walk-up counter and a handful of tables, walls dingy with time and grease and covered with photographs of famous Italians and smiling customers. Dahlia ordered a slice of pizza and a bottle of water and took it to the table farthest from the door, where an alcove between the counter and the wall created enough space for a dart board and an old arcade machine.

She ate quickly so as to have time to take one last walk along the beach before packing up and heading home early. She drained the last sip from the water bottle and collected her trash, and scooted out of the booth to throw it away. She walked a few steps to the trash can and tossed it all in, then turned back toward her table to make sure she hadn't forgotten anything.

Her brow furrowed, and she stepped closer.

Above her table in a thin black frame was an old photograph. In the photograph was a stout middle-aged man in an apron that said "Giuseppe's Pizza." He had his arm around a young man with floppy dark hair, and a wide smile that made one corner of his mouth lift slightly higher, giving him a playful, knowing appearance.

Dahlia stared at the photo with widening eyes and quickening heart. Then she turned to the counter and started talking loudly at no one in particular.

"Excuse me, do you know anything about the man in this photograph?"

The two men behind the counter stopped chatting and looked at her. She was standing in front of the counter now, with her arm extended and her finger pointing toward the wall.

The older of the two stepped closer and squinted.

"Oh, yeah," he said, and when he smiled Dahlia saw that he was the other man in the photo. "Of course I remember that guy. He was the darts champion that one year." He tapped the other man on the arm. "You remember, Johnny?"

"Yeah, I loved that guy." The younger man was stout but less stout, and also in an apron, and was clearly the older man's son. "He's the one who gave me all that taffy. Every time he came in here he pulled a piece of taffy out of his pocket." The man laughed. "By the end of the week all the cousins would be crowding around him for candy. He was pulling taffy out of his pockets left and right."

"Yeah, yeah, that guy. I forgot all about that. When was that, twenty, twenty-five years ago?"

"Nah, more like thirty," the younger man said. "I was ten. I remember because he asked me how old I was."

The older man had come out from behind the counter and joined Dahlia by the photograph. He folded his arms across his chest and stared at it wistfully.

"We had a darts tournament every year, back then," he said, gesturing toward the dart board with his finger. "The guy in that photograph, he didn't want to play. But he came in here with a bunch of buddies, and they goaded him into it. He was quiet, like, and they got their kicks from putting him on the spot. Good-natured stuff, you know what I mean." The man laughed heartily. "He beat all their asses, like outta nowhere. Boy, were they surprised! And then his girlfriend, she beat all their asses, too."

"His girlfriend?"

"Yeah, he was in here with a girl, some girl he'd brought from home. Maybe a wife, I don't know. But you know, it made him a target, like. It seemed all in good fun."

"Do you happen to know his name?" Dahlia's chest had tightened, and her stomach was clenching; she had the dizzy feeling of standing at the edge of a great cliff. "Is his name on here? Does anyone remember his name?"

"Yeah, yeah," said the older man, ticking his finger against his face, thinking. "It was Christopher, or Chase. What was it, Johnny? Something with a 'C.'"

"It was Colin." This from the younger man, who was bagging up a to-go slice of pizza for a customer who'd entered the shop. "Colin Hennings."

"Colin, that's right. He's got a memory like an elephant, that one." The older man had drifted back behind the counter and was ringing up the customer on the register. "Always had a thing for names."

Dahlia couldn't believe it. "Colin Hennings? Are you sure? You even remember his last name?"

"Pretty sure, yeah. Like Pop said, I'm really good with names."

"You looking for this guy?" The father was working on some pizza dough now, moving it around on his fists. "You know him or something?"

"Yes, I mean no. I mean, it's a very long story." She looked at the photo one last time. Heat had flushed her face, and she felt a physical lightening that coincided with a rapid fluttering in her chest. "Yes, I've been looking for him."

"He's not in any trouble, is he?"

"No, no, it's nothing like that." On a whim, Dahlia pulled her phone from her purse and took a quick photo of the picture on the wall. Then she turned and faced the men at the counter. "He did something nice for me, a really long time ago. I'm trying to find him so I can thank him."

"Oh." The older man had stopped working the dough for a moment, and was looking at her thoughtfully. He resumed his motion, and shrugged. "I guess I'm not too surprised to hear that. He seemed like a real nice guy. Hey, I hope you find him."

"Me, too. Thank you so much. Really, both of you. I mean seriously. I don't know how to thank you."

"No need, sweetheart. And hey, if you find him, tell him Giuseppe and Johnny say hello."

Dahlia promised that she would and left the shop in a rush.

She nearly ran back to the Old Victorian and up two flights to her room. Once there, she threw her jacket on the bed and pulled her phone from her purse. She opened Baila's last email and typed in a frantic burst:

Hi Baila.

Quick question, can you tell me if you had a member named Colin Hennings, and if so, was he at the retreat?

Thank you,

Dahlia

She continued to pace for a time, checking her phone every few seconds to see if by chance Baila had seen her message right away. After a while she accepted that she was going to have to wait. She attempted to distract herself with one of her shows. She made herself some coffee and sat on her bed, trying to act as if it were a normal day and to ignore the energy flushing through her like the claws of crawling creatures.

It wasn't until after three o'clock that Baila's email finally came through.

Dahlia sat up straight and leaned over her phone, her gut twisting.

Hi Dahlia,

We've checked our membership lists. There is no Colin Hennings; however, there is a Colin Henninger. He was a member at the time, and he was at the retreat that week.

Do you think that could be him?

Baila

Dahlia read the email over a few times to make sure she'd gotten it right. She laughed out loud and ran her fingers through her hair, and sat back down on the bed, nearly wild with excitement and relief.

Thank you so much, Baila. Yes, I'm sure that's him. Is he still a member? Is there any chance you can tell me where to find him?

While she waited, she began packing; she didn't know where she was going, but she knew her time at the Old Victorian was over. She was onto the next phase; she was finally getting close.

Baila responded about a half hour later.

Hi Dahlia, I'm so glad to hear that! Unfortunately I don't have that information, and I couldn't share it even if I did. But I can tell you his membership lapsed years ago and he appears not to have renewed. He must have moved some time ago because our mailings were returned to sender.

Please let me know there's anything else I can do.

Baila

Dahlia sat pondering this response, because something had occurred to her.

She had reached a point in her search where she would begin to toe the line of appropriateness, where she was beginning to invade his privacy. Anything she did from this point forward would be venturing into the personal. She'd been so fixated on fulfilling her father's wishes, not to mention the fact that, as it turned out, she was enticed by the idea of gaining closure. Not once had she considered the man himself, that he may not want to be found, and that even if he did, he may be made uncomfortable by the methods by which she found him. Until now, she was sifting through multitudes for a name. Now that she had a name, anything she did going forward would be diving not through archived newspapers and membership lists but through an individual person's life.

She stood for a minute or two in thought, wondering what to do next. Her first instinct had been to call Imani and take some time off, responsibility be damned. But she didn't really want to do that to Imani. And maybe going home for a while and absorbing this new information would help the answer surface.

Dahlia would be waiting, yet again, but she felt more at ease knowing that she would not have to pull the trigger on an ethically questionable decision right away. Maybe her instincts were right. Maybe the comforts of her apartment, the familiar sights and safety, would put her on the right path, just as coming to the beach had, too.

It was a couple of weeks later when she was visiting her parents that she put her toe over that line.

It was Monday and her day off, and Tara was there without the girls. Tara and Dahlia were cleaning up in the kitchen while Vera was out for a rare brunch with some girlfriends. Tara had just closed the dishwasher and punched the start button when she asked Dahlia how her search for the stranger was going.

"Oh," said Dahlia, an immediate tightening in her chest. She was putting away a grocery order that had arrived a few minutes before. "Oh yeah, that. It's going okay, I guess."

"Any progress?"

"Not really," Dahlia replied, hesitating a shadow of a second.

But it was a shadow of a second too long. Tara faced her, her eyes sharp. "No progress at all?"

"Nothing super meaningful."

"Are you sure about that? Because you don't sound sure about that."

Dahlia shrugged as she reached to put some pasta in the pantry. "I guess it depends what you mean by progress."

"What happened?"

Dahlia bent to pick up a few cans of beans. "I mean I went down to the beach a couple of times, just to kind of see if I could find anything."

"And did you?"

Dahlia sighed as she reemerged from the cabinet. She looked at Tara. "I found out his name. But I don't know where he is."

Tara's eyes rounded, and her jaw dropped open. "You found out his *name*? What's his name? Who is he?"

"I think his name is Colin Henninger."

"You think?"

"I mean it is, his name is Colin Henninger. Unless I got something wrong, which is possible. I mean there have been a lot of moving pieces, I might have gotten misdirected."

"Well, what happened? How did you find out?"

Dahlia went through the story for Tara, now and then picking up a food item and storing it in its proper place, both as a pretext for avoiding Tara's gaze and also in the hopes of appearing casual. She knew Tara's next question would be about why she hadn't said anything before; she knew she'd tell her she should have mentioned it, that time was running short and that she'd been keeping everyone waiting, and she knew that she'd be right.

"So now I guess I should start trying to find him."

Tara's brow furrowed crossly. "You haven't tried to find him?"

"No, I mean how do you even start?"

"Well, have you looked him up online?"

Dahlia felt a little sick. She forced the word out. "No."

"Okay, well," said Tara, in a brusque movement striding to the table and sitting down with her phone in her hands, her arms resting in front of her. "Let's go ahead and do that right now."

Dahlia joined her in silence, taking the seat beside her and folding in on herself sheepishly.

Tara scooted closer so they could look at the phone together.

"Lots of Colin Henningers here," she said. "What state do you think he's from?"

"No idea." Dahlia drummed her fingers on the table. "Try New Jersey?"

Tara added "New Jersey" to the search.

"Hard to tell," she said. "Some of these are just about random Colin Henningers who happened to have some kind of connection to New Jersey."

Dahlia had an idea. "Try adding 'hiking.'"

Tara deleted "New Jersey" and added "hiking."

A series of results popped up, most of them involving two of the three words, with one of them crossed out beneath, indicating that word was not included.

"Try 'Northern Horizons Alliance.'"

Dahlia had hope this one would have the answer, but no Colin Henningers came up.

"He must have been just a random member," said Tara. "No leadership position or anything like that."

"Try 'hiker' instead of 'hiking.'"

Tara did.

The first result was for Henninger Roofing in Dunbridge, New Hampshire. A menu appeared showing links for Home, Design, Materials, Gallery, About Us, and Contact Us.

"Click 'About Us.'"

Tara clicked it.

At Henninger Roofing, we bring over 30 years of experience and a personal touch to every project. Founded by New England native and avid hiker Colin Henninger, our company combines expert craftsmanship with a deep commitment to protecting your home. Whether it's a small repair or a full roof replacement, you can count on us for reliable, detail-oriented service.

Tara said, "Look, there's a photo."

Dahlia looked.

"Is it him?"

Dahlia stared at the headshot on the screen. He appeared to be in his fifties, with a full head of salt-and-pepper hair. He had well-set eyes and a straight, strong nose, a full, easy smile and a square, angular jaw. His smile was in every line of his face, deepening the creases around his mouth and eyes. The smile was more tempered than it was in the black-and-white photo; he was much older, now, and perhaps not so carefree. But the smile had pulled up and accentuated his cheekbones, and one corner of his mouth was slightly higher, giving him a playful, knowing appearance.

"Yes." The word came out as a whisper. It was surreal. For thirty years she had known him only in her mind, as the young man who'd saved her. But in those thirty years he'd aged, loved, changed, probably suffered. Seeing him now—present day, in color, on a website for his business, which she could locate in a handful of seconds—irrevocably altered the way she thought of him; it wiped out her memory and left in its place something complex, startling, and new. In an instant he was more real to her, and also less real, than he had ever been. Dahlia closed her eyes. She simply couldn't handle it. The intensity of feeling inside her was crushing, and too much to bear.

Tara was looking at the photo thoughtfully.

"Well then."

They both sat for a minute or two, the photo between them.

Eventually Tara pulled her phone back and began typing.

She shook her head and frowned. "I don't see him anywhere on social media," she said. "Colin Hennings, Colin Hennigan, Colin Hanningan. No Colin Henninger at all." She put her phone down. "He must be a pretty private person."

Dahlia rubbed her lips together. She wasn't sure what was coming.

Tara leaned her elbow on the table and turned to her frankly.

"I'm sure there's a reason," she said, not without gentleness, "that you didn't say anything about this."

Dahlia didn't know how to respond. There undoubtedly were

reasons, but she didn't know what they were. Something about fears, and comfort zones, and wanting to be by herself.

"Dahlia, I know you've been struggling a little," Tara said then, and Dahlia looked at her with surprise. "I'm not upset with you for keeping this to yourself."

Dahlia studied her sister's face for a sign of how she should interpret what she'd just said. Whether Tara was being concerned, or condescending, or simply matter-of-fact was yet unclear. Mostly Dahlia was taken aback, both by Tara's honesty and by her perceptiveness. Up until recently even Dahlia herself didn't see herself as "struggling." She'd only just acknowledged it in herself and was alarmed by the possibility that other people had seen it before she did. Now it seemed like everyone around her was worried about her. She didn't mind being seen as quiet, and passive, and even meek, but the thought that she was seen as vulnerable filled her with a sick kind of feeling very like shame.

"It's okay," said Tara, and Dahlia looked down at the hand now on hers. The look of the hands was jarring; they appeared knobby and wrinkled, and old. "I'm not trying to push you to talk about it. I'm just saying I see you, and I care."

"Okay." Dahlia's face was flushed. She pushed her hair behind her ear and scratched a little at the back of her neck. "Thanks."

"But you can talk to me if you want to."

"Okay. Thanks."

Dahlia stood.

"I think I...I'm going to go say good-bye to Dad."

She fled the room. Tara didn't follow.

"Hi, Dad," Dahlia said, smiling sweetly. She found her father sitting in an armchair reading. He'd been looking well lately, and discussion about his treatments had been lighter, but Dahlia knew it could all be an illusion, and she sensed everyone else did, too. "I think I'm going to head home."

"Okay, kiddo." He lifted his face to meet her kiss on the cheek, and kissed hers in return. "Thanks for coming, and thanks for the book," he said, gesturing with the book in his hand. "Will I see you tomorrow?"

"I think so. Hey, I wanted to mention something."

"What's that?"

Dahlia shifted her weight, then sat on the edge of the bed to face him.

"I'm pretty sure I found him," she said. "You know. The stranger, from the beach."

Edward dropped the book, and his brow shot up high. Dahlia's heart broke at the brightness in his face. "You did? Wow! That's amazing!"

"Well, I mean, I think I did. I'm not one hundred percent sure. But I think I have his name."

"What's his name?"

"Colin Henninger."

"Colin Henninger," Edward repeated, enunciating the syllables slowly, with reverence in his eyes. He smiled at her; Dahlia hadn't seen him this animated in months. "So, where is he? Did you talk to him?"

"Tara and I looked him up," she said. Truthfully, she hadn't intended to tell her father today, but she was afraid Tara would now that she knew, and she didn't want her father to think she was hiding it from him. "Looks like he's in New Hampshire. He has a business up there."

"So you can call him."

Dahlia frowned. "Listen, Dad...I'm nervous. Like...isn't it weird for me to track him down? Isn't it an invasion of his privacy? Won't he be creeped out, or something?"

Edward considered. Then he shook his head. "I see your point, but in this day and age I think most people understand they can be found."

"But what if he doesn't want to be? What if I offend him?"

"Listen, honey." Edward took her hand and looked up at her, and Dahlia instantly softened. "I understand your concerns on this. And knowing who he is is enough. If you don't want to contact him, I can live with that." He smiled soberly. "If you did, though, I think that would be fine."

"Maybe if it were a woman and not a man."

"Well, I'm a man, and in his shoes I'd appreciate it."

Dahlia thought about this. Deep down she knew he was right. She'd appreciate it, too. And it was true, what he'd said about everyone being findable. Dahlia wondered, not for the first time, how much of her hesitation was related to Colin's discomfort, and how much of it was her own.

"Okay, Dad," she said, and smiled sincerely. "I'll think about it."

She kissed him again, promised to come again soon, and took her leave. She peeked warily into the kitchen for Tara, but Tara wasn't there. Dahlia didn't know which was more awkward, leaving without saying goodbye or seeking her out to force a conversation. She stood for a fleeting moment in indecision, then hurried out the door. If it would be awkward either way, she'd might as well.

PART III
THE MOUNTAIN

CHAPTER THIRTEEN

*W*inter began turning into spring. Clusters of robins congregated on lawns, and morning commutes were a little bit lighter. The bite in the air withered into a chill with the promise of warmth. The ground was marshy with the last remnants of melted snow.

Dahlia had not yet been able to bring herself to contact Colin Henninger of Dunbridge, New Hampshire. She knew that once she hit that "send" button, her life somehow would change. The clashing of worlds would end a secret part of herself. First it was her memory that had been exposed to the light. Now the searching she'd embarked on by herself was about to become something entirely different, something that would open her to more people she didn't know and emotions she hadn't had. She didn't know what to expect on the other side of that communication. And she wasn't ready to take that leap into the unknown.

In the meantime, the trip to Los Angeles was fast approaching, and Imani informed her it was time to book their flights. Dahlia had put off thinking about it, oscillating between denial and desperate hope that something would happen to get her out of it. But her time had finally run out. Imani sat her down with a calendar one day and attempted to go over their schedule.

"The conference technically begins on Wednesday," she said, scrolling down the itinerary. "But most people are arriving Tuesday, or even Monday. The last session is Saturday morning, but I'd like us to stay until Sunday because people will be having dinner and discussions Saturday night. I've already added a couple of nights to our hotel reservations." She pulled up the website for flights. "Direct is best, but if the timing doesn't work out I don't mind if we have to connect."

Dahlia had become more breathless with every word Imani said; she was beginning to sweat on her face and under her arms, and her heart was pounding in alarm.

"Wait, Imani, wait," she said, without even meaning to. She was propelled forward by an unknown force: as pressing as her anxiety over disappointing Imani, her anxiety over the trip was even more so. "I'm not quite ready to commit to this yet."

"All right then, go ahead and check the dates and get back to me, that's fine. But try to let me know as soon as possible, okay? I'd really like to get this taken care of."

"No, I mean..."

Imani looked at her, waiting.

Dahlia gathered her strength. "I mean I'm not...I mean I'm not ready to..."

Imani blinked. "Is everything okay?"

Dahlia didn't know if it was or if it wasn't. "Yes, everything is fine."

"Is there something you're not telling me?"

Dahlia swallowed. "I mean I'm not...quite ready to commit to the whole thing."

"What whole thing?"

Dahlia had reached the limits of her courage; she needed Imani to read between the lines so she didn't have to say the words. If Imani was stopping there, then so must she.

"Nothing, nothing," she said, not unrelieved to kick the can down the road. "I'll check the dates and get back to you. Thanks, Imani."

Her relief was short-lived, however. The necessity of facing the inevitable continued to wear on her; she was plagued with it day and night, and she constantly turned it around in her mind, contemplating how to word her refusal just right, or working out how she might get out of it without having to refuse at all. The simmering was now at a constant full boil. She found herself unable to eat and unable to sleep, even unable to breathe: her lungs, it seemed, had never fully regained their former capacity, and while she had been able to live with it, to tell herself it was nothing or that she was just getting older, her constant feeling of suffocating and the unrelenting need to consume air in unwieldy gulps had taken its physical toll. Which only made the mental toll that much more unbearable.

On Monday she attempted to discuss the situation with Gita.

"Would you like to work on some exercises?" Gita asked, her voice gentle and kind.

But Dahlia was impatient.

"What I really need is a way to get out of this, without having to directly tell her I want out of it."

Gita's expression turned sympathetic—the divot between her eyebrows had creased, and she was smiling, but the smile was sober.

"Well," she said, with a throaty little exhalation of breath, a quick scoffing sound that seemed to Dahlia a tad dismissive, "unfortunately I can't advise you to lie or to manipulate. I really think you'll need to tell her the truth, though honestly, Dahlia, I'd like to at least explore the possibility of your going, and how you might get through it."

"I'm not trying to manipulate," said Dahlia. "I just feel like there are ways of getting out of this that can satisfy both sides."

"I'm afraid I don't agree. I'm sorry. I think finding an excuse or sugarcoating your feelings will only delay dealing with the issue at the heart of all this. Not to mention the fact that it isn't fair to Imani."

"What's the issue at the heart of all this?"

"I really think anxiety is holding you back. I know you don't like to call it that, and I understand that completely, I do. But there comes a point where you want to feel better, right? Look," she said then, holding her hand out in appeasement as Dahlia shifted in her seat, and frowned. "I have to be honest, I'm really torn here. On the one hand, I want to do this at your pace. That's why I'm here. My job isn't to stress you out further, it's to make you feel safe and to meet you where you are. But I also feel like as your therapist, I'd be remiss not to put these ideas to you, when I think they can help. I care about you, Dahlia, and really think we can do this. I just see a strong, beautiful, talented, and incredibly kind woman sitting in front of me, and I want you to know all that about you. Does any of this make sense? I just want you to know that it doesn't have to be this way."

"What are you saying?"

Gita hesitated for a moment or two. "Would you consider a consult with one of our psychiatrists or nurse practitioners," she said then, and her voice was higher, and quieter, than normal, as she predicted, correctly, that Dahlia would resist, "someone who can talk to you about medication? Just a consult, that's all, no commitment whatsoever."

"What?" Dahlia's mouth had opened wide, then closed, and her eyes turned cross. "Medication for what? I'm not like that. I don't need medication."

"There's no shame in it, Dahlia. Lots of people have meds to help manage their anxiety and depression. It's a medicine like any other."

"No, it's not."

"Why not? If you had strep throat, you'd take an antibiotic. It wouldn't be something you could control, but it would be something you could treat. Right? There's no difference here. You might just need a little something to help you along in your process. There's only so much talk therapy can do."

Dahlia's vision was blurred by embarrassment and anger. She saw Gita's suggestion as an implication that she was weak, that she was incapable of managing her feelings independently, and as someone who took care of herself—granted, she was a mess, she saw that now, but she was responsible, she was on top of her business, she never let any balls drop—the idea that she could need medication conflicted with all her beliefs about her identity. She solved her problems, she didn't take the easy way out—and besides, any struggles she had were the result of her own choices. She already felt bad enough about herself; going down the path Gita was proposing meant acknowledging something even worse, and if she couldn't figure it out herself then she didn't even deserve it.

"If that's true, then why am I even here?"

Gita seemed stumped as to how to respond. Dahlia took the opportunity to gather her purse.

"Honestly, I think I'm going to go. No offense to you, I appreciate your help. Let's hold off on the next appointment for now," she added when Gita turned to her laptop. "I need some time to think."

Gita had stood; frown lines wore deep into her face. "I can't stop you from leaving or from taking a break, but let me just plead with you, just once. It doesn't happen right away. It's a long game, right? Can we at least meet in two weeks?"

"Let's see what happens." Dahlia's heart was beating so fast her face was turning red. She was mortified with herself for taking this bold action, which she hadn't thought through and was sure would hurt Gita's feelings, but she couldn't care about that now. "I'll be in touch." She held up a hand in goodbye, and attempted a weak, sideways smile. "Thank you for your help."

She walked out the door and out of the office, and down to her car.

~

THE IDEA CAME to her before she even pulled out of the parking lot.

She called Imani from the car.

"Hi, Imani," she said, surprised to find herself not even steeling for the impact. "I really hate to do this to you. But I was thinking of taking my two weeks of vacation."

"Of course, sweetie. You're entitled to your vacation! I'm glad you've decided to use it, finally. You don't have to feel bad about that."

"But the thing is, I'd like to take it right now."

There was silence on the other end. "Okay," Imani said finally, though it was clearly less a capitulation and more an expression of her attempts to absorb what she'd just heard. "Is everything all right?"

"Yes. I mean, no. I mean, I'm just dealing with some personal things I really need to take care of."

"Dahlia." Imani's voice sounded funny. She was confused: Dahlia had never seen her confused. "This is of course not a lot of notice."

"I am so sorry, truly," said Dahlia, and she was, but her focus was already way ahead. "I just don't have a choice."

"Dahlia, what is going on? You haven't been yourself lately, at all. Did something happen at the store? Are you upset with me for some reason?"

"Oh, no, no, Imani, no." She hoped she sounded as sincere as she was; if there was one thing she couldn't bear, it was Imani doubting her respect for her. "I'm really not ready to talk about it. But it has nothing to do with you, or the store."

"I wish you'd tell me what they were. I have to be frank, it's hard to be put in this position without having some kind of concrete reason. Honestly, it feels like you're flaking out."

"I'm not." A small voice inside her agreed that she was, but she ignored it. "Do you think you can swing it without me?"

She wasn't sure what she'd say if Imani said she couldn't. Imani thought about it for a few moments before responding.

"It's going to be tough, I won't lie."

"I'm sorry."

Imani was silent for a moment or two.

"Do what you have to do, Dahlia," she said finally. "It doesn't sound like I'm going to stop you anyway. I need some time to think about all this."

"I understand." Dahlia had an uneasy sense that Imani might actually fire her, and a vision of the inside of the store flashed in front of her eyes. She loved that store; it was a safe, familiar place for her, one that reflected her vision just as much as Imani's. She'd taken refuge there, had made it her own; she had experience, seniority, and leverage, and it was mere steps away from her own home. She knew she'd never find another job as perfect as this one.

But the fact that she kept going told her that this was now out of her control.

"I'm so sorry," she said, and her voice caught on tears. "I really am. I wouldn't be doing this if I didn't know it was necessary."

"Dahlia." Imani's voice was softer now, and kind. "I wish you'd tell me what was going on. I'm your friend. I care about you. You know that."

Dahlia swallowed and sucked in her breath, barely managing to subvert a burst of emotion. She knew she could trust Imani. The problem was, she couldn't trust herself. She was pure emotion now, no logic; she'd been taken over by a part of herself she hadn't known existed. She didn't even know what she was doing. How could she explain it to anybody else?

"I know that. And I care about you, too."

"Is there anything I can do to make you change your mind about this? Or at least let me in on what you're going through?"

Dahlia stared at the road before her. For one last moment, she faltered.

Seriously, though. What the hell are you doing?

But it was no use. Something had changed.

"No," she said, overwhelmed by a rush of inexplicable anger, at nothing in particular. "I'm sorry. I'll make it up to you, I promise." She paused. "Thank you for understanding."

She hung up the phone and turned into the parking lot, and scrambled up to her apartment with shame curdling her blood and tightening her stomach like a ball of pulled thread.

SHE WAS HAVING what felt like an out of body experience. Her uncharacteristic behavior in Gita's office had opened the gates; once she stood up and announced that she was leaving, she became enmeshed in a snowball effect of guilt and fear and desperation, in which she had to keep going, and keep escalating, to drown out the memory of what she'd done only minutes before. The only way to justify being brash was to continue being brasher. She had run from Gita's office, she had run from Imani—and now she was running from her entire existence, her suitcase on her bed and almost every item of clothing she owned being halfheartedly folded and thrown in a pile on top.

She collected a bag of toiletries and threw some books in a canvas bag; she packed up her laptop and grabbed a handful of comfort items—a favorite blanket, a pillow, her slippers and her favorite mug. She lay these items together in the center of her living room and stared at them, ticking off a list in her mind and making sure there was nothing else she needed. At the last minute, she spied her father's green glass bowl on the window sill, and her heart stopped. She snatched it from its place and held it close to her heart, with a sigh of relief. She couldn't believe her oversight. She couldn't leave that here, even for a couple of weeks. Besides, he was the reason she was doing this in the first place. Being strong enough to meet this challenge was her purpose now —and the bowl was a quiet reminder.

Most importantly, he'd told her he was worried about her, that he didn't want her to be afraid. Well, she wouldn't be. She wouldn't add to his burden or his troubles. She wouldn't disappoint him or worry him again.

Satisfied, she brought the items down to her car in two shifts, then locked up and made the final trip to her car, glancing longingly inside the store on the way. She turned the corner around the building and climbed quickly into her car. Then she pulled up a location on her GPS.

"Henninger Roofing Dunbridge NH."

IT WAS HOURS LATER, after she'd driven from Pennsylvania into New Jersey and traveled up the Turnpike, then through New York City—a tense, harrowing forty-five minutes that left her breathless and shaking—that Dahlia was calm enough to think about what was happening and about what exactly she had done. It wasn't until she was well into Connecticut, past the New York City commuters and the construction, past the busy and twisty highways of the city's immediate suburbs, that the road grew straight and simple, that she didn't have to keep a constant eye on her GPS for quick exits and lane changes. The sun was already setting by the time she crossed into Massachusetts, where she stopped for gas and a quick to-go dinner, and sat in the convenience store parking lot staring at the dashboard in a kind of stunned silence.

It had occurred to her that she was here because she was avoiding one discomfort by running straight toward another. *Why didn't I just call him?* she thought, though the answer was already clear. She'd driven up here to avoid making that call. She'd driven up here to avoid booking her flight to LA. One delay fed into another, gathering weight and momentum like a snowball plummeting downhill. She would drive four hundred miles if it bought her a single day's reprieve from facing what scared her. For the first time, she saw her actions for what they were—a labyrinth of pretenses she'd constructed to evade the things that were scary and to justify excuses that sounded unreasonable even to herself.

Her father's request had forced her to confront everything she'd been avoiding. It was in direct conflict with how she'd been living her life. And that was why it was so hard. It was why she could fail them both.

The breathless feeling had returned; the increased pounding of her heart was making her lungs feel empty when they were full. She tried to inhale, but the breath wouldn't catch, and the suffocating sensation made her heart beat even faster. Eventually she began sweating and growing lightheaded. Dizzy and panicked and frightened, she pushed the seat all the way back and put her head between her legs, which helped somewhat.

Her breathing became easier, and her heart slowed. She emerged back into reality, feeling the seat beneath her thighs and her hands on the skin of her face, hearing the slamming of car doors and the chattering of voices around her. She pushed her seat forward and took stock of where she was and of what was happening. A sense of sadness overwhelmed her as she watched the people walking in and out, carrying various packages of quick foods and colorful drinks. She looked at the people getting gas and wondered where they were going. She wondered if anyone was looking at her, if anyone even noticed.

Well, I'm in it now, she said to herself, and drove out of the parking lot back toward the highway.

SHE CROSSED into New Hampshire at around ten o'clock, well after the sun had set. She had about an hour left to go. It would be a straight shot now up to Dunbridge, about fifty miles up a singular highway until she took an exit, with only one local turn.

It felt different even in the dark. It was wilder up here, the trees somehow thicker and the night heavier. Being from the suburbs of a larger city Dahlia had not felt much of a change in atmosphere even so far as Massachusetts; the highway had been flanked on either side by housing developments and commercial centers, similar to what she saw every day back home. But the signs of human day-to-day goings on had faded, and while life was teeming here it was a different kind of life, one of forests and hills and untamed wilderness. The change in the air was palpable. Dahlia felt simultaneously enclosed by the dense woods around her, and intrigued by them. There was subtle ominousness in the terrain; however, Dahlia did not feel it was threatening. It was mysterious rather than daunting, dangerous but not forbidding.

She continued on until the trees cleared and the road opened. She was surprised to find a series of mountains before her in the distance and that in fact she was driving along a cliff's edge. As the road curved around the side of the slope Dahlia let her gaze drift to the left toward the wide expanse of sky—against the horizon the mountains rose in great, sharp heaps, rolling in on themselves like the humps of sea monsters swelling with the waves. Above, a sea of of stars spilled across the heavens in an endless cascade that seemed to cradle the earth itself. Dahlia swallowed, a bit taken by the scene. In daylight it must be majestic, a picture of nature's grandeur and beauty. But it was shady and somber, layers of purple and indigo nearly indistinguishable from each other, suggestive of obscurity and secrets.

The thickness of woods returned, and she entered the wilderness once more, catching only fleeting glimpses of the cliff-lined chasm she now knew existed on the other side. The road dipped and rose, and as the mountains once again came into view she felt that she was part of the landscape, a minuscule midnight creature among millions. Before long her headlights illuminated on her exit sign, which itself loomed sinister in a thicket of trees. Dahlia drifted to the right and flicked her brights on as she rounded the curves of the ramp, encased in darkness.

At the bottom of the curve she made a right-hand turn onto a small local highway that at this time of night was completely deserted. There was not much here for anyone to need at this hour. Small nondescript structures occasionally rose into vision from the depths of the dark—an insurance office, a convenience store, a collision center. The silence was as tangible as the darkness, which was broken only by the narrow scope of her headlights and by the blanket of stars in the distance above.

She was coming up on her destination, and she slowed to almost a full stop as Henninger Roofing came into view. It was a rectangular structure made of neat cinder blocks, with a yard for materials in back and a parking lot with a dozen or so spots on the side. The door was squarely centered. A white sign reading "Henninger Roofing" in blue letters sat on top.

Dahlia stared at it for a minute or two in strange suspended emotion. She was exhausted from the drive, but it was more than that. The fact was, she didn't even know for sure that she'd tracked down the right person, and if she had, that he'd be the person she'd realized she wanted him to be. Until she looked at the name on the building she hadn't understood the weight of her expectations; now that she was here, in his proximity, and that a face-to-face confrontation was imminent, a quiet fear of disappointment crept through her. Part of her had begun to wonder if it was really about him at all.

Dahlia took a breath and faced forward. She lifted her foot from the brake and moved on.

She drove for a time without finding anywhere to stay and realized how poorly she'd thought this through. After several lonely minutes she was forced to pull over so she could look up the closest hotels, only to discover that the closest commercial hotel was almost twenty miles away. She looked about, growing a little frightened at the obscurity of the night and of the inscrutability of the landscape. Tasked with the necessity of making a quick decision she opted to check into a roadside motel two miles farther up the road, relieved to be able to settle for the night and then dejected to learn that the office was closed. She sat in the parking lot investigating accommodations until she found another motel a mere half mile away; she pulled quickly out of the parking lot and down the street, and sighed gratefully upon spotting the neon "Open" sign in the window.

She grabbed a bag from the backseat and made her way to the office. It smelled of dust and cigarette smoke, and she tried not to be fearful of what she would find in her room. She thanked the clerk and made her way to Room 7, where she opened the door and flicked on the light, locking the door quickly behind.

The room was old and dingy but, on first glance, clean. Dahlia exhaled. It would do. She quickly changed into pajamas and washed up, then climbed into bed with her book and her phone. She messed around watching videos for a time, until her eyes grew weary; then she placed the book and the phone on the end table and stared into the darkness of the room.

It was very quiet. Even at home in her upstairs apartment by the bookstore there was always some noise from the street—late stragglers on the sidewalks, night commuters returning home, the train pulling through the station a couple of miles away. The silence in the room was as palpable as the darkness had been outside. Dahlia watched with wide eyes the stillness of the silhouettes of the furniture. Heaviness gradually fell over her eyes, and she fell unknowingly asleep.

She awoke with the light of day on her eyelids and took in the sight of her room before rising. It was obviously rundown but not wholly uncheerful. From her bed she noticed the grime in the corners and the stains on the carpet, the way the wallpaper was peeling at the seams and the evidence of leaks on the ceiling. But she had been undisturbed all night, and the bathroom smelled as if it had been cleaned before her. Dahlia could not complain.

She showered and dressed and then moved the rest of her things into the room. Then she climbed into her car in search of breakfast, stopping at a greasy spoon not far from the motel.

After she'd delivered her order and thanked the server she sat back and took stock of her surroundings. The diner, like the motel, was aged and clearly well used and well visited. But it was surrounded on all sides by large windows above every booth, and copious sunlight bathed the room in a warm, comforting glow. Dahlia looked out the window of her own booth. Her view was of an empty meadow next to the restaurant, where grasses and shrubbery spilled untamed into an uneven field that sat beside the road. On the other side were layers of forest, rolling in a jagged green carpet all the way to the mountains, which in the faint haze of morning stretched across the horizon like ghostly silhouettes. In the light of day, the landscape had lost none of its harshness or its mystery. But as she gazed at it Dahlia grew lulled by its unrelenting beauty, almost mesmerized by its unrepentant, unknowable quiet.

She enjoyed a hot breakfast and then made her way out into the sunshine. She stood by her car a moment, thinking. There was no other structure in sight; Dunbridge was a rugged, rural town nestled into the mountain and marked by one two-lane highway serving as the primary route connecting towns, with a handful of smaller streets branching out into what Dahlia presumed were farms or sparse neighborhoods. She checked the time on her phone: it was a little after eight-thirty. Her gut tugged a little at the reminder that she was here for a purpose and that she hadn't thought through to the next step. She decided she'd do a little bit of exploring. Maybe a drive in the sun would inspire a clever idea.

She climbed into her car and drove up toward the main road. From there, the motel, and then Henninger Roofing, would be to her right. She didn't know what was to the left. She flipped on her lefthand turn signal and eased out in that direction.

The road was more or less a straight shot, with frequent curves or rises and falls of elevation. The buildings were few and nondescript, but the scenery was sublime. As she followed along Dahlia was taken in and out of forest thickets; sometimes, it was thin enough for her to spy through the trees. She slowed down and attempted to glimpse what was beyond. Often these peeks were rewarded by a view of a stream ragged with rocks and waterfalls, flanked on either side by lush woodland that was dark with shade and shadows. She drove on, rolling down the window and savoring the sun on her skin. Her music had been on, but she flicked it off, preferring to take in the sights in silence.

At one point a natural clearing broke the line of trees; it was a small, bare patch of earth, just wide enough for a car to pull over. On a whim, Dahlia crossed the road and swung her car into it, then opened the door and climbed out, staring into the thicket out toward the stream beyond.

She stepped carefully into the trees and around boulders and upturned roots, and made her way down toward the edge. The woods descended, but it was not too steep, and before long she was standing on the rocks beside the stream. The air was alive with the sound of rushing water. Dahlia inhaled it deeply, lifting her chin. The air itself smelled different here; it felt different, also, in her lungs. It was clear and clean, pure like the water itself, which sparkled as it cascaded over the rocks. Dahlia stood and watched the stream ripple and jump around the stones, forming endless pools and rapids like nooks in an enchanting old house. She bent and touched her fingers to the water, unprepared for its biting cold; but she submerged her hand even deeper, feeling the movement as the water hurried downstream.

Dahlia rose and listened for some time, staring up the mountain, her mind adrift. Finally she returned to her car, no more enlightened, but somehow calmer.

She drove back the way she came but passed the motel, driving farther up the road toward Henninger Roofing. She slowed as she passed: this time, there were a few cars in the parking lot, and a couple of trucks. She drove up the road for a time, passing the exit to the highway and then a small preschool, a gas station, a liquor store, and a bar. Beyond that there was nothing, only the trees on either side and a couple of turnoffs that offered no glimpse into what lay beyond. Dahlia made a U-turn in the parking lot of an abandoned structure and made her way back where she came from. She passed Henninger Roofing one more time but didn't see anyone. She took the opportunity to turn around in their parking lot, and drove back the other way until exiting onto the highway.

Dahlia decided to head farther north into the mountains. The road was wide and open here, the sun bright in the clear blue sky. Her body felt alive as she sped over dips and around curves; she opened the window further, letting the wind rush over her skin and through her hair. Exits were few and far between. In the meantime, she enjoyed the views of the rocky streams from the overpasses, and of the green mountains that stood straight and proud on the horizon.

At one point the trees dissipated, and the road curved around a towering cliff. As the edge of the precipice came into view Dahlia gasped aloud with awe. The vision beyond was like none she had ever seen. To her right was the forest, its canopy a rich, verdant sea. But to her left, a breathtaking panorama unfolded—a vast expanse of mountains undulating in waves of green, their shadows rippling like waves across the landscape. Further still, jagged peaks pierced the clouds, each ridge more ethereal than the last until they seemed to fade into heaven itself.

The mountains disappeared behind rises and falls of the terrain as Dahlia continued along the highway. Every so often a car would appear, and she wondered if they were as awestruck as she. Up ahead she could see where the road rose over the next hill. The cars were mere pinpoints, insignificant—it was hard to believe they contained entire human beings, with lives and hopes and fears just like hers.

Finally a large brown sign came into view, reading "Hanford Notch State Park" in white letters. She passed signs for a picnic area, an information center, and a couple of lookout points; farther up they had more nebulous meaning, indicating places such as "Hollow Lake," "The Stag," "The Castle," and "The Cauldron."

Dahlia was tempted to investigate "The Cauldron" but was concerned about parking and navigating a new place alone. She continued up to the next exit and turned around, taking in the sights from the other direction as she made her way back to the motel.

She approached Henninger Roofing a third time. This time, two men were talking out front. Dahlia's stomach jumped into her throat. She slowed enough to observe more closely but not enough to arouse suspicion. As she drew nearer she kept her head straight, looking at them only out of the corner of her eye.

Both men clearly worked there. One of the men was a little younger and was wearing khakis and a maroon polo shirt with a logo on the chest. He looked to Dahlia like a supervisor of some kind. The other man appeared to be in his fifties, with a full head of salt-and-pepper hair; he was wearing jeans and a flannel shirt, tucked in. He was carrying a clipboard, and he had a laptop bag slung over his shoulder.

Dahlia couldn't get a good look at his face at this angle or this speed. But it was enough. She could see it in the particular crinkle of his eyes. She could see it in the lines of his cheekbones and in the slight uptick of one side of his mouth.

Her heart was pounding. She took a breath, opening her mouth to invite in the air that would fill her empty lungs. She accelerated and drove on to the motel, where she spent the day reading and staring out the window, missing the busy and familiar street of home.

~

DAHLIA HAD BEEN SO SWEPT up in her decision and in the frightened analysis of what she had done that she had not, the night of her drive, even considered contacting her family. Even upon waking up her first morning in the motel she felt she couldn't face the reality of what she had done. It was bad enough that she had abandoned Imani. But she'd also rushed off and left her family, without a warning and without a word. She'd heard the way her mother talked about April's absence, and the thought of being on the receiving end of this disappointment filled her with shame and with dread.

But most importantly, while part of her felt whatever journey she was on was one she had to complete herself, a bigger part of her simply couldn't vanish from their lives, especially from her father's.

"Hello, Dad?" she said tentatively when he had picked up his phone, relieved that he had answered, and not her mother in his stead. "I hope I didn't wake you."

"You didn't, kiddo, and in fact you're calling at just the perfect time. Your mother's stepped out, and Tracy's here helping me get ready for a walk." Tracy was one of the nurses, and one of Dahlia's favorites. A small part of the weight fell from off her chest. He was in good care, and he was up for a quick chat.

"Oh, good," she said. She cleared her throat. "I just wanted to tell you something really important. I'm doing it, Dad. I'm finding Colin Henninger. I'm in New Hampshire. I drove all the way up here last night."

She waited in agony through a few tense moments of silence. "Wow," he said finally, the surprise evident in his voice. "Oh, wow, that really is big news! You drove up last night? All alone, all by yourself?"

"Yes, I just had an urge to do it, and I wanted to take advantage of it before it went away. I'm fine, I'm doing well. I'm in a decent room, and it seems like a nice little town."

"Well, that's wonderful." He paused; he seemed to be absorbing what she'd told him. "I'm so proud of you, kiddo, and so grateful. But I do hope I didn't push you too hard."

"No, no, no, you didn't." The last thing she wanted to do was make him feel guilty; she had to put an end to this line of thinking, and quickly. "It was really just the next most likely step. You know? And I wanted to do it. I wanted to do it for you."

"Well, I appreciate it. More than you can know." His voice was soft and tender, and for a moment, Dahlia's eyes stung with tears. "So what's the plan now? Have you met him?"

"I haven't met him yet, no," she said, "but I'm going to try to soon. But listen, I'll be gone for a while. I don't know how long. I just didn't want you to worry. You, or Mom, or Tara, or the girls."

"Well, you know us, we'll always worry," he said, with a laugh. "But you're a strong young woman. I know you know what you're doing."

I don't, she thought, but she couldn't say that, of course. "Thanks, Dad. I promise I'm going to find him. And I promise I'll be in touch."

"I know you will."

Dahlia heard Tracy whispering as she eased him into his wheelchair—it was time to end the conversation, and just as well.

"I love you, Dad," she said, speaking more loudly to disguise the shaking of her voice. "I love you so much."

"And I love you, kiddo. More than all the world and back."

CHAPTER FOURTEEN

*D*ahlia spent the next two days much like the first. She ate in the diner on the little side street by the motel or picked up some meager groceries in a market she found in her GPS, then passed by Henninger Roofing a couple of times before taking a scenic drive up Hanford Notch. She never stopped. She had grown increasingly curious about the oddly named landmarks of the Notch and had looked them up online, finding them to be local nicknames for such innocuous attractions as a waterfall, a rock formation, and a chair lift up the mountain. She was intrigued by these attractions but intimidated. She wished she'd have an opportunity to explore them before she departed.

The thought of departing filled her with dread. She still hadn't figured out what she was going to do here, how she was going to approach Colin Henninger and if she was going to do so at all. She was afraid he would think she was stalking him. She was uncertain about how she would introduce herself. She was frightened of the emotional import of all this, unable to predict what feelings would arise in her and how he would react to her after all these years.

But every time she looked at the little glass bowl on her night-stand she knew that it had to be done. Every time she thought of her father telling her not to be afraid she was ashamed of her own inaction. Somehow, some way, she was going to talk to Colin Henninger. She couldn't return to her father without having done that for him. And she couldn't talk to her family until she'd proven that she could do it.

Tara and her mother tried to call her; Dahlia let them go to voicemail, and texted them tersely back. She reassured them about where she was and that she was safe, and that she'd be in touch whenever she could. But she had to have some success first. She had to make some connections with herself before she could explain herself to them.

On the third day, Friday, she was turning around in the parking lot, pulling out of a spot she'd briefly swung into and preparing to drive forward onto the road, when she jumped at the vision of a face in the driver's seat window.

She stared at him a moment, utterly breathless. She had enough presence of mind to put the car in park, and to open the window, attempting a pathetic shadow of a smile.

"Morning," he said, looking her right in the eye. He was bent to meet her gaze; his face was about a foot from hers, and from this angle Dahlia lost all doubt she'd had about whether he was the man from the photo. "Can I help you with something?"

Dahlia said nothing for a second or two too long. Her mouth was dry, her palms damp with sweat. She blinked a few times. "I, um...I'm sorry, I was just turning around."

"I've noticed you out here the last few days," he said. His voice was firm, matter-of-fact. "Kind of driving back and forth, slowing down, pulling in and out of the parking lot. Were you looking for something? Because it seems like you've been watching the place."

"Oh, no, no." This was already going very badly. Dahlia tried to think quickly, but she kept getting distracted by his face. She couldn't believe she was here, that she was looking at him. It was surreal, but also, painfully mundane. After all these years of dreaming about him, after seeing him as a handsome young savior...here he was, a gray-haired roofer with khakis and a clipboard, in a parking lot on the side of the road in this backwoods town in New Hampshire. "No, I...I mean, I...It's just that you..."

"Look, I don't want to be that guy," he said, in a tone not unfriendly, but hard. "But I'm going to have to ask you to stop. The guys have noticed it, too, and it's making them uneasy. Now, if there's nothing I can help you with..."

Dahlia's heart crumpled painfully at his words. They surprised her in their boldness, and for a moment, she wondered if she'd tracked down the wrong man. "I'm sorry, I'm so sorry," she said, flushing furiously. "It's just that, I mean, I think I know you, and I was...I mean I was trying to work up the nerve to talk to you."

His brow furrowed, and he studied her. "Have we met before?"

Dahlia's eyes were locked on his.

"It was...a long time ago. Did you...did you ever save a little girl from drowning?" She swallowed. "You know. At the beach."

His expression slowly changed. His mouth straightened, and his eyes widened; his entire body seemed to tense. "I did." His gaze turned sharp. "How did you know about that?"

Dahlia looked up at him as she had that day. Abruptly her eyes clouded with tears.

"I'm the girl. You saved my life."

His face remained still, his expression unreadable. Then his jaw tightened, and his muscles shifted with a deep intake of breath. The corners of his mouth had dragged downward, as if frowning—but a faint shimmer had touched his eyes, and his eyebrows had lifted as recognition registered.

"Go ahead and park," he said, his voice now shaky and low. "Why don't you come on inside."

He backed away to allow her space, and waited for her on the sidewalk beside the building. She swung slowly into a spot and climbed out of the car, then stepped toward him, glancing up at him nervously.

He began moving up the sidewalk when she was still several feet away. "Just this way," he said, gesturing awkwardly with his hand. He walked ahead of her, with quick steps; Dahlia followed hastily behind.

When they reached the front of the building he promptly took the door handle in his hand and swung backward to hold it for her. Dahlia thanked him, tucking her hair behind her ear.

"We could go to my office," he said, leading her to a little sitting area to the side, "but we'll probably be more comfortable out here."

"That's fine." She sat on a low couch with a metal frame and blue tweed fabric, and took quick stock of the place while he sat in the armchair beside her. It was a small office, with a wooden desk in the corner and samples of building materials on neat displays all around. A hallway leading to a couple of rooms lay just beyond. Against the wall by the window was a little station with a coffee maker and water cooler. A sign above the desk read "Henninger Roofing" in tall all-caps lettering.

"Can I get you some coffee? Water?" he asked her.

"No, thank you, I'm fine."

He was clearly unsettled and nervous. He was leaning forward in his seat, intimately, to invite conversation, but his hands were fidgeting with each other, and he was rubbing his lips together, or clenching and unclenching his jaw.

"Well," he said, with a smile, and Dahlia's breath caught as memory hit her like a gust of wind. "Imagine seeing each other after all this time. How have you been?" He laughed, a little awkwardly, and ran his fingers through his hair. "I guess that's kind of a funny question to ask. It's been what, thirty years?"

Dahlia was fixated on his eyes, his cheekbones, the movement of his lips as he spoke and had barely heard what he'd actually said. She blinked a few times, collecting herself.

"Yes, thirty years." She uncrossed and recrossed her legs, and shifted in her seat, trying to find the most casual position. "I've been good. I went to college, got a job. I have a little apartment. You know."

"What do you do for a living?"

"I manage a little independent bookstore."

"Oh, wow." He was making his best efforts to be interested and kind—he was nodding along with her answers, and his eyes were round with attention. He smiled more warmly. "Do you like your job?"

"I love it." Dahlia's smile turned more natural now that she was talking about the shop. "I love books, always have. I'm kind of a quiet person. I spend a lot of my time reading, and I'm kind of a homebody, so it's a good job for me."

Too much too soon, she scolded herself.

"I see." He was nodding again, his tone serious but soft. "That's wonderful. I'm glad to hear it." He rubbed his hands together and swallowed. "So where do you live?"

"I live outside Philadelphia. That's where I'm from. It's where I lived back when..."

She stopped. Neither of them said anything.

"You know," he said then, clearing his throat, "I've thought of that day over the years. I really should have made sure you were okay after. Should have looked for your parents, at the very least."

"Oh, no, you were fine." Dahlia was shaking her head adamantly. "You did enough just by saving me."

"Well, I was young back then. I didn't know anything." He laughed, and his eyes crinkled. "It just didn't occur to me." He spread his hands. "I don't know why."

"It was fine, really. I was fine."

A tense silence passed between them. He was rubbing his lips together again, maybe thinking of something to say.

Dahlia said, "How have you been? This is a very nice office."

"Oh." He looked around and made a dismissive gesture with his hand. "This old place. It definitely could use a refresh, that's for sure."

"No, no, it's very nice. You're a roofer. That's a great business."

"Yes, the business is good. I've been doing this for a long time, you know? Moved up here from Mass a long time ago, not long after that day at the beach. That's where I lived back then, Massachusetts. I moved up here shortly after my son was born."

"The woman." Dahlia had said the words before she'd had a chance to stop herself. "In my...in my memory, I saw another pair of legs. Women's legs. At first I wasn't sure if she was with you or not."

"Cindy." Something had happened to his face: the smile had dissipated, and the smile lines had turned hard. The divot between his eyebrows creased, as if in disbelief. "You remember Cindy."

"Cindy?" Dahlia's voice was soft; she felt that she was intruding. "Is she your wife?"

"Yes. No. Yes, she is. Yes, she was." His hands continued fidgeting. "Cindy is my wife. She was my wife. She passed away a few years later."

"Oh, I'm so sorry." Dahlia's face rushed with heat. "Maybe I shouldn't have said anything."

He was watching her intently. "No, don't apologize," he said, relaxing once more. "I'm just surprised." He smiled again. "It's nice to know this, actually. I like the idea that you remember her."

Dahlia paused a few moments, both to let him gather his thoughts and to gather her own. She was suffering a little pang of grief, deep in her core, knowing the woman in her memory had died, and so young. Emotion pricked in her eyes, but she took a deep breath, and restrained it.

"So," he said then, "how did you find me?"

Dahlia blinked and resettled in her seat. "Oh. It's such a long story." She swallowed and returned his smile, affecting a nonchalant tone she was sure was transparently contrived. "I had this memory. But I didn't remember a lot of details. Someone suggested I try hypnotherapy. I was skeptical at first, but it worked, because I remembered that symbol on your hat."

"My hat?"

"Yes, you were wearing a cap, and it had a symbol on it. For the Northern Horizons Alliance."

"Oh, right," he said, smiling more warmly, now leaning back in his chair. "Of course, I should have guessed."

Dahlia smiled and shrugged. "Once I remembered that, it was easier. I was able to find the symbol, and then I found out about the trip." She was going to add that she had been in days of conversation with the organization, that she'd visited the reporter who wrote the article, and that once she'd discovered his name she and her sister googled him to find out where he lived. But going over it all now in her mind she realized how deeply she'd dug into his history. She shrugged again. "It kind of all happened from there."

He was listening attentively. "And can I ask," he said, with what was clearly deliberate care, "is there...or was there something..." He scratched his head and refolded his hands. "I guess I'm just wondering, was there a particular reason you wanted to find me now? Do you need something? Are you in trouble in some way?"

"Oh, no, I'm not in trouble. I'm good, I'm great. Thank you so much." Dahlia kicked herself. At first she'd thought he wanted to help her, but as the seconds passed she wondered if he was only trying to gauge the situation. Her stomach dropped at the thought that she'd been presumptuous and that he'd picked up on it, but there was nothing she could do about that now. "I guess I just wanted to thank you. And also..."

His eyebrows rose as he waited.

Dahlia looked away for a moment, then played with the strap of her purse. "And also, my father asked me to do it. He isn't well. He's sick."

Colin's face creased with sympathy. "I'm really sorry to hear that."

A ripple of warmth enveloped Dahlia's heart like a hug. "Thank you." She hesitated, then took a chance. "I knew the man who'd saved me would be nice," she said, and smiled.

An almost unnoticeable pause, then he smiled in return. He didn't say anything. Dahlia couldn't read his expression.

He was folding his hands together, looking at the table between them. Dahlia looked at it, too. It had a tissue box, a remote control, and a neat array of magazines arranged in a fan.

"Um," she said, scrambling for something to say. "What did it feel like? Saving someone's life, I mean."

The question made him smile in earnest, and Dahlia was pleased.

"Oh, I don't know," he said, and chuckled. "I didn't really think about it at the time. Like I said, I was young. I wasn't a super thoughtful person, I guess."

"I'll bet you were," said Dahlia. "A person who wasn't thoughtful wouldn't realize what was happening."

"Well, maybe that's true."

A few moments of silence passed.

"It's good, though," he said then, more quietly. "I mean it's nice. To know I...saved someone." A whisper of color touched his cheeks. He paused again. "Have you had a good life?"

Dahlia blinked, then nodded. "Yes," she said, because she had, though she felt her answer wasn't entirely truthful, and she couldn't identify why.

"Good, that's good," he said. Dahlia's eyes were drawn to his hands, which were fidgeting again; he noticed her watching them, and stopped. He checked his watch and began to stand. "So listen,

I really hate to do this, but I have a client coming in any minute. Can we continue this conversation another time?"

Dahlia had risen when he did, and stood facing him. "Sure, of course."

"I'm sorry. If I had known you were coming I certainly would have—"

"No, no, it's fine. I understand."

"Thank you, I appreciate it. Look, why don't you take my card," he said, striding with quick steps to the reception desk and retrieving a business card from a holder, "and shoot me a text. Then I'll have your number. Maybe we can meet for a drink."

"That would be great." She took the card gratefully, and looked up at him with a smile. "I really appreciate your time."

"I appreciate your seeking me out," he began, and then his eyes widened. "I'm sorry," he said, and laughed nervously, and loudly. "I never even asked you your name."

"Oh, I'm sorry!" she said. "It isn't your fault. I should have introduced myself. My name is Dahlia, Dahlia Polinski."

"Dahlia." He said the name slowly, then stuck his hand out. "Well, it's an honor to meet you, Dahlia. Thank you for coming."

"Thank you." She shook his hand, holding a second too long before releasing. "I really am grateful for your time. And for the fact that you saved my life."

He laughed again. "Well. You're welcome."

"Okay, thank you." She held up the card in her hand. "I'll text you."

"Sounds great. Thanks, Dahlia."

"Thanks."

She turned and walked toward the door, then pushed it open and stepped out. She looked back inside before closing it. He was standing where she'd left him, and he waved.

Dahlia walked back to her car with a spring in her step and a wide smile on her face. It was over; she had done it. She had met him, and she'd said what she'd wanted to say. He was appreciative of her being there and was clearly a kind and decent person. Her task was accomplished, and her memory was intact: it was a great success, and the best possible outcome, and the relief she felt at having accomplished all this made her feel she could climb the tallest mountain or run a hundred miles.

I did it, Dad. I did it all for you.

~

SHE TEXTED him a few minutes later, as soon as she was back in her room.

Hi, this is Dahlia Polinski.

She had agonized over how much she should say, whether she should merely text him so he had her number, as he had asked, or if she should tell him it was nice to meet him, or if she should go even further and tell him how much it meant to her to find the man who'd saved her, after all these years. She sat staring at her phone for ten minutes or more, typing and retyping and analyzing all the possible ways her hypothetical words could be misinterpreted. When she first prepared to send her message, it had seemed silly, and she worried if she should add a reminder that she's texting because he'd asked. But then she didn't want to insult him by suggesting he couldn't remember something he'd said only fifteen minutes before.

He texted her back a few hours later and asked if she wanted to meet him for a drink after he got off work.

Dahlia was happy to do this and waited a minute or two to accept, so as to avoid appearing too eager or too impatient. He told her there was a tavern a little further up the road, just a couple of miles, called Moose and Lantern. It didn't take long for her to realize this was the bar she'd passed every day before she exited onto the highway that had led her to Hanford Notch State

Park. She spent the rest of the afternoon in her room reading, eating a light lunch, and rewatching one of her favorite movies, to calm herself.

Shortly before she was to meet Colin she changed from her t-shirt into a floral blouse, tidied her hair, and stared at herself in the mirror, watching her own reflection. She blinked a few times, paying special attention to her eyes. The longer she gazed at herself, the older she looked, and the harder it was to believe she was the person staring back. Dahlia was reminded of how saying a word to yourself over and over makes the word sound alien, and strange. She stared amazed at her own face, not recognizing it, wondering if this is the person other people saw when they looked at her, or if it was the other person Dahlia saw, herself.

THE INSIDE of Moose and Lantern was very much what she'd expected. It was dimly lit, with wood-paneled walls and dated decor and a well-used pool table in the corner. The hardwood floor was heavily scuffed, and the air smelled of beer and fried food, as well as the faint scent of stale smoke from days long gone. It was occupied by a half dozen patrons who were clearly locals, with the hum of light laughter and low conversation hovering beneath the low ceilings.

"Dahlia."

Dahlia turned in the direction of the voice. Colin was half-standing in a booth, having risen upon seeing her, and holding his hand up to get her attention. She waved and joined him, sliding into the other seat and watching as he settled himself back in.

"Hi, how are you?" she asked, placing her bag on the table, and then moving it to the booth beside her. "How was the rest of your work day?"

"Good, busy." He smiled kindly. Dahlia noticed how it made his eyes narrow and sparkle, how it brought out the angular lines of his face and a dimple on his right cheek. One corner of his lips was just higher than the other, in the jaunty, charming manner of the photograph. He already had a glass of beer in front of him; he turned it absently on the table. "This is a busy time of year for us. In fact a client was running a little late today, and I had to cut it short."

"Oh, I'm sorry." Dahlia was instantly contrite, her stomach contracting with nerves. "I didn't want to impose on you. I wouldn't have minded if you were late, or even if you canceled. I understand."

"Nah, he was talking my ear off," said Colin, waving the thought away. The corner of his mouth lifted even higher, in playful good humor. "You did me a favor."

Dahlia smiled gratefully. Her mind was transposing the images of him, the one from her memory and the fleshly presence right here. Her eyes yearned to soak him in. She made a point not to stare.

He took a long swig of his beer. A server came over and took her drink order. She ordered a glass of white wine.

"Are you hungry?" he asked, opening his menu and resting it on the table as he browsed. "I don't even know why I'm looking at this. I know it like the back of my hand."

"Is it the only place in town? Well, there's the diner, I guess."

"There are one or two places up along the road, but you have to go pretty far." He closed his menu and laid it on the table, then wrapped his hands around his beer again. "There's the resort, of course, but I hardly ever go up there."

"The resort?"

He swallowed another drag of beer and nodded. "Goose Wing Mountain. There's a hotel and ski resort, and all kinds of shops and restaurants. About fifteen miles up that way," he said, flicking his finger toward his right to indicate the northernly direction.

"Oh, that's nice. You don't go there?"

He shrugged, staring into his beer. "Never have reason to. It's all tourists up there, anyway."

The server brought her wine; Dahlia thanked her and took a small sip. They delivered their orders, then sat in silence for a minute or two. Dahlia nursed her wine, looking around, her mind working for something to say.

"So you're from Philadelphia," he said, his eyes on the TV screen on the wall behind her. His gaze turned to her. "You were born there?"

"Yes, I was."

"Same house?"

"No." Dahlia rubbed her lips together. "My parents are in the house I grew up in. I have my own apartment."

"That's right. You said you have an apartment. Sorry."

"No, it's fine."

They leaned back as the server placed a burger in front of Dahlia and a sandwich in front of Colin. They thanked her and took a few moments to begin their meals.

Dahlia swallowed a bite and glanced up at him from behind her burger. "You used to live in Massachusetts?"

"Hmmhmm." He swallowed and wiped his lips on his napkin. "I'm from Mass originally, and that's where I met Cindy. We grew up together."

Dahlia frowned. "I'm sorry."

A flicker of acknowledgment, and he took another bite. "After she died I needed a change. Just wanted to get away." He sipped his beer. "Cindy and I used to hike here," he said, flicking his finger in the general vicinity of outside. "It was really the only choice as far as where to go. I figured it was as good a time as any to branch out on my own."

"You started your business here?"

"That's right. I worked for a guy down in Mass, a larger company. It was easier to do my own thing up here, anyway. Not as much competition, as I'm sure you've noticed."

Dahlia looked around the bar, and out the windows at the empty stretch of road and the wide expanse of untouched landscape. "It's nice and quiet up here," she said. "Do you like it?"

He shrugged and swallowed, took a long sip of beer. "It's a good little town. A little harsh in winter, I guess, but I manage. We're all used to it up here."

"I've heard that," said Dahlia. "About New England winters being especially harsh."

"Worst part is it aggravates my sinuses." He rubbed his throat. "It's that nasty dry air."

"Oh, no." Dahlia put her food down and looked at him with a frown. "How terrible. Are you okay? Is it manageable?"

"Yeah, it's okay. I figure it out."

Neither said anything for a moment or two.

Colin swallowed a bite of his burger. "You ever been up here before?"

"No, never. I'm not a big traveler."

A little time passed in silence.

Dahlia said, "Do you like to read?"

He was taking a long drag of his beer. "I'm not a reader, no."

"Oh." She chewed a bite, and swallowed. "I just finished *The Night Flower*, and it was wonderful. If you were ever looking for a good book to jump into, I'd highly recommend it. We could talk about it."

"Okay." He smiled politely and dove in for another bite. "Thanks."

They said nothing more for a time, each absorbed in their own dinner. Dahlia didn't mind silence but was worried it was growing awkward. She tore her mind apart trying to find appropriate things to say to him. She had so many questions—about his life, his background, his family—but she didn't want to pry. And though she was normally hesitant to talk about herself she felt she would tell him anything at all, if he asked.

They finished their meals in spotty, sporadic, topical conversation. When the bill came, Dahlia reached for it, but Colin swiped it first.

"On me," he said, pulling his wallet from his pocket and removing a few flat, neat bills. "It's the least I can do after you drove all the way up here."

"It would be the least I could do after you saved my life," said Dahlia, with a smile. "But thank you so much, that's very nice of you."

He laid the payment on the table and began to slide out of the booth. Dahlia's stomach sank. She'd been hoping to have a more meaningful conversation—about what, she didn't really know. The disappointment of parting as strangers making smalltalk was a physical ache in her chest. She rose reluctantly and followed him out of the tavern, watching as he waved and nodded to the hostess and to a couple of other customers he clearly knew.

They made their way to the parking lot and stopped in front of his truck.

"Colin," she said, mortified by the shaking of her voice, "I really just wanted to thank you again for what you did. I feel like...sometimes people do things without really thinking about them, like we all make small decisions every day, or like we're in the right place at the right time, in a way. But sometimes people don't realize how important they are." She could feel the color in her face and only hoped her obvious emotion evoked sympathy in him, rather than pity. "Anyway, it was important, to me. Thank you."

His brows were furrowed as he watched her; when she was through, he offered a small nod. "I appreciate that. But you don't have to thank me. Anyone would've done the same."

"Not necessarily."

He shifted his weight awkwardly, and rubbed the back of his neck. "Well," he said. "I'm just glad you're okay."

She studied him perhaps longer than she should have: he was looking here and there, evidently avoiding her gaze. Dahlia gathered she had embarrassed him, and she was sorry about it—but she was fixated on his face, the face of her savior, of her cryptic recurring dreams. She'd caught glimpse of it for only a moment, so many years before; now it was a whole different time, and they were entirely different people. Dahlia couldn't discern whether he was indifferent, or whether it had meant something to him, as it had to her, and he was simply too humble—or too overwhelmed —to say. She was desperately trying to connect the young hero from her dreams to this reserved, cautious man in front of her; it was one man, but two visions, and she didn't know which was real.

He looked up at her suddenly.

"*Are* you okay?"

His expression had turned serious, his brows furrowed and his lips in a somber straight line. His gaze was heavy and sharp, but Dahlia couldn't parse what she was seeing there. They were facing each other, with several feet of empty space between them; Dahlia wished they were closer, but to close the gap now would be too abrupt, and too intimate.

"I'm...okay," she responded, cocking her head. "Why?"

"I don't know." He shrugged and stuck his hands in his pockets, frowning. "Something told me to ask."

Is it me? Or is it you? she wanted to say, but didn't. Instead, she forced herself to smile.

"Well, I'm okay." She slid her purse strap further up her shoulder. "Thank you."

He smiled mildly. "Okay." He pulled his keys from his pocket. "How long are you in town?"

"I'm actually not sure." She moved out of the way for a car headed out of the parking lot, and took the opportunity to take a few steps toward him. "I'm using this time as a bit of a reset. I don't have any definite plans."

"You have a room somewhere, then?"

"At the Mountain View Motel, just down the road."

His expression instantly flattened. "Oh." His lips drew back into a grimace that tensed his jaw and tightened the cords of his throat. "Is that really where you're staying?"

Dahlia's eyebrows lifted. "Yes. I don't need anything fancy." Her eyes narrowed. "Is it dangerous?"

He scratched his head again. "Not the nicest place, but it's fine." His eyes softened, brows drawing together. "I'm sorry, I can't offer to put you up."

"Oh, I understand!" Dahlia waved her hands back and forth in protest. "I would never ask or expect that of you." She hesitated. "Is it okay if I see you again?"

"Sure. How about I'll shoot you a text this weekend."

"Okay, that would be great." Her smile turned warmer. "I'd love that, thanks."

"All right." Abruptly, he jerked forward and moved his hand to her back in a stiff, clumsy hug. Dahlia slipped her arm around him and pressed her hand to his shoulder. He gave her a couple of pats and quickly withdrew, and so did she; but the heat of him remained under her fingers, the woodsy scent of him in her nose and in the air. She was stilled by a sharp intake of breath. With that touch, he was no longer just a memory—he was solid, human, warm beneath her hand.

He lifted his hand in a wave and smiled, his eyes crinkling, one corner of his mouth just a little bit higher than the other. He took a step back toward his car.

"Take care of yourself, kiddo."

Dahlia straightened, taken aback. "What did you say?"

"Oh." He stepped back toward her. "Sorry," he said, shaking his head. "That's probably condescending." He laughed. "I guess in my mind you're still six."

"No, it's fine." She opened her mouth to say more, but stopped. Hearing him call her "kiddo" felt serendipitous; saying it out loud would strip the magic away. She didn't want to discourage him from saying it. And divulging the fondness she felt at his saying it would expose her in ways she herself didn't fully understand.

They waved and said goodbye. He climbed into his truck, and she fell gently into her car. He waited for her to leave, then followed her out of the parking lot; she turned left, and he turned right, and she wondered where he lived and what kind of home he had, what he was returning to right now, what he'd do when he got there and whether he'd think of her, as she knew she'd spend all night thinking of him.

CHAPTER FIFTEEN

*H*e didn't text her the next day, or the day after that. Dahlia spent her time reliving their conversation in her mind and rationalizing why it was taking him so long to be in touch with her. She knew he had a business to run, and a son somewhere, though she didn't know where the son lived, what their relationship was like, or what his name was. *He must be very busy,* Dahlia told herself. *Or maybe he's trying not to push too hard, just like I am.*

Dahlia sat in the armchair in her motel room staring out the window at the handful of cars in the parking lot and the empty road beyond. Across the street was an uneven row of trees, and even further beyond, the mountains. She imagined what it was like to live here, for this landscape to be part of the background of a person's everyday life. It was tranquil enough to feel desolate, the quiet heavy in the air. She realized how used she'd grown to the hubbub of the city, how dependent she was on having choices —in food, in entertainment, in everything.

She thought about her drive up the road and remembered that it actually wasn't quiet at all. With the windows down, she'd heard the rushing of the stream and the chirping of the birds; there was the rustling in the trees and the crunching of the foliage under her feet as she'd trudged through the woods down toward the water. There was the music of the tavern and the buzz of conversation—which against the placid background in fact seemed more animated, more meaningful, more alive.

Thinking of the tavern brought her mind once again back to Colin, who like everyone else in the tavern was part of the landscape itself. He belonged here, had built his life on the lurking quiet of the woods; and like the woods he was enigmatic, but not without softness. Dahlia recalled the way he'd smiled when insisting on paying for dinner, the way he'd asked if she was okay. There was something protective in it, something endearing in his extending his hand despite his own lurking quiet.

In her memory he was lithe and upbeat. Her vision of him conflicted with the wary man she'd met. But beneath his wariness was obvious kindness, and that did not conflict.

She frowned as she gazed absentmindedly at the scene on the other side of the window, then glanced down at her phone. She worried over how long she should wait to contact him. She worried over whether he didn't want to see her again, or whether he'd simply lost track of time. She worried over the possibility that he was humoring her. She worried over her failure to ask if he, too, was okay.

ON MONDAY AFTERNOON Dahlia texted him herself, the pounding of her heart making her almost physically sick.

> *Hi Colin. I hope you had a good weekend. I was wondering if you'd be up for meeting again. I just thought it would be nice to talk a little more before I head home. But no pressure.*

She wasn't considering heading home yet and had carefully

worded her message to avoid lying—after all, she would be heading home at some point. Still, she felt guilty for what she acknowledged was a deliberate attempt to create a sense of urgency. But she was afraid that without it, she didn't have an excuse to ask to see him. Her fear that he'd think she was crossing a line was matched only by her fear that she was, and the two wrestled with each other, keeping her in a constant state of simmering anxiety.

Her phone pinged about an hour later.

Hi Dahlia. Apologies for the delay, things hectic at work. I'd be happy to see you again. How about The Timberline on Carver Rd, 6-ish.

Dahlia happily agreed and promptly pulled it up on her GPS. It was off a smaller road between the motel and his office. It would take her only five minutes to get there.

She took a long walk to the diner for lunch, then returned to the room and spent the rest of the day reading. She was changing her clothes and preparing to leave to meet Colin when he texted her again.

Hey Dahlia, I hate to do this but my son's having car trouble, and he's waiting at my place for me to help him out. Looks like I'll need to reschedule. Unless you want to come here though I doubt that's what you had in mind.

Dahlia's heart dropped, then rose again with relief. She'd thought he was cancelling, but he was only trying to be nice. She immediately began typing her response.

Hi Colin. No problem at all, I'm sorry he's having car trouble. I really don't mind meeting you there so you don't have to worry about rescheduling.

She watched for his reply, but it took him a long time. Dahlia kept expecting to see the three dots, but they never came. She figured he was talking to his son, or to a client. She put her phone on the table and picked up her book, content to wait.

Finally he wrote back.

Okay I'm at 451 Oak.

Dahlia stared at the words for a moment or two. For a fleeting moment she worried that he'd actually been trying to cancel and that her acceptance had taken him off guard. She blinked a few times, trying to pick up on anything about their meeting that would suggest he didn't want to be there. She recalled their conversation, over and over, but no matter how many times she thought about it she couldn't isolate any evidence to validate her concern. She chalked it up to her tendency to overanalyze, and picked up her purse to leave.

From what she could tell the drive to his house was going to be more or less a straight shot from the motel, past the office and Moose and Lantern and further along the tree-lined highway. Dahlia made a left out of the parking lot and drove by the now familiar landmarks, and slowed a little as she passed the tavern. Colin's home was another six miles up the road. Dahlia had, a few days earlier, begun to drive up this way but had turned around at an abandoned garage because there hadn't appeared to be anything here.

She passed some kind of construction business set back a little from the road, and also a rickety gas station and convenience store. Finally a clearing came into view, and Dahlia could see the first signs of a housing development. She made a left into the parking lot to find a cozy maze of modest white townhouses, all two-story with four steps in front and a single-car garage and driveway to the side. The feel was light and inviting. The grounds were nicely maintained, the landscaping careful but abundant in the way that greenery in well-planned developments often is. It was nestled in the surrounding woods, which made it feel safe and welcoming.

Dahlia turned right onto Oak Street and followed the numbers down, until her eyes lighted on two people standing in the driveway of a townhouse toward the end. It was Colin and another man, whom Dahlia presumed to be his son. It was a bright, sunny day, and they were standing casually around a small blue sedan with the hood up, clearly in conversation as they worked.

They glanced over as she approached, and she waved, a spark of adrenaline flickering in her blood. There were guest parking spots across each home, in sets of two, separated by narrow patches of grass. Dahlia slowly pulled into one and grabbed her purse, then stepped out of the car with her heart in her throat.

Colin was saying something to his son, who was watching him, but turned to her as she crossed to the sidewalk. Dahlia met his eyes and offered a polite smile, and quickly directed her gaze to Colin, who'd returned his attention to the open hood. He was twisting something, giving it a few hard squeezes; when he was through, he rose and looked at Dahlia, and smiled.

"Hey, kiddo," he said, rubbing his hands on a cloth to remove the grease. "Good to see you. Sorry again for the last minute change of plans."

"Oh, it's no problem. Thanks for having me." She indicated her car with her hand. "Is it okay that I parked there?"

"Yeah, that's fine. Dahlia, this is my son Ethan. Ethan, this is Dahlia."

Dahlia turned back to Ethan as Colin took one more look under the hood. Ethan was still looking at her. He appeared to be about her age, perhaps a little younger. He was wearing light-colored jeans and a white t-shirt with some kind of abstract design, a band logo of some sort. He was very thin, and the shirt fell flat over his chest. His hands were in his pockets as he stood a few feet behind his father; he was not tall, in fact bordering on short, and between his slight frame, his hesitant posture, and his position in the shadows Dahlia's first impression was of someone finding his footing, maybe awkward in his own skin.

She looked at his face, and was taken aback. It was not a face that matched the body. His eyes were large, strikingly so, and had the wide roundness of a child's. Though his features were soft, almost fragile—a pert nose, thin lips—his cheekbones were his father's, angular and sharp, even sharper in its thinness. But nothing was more remarkable than his hair, which while short, was thick, unruly, and blond, and in such wide, tumbling curls that Dahlia was reminded of a cherub, or a Renaissance angel.

The large round eyes were watching her, the lips pulled into a straight, thin line. Above, blond eyebrows were slightly raised, imparting to the face a kind of lost, thoughtful look.

Dahlia was unnerved, but not alarmed. He was disarming without being threatening.

They were too far away from each other to comfortably shake hands.

"Hi," she said shyly, lifting her hand in greeting. "It's nice to meet you."

"Hi," he said in return. "You too."

"All right," said Colin, standing back and wiping his hands off one more time. "Battery's charging. It'll take a couple of hours. That way at least you can get to the shop to replace it."

"Thanks," said Ethan. "Sounds good."

Colin turned to her. "The battery died not far from here. He was able to get a jump, but it's on its last legs. Nearest shop's twenty miles from here, so we didn't want to take any chances." He coughed a few times, his face in his elbow, turning away for a moment or two.

"I completely understand." She frowned. "Are you okay?"

"Fine, just all this damned pollen. We'd might as well go inside anyway." Colin waved them toward the front door. "Come on."

Dahlia and Ethan looked at each other, each waiting for the other to go first. They began moving at the same time, then stopped, then did it again. Dahlia laughed awkwardly. Ethan stepped backward, conceding. Dahlia tucked her hair behind her ear and followed Colin up the steps.

The inside of Colin's townhouse was not what she'd expected. Based on his office and the reserved quality of his demeanor, she'd thought it would be sparse, outdated, maybe a little glum. Instead, it was bright and airy, with light gray walls and light-colored furniture, crisp carpet and tasteful art on the walls. The occasional vase or ceramic planter appeared on mantels or simple iron stands. It was understated and modern, without a lot of frills but cheerful, and obviously very clean.

"I'm sorry, I wasn't expecting to do any entertaining today," said Colin, from a room toward the back that turned out to be the kitchen. "I'm afraid I don't have a lot to offer you."

"Oh, no worries at all, really." Dahlia stepped cautiously toward the kitchen. It was a more open floor plan, and the wall separating the kitchen and dining room was at half height, with a counter for bar stools on the dining room side, cabinets in the kitchen. Dahlia stood in the dining room and watched as he fussed with this door and that, evidently taking stock of what he had. "There's no need to put yourself out, and I'm very easy, anyway."

"Here, Dad," said Ethan as he walked up from behind. He bypassed her and joined his father in the kitchen, patting him on the back and moving toward the refrigerator. "Go ahead and sit down. I'll figure something out."

"Nah, you've had a long day."

"I haven't. I'm sure your day was longer than mine."

Dahlia stood back, not wanting to get in the way. After a little back and forth banter with his son, Colin turned to her.

"Can I get you something to drink?" he asked, eyebrows

raised, hands spread with a question. "Water? Wine? I can make you a cocktail, if you're feeling fancy."

Dahlia laughed. "I'm not fancy. Wine would be great."

"Red or white?"

"White, if you have it. Thanks."

Colin reached for a glass and poured her what seemed to Dahlia like quite a lot of wine. She thanked him as he handed it to her and watched as he helped himself to a neat pour of whiskey from a well-stocked bar cart in the corner.

He walked to the other side of the counter and gestured toward the stools.

"Thank you." She took a seat beside him. "Do you need any help with anything?"

"Don't worry about it. Ethan here knows his way around the kitchen. He's a whiz at this kind of thing."

"You mean making shit out of nothing, doing things at the last minute," inserted Ethan, bent over a shelf in the refrigerator, his arm extended as he reached for a bag of spinach. "I guess that tracks."

Colin sipped his whiskey and smacked his lips together. "You're too hard on yourself, bud."

"Colin," Dahlia said gently, "are your sinuses very bad?"

He swallowed another sip. "I don't love it, but I live with it."

"Are you getting good care? You take care of yourself?"

He downed the rest and placed the glass on the table with a clink, and smiled. "Yes, I do, kiddo. Thanks for your concern."

Ethan emerged from the refrigerator with the spinach, some mushrooms, a tub of parmesan cheese, and a bottle of heavy cream. From the freezer, he withdrew a couple of bags of tortellini.

"Turns out you're pretty well stocked."

Dahlia was taking careful sips of wine. "You guys really don't have to do this."

Ethan laid the food on the counter, and looked at her. "It's fine."

He smiled, and his face turned unexpectedly bright. Dahlia blinked and smiled back, then broke their gaze, unsettled.

They chatted for a time about their day, their weekend, the weather. The mood was light and easy, the conversation flowing, if subdued. Ethan worked mainly with his back to them, chopping vegetables and stirring sauce on the stove and speaking over his shoulder when he had something to say. Dahlia had turned her body a little toward Colin in the hopes they might continue their discussion from the previous night. She had so many questions for him, so many things she wanted to know about his life. She'd envisioned an emotional heart-to-heart in which they shared feelings, shared everything. She'd envisioned learning about him, and helping him learn about her. It seemed only right, for him to know all about the life he'd saved. She'd had so much hope for returning triumphant to her father, for having carried out the task he'd set before her with total and complete success. She supposed she'd set her expectations too high. But she wanted to make the most of this experience, both for her father and for herself.

"Your condo is very nice," she said, easing into it. "Have you lived here a long time?"

He'd replenished his whiskey and reclaimed his seat at the counter. He swallowed a sip and turned his body a bit toward her; Dahlia leaned her arm on the counter casually, pleased. "I've been here about fifteen years," he said. "I had a little cabin closer to the mountains when I first moved up here. But after a while I just wanted something easy."

"He waited until I moved out," said Ethan, over his shoulder, as he tended to dinner. "Too bad. I would have liked all that indoor plumbing, too."

"Knock it off, bud," said Colin, but there was no malice in his voice. Dahlia glanced over at him: he was smiling. "We had indoor plumbing. It wasn't that bad."

"No, it wasn't bad. It was fine. Roughing it just isn't my vibe."

"You can't say it wasn't beautiful, though."

"It was beautiful. I'll give you that."

Ethan walked by them to put a trivet on the dining room table, then placed the simmering sauce pan on top. Dahlia inhaled the rich, sweet scent of parmesan cream sauce, infused with the heady earthiness of mushrooms, spinach, and peas. She glanced over her wine glass at Ethan, surprised. He hadn't struck her as someone who made gourmet dinners on the fly.

"Do you cook much, Colin?" she asked, as Ethan distributed plates around the table. "I'll bet there are a lot of good farms around here."

"I cook, from time to time." They took their seats at the table; Ethan brought them each a glass of water. "But I live alone. I'd cook more, but it would all go to waste."

"My dad's a decent cook." Ethan had returned and was lifting a heaping scoop of tortellini out of the pot. "I ate pretty well growing up. Here." He reached his other hand out toward Dahlia, and wiggled his fingers. Dahlia stared at him, confused.

He blinked, those big eyes shutting, then rounding once more. "Your plate."

"Oh." Dahlia handed him her plate, and he dropped the pasta on. "Thank you. This looks great."

After dinner Colin began to collect the plates. Dahlia and Ethan rose to help him.

"No, sit," said Colin, balancing plates in both hands. "You cook, I clean."

"But I didn't cook," said Dahlia.

"You're a guest. Go ahead and relax."

Dahlia and Ethan sat across from each other in silence. Dahlia was looking around the townhouse, taking note of little details here and there—a little abstract sculpture sitting on an end table, a house plant that appeared in need of watering, a wall with four evenly spaced photographs too far away for her to see who was featured. Dahlia sighed and took a sip of wine, then shifted her eyes across the table to Ethan, who was staring at her.

Dahlia straightened and rubbed her lips together. A corner of her mouth twitched upward in a poor attempt at a smile.

"It's quite a story," said Ethan.

Dahlia looked at him and blinked. "Story?"

"Yeah, how my dad saved you. I guess I shouldn't say 'story.' I mean it's quite a thing, that it happened. It's an event and not a story, is what I'm saying." His face had turned red. It contrasted dramatically with the yellow gold ringlets of his hair. "Sorry. I worded that badly."

"No," said Dahlia, relaxing a little, and turning fully toward him. "It's fine. I know what you mean."

"How on Earth did you find him?" His face was still flushed, but his voice had grown more casual. He was sitting very straight, his arm resting on the table. "You only saw him for a second or two, right?"

"Yes." Dahlia could hear Colin in the kitchen, cleaning up. The sink was running, and he was listening to the news on his phone. "I'd seen the symbol on his hat," she said. "I was able to remember that after...after thinking about it."

"My dad said something about hypnotherapy."

"Yes." She was wary of relating the long process by which she'd found out who Colin was. But she was happy to hear Colin had talked about her with his son. "The hypnotherapy helped me, a little."

"That's pretty cool." Ethan's expression had loosened, and his voice had become more animated. "I tried hypnotherapy once, but it didn't do anything for me."

"Oh, really? What happened?"

"I was writing about it in a short story," he said, mindlessly fidgeting with his napkin on the table. "I did it for research, like to make sure I knew what I was talking about. But it didn't work. I had to kind of wing it. Hopefully I got it right. But no one's ever complained." A smirk touched the corners of his lips. "Then again, no one even read the story, so who knows."

"You wrote a short story?"

"I have a short story collection. It was published years ago."

Dahlia cocked her head with interest. "That's great. What's it called? Maybe I've read it."

"I guarantee you haven't read it. To say it was a small press is an understatement. But it's called *Nowhere to be Found.*"

"*Nowhere to be Found.*" Dahlia committed the title to memory. "I'll have to look it up."

"My dad has a copy." He paused. "Do you want to see it?"

"Sure."

He rose, and she followed him into the living room. She stood a little behind him as he searched a moment and then pulled a book off a shelf. It was a slim volume, a hardcover, with a yellow spine and a cover depicting a watercolor painting of a forest. It read *NOWHERE TO BE FOUND*, and underneath, *Short stories by Ethan Henninger*, in simple white text.

Dahlia took it from his outstretched hand and opened the cover to read the dust jacket. From what she could tell, it was a collection of unrelated stories on a similar theme, that of finding oneself, and losing oneself, both in nature and among other people.

"It sounds fascinating," she said, flipping through the pages. She looked at him. "Which is the one with the hypnotherapy?"

"It's in the title story. I could tell you what it's about, but then you wouldn't read it."

"I'll still read it." She handed it back to him. "I'll order a copy to the store."

"The store?"

"Yes, the store where I work. I work in a bookstore."

"Oh wow. That's cool." He stuck his hands in his pockets. "So you're a big reader then."

Dahlia laughed. "You could say that."

"What's your favorite book?"

She scrunched up her face. "As a reader and a writer, you should know that's an impossible question."

"Fair enough."

He smiled. She smiled a moment, then tucked her hair behind her ear.

"Okay, then, let's compromise," he said then. "What's been your favorite book this year?"

She thought about it. "It's only March. Can I tell you my favorite book of the last year, like the last twelve months?"

"Go for it."

"Then I'd have to say *The Night Flower*."

His eyes widened, and his brow rose. He stuck out his finger at her. "Terry Yang."

Her head tilted. "Have you read it?"

"Oh, my God, yeah. I love Terry Yang. I had it on preorder and read it the first day it was out."

"Well, I've got you beat," she said, with an unintentionally coy grin. "I read it before it was released. A perk of the job."

"Aw, man." The words were playfully raspy, as if he were lamenting having lost, and he snapped his fingers in jest. "Unfair advantage."

"Yeah, I guess so."

He put his hands back in his pockets and studied her. "It must be tough to work in a bookstore. You know, too tempting to slack off and read all the time."

"A little, maybe, but I like the job." A pang of longing pulled inside her at the thought of her beloved bookstore, as well as a twinge of guilt. She smiled, determined to stay in the present. "And I'm always the first to see what's new and what's coming."

"Maybe I should work in a bookstore. I could quit my editing job, which I hate."

"You're an editor?"

"I said I have an editing job. I'm not really an editor. I work for a study guide company. I oversee the projects. And I hire all the new writers."

"That sounds interesting." Dahlia regarded him curiously. "Why do you hate it?"

"I don't know," he said, shrugging. "I guess it's okay. But writers are finicky people. Even the ones writing study guides. They don't like a lot of feedback. And the pay is pretty low for the writers, so there's a ton of turnover. I just want to write, you know? I feel like such a hack. But I have to pay the bills. At least I get to work from home."

"Are you still writing?"

A shadow crossed over his face. "Theoretically."

He didn't say any more about that, and Dahlia didn't ask. She was just about to suggest they rejoin Colin in the kitchen when he changed the subject entirely.

"You know," he said, "we've already met."

Dahlia stared at him. "Who?"

He gestured between them with his finger. "You and I."

Her brow furrowed. "No we haven't."

"Yes, we have."

"I think I'd remember."

"No, you wouldn't."

Dahlia frowned, impatient. "What are you talking about?"

A spark of mischief twinkled in his eye. "My mom was pregnant on that trip to Seashell Cove."

Dahlia's lips parted. A little gasp of surprise escaped her lips. "Oh. I...I didn't know."

"They didn't know either, at the time."

Dahlia pressed her lips together, and her gaze drifted as the old memory of Colin and Cindy sprouted new branches, transforming right before her very eyes. She hadn't realized how special that memory was, until reality began chipping away at it bit by bit, leaving it to disintegrate slowly into nothing. The information Ethan had shared with her made Colin and Cindy more fully dimensional, had made the memory more vivid—but simultane-ously, it left her with an aching sense of loss.

She glanced toward the kitchen, toward the sounds of dishes clanging and cabinets closing. She wished Colin would finish; it was precisely the kind of conversation she'd hoped to have with him. She wanted to learn all this from Colin, not his son. And somehow hearing it from him would help her reconcile her memory with the new images she was gathering.

"Something wrong?"

Ethan's voice pulled her from her thoughts.

"No, nothing."

"Kind of funny that we've all been together. Even if I was an embryo at the time."

Dahlia laughed, a little uncertainly.

Ethan turned to the bookshelf. He reached for a photo in a simple white frame.

He handed it to Dahlia. "This is Mom."

Dahlia took it, holding it carefully as she studied the woman in the photo. Cindy's face wore a brilliant smile, which shone in her eyes and lifted her cheeks. Even though they were narrowed in laughter Dahlia could tell her eyes were round and wide, and in perfect symmetry with the rest of her features. She had mid-length blond hair that fell in thick, wavy ringlets. She stood straight, and with confidence, staring directly into the camera, appearing to dare it to come along for some fun.

Dahlia brushed the image's cheek, then handed it back to Ethan.

"She's very beautiful."

Ethan said nothing. He looked at the photo for a moment or two, then placed it gently back on the shelf.

"I was only two when she died," he said. "Sadly, I don't remember her at all."

"Oh. I'm so sorry." Dahlia frowned, a painful ache in her gut. "I really am. I wish I had words."

"Don't worry about it. There aren't any." He placed his hands back in his pockets and looked at her. "She had a heart condition. It was never far from their minds."

Dahlia was at a loss. It opened them up, fleshed them out to her in ways that, as it turned out, she wasn't quite ready for. Part of her felt it was an intrusion. But she was drawn to the story, and to them.

"Thank you for sharing all this," she said, quietly, as Colin turned off the news in the kitchen. "I'm sure it isn't easy."

"I wouldn't say it's easy. But it's not hard, because I don't remember. And that's the hard part. You know?"

Dahlia looked at his face which, like his voice, was neutral in tone. But there was a layer of sadness behind it, almost as if it were always there, as if the loss had been embedded in his otherwise angel-like features. In an instant she saw him as a sad, confused toddler, a somber little boy, a lost teenager. There was a playfulness about him, a pleasantly quick wit; but the playfulness was subdued, the wit hard. She imagined the two young men, growing through the years together and alone, and she was heartbroken for both of them.

"I can't imagine," she said. "I'm so sorry you've been through this." She hesitated. "My father is sick," she said then. "We're very close, so it's very hard. I guess it's hard in a different way."

"'We are all in the gutter, but some of us are looking at the stars.'"

Her eyes grew alert, and she smiled. "Oscar Wilde."

He smiled in return. "You're good."

"That's a great quote. It's so typical of him, too, this kind of intermingling of the beautiful and the painful."

"Right on."

They exchanged a curious look. Dahlia focused on those round, wide eyes, and furrowed her brow. There was something else there, something tempering the sadness, but she couldn't tell what it was.

"All right, we're all set," announced Colin, breaking the stillness, and Dahlia and Ethan both turned in his direction.

Dahlia broke into a wide smile as he approached. "You've gone to so much trouble. I wish you would have let me help you."

"No trouble at all."

"Next time you'll have to let me take on the work. I'm happy to cook, and to clean. I'd love to prepare a meal for you. Anything you need."

Colin smiled politely and turned to his son. "We can check that battery now. It's probably just about set."

"Cool."

They headed outside, Dahlia following behind. She stood back as Colin and Ethan tended to the car, joking and chatting and making a few inside jokes. Without anything to do, she made pretext of admiring the sparse landscaping, the infrequent patch of flowers and the view of the forest, which at this time of the evening was little more than a band of hazy silhouettes against an indigo, star-studded sky.

"I guess I'll get going," said Ethan. "I should at least try to get some work done." He turned to Dahlia. "Nice to meet you, Dahlia. Maybe I'll see you soon."

"Yes, maybe. It was nice to meet you, too."

"Thanks for coming," said Colin, regarding her with a kind smile. "Glad it worked out."

"Yes." Dahlia put her hands in her pockets , leaning her weight on one hip, in an attempt at a casual, nonchalant stance. "It's still pretty early—did you want to grab some coffee, or something?"

"Oh." Colin's face dropped, and his smile grew rueful. "I'd love to, but I have an early day tomorrow. But thanks for the invite."

"Okay, no problem." She was disappointed, but she tossed her hand up as if it were nothing. "Another time, then. Thank you so much for dinner. It was delicious. And thank you for the hospitality."

"My pleasure. Glad you could come," said Colin.

Beside him, Ethan was staring at her blankly.

Colin held out his hand for his son. "Good to see you, bud. Keep me posted on that car."

"Will do. Thanks for the help."

Father and son clapped each other on the back and embraced. Dahlia lingered as they said goodbye, then waved to them and headed reluctantly to her car. Colin waited for them to pull away, waving as they drove off before returning inside.

Ethan followed her out of the parking lot and continued on behind her before exiting onto the highway, headed south. A handful of minutes later Dahlia was cozy in her motel room, the television on and the lights dimmed as she prepared for bed. It had been a pleasant evening, she thought, even if they'd had unexpected company. Colin's son seemed pretty decent, clearly smart and relatively friendly, though evidently less focused than his father. They were a likable pair, though unalike in many ways, and Dahlia wondered if the son's early loss had prevented him from acquiring the bolder, more confident, quietly alluring strength of his father.

DAHLIA WAS RECEIVING texts from her family wondering how she was and what was going on. She continued to vaguely assure them that she was safe and comfortable and that she promised to be in touch when she had something to report. Her father had seemed to accept this; her mother was worried and upset. Dahlia couldn't get a read on Tara, who was understanding but curt in her response.

She knew she owed them more, but she couldn't bring herself to give it. Part of her wanted to prove she could do this by herself. Part of her was afraid of failing. But mostly she was beginning to sense something in herself unraveling. The thought of revealing this vulnerability—which she barely understood herself—brought visceral, physical anguish. Also, relating details would require her to assess and characterize her experiences, and she didn't know how to do it, and was afraid of what it would look like if she could. She told herself they were better off not hearing from her, that she was doing them a favor by sparing them from her mess. But every unanswered message made it harder for her to respond. The longer she waited, the heavier the guilt felt, until the silence stretched too long, and breaking it was so terrifying that she fled from the task even faster. By worrying about failing them, she had failed them. The irony would have been amusing, if it didn't make her so pathetically, desperately weak.

CHAPTER SIXTEEN

Hi Colin. Please let me know if you're getting tired of me! I was just wondering if you'd have any time to meet up in the next couple of days.

$\mathcal{D}$ahlia sent the text around one o'clock the next afternoon, against her better judgment. She would have preferred for Colin to initiate their next meeting himself; however, she had gathered that he was reserved by nature, and she chalked his passivity up to wariness. Also, though they had had only a handful of interactions, she sensed that, understandably, he had been wounded by Cindy's death so many years before, by losing his wife so young and becoming a single father, to boot. She didn't know what his romantic life had looked like since Cindy's passing; it was one of the many questions she had about him. She hoped he'd open up to her in time. In any case, he had demonstrated kindness toward her, and had been welcoming, despite this. He was not uncaring; he seemed to want to protect her. Dahlia appreciated this and assured herself she was not imposing.

He responded about an hour later.

I could do lunch Thursday.

It was currently Tuesday. Dahlia had hoped to see him before then. However, she eagerly accepted, and they arranged to meet back at Moose and Lantern.

Dahlia spent the time in between quietly, preferring to stay close to the motel rather than exploring. Her room was actually quite bright during the day, with a large window facing directly east, which meant the early hours of the day were perfect for sitting in the armchair reading with a cup of tea or coffee on the end table beside her. In this light, which bathed the mountains in a sea of gold and trickled through the tree branches in extravagant patterns, her room felt homey rather than drab, the dreary colors muted and soft.

Still, there was a feeling of waiting, of being somewhere she didn't belong, on a task she hadn't fully defined. She supposed she could bid farewell to Colin, now that she had found him; she could return to her father with the information he craved, could deliver her savior to him the way her savior had delivered her.

But she couldn't tear herself away. There was a comfort in being here, a strange fascination that compelled her to push further in. It wasn't enough to have met the man who saved her. She needed a connection, some kind of closure she hadn't yet found. There was something left undone. And while she couldn't clearly define it, she knew her time here wasn't complete.

She swallowed against a lump in her throat and called Imani.

"I'm so sorry, but I'm not ready to come home yet," she told her after a few quick moments of chit chat, touching her fingertips to her forehead as she braced for Imani's response. "Can Marilyn fill in? I'm going to need more time."

"More time." Imani's voice was tight and formal, unfamiliar. Dahlia knew their relationship was changing with every word she said, but she had resigned herself to this inevitability, and pushed forward.

"I wish I could explain it," she said. "But I just can't go back yet."

"You know I'm not going to deny you what you need," said Imani. "But I think I deserve an explanation. I need you to tell me what's going on. Otherwise it just isn't fair to me, to your colleagues, or to our relationship."

Dahlia wrestled with what to tell her. She didn't want to burden her with her sad, pathetic life, and she was protective of her father, and of herself. But she understood Imani's point. And she hadn't shed so much of herself that she didn't feel the pull of responsibility.

"My father is very sick," she said. "I haven't mentioned it before. But he may not have very long."

"Oh, Dahlia." Imani's voice was heavy with sympathy, and something else, something like pity, or guilt—a tremble of disorientation. "Why on Earth didn't you say anything to me?"

"I don't know." It felt wrong even now, this revelation of her life, the bleeding of her heart into the outside world. "I'm sorry."

"I'm sorry you've been going through this. I wish you'd let me know sooner. I could have been there for you, as a shoulder. You could have alleviated a little bit of burden."

"Thank you." She wanted to stop talking about it as soon as possible. "I just didn't want to put it on you."

"You're a person, Dahlia. You're allowed to be human." Imani sighed. "So I assume you've been tending to him, and helping your family."

Dahlia inhaled against a new wave of shame. "Yes," she said, "I've been doing that. But I have to be honest, that's not what I'm doing now."

Imani said nothing. The silence was heavy through the phone.

"The truth is, Imani...I'm up in New Hampshire. It's a really long story. But I'm connecting with a person from my past, someone important to my father. He wanted me to find this person, and it was like I couldn't let him...I had to do it before..."

Her throat was choked with the promise of unshed tears. She swallowed. "Can I explain when I get back?"

Imani said nothing for a moment or two. "Well," said Imani, "I can understand that. I certainly won't push you before you're ready. Take the time you need. Marilyn's happy to fill in."

Dahlia's eyes were prickling with tears. She cleared her throat and straightened her back. "Thank you. I'm sorry. I'm really sorry. And Imani." A few tears escaped, and she quickly wiped them away. "I understand if you can't hold my job. I really, really want you to," she added quickly, panic already squeezing her tight. "But—"

"Nonsense," said Imani. "It's not like that with us, and you know it. Take care of yourself. I'll figure it out. Just be in touch with me about your plans and how things are going."

"I will. I promise. I absolutely will."

"Great. And Dahlia," Imani added. "Thank you for your honesty."

After they hung up Dahlia placed the phone on the table, then sat very still for a few minutes of recovery. It had gone as well as she could have hoped, and she'd learned something in the process. She'd opened up, she'd trusted someone, and it was going to be okay. Still, she was left with a sick feeling in her stomach. She knew she had pushed it too far, that she was walking farther and farther away from her cherished stability. She just had to trust she was making the right decision, and focus on the connection she was building with Colin.

"How is your day going?" she asked him as they sat down in a booth that looked out onto the parking lot. "Is it busy?"

"Bit of a slower day today. The whole week's been slow. Makes me nervous, but we're up for the month, so I'll take it."

Dahlia asked him if he himself went on the roofing jobs or if his role was more administration.

"I'll often go out and do the estimates," he said as a server slid two glasses of water onto the table. "But I spend a lot of time in the office. You won't find me climbing ladders so much anymore. I did that for years, even after I started the business. But I've got a team now for most of the hard stuff."

They ordered their lunches and sat back for a minute, looking out the window, or checking their phones. Dahlia told him she'd looked into Northern Horizons Alliance and that it seemed like a very good organization.

"I enjoyed the Alliance," he said, shaking ketchup onto his plate. "They're a solid group. Very organized, they ran some good programs. I did a couple of events a year with them, until the move."

She told him she'd found out about the group by accident, when she'd randomly come across the logo on a book.

He smiled at that. "I guess your interest in books paid off."

They discussed her job, what she did for Imani and what she found most interesting about the way the shop ran. He asked her what she liked about it and what were some of the challenges. She told him Imani wanted her to go to Los Angeles, but she had so many reservations.

"It'll probably be fun," he said, taking a bite of his sandwich. "See a new place, do some new things."

The conversation was comfortable but no less formal. By now they had met three times. Dahlia had hoped he might open up to her a little, talk to her about his background or education, his time with Cindy, his thoughts on being a father and on running a business here in the mountains of New Hampshire. She wanted to know how he liked it here, whether he still hiked as he used to, what he did in his spare time. She wanted to know about his favorite foods, his favorite color, his favorite movie or book genre, his favorite kind of art.

Most importantly, she wanted to know if he'd ever thought of her over the years, if she'd ever appeared in his dreams as he'd appeared in hers; she wanted to know what he felt like after he saved her, whether he understood the magnitude of what he'd done, what he'd seen that day when he glanced out at the ocean. She wanted to know what he'd been thinking, whether he'd felt a sense of urgency, whether she'd felt light in his arms or heavy, whether he'd noticed the expression on her face. She wanted to know what it felt like to be a savior. She wanted to know what she'd looked like almost drowning.

And yet there was something warm about his treatment of her, despite the aloofness. He smiled when she talked about her life, narrowing his eyes in that charming way, the corner of his mouth lifting just a little higher than the other. He seemed protective of her, making sure the motel was safe and asking whether she enjoyed her job. And he always assured her everything would be okay. As she watched him from across the table her heart opened further to him. He was complex and complicated, firm and steady but wounded, and vulnerable. There was something endearing about it, and heartbreaking, and she was moved as she imagined the process by which he'd learned to move on after grief, the defenses he'd built and the little ways he revealed cracks in the wall. He was rugged and sharp-edged, with moments of softness; it was even reflected in his face, angular and strong featured, but gentle in the eyes and lips.

He's like the landscape itself, she realized, and it drew her to him even more. She saw the mountains in the sharp lines of his face, the rippling water in the depth of his eyes. He had a pensive, wise look to him, but there was sadness there, too. More and more, tenderness simmered in her stomach and trickled through to her heart and skin and fingers, and she wanted to be near him, like she wanted to explore the beauty of the land around them.

When he'd swiftly lifted the bill from the table and once again refused to let her pay for anything, Dahlia nervously breached a topic she'd been thinking about since the day before.

"Have you ever been to Cobblestone Park?"

Colin laid a few bills on the table. "Sure, up in Hollow Hill."

"It looks really pretty. Is it as pretty as it looks online?"

"Sure, it's pretty."

He took a deep sip of his coffee. Dahlia pulled her purse strap over her shoulder, both in preparation to leave and in an attempt to pretend this was an off the cuff question. "I'd kind of like to check it out. Would you want to go with me, sometime? Maybe tomorrow, after work?"

"Oh," he said, nodding, his eyebrows raised. He didn't say anything for a second or two, then offered that rueful smile. "That's a nice idea. Thanks so much for the invitation." He took another sip of coffee, then furrowed his brow and frowned. "I don't think I can, though. Fridays are kind of hectic, and I never know what time I'm getting off work."

"Okay. I totally understand." Dahlia shrugged nonchalantly and tried to ignore the ache of disappointment pulling inside. "It's pretty last minute. I knew it was a long shot."

She slid to the edge of the booth, and he followed, but slowly.

They walked out to the parking lot. As they approached their cars, he turned to her.

"How about I meet you there after work," he said. "I'll make sure I get out on time."

"Oh, I don't want to put you out at all," said Dahlia, sincerely; the shame she'd feel for inconveniencing him was far more devastating than the disappointment. "We don't have to do it."

"It's okay. I'll figure it out."

Hope fluttered in her chest. "Are you sure?"

"I'm sure." He smiled. "I'll let you know when I'm leaving."

"Okay. That's great. Thanks."

They smiled awkwardly and parted ways, Dahlia glancing back at his tail lights in her rear view mirror as long and as safely as she could. She stepped into her homely room and flicked on the lamps, and the hushed glow against the walls felt pleasantly comforting and cheerful. She changed into her pajamas and brushed her teeth, and wondered at the little flutter of her heart as she thought of him, then fell asleep with images of him shuffling through her mind like ripples on the stream.

FRIDAY WAS WARM BUT OVERCAST, with the tense humidity of the hours preceding rain. Dahlia spent the afternoon in her room and left for Cobblestone Park a little early in case she got lost or missed her exit, and to ensure she was able to park and acclimate herself to a new place before Colin arrived. She wanted to have plenty of time to be nervous by herself and to conduct all the little rituals she needed to feel safe, without having to explain them or worry about what he'd think.

As it turned out, the twenty minute drive required nothing more than veering onto the highway and then making a single right off the exit ramp, then continuing about a mile up the road. She arrived quite early and parked on the street with no trouble, then decided to walk around the town of Hollow Hill, which from what she could tell catered to locals seeking a little charm and upscale dining and to visitors interested in being outdoors without the hubbub of the ski towns farther north.

Hollow Hill's attraction was Main Street, about a half mile of bed and breakfasts, quaint restaurants, and artisan shops featuring pottery, jewelry, and chocolate made in homes nestled in the nooks and crannies of the mountains. Tucked beside an inn was a gazebo with a pathway leading downward into the woods, with a sign reading "Cobblestone Park" along the sidewalk. Dahlia could see the rushing of the stream through the trees, and the air had the fresh, healthy crispness that it often did near water. She ate lunch in a café and enjoyed an ice cream cone from the stand next door, then poked in and out of the shops, treating herself to some chocolate for her room, which she stored in her backpack to take back home.

She walked up and down the street a few times, admiring the scenery. She wondered once again what it must be like to live here among the mountains and the streams, to have them always present in the backdrop of one's life. People here went about their days as if it were normal, as if it were everywhere. She wondered if they even noticed it, or if it were simply the mundane images of their lives, just like the buildings and chimneys were to hers.

About ten minutes before she expected Colin she found a bench near the gazebo and waited. She was sitting in the shade, and the air was alive with the scent of pine and moss. She watched people walking by, milling about with their families or chatting intimately with friends. There was an ease and a familiarity between them, a sense that whoever they were with, they belonged. She watched them from the shadows, without speaking, and they drifted by her without noticing, an unknown and invisible figure among so many more beautiful, more interesting sights.

She looked back out to the mountains. They were ancient and unchanging. Everything here seemed to have a role, a place, a purpose. Though the clouds moved around them, the weather changing day by day, the mountains stayed the same. It made her feel insignificant, and small—but there was a peacefulness in the feeling, a sense of being a part of something bigger. She dared have hope that she could one day feel this purpose, too.

Her phone pinged: a text from Tara.

Hi. Just thinking about you. Any chance you're ready to talk?

Dahlia's stomach clenched. She'd been here for almost two weeks. To tell Tara now everything that had happened would certainly, and understandably, invite disbelief and outrage. She'd been preserving herself so fiercely as to create legitimate reasons for disapproval. She knew she couldn't wait any longer. She carefully worded her response.

I'm still here. I've met Colin Henninger. I don't blame you if you're mad, but please don't be too mad. I can't explain but I had to do this by myself. I'll tell you all about it, I promise. Please believe me when I say that I just can't do it now.

Out of the corner of her eye emerged a figure veering off the sidewalk and onto the path. She turned off her phone. She'd stress about Tara's response for the rest of the day, but at least she could control when she dealt with it.

She stood to meet Colin.

"Hi," she greeted him, a little thrum in her heart as she took in his particular gait, the way his hips and arms moved, the casual tidiness of his dress—all charmingly familiar to her now. She rose and smiled. "It's so good to see you. Thanks so much for meeting me here."

He took a moment or two to respond. Dahlia looked at him with a vaguely unsettling feeling. Something about his face was different today; it was the same face, but tense.

"No problem," he said, but there was no brightness in his face, and Dahlia wasn't convinced.

"Are you sure?" Dahlia frowned, immediately seeking to alleviate his displeasure or inconvenience. "If it isn't a good time, then—"

"No, we're here now," he said, and extended his hand toward the park before Dahlia could respond. "Shall we?"

She was unnerved, but wary of pressing him further. She nodded agreement and moved forward.

Colin and Dahlia made their way down the path toward the

stream. Around the curve it became steep quite suddenly, and unpaved.

"Watch that tree root," he said.

At the bottom of the slope they landed on a wide flat layer of rock. Dahlia looked up and down the stream, marveling at the untamed beauty.

"Wow," she said, uplifted. "This is incredible."

The water was clear as glass as it spilled over a chaos of cobblestones, which piled on top of each other in myriad shapes and colors, forming pockets of whirling water that trickled into those below. Dahlia wanted to sit in all of them. It seemed like each little pool was a world of its own, with corners and secrets and creatures too small to see.

She turned back to Colin, who was looking at his watch. When he noticed her gaze on him, he straightened, smiled, and stuck his hands in his pockets.

"So, this is the park," he said, and his face had melted into the more friendly face she was used to. He stood with his legs apart, facing downstream, where the waterway narrowed and the trees appeared darker and more impassable. He looked at her, his eyes creased warmly. "Does it meet your expectations?"

"I didn't really have any," said Dahlia, "but yes."

They stood in silence for a moment or two, listening to the water. The natural chorus around them had dispelled the tension, and Dahlia felt more at ease.

"You've been here before?" she asked.

"Many times," he said, and kicked at some pebbles at his foot. "It's a local landmark, really. If you live here, you haven't missed it."

"How does it feel?" asked Dahlia, turned in his direction, but not looking at him. "To belong here. To belong anywhere."

He lifted his gaze once again to her face, and studied her with lips stern and straight. He seemed to be considering what she'd said.

AMANDA GALE

"I don't know," he said finally, a little warily. "Do I belong here?"

She watched him with interest. "Do you not?"

He was looking out onto the stream. "I guess I hadn't thought about it before."

They said nothing for quite some time. Dahlia stepped around the platform, crouching to dip her hand in the water, icy and glimmering on this early spring day. She walked to the edge of the boulder, then gazed downward over the rocks.

"Are people allowed to step into the water?"

He stared at her, and a smile tugged at the corners of his lips. "Yes."

Dahlia turned once more toward the stream and began inching her way across the cobblestones.

She held her arms out for balance as she went, strategizing her path with each step. Many of the rocks were wet and moss covered, and she learned quickly which were safe and which she should avoid.

"Careful," he called after her. "It's gonna be slippery down there."

She sat down and removed her sandals, placing them gently on the rock beside her. Then she stood and lowered her foot into the water. It was bitingly cold, but rejuvenating and pure. She shivered at its touch, and yet she felt she could immerse her entire body into it and emerge feeling refreshed, and happy.

"Don't go out too far."

Dahlia delighted in this concerned, protective instruction, and her heart lightened and flew, sparking her enthusiasm further. She continued stepping across the rocks, feeling their ungainly roundness on her soles, her arms straight out at her sides as if they were wings.

"Well, look at you."

She was as far as she could go before a steep, jagged drop. Dahlia stopped, but peered into its depths. She estimated it was about as deep as she was tall. She could certainly swim it, if she weren't fully clothed, and she wished she'd brought a bathing suit with her from home. Maybe she'd buy one in a store up here. Maybe she'd come back and go swimming one day soon.

"Hey," said Colin, taking a few steps forward. "You might want to stop there, eh?"

He was tall and straight on the rock; the sun behind him made his figure a shadowy silhouette. She could make out the angular lines of his jaw, the hard lines of his form.

She beamed up at him, warm all over, despite the cold of the water. "Don't worry, I will."

She tiptoed back to the edge, then scrambled back up toward the platform.

On her last step, her left foot hit a patch of mold, and she slipped, her ankle turning over the rock from which she'd just come. She cried out in pain, sinking to the rock below.

"What happened? You okay? Dahlia?"

"Oh yeah, I'm fine," she responded, too cheerily, flushed with mortification. She began to stand. When she placed weight on her foot, pain shot through her leg, and she crumpled.

"Hold on, I'm coming," he said. "Shit."

She rose again, stifling a grimace, pretending her foot wasn't throbbing in agony. "Really, I'm fine. I've got it."

She faltered trying to climb. He joined her on the lower bank, and crouched low to look at her ankle.

"That definitely looks twisted," he said, cradling it gently in his palm to turn it. "It's already red and swollen."

Dahlia grumbled at her own stupidity. "I can't believe I did that. I'm sorry."

"What are you apologizing to me for? Come on, let's get you out of here."

He moved in closer and wrapped his arm around her back, signaling she should lean on him, which she did. Her arm found its way over his shoulder and the back of his neck, and he supported her as she hopped on her right foot, putting only the slightest pressure on her left. Thus they made their awkward way up the embankment of rocks until they were safe on the original platform; then he led her to the gazebo, where he sat her down to look at her foot again.

He examined it, careful of the tenderness, and squinting. "Looks a little gnarly, but you'll be all right. Just keep some ice on it. Elevate it as much as you can."

She smiled down at him. "You sound like a doctor."

"Nah," he said, pushing up off his thighs into standing. "Just been there, done that. Someone's always twisting something on a hike."

Dahlia brushed her fingers over the ankle, tracing the line where his hand had been. Her heartbeat had quickened, and she was still tingling from her contact with him. He'd been warm and vibrant against her, strong and sure, agile and competent and smelling of the earth and the trees. A funny thing was happening in her stomach, little pitter patters of energy like the heat of sparklers against a cool summer sky.

"Thank you for helping me," she said shyly, blushing again. "I'm so embarrassed."

"No need, don't worry about it."

"You told me to be careful, and I wasn't. I should have listened."

"Forget it."

Dahlia continued rubbing her foot, listening to the gurgling of the stream below. She gazed out onto its beauty, grateful for having seen it, despite her mishap.

"I really appreciate that you came out here with me. And I appreciate your kind help," she said, a subtle, almost involuntary smile playing at the corners of her mouth. She felt warm, and a little dazed. Her eyes took him in, lingering just a little bit too long.

His expression shifted, his eyes widening slightly and his

mouth pressing into a tight, thin-lipped line. His jaw tensed, and he swallowed, his shoulders suddenly stiff.

He cleared his throat and glanced around, seemingly at everything but her. Then he pulled his keys from his pocket.

"You probably can't drive on that," he said. "I'll take you back. We'll figure out your car."

Dahlia looked at him. His voice had sounded forced, almost reluctant, but Dahlia couldn't be sure. She shrugged it off as concern.

She slipped back into her sandals and slowly stood, hopping on her right foot. She lowered her left foot down with caution, trying to assess how badly it was hurt.

"It feels a little better," she said, surprised and relieved to find it could hold more weight than she'd thought. "It's actually really okay."

"I don't know, Dahlia. I don't want to be responsible if something happens."

"You wouldn't be. But I'll be okay."

He looked generally ill at ease. He was fidgeting with his keys, and he wouldn't meet her gaze.

"Okay," he said. "Well, I should get back. I'll make sure you get to your car."

They made their way toward the street, slowly, Dahlia being careful to keep her full weight off her injured ankle. They arrived at her car and faced each other.

"Thanks for the invitation," he said, with a stiff smile. "Sorry about your foot."

"Oh, it'll be fine." She ran her fingers through her hair and gestured with her hand to indicate it was nothing. "I'll do as you said and ice it. I'm sure it'll be good as new in no time." She considered his worry over her, his gentleness in checking her foot and his ensuring she make it home safely, and took a chance. "Would you want to grab dinner somewhere? By any chance?"

"I can't, kiddo, I'm sorry. I've got a lot to do back home."

"Absolutely no problem." A tumult in her stomach, and the old dread at having embarrassed herself, but she smiled. "I understand."

"I'll at least follow you back," he said. "At least to the fork at the exit."

"Okay." She smiled warmly. "Thanks for looking out for me."

Colin didn't respond. She hobbled to the driver's side door and waved, then gingerly lowered herself inside. He strode to his own car a little down the road and waited for her to pass him, then pulled out of his spot after her. He trailed her to the highway and down to their exit, then turned left at the bottom when she turned right. She held her hand up to the mirror to wave in case he was looking, then drove the remaining couple of miles to the motel, where she parked in her usual spot and walked clumsily to the door.

Once inside she turned on her phone and braced herself for Tara's text.

I had a feeling. Look I can't pretend I understand it, but I guess I have to accept it. I trust that you know what you're doing and that you'll give me the whole story one day soon. I hope you know that you can. I won't judge you. In the meantime, what should I tell Mom and Dad? Love you.

Dahlia's eyes filled with tears, which she brushed away with her sleeve. She stood frozen still for a moment or two, struck by a sudden urge to call her. She knew she could be honest with Tara. She knew if she explained herself, that Tara wouldn't be angry.

She responded,

Thank you so much for saying that. It means more to me than you can know. I promise I will tell you everything. And I know that you won't judge.

As for Mom and Dad you can tell them I've met Colin and that he's really very nice. I'm sure they're worried. Tell them I'm sorry I've been so bad about calling them back.

I love you too. Thank you for seeing me.

She had more to say but couldn't say it. She was wracked with guilt over it, over everything. For all her family had done for her, she couldn't even update them on this extremely important event. But more and more it seemed that achieving this for her father was a catalyst for something about herself. She wasn't ready to face it. She'd asked Tara to trust her, and that meant she had to trust herself.

She treated herself to a dinner delivery, and spent a cozy evening watching her shows and reading her book while enjoying her meal. She even ordered a slice of cake for dessert, and indulged slowly, pondering on the day. She sat at the table with her cake and a cup of tea, looking outside into the blue, shimmering dusk. Finding the man who saved her as a child had closed up a hole in her that she hadn't been expecting. He'd been there for her at a time when she'd felt invisible and unsafe; seeing him again made her feel seen again, and valued. She hadn't even realized she'd needed it until she'd seen his face again.

But with the filling of the emptiness came the weight of survival. She wanted to give him something in return. She wanted to show him that his saving her wasn't for nothing. She now had a new purpose, a new sense of urgency. Her life had to be for something. It had to matter; it had to make a difference.

She'd taken bold action when she'd left her job and her family and driven up here, determined, by herself. There had to be a purpose in her leaving everything she knew behind. It felt like fate, like something as stable and true as the mountains outside her window. Her connection with Colin had a purpose; it was bringing her full circle. It meant she was part of something bigger than she was, that she could find her place in the universe.

Dahlia finished dinner feeling calm and more free, and she cleaned up and prepared for bed with hope in her heart and a smile on her face. She didn't know what the future held for her or how this adventure would change the path of her journey. But for the first time, the unknowing felt promising rather than threatening; it felt exciting, and full of possibility, and the fact that she had something to look forward to was the most exciting thing of all.

CHAPTER SEVENTEEN

*D*ahlia woke up the next morning to the sound of rain pattering on the asphalt outside. The room was dim and gray through the curtains. She stayed in bed a while, stretching and thinking and preparing for the day. She rolled her ankle back and forth, relieved. There was barely any pain.

After a time, she stood and walked to the window, then pulled the curtain aside and peeked at the scene on the other side. A hazy fog was hovering over the ground, obscuring the tree trunks and enfolding her car in a ghostly cloud. The parking lot appeared covered in glass, the raindrops piercing the surface and creating a chaotic symphony. She watched the scene for a minute or two, soothed by the sound. She didn't mind the rain, which created a special kind of coziness, though rain accompanied by wind and storms frightened her.

A little after noon she received a text from Colin asking after her ankle. She assured him it was fine and thanked him for checking on her, then sat at the edge of her bed concentrating on the fluttering in her chest. She brushed her ankle with her fingers. In the pensive, dim light of the new day Dahlia recalled the previous day's excursion with renewed warmth. His concern for her—the tenderness with which he'd handled her foot and his worry over her driving home—were so consistent with his having protected her as a little girl, and she smiled. Now that she was an adult she could truly recognize and appreciate this kind instinct in him, and her stomach tumbled at the thought that he cared about her. She hoped to spend more time with him, but she refrained from asking.

Dahlia was getting ready to venture out for the first time so she could place a takeout order at the diner when her phone buzzed on the table. She picked it up, and her heart skipped a beat. It was a text from Colin.

If you'd like to come to my place for dinner you're welcome to. Any time after six.

Dahlia was elated. He wanted to see her again. She felt like she was cracking the wall, that he was growing more willing to open up to her. The thought that he could feel the way about her that she felt about him made her trill and tingle inside. She texted him back right away to tell him she'd be there, and to thank him.

Around six o'clock she pulled out of the parking lot and drove north toward Colin's house, adrenaline making her heart pound and her blood rush. She took a deep, steadying breath as she made the lefthand turn into his complex. Her stomach dropped when she spotted Ethan's car parked in one of the guest spots on the other side of the road.

She parked in the spot beside it and stared at it for a moment or two, then walked toward the house.

The front door was open, and she rang the bell from the other side of the screen door. She could see Colin and Ethan at the back of the house, between the kitchen and dining room. At the sound of the bell Ethan turned, said something to his father, and walked toward the door to let her in. Dahlia sought out the sight of Colin as Ethan approached. Colin was back in the kitchen, probably working on dinner.

"Hey," said Ethan, holding the door open for her as she entered. He was a controlled mess of blond curls in an understated pair of jeans and black t-shirt. "You're upright."

She tilted her head. "Excuse me?"

He closed the door and gestured toward her foot. "Your ankle."

"Oh." She chuckled once, awkwardly. "Right. It's fine."

"My dad said you twisted it pretty bad yesterday. Ouch."

"Really, it's fine."

"I'm glad it didn't keep you from coming over."

She smiled. "Thanks." She cleared her throat. "It's good to see you again," she offered.

"Good to see you again, too. I told my dad it was worth asking."

She blinked. "What do you mean?"

"I saw you texted him earlier and asked if he'd seen you, and he told me what happened yesterday. I said he should invite you to have dinner with us. He didn't think you'd come, but I figured it was worth a shot."

Dahlia went very still. She let several moments of silence pass. "You okay?"

Her fingers had tightened around the wine bottle in her hand. She was trying to reconcile what he had told her—that Colin had not, in fact, been behind her invitation—with the hope and excitement that had been building in her all afternoon. *So*, she thought. *It wasn't Colin who wanted me here.* She suffered a wave of nausea at her own foolishness, and a sudden, urgent instinct to leave. She'd been so hopeful this morning. But maybe he was just being polite after all.

The familiar burn of shame roiled around in her stomach. The possibility that he was merely tolerating her made her feel pitiful and small.

Well, I'm here now. She forced a small smile. "Yes," she said. "Of course."

Ethan led her to the back of the house, where Colin was putting the finishing touches on a big plate of what appeared to be fish tacos. There was cilantro and cabbage on top, and neatly arranged sliced radishes.

"That smells delicious," Dahlia said politely, hanging back.

"Oh, hey there, kiddo," Colin said, glancing back at her over his shoulder. "Just in time."

He seemed in a decent mood; he didn't seem upset that she was there. She was heartened slightly.

"Colin, did you make all this yourself?"

"Nah, I had lots of help."

"A little help." Ethan was carrying a bowl of rice and a bowl of beans from the kitchen into the dining room. "I barely did anything."

"Here you go." Dahlia approached Colin at the counter and held out her wine. "This is for you."

"Aw, thanks, kiddo." His hands were working quickly over the food; the sleeves of his shirt were rolled up over his wiry forearms. He looked up quickly enough to shoot her a smile, then nodded back toward the dining room. "You can put it on the table."

Dahlia returned his smile, but his attention was already back on the food. "Thank you for having me."

Ethan and Dahlia brought items across to the dining room as they were ready. As they did Dahlia paused a moment to appreciate the scenery outside the sliding door that led into the backyard. There was a small patio of white stone slabs, with a wrought iron table and an umbrella in the center. A single plant stand stood on the other side, with a couple of flower pots of generic green plastic. The backyard itself was small and sparse, but open and sunny before the shade of the evergreens beyond. Late-day sunshine spilled unfettered into the house, casting the space with a warm glow that couldn't help but cheer her.

Colin brought in the tray of tacos and sat at the head of the table. Dahlia and Ethan sat on either side, across from each other, as they had the last time Dahlia was there.

Ethan picked up a pair of tongs. "I'll do the honors."

He waited for her plate. She picked it up and thanked him.

"One? Two? Three?" He raised his eyebrows. "Four?"

"Two is great," she said. "Thanks."

"Do you need to put your foot up?" he asked, placing two tacos carefully on her plate. "Do you need some ice?"

"No, I'm good. But thank you."

Ethan placed three tacos on his father's plate and then three on his own. They passed around bowls of sides and toppings. Colin took a corkscrew to Dahlia's bottle of wine.

"Say, how about a margarita?" asked Ethan suddenly. He turned to Dahlia. "No disrespect to your wine."

"Not for me," said Colin, filling his wine glass.

"Dahlia?"

"Oh," said Dahlia, pleased to see Colin enjoying her wine. But she was tempted by the thought of a tart, chilly margarita washing down the tacos. "That sounds good, actually."

Ethan smiled with pleasure, then rose to fix the drinks. Dahlia took the opportunity to spark some conversation with Colin.

"How was your day?" she asked him. "It's a busy time of year, right?"

"Mmmhmm." Colin had his mouth around a taco; he took a bite and chewed as she watched him, awaiting a reply. He swallowed and dove in for another. "Very busy."

"Do you have any interesting projects going on right now?"

Fleetingly, Colin's brow furrowed, as if it were a strange and unexpected question. "We do mostly residential structures, some standard commercial. Pretty rare we get anything worth reporting about."

311

"Your margarita," said Ethan, who had returned to the table and was holding a glass in his extended hand.

Dahlia took it. It looked delicious, pale green and cool, with a salt rim and a lime wedge.

"Wow, thank you," she said, her mouth watering. "This is very nice."

Ethan took his seat, his own margarita in hand. "I bartend here and there. Just helps with the bills, you know?"

"Mmm." Dahlia took a sip. Her senses were brightened by the sharp sweetness of the drink, and she savored it a moment, inhaling the scent. "Does it pay well?"

He laughed darkly. "Better than my actual job, if you can believe it."

She looked at him. "Really? Is that true?"

A corner of his mouth ticked upward as he took a long draw from his glass. "Writing doesn't pay crap. But editing doesn't pay shit."

"Why do you do it, then?"

"Good question," mumbled Colin, his mouth around a taco.

Ethan placed his glass down with a satisfied sigh. He picked up a taco. "I need to do something with words, even if it sucks. I'm a masochist. Most writers are."

Dahlia raised her eyebrows at him. "I don't believe that."

He grunted around a bite of taco, then cleared his throat. "Think about it. You pour your heart out onto the page, bleeding your guts and blood and exposing yourself to your own darkest impulses, and that's on a good day. On a bad day you stare at the screen in a dead-eyed panic, wishing the pain would hit you, desperate to feel something, anything, just so you can meet a deadline, just so you can feel human. That's when you realize you're nothing more than a drone and that the passion of your soul has become commercialized and capitalized, making money for other people, or worse, falling into obscurity with centuries of other starving artists erased by the weight of history. And when you don't, you run headfirst into fire for criticism, appeasing agents, editors, reviewers, who promptly move on to the next spectacle, leaving you scrambling gratefully for crumbs."

Dahlia stared at him in silence. Colin snorted, shaking his head.

"It doesn't sound like you like writing very much," she said at last.

"Oh, I love it," he said, rather brightly. "Best job in the world."

He was casually drinking margarita and chowing down on tortilla chips. Dahlia watched him for a minute, at a loss.

He looked at her. Catching sight of her face, he chuckled.

"Don't feel too bad," he said. "At least it builds camaraderie."

"Like the Bloomsbury group?"

His head snapped up from his plate. A grin spread over his face. "Exactly. Or the Pisan circle."

"The Algonquin round table."

"The Dymock poets."

"The beat poets."

"The lost poets."

"Enough, folks," said Colin, waving his hand up. "It's dinner, not a dissertation."

They made light conversation over the tacos, which Dahlia thoroughly enjoyed. The fish was fresh and perfectly crisp, and she appreciated the balance of savory flavors that complemented its buttery richness.

"Where is the spice coming from?" she asked Colin. "The cabbage?"

"The corn," said Colin, swallowing. "Special corn salad."

"It's delicious. You're such a good cook. Thank you."

Colin finished the last bite of his taco, then cleared his throat and wiped his fingers on his napkin. "It's his recipe," he said, swallowing, and nodding toward his son. "Thank him."

Dahlia turned toward Ethan. He was eating slowly, his elbows on the table, taking leisurely bites. His eyes met hers, and he shrugged.

After dinner they cleared the table together. The house, which in the golden glow of sunset had been flooded with light, was now awash in the soft lavender of the oncoming night. Dahlia observed the tentative peeking of stars over the trees, and the flurry of birds in their evening hunt. She paused for a moment on the way back into the kitchen, a dish in each hand, to watch an owl swoop toward a tree and perch on a high branch, unseen.

"Pretty nice out," said Ethan, noticing her pause. "Want to step outside?"

"Oh." She allowed Colin to remove the plates from her hands so he could wash them. "Okay. Sure."

Ethan pulled the handle and slid the door aside, then closed it after her. They stood on the little patio, side by side, taking in the cool evening air and the soft tension of the transient time between day and night.

"This is a really nice property," said Dahlia, looking around. It was so quiet out here, so far removed, even from the sparsely driven road that ran through the barely existent town. It was an enclosure within an enclosure, a pocket of respite in a pocket of the mountain. "Does your dad use the backyard a lot?"

"I don't know." He seemed distracted; he was staring absently into the line of trees.

He turned to her suddenly.

"So do you like it here?" he asked, his eyes wide and his smile kind. Dahlia looked at him. Beneath the mess of curls, his face was a study in contradictions—angelic yet sharp, delicate yet defined. His wide, impossibly large eyes gave him an almost ethereal or otherworldly quality, but the strong lines of his cheekbones and jaw made this softness an illusion. It was too fine to be rugged, too sharp to be delicate; the features were soft, but the structure was firm, composed subtly, and quietly—much like Ethan himself.

He was taller than she was, but not by much, and thinner; he had the look of someone creative, maybe a little angsty—of a writer, she thought with a smile. She could easily picture him sitting in a café or on a park bench, scribbling on a napkin or furiously typing, oblivious to the goings-on around him. He looked like the kind of person she might have hung out with back in high school. They would have made mix tapes, listened to new music. Mused too cynically on the constraints of the industry.

He was waiting for her to reply. She sighed and ran her fingers through her hair, and turned back to the natural scene before them.

"I do like it," she told him, sticking her hands in her pockets against the chill. "I like it a lot, actually."

"Oh, yeah? Why's that?"

She looked at him again. "You don't like it?"

"No, I like it." He nodded at the landscape, in acknowledgement, or acceptance. "I've got no complaints."

Dahlia watched a pair of squirrels chase each other through the trees. "It's so different here than it is back home."

"How so?"

She thought about it. "In every way. I mean of course there's the obvious, the mountains, trees, rivers. I live above a bookshop on the main street of town. The view from my window is very different." She thought about her cozy little apartment, the familiar line of buildings that had almost become her friends. For a moment she grew homesick. "But there are other things, too."

"Like what?"

She turned to him. He was watching her now, his round eyes alert. He was very intense; she felt there was always so much beneath the surface, that there was a low humming in him, something he was living with, but wasn't revealing.

She inhaled, pensive. "The air's just different here. It's fresher, like it's cleaner. It probably literally is. Cleaner, I mean."

"Hmm," he said. "Interesting."

"And the quiet," she went on. "Even when it isn't quiet. I mean I've been here a little bit, now, I know it's never quiet. But the sounds, it's like they're deeper—you know? Like it's quiet out here, but in there..." She was looking at the trees, at the mountains. She eyed him warily. "That probably doesn't make any sense."

"No, it makes sense," he said. "The quiet conceals, like the inner workings of the body though the limbs remain still."

She looked at him again, and blinked. "That's a good way of putting it."

"You think?" He met her gaze, then faced the yard. "It's a line from one of my stories."

"Really?" Dahlia watched him curiously, impressed. "It's beautiful."

"Thank you."

"Which story is it from?"

He hesitated. "It hasn't been published yet."

They stood in silence for a moment or two.

"You said the other day that you're writing another book 'theoretically,'" she said then. "What does that mean?"

He shifted his weight and stuck his own hands in his pockets. "You know. It's hard to find the time, sometimes, or the motivation."

"Do you have a deadline?"

"Nah. I got a one-book deal for *Nowhere*, with a small but respectable press. And they liked it. My agent was invited to submit to the editor when the second book was done. But *Nowhere* didn't make much money, so..."

He didn't say anything more than that. Dahlia didn't know how much she should push him.

"What's the new book about?" she ventured.

"Beats me." He laughed, a little darkly. "I've got a few solid ideas for stories. But I'm trying to figure out the umbrella, you know? What is it at its core? Like, what does it all *mean*?"

Dahlia could understand that. She gazed up into the sky, which was now in the first stages of true night. The stars had grown brighter, and the birds that had been circling above had found somewhere else to be.

"I'm not a writer," she said, "so I don't have any advice. But maybe you just have to keep writing it. Maybe the answers will become clear."

"Maybe."

He stared with her into the trees, now a dark band of shady spikes and swells.

"I just feel," he said then, and Dahlia looked at him—he was holding a hand out, as if to hold the weight of the feeling, "like it's spinning its wheels. Maybe it's fitting. I'm spinning my wheels, too. I'd love to quit editing and write full time. It's hard to stay in the zone."

"Editing is very technical. I can see how it would distract you." The nighttime serenade of crickets had started; she paused for a moment to listen. "I do a lot of editing myself, kind of informally. For the store, I mean. Not professionally."

"What would you be doing, if you could do anything?"

Dahlia blinked into the night. "I'm not sure."

There was a rustling in the trees, and they both looked. Dahlia couldn't see anything. Then he nudged her with his elbow, and pointed.

"Check it out."

From the darkness emerged a huge figure, lumbering slowly between the trees. Dahlia squinted.

"Is that a..."

"Moose," said Ethan. "And a massive one, too."

"Oh, my God," she breathed, her eyes glued to the meandering creature. "It's huge! I had no idea they were that big! Look at its antlers."

"Yeah. Don't get in the way of those things."

Dahlia watched it with awe until it disappeared back into the woods. It was like something out of a fairytale, impossibly large and majestic, something elusive she was grateful to have seen.

"Thanks for pointing that out," she told him, overcome with the magic of the experience. She looked at him; he was now a dark outline in the violet moonlight, rather mystical looking himself, in profile. "And...if you ever want anyone to read any of your manuscript," she said, braver, now, under the cover of the oncoming darkness, "I'd be happy to take a look. Not that I know anything. But I have read a lot of books."

He turned to her. "That's really nice of you. Thanks." He faced the yard once more. "But it's a dumpster fire. It's in no shape to be seen. I get nervous about showing people my drafts. Especially people I respect."

"I understand."

They exchanged a kind of meaningful look, one Dahlia found surprising and confusing. In the darkness, she could perceive with clarity only the straight shadow of his form, the whimsical waves of his curls, the consideration in his perpetually round eyes. Something flickered somewhere distant, maybe a firefly in the trees, a star twinkling in the night. Dahlia tucked her hair behind her ear and smiled awkwardly, and turned back toward the yard.

It had grown quite chilly, and they headed back inside. Colin was sitting at the table with a glass of whiskey, reading the news on his phone.

"You kids get some fresh air?"

"Mmm," said Dahlia, with a smile. The brightly lit apartment appeared even more charming after the darkness outside. "The air is so wonderful up here. I feel cleansed."

"Can I get you another drink, Dahlia?" asked Ethan, eyebrows raised, on his way to the bar cart. "A little poison to ruin all that cleansing?"

"Oh, no, thank you. I have to drive home."

"Sure. Right." Ethan looked disappointed, but he nodded and tapped his head, as if he'd forgotten. "What was I thinking."

Colin put his phone down and looked at her with a smile. "Heading out?"

"Oh." Dahlia hadn't intended to leave right away—she'd been hoping to take the opportunity to talk a little more with Colin—but she didn't want to overstay her welcome. "Yes, I probably should."

Colin stood. "Well, thanks for coming. And thanks for the wine, it was very good."

"I'm so glad you liked it."

"There's a really good wine store up in Woodrow," said Ethan, from behind them—he was standing nearly against the wall, with his hands in his pockets, and he practically blended in with the furniture. "They do tastings all the time. Kind of fun."

"Woodrow's nice." Colin turned to Dahlia. "That's the ski town I was telling you about."

"I passed a sign for Woodrow on the way to Hanford Notch. Oh, speaking of which," she said, looking directly at Colin. "I'd really like to check out some of the sights up there. Like 'The Cauldron.' It sounds so interesting."

"Yeah, the Cauldron's kind of neat," said Colin, now walking ahead of her toward the door. "You should see it."

"Would you have any interest in going with me?" The words were high and quiet, tentative in a way she hoped conveyed informality. She forced a laugh. "I promise not to twist any limbs."

"You know, I think I'm going to have to pass on this one." He stopped a couple of feet from the door and faced her. "I'm gonna be swamped with work this week."

"I'd go with you."

This from Ethan, on the other side of the room. He pushed himself off the wall and ambled toward them, hanging back a little before stopping.

"Well, there you go," said Colin, gesturing toward Ethan with his hand. He smiled at Dahlia. "Looks like you've got some company after all. Thanks, bud."

"It's no problem. I haven't been to the Notch in a while. One of those things you live near but never see." He directed his gaze at Dahlia. "Is that okay?"

"Oh. Sure," she said, exasperation like fire smoldering in her stomach; going with Colin was part of the point, but she didn't really have a choice. Besides, she guessed going with Colin's son could only help her get closer to Colin himself. "Thanks, Ethan."

"I'll have my dad send me your number," said Ethan. "As long as you don't mind."

"No, that's fine. Great."

"I'll walk you outside."

Dahlia smiled at him in acknowledgement, then turned to Colin.

"Thank you so much for having me, once again. I really appreciate the invitation, and it was so nice to see you."

"My pleasure." He reached out for a brisk, awkward embrace, then pulled away quickly and moved backward several steps. "Take care, drive carefully."

Dahlia said goodbye and walked with Ethan out to her car.

"Hey," he said as they made their way down the steps. "I hope you don't mind that I shoved myself into your plans."

"Oh, no, it's fine. I'd like to go anyway. And I'd rather not go alone." It was the truth. She wanted to keep at least one promise to herself, and she'd regret leaving before she saw the Cauldron. Ethan wasn't exactly relaxed, and he wasn't without-a-care; she continued to feel there was something simmering beneath the surface, some kind of pain or worry that was hidden deep inside. But despite this, he seemed easygoing and free, if not in his thoughts then at least in action. She had a feeling he'd be a good companion. They did have a number of things in common. And he was interesting, despite his strange, somewhat dark wit, and his tendency to intervene in the time she hoped to spend with Colin.

"Cool." He stood by her at her car, not saying anything else.

The two looked at each other for a minute or two before Dahlia opened the door.

"Okay. Well, text me tomorrow, I guess."

"Will do."

She waved awkwardly, and smiled, then fell into the car and drove off. He backed up to give her room, and watched her go down the road for a bit before turning and ambling back inside.

CHAPTER EIGHTEEN

*E*than texted her at around nine o'clock the next morning in a series of short messages sent in quick succession.

Hey! This is Ethan. Colin's son.

Sorry if it's too early. I didn't know if you were a morning person. I'm usually up by seven.

Looks like it's going to be a nice day today. Wanna check out the cauldron?

I'm supposed to be doing word stuff today but to hell with it.

Lmk.

Dahlia had already been to the diner for breakfast and was back in her room reading. She had nothing else to do that day and had no immediate plans to see Colin again. It would be as good a day as any to do a little exploring.

Sure, sounds good. What time do you want to meet?

He responded,

How about I pick you up?

Dahlia held back for a minute or two as she thought about this. She didn't know why she was hesitating. It wasn't that she was afraid of him, or that he was threatening, at least not in a physical, practical sense. She was trying to put her finger on her feelings when he texted her again.

Or not. I get it. I just thought there was no point in taking two cars.

And again:

No worries.

Dahlia responded quickly.

No that's fine, you're probably right. I'm at the Mountain View. Room 7. How about 1:00?

He agreed to this plan and signed off with a jolly, "Cheers." Dahlia put her phone back on the table and spent a little time gazing out the window, letting her thoughts drift.

She spent the rest of the afternoon reading and eating a light cold lunch in her room. Just before one o'clock, she noticed his car pulling into a spot next to hers. She closed her book and slipped into her sneakers, and picked up her small backpack with her wallet, water bottle, and keys.

She opened the door before he'd had a chance to knock: he was just closing the car door when she stepped outside her room.

"Oh, hey," he said as she locked the door. "Looks like you beat me to it."

"I'm all set. Thanks for picking me up. I guess you live pretty close by?"

"I live in Porter's Landing, about fifteen miles south. So it's no big deal."

The day was especially bright and warm. He looked the same as he always did, slight in stature but standing firmly, a little further away as if hesitant to bother anybody. He was wearing jeans and another dark t-shirt, with an abstract design in blue. As usual, his defining feature was his hair, which crowned his head like a gold halo of curls. But today it shimmered in the almost aggressive sunshine, which illuminated the ringlets' shadows as if he'd stepped off the canvas of an oil painting. There was something simultaneously wholesome and devious about it. Dahlia wondered if he even realized it.

She stepped toward the passenger side, and they both climbed into the car.

"All right," he said, looking behind him as he backed up. "Here we go."

He pulled out of the parking lot and back onto the road. The windows were half open. Their hair blew around their faces, red and gold.

"Too windy?" he asked her as he exited onto the highway. "You can close the window if you want."

"No, it's good." She looked through the window at the majestic scene beyond. The highway rose and dove before them; in the distance, the land became a chasm between mountains, like in a science fiction novel. From her trip up this way her second day here she knew a particularly impressive view was coming just around the curve, and she watched with anticipation, a wide smile forming on her lips as they rounded the cliff and the terrain's majesty came into view.

He glanced in her direction and smiled. "Pretty cool."

Dahlia appreciated the way the people here seemed to work with the landscape, conforming to its movements and using its nooks and crannies, rather than transforming it. They lived inside it, and among it; there was a respect for the earth here, a coexistence.

"It's really beautiful," she said. "I'm glad I came up here to see it."

"Do you like where you live?"

"I do like it." She paused. "Though I've never lived anywhere else."

They drove on. Eventually the signs for the state park appeared. Dahlia watched with excitement as they drew closer to the sign bearing the words "The Cauldron." When she'd first seen it, she hadn't known if she'd come back. She was eager now to find out what it was.

The parking lot was a half-circular clearing along the highway. There were a handful of other cars already there. Ethan pulled into a spot, and the two stepped out of the car into the sunshine, Dahlia already peering into the dark of the woods before them.

"Have you been here before?" she asked him as they made their way onto a path.

"Tons of times," he said. "It's just one of those things."

The path was marked by raised roots and makeshift steps. The two carefully marched onward into the trees.

"I love the smell of the air in here," she said. "It's kind of mossy, very fresh."

He didn't say anything for a moment or two. "Yeah, I guess it is."

She looked backward at the entrance to the path. "It's funny how it's so bright out, but it doesn't even make it through the trees. It's like we're in a house, or a castle."

"There's another Notch landmark called the Castle. We can check that out, too, if you want," he said. He had his hands in his pockets; his gaze was directed downward. He looked up and pointed straight ahead. "The Cauldron's up this way."

There was a small crowd gathered on a rise in the hill. Dahlia could see a wooden bridge over a stream, and a guard rail blocking the people's way. They climbed the rise to the sound of rushing water, and found a spot for themselves along the rails.

Dahlia gazed downward at the humongous blue-green pool.

"The Cauldron."

It was essentially a natural bath, filled with swirling water and constantly refreshed by a waterfall above. All around were smooth rock walls like the secret hideaway of a forest nymph. Dahlia stared, bewitched of the color. The motion of the water transfixed her, and she imagined what it would be like to be carried away by it, to let it take her to faraway new places and see parts of the mountain nobody ever had.

But would she do it, even if she could? Probably she'd be too afraid. It wasn't the first time she'd marveled at the allure of the water up here. And yet, she'd dipped her toes in, or her fingers, and nothing more.

"It was formed by glaciers," said Ethan, and Dahlia looked at him. He was leaning forward casually, his arms resting on the railing. "Apparently."

"Apparently?"

"I don't remember the full story."

There was a sign a few feet away explaining the creation of the Cauldron. Dahlia took a few steps in its direction, and stood reading, the sounds of the whirlpool behind her.

When she turned, Ethan was standing there watching her. His legs were at attention, and his hands were in his pockets. His lips were long and straight, his impossibly large eyes wide and soft.

She smiled warily. "You okay?"

He blinked. "Yeah."

She gestured toward the Cauldron. "This is really neat. Thanks for coming up here with me."

"There's more to see, up that way," he said, himself again. He gestured behind him to another path leading further up the mountain. "Maybe a quarter mile."

"Okay, let's go. Actually, hang on." She pulled her phone from her pocket and smiled sheepishly. "Just going to get a quick photo. I hate to be that person."

"You're not that person. Go ahead."

She snapped a couple of quick photos, then faced him. "Thanks."

"Want me to get one of you?"

"Oh," she said, handing her phone to him. "Sure."

She stood awkwardly before the Cauldron, hands at her side, a forced smile on her face.

"I got a few," he said, handing it back.

"Thank you so much. Do you want one, too?"

"No thanks, I'm good. I've been here a million times."

They moved on. The path became more narrow, and they could no longer walk side by side. They both stood there in mutual hesitation, neither wanting to be rude by cutting the other off.

He stuck his hand out. "After you."

She smiled awkwardly and went.

"Do you have work to do today?" she asked him.

"Yeah, I'm really behind," he said. "But I'm always behind."

"Oh, no. I feel bad for making you come with me then."

"It's fine. I'd be procrastinating anyway."

They continued walking for a minute or two, until the path widened and he joined her at her side.

"Are you procrastinating on the writing or on the editing?" she asked.

"Yes."

Sunshine began filtering through the trees, and they found themselves beside a clearing. Dahlia stopped short, and stared.

"Oh! Wow."

He'd kept on walking, and he turned back and smiled. "Come on," he said, motioning toward the clearing. "Let's have a seat."

Dahlia followed him onto a series of shelves of rock, like a downstream riverbed that had been drained of all its water. Small trickles of streams carved through the stone and down the mountain. Dahlia turned back and looked at the scene before her. The platforms extended seemingly all the way down the side, a split in the forest with a perfect view of the sun between.

A smattering of visitors were sitting on the rocks or dipping their fingers in the water. Ethan had found a spot in the shade and was sitting with his feet flat on the rock bed, his arms around his knees.

Dahlia sat beside him, her legs flat and her feet pointing upward toward the sky. She leaned with her hands behind her back, taking it all in.

"He's not that emotive," Ethan said suddenly. "My dad."

Dahlia was surprised, and her heart thumped at the thought of Colin. It felt strange to be here without him. Talking about him brought comfort, a sense of safety that anchored her to her time here.

She didn't know what to say. "He seems reserved."

"Yeah, I guess." Ethan now leaned back as she did, his hands on the rock behind him, his chest facing the sun. "He's always been a little tense."

"What do you mean?"

He shrugged. "I don't know. Just one of those guys, you know? Though I think my mom dying had a lot to do with it."

The emotionless way in which he talked about his mother was jarring. Dahlia glanced at him. His expression was serious and thoughtful, flat as the rocks they sat upon.

She faced the horizon once more. "I guess that makes sense."

"They had a really solid relationship," he went on. "He doesn't like to talk about her. But you can tell from the photos."

She looked at him. "He doesn't talk to you about your mom?"

"Not really. He never has."

For some reason Dahlia was not completely surprised. It seemed to explain so much about both of them.

"I'm sorry," she said gently. She hesitated. "You probably would have loved to hear about her."

"It would have been nice, yeah." He shifted where he sat, and crossed his legs. "I don't have any memory of her. It bothers me, if I'm honest."

She looked at him warily. His expression was still as blank as the stone around them, but there was new gravity in his eyes.

"I wanted to know who she was," he went on, "what she was like. But whenever I asked questions it seemed to piss him off. So I stopped."

"I'm so sorry, Ethan," she said. Her stomach roiled with nerves. It was about as serious a confession as he could make. She wanted to show support and sympathy; she was terrified of compounding his pain by saying something wrong. She thought carefully before responding. "That's a tough thing to carry. It makes sense that it bothers you. She's a part of you, though." She swallowed. "I know that's small consolation. But she helped shape who you are, even if she had you for only a short time."

"Maybe. I wouldn't know, since he won't tell me."

"I know." Her voice was soft and hesitant. She didn't want to minimize what he'd said. "I think it must be there in ways that you don't realize."

He took a breath. "Thanks. I'm sure you're right."

Dahlia didn't press further. She was certain Ethan's wounds ran deep; their conversations had revealed to her how complex he really was. She could understand how his experiences had perhaps made him feel more comfortable in the shadows, or less sure of himself. She could also understand the forces of grief that would make a person afraid to talk about someone they loved deeply, and then lost. Surely walls were constructed, defenses built. Colin was guarded for a reason. She guessed forcing it into the past was the only way he knew how to move forward. But of course, great love, even when lost, is never left in the past.

Her heart ached to imagine his pain, and Ethan's. "It must have been so hard for both of you."

"He hasn't really had anything serious since then." He watched as a chipmunk scurried by a few feet away. "He dates around, you know. Casual stuff. That kind of thing. But he only puts himself out there to an extent. And I don't just mean romantically."

Dahlia absorbed this information with sadness. She could only imagine what it was like, to be so young and to lose someone you loved so much. She understood why the wall was there; she understood why, until now, he hadn't let anyone else in.

"I'm only telling you this because you came all the way up here to spend time with him," said Ethan finally. "If you're looking for him to open up or, I don't know, be more enthusiastic, you might be disappointed."

"Oh." Dahlia thought about this, and wanted to step carefully in this delicate conversation. She looked at him. "Is he like that with...I mean, has he always been..."

"Is he like that with me?" He shrugged again, then sat up straight and leaned forward once more. "He's a good dad, he raised me well. Always took care of me. Still does." He picked at some pebbles on the ground, turning them over in the palm of his hand. "There's a hardness to him, though."

"What do you mean?"

"Don't get me wrong, he's a nice guy. He tells me he loves me and all that shit." He tossed the pebbles aside. "I think he wanted more for me, though. Or from me. I'm not sure."

"What makes you say that?"

"He wanted me to go into business with him. Henninger and Son. But that stuff was never for me. I was always less of a doer, more of a thinker."

Dahlia wanted to ask him if those were words his father said to him, or merely words he said to himself, but she felt she knew, and she didn't want to pry.

"Anyway, don't take it personally," he said. "He's just got a wall up. That's all."

She stared forward, watching the water jump over the rocks and cliffs. She wasn't sure what this meant for her, whether it was true, or whether it was just his son's interpretation. She felt though that she was there for a reason, that something had brought her and Colin together and that if there was indeed a wall there, maybe she could break through, for her own benefit but also for his.

"I can understand why he has a wall up," she said. "He's probably used to defending himself that way. I guess if I'd been through what he has, I'd probably have a wall up, too."

He sat thoughtfully for a moment or two. "I'm sorry your dad is sick," he said. "It seems like you're close to your family."

"Thanks. Yes, I'm very close with them." Her heart tugged at the thought of her kind parents and vivacious sisters; she thought of how little she'd spoken to them lately, and a pang of guilt pained her. "I'm pretty lucky. I'm from a tight family, and they're very open with their affection."

"That's really great." His smile widened and warmed. "I'm really happy for you."

"My parents also have a good relationship," she said. "It's been so hard for my mom to see my dad this sick."

"I'll bet. Do you live close to them?"

"They still live in my childhood home. I live about a twenty minute drive away."

"I'm sure it's been hard on you, too, then. To take care of your dad, I mean."

"It is hard. Tara does so much, though; she takes a lot of it onto herself. That's my sister, the oldest of the three."

"Ah."

Dahlia inhaled deeply, inviting the crisp mountain air to fill her lungs. She looked at the trees, the rocks, the mountains, all the things that were teeming with life but that constantly stayed the same. There was honesty here, a kind of stripping down to the bones that was refreshing, and inspiring, too. She was reminded of his honesty and decided to meet his honesty with her own.

"Sometimes I feel a little lost," she said, surprised by the way she had worded this statement. "In my own family, I mean."

"You do? How come?"

"Well, there are five of us. Not a huge family, but not small. Sometimes it's like…it's like everyone has their role in the family, except me."

"What are their roles?"

"My mom is the matriarch, the one who makes all the household decisions. She's the one who disciplined us, the one who tells us how things are going to work. Then there's my dad. He's kind of the moral center of the family. He's the artist."

"Your dad's an artist?"

"He's a glassblower. I know it doesn't sound like a serious job, but he does well. He's got a gallery, and his pieces really do sell. He's brilliant."

"I don't doubt it. That's awesome. Good for him."

Dahlia took another breath. "My mom supported him as he built that business. She worked hard all through my childhood. It totally paid off because my dad's really made it."

"I admire them both. Well done."

She picked up a leaf and fiddled a little with the stem. "My middle sister April's the sophisticated, worldly one, even if we don't see her all that much. And Tara's tough as nails. She's the nurturer, the one people go to when they have a problem. She's put her life on hold to help my mom take care of my dad. She has a husband and three daughters, my nieces, who I adore. I don't know how she finds the time for it all."

"And you?"

She rubbed her lips together. It was more than she'd intended on sharing. Part of her felt that it wasn't even true, that her mind was simply jumping from step to step like the stream falling between levels.

"I'm just there," she said, thinking of her second-floor apartment that nobody ever saw, the bookstore job mere steps away from her home, the way she was always a side character in other people's lives. "I'm like...the quiet one. The one tagging along." She tried to laugh. "I probably sound pathetic. I shouldn't even be saying anything."

"No, it's good, you should say it." He was staring into the mountains; then he turned to her with a sly, crooked smile. "I'll bet you're the cool aunt. Are you? Are you the cool aunt?"

Dahlia laughed in earnest. "No, not even close. I've never been cool, never will be."

"Now, I know that's not true."

They sat in silence for a moment or two.

"The thing is," she said finally, "I don't want to do anything so impressive. I don't even want to travel a lot, or make a lot of waves. I just...want to do *something*. Anything. I guess I just want to know that I *could* do them, if I wanted to." She hesitated. "My therapist says it's anxiety."

"Could be." He was looking around at the landscape; Dahlia couldn't see his face. "Anxiety's a bitch."

"Maybe it is anxiety, I don't know. I mean I like my life, though. Things scare me, yeah, but still, I like to be home."

"There's nothing wrong with that," he said. "You can be introverted, and anxious, and they can be two separate things. You can want to do a little. You don't have to do a lot. And just because what you're doing now isn't enough, it doesn't mean you have to do it all."

Dahlia thought about this.

"My sister April did a lot," she ventured, working it through as she was saying it. "I mean she moved far away, built a whole new

333

life, became an entirely different person. Last time I saw her was at Christmas. She didn't seem super happy."

"Well, people make all kinds of choices. It isn't all or nothing. You don't have to follow in anyone else's footsteps."

She didn't think she'd ever had this kind of conversation with anyone, certainly not this honestly, certainly not this fast. It was interesting the way it had led here so quickly and so naturally, how he was talking with her about their deepest feelings without any care or hesitation at all. She'd always seen revealing oneself as scary or dangerous, or self-indulgent at the very least. The freedom was refreshing, like the cool mountain stream beside them. She felt she could be frank with him, that her frankness wouldn't faze him—and the idea of speaking without over-thinking was more alluring than she could resist.

"Can I tell you something really deep, and really messed up?"

He turned to her. His round eyes locked into hers.

"Of course."

It was there again, that intense introspection of his eyes. In this brief moment of scrutiny Dahlia saw how his cognizance ran layers and layers deep, and it was now directed at her. She was gratified but timid. Once again something flickered, but it was the middle of the day now, and light. Dahlia blinked, and it was gone. She shrugged and pushed these thoughts aside.

She swallowed and turned away from him, facing the expanse of peaks before them.

"I feel like no matter how many people tell me I'm good," she said quietly, "and no matter what kind of evidence I have, I only see the bad, like if people only knew me they'd know I wasn't worthy."

"Like who?"

"Like everyone. Like my family." The simmering grew a little higher, building bubbles of heat in her stomach. "I know they love me, but it's like, they don't know. Boyfriends, too."

"What about boyfriends?"

"It's like...they don't stick around. Emotionally. I mean maybe they just know, only they have no obligation to stay."

"You think the people who love you don't know you, and you think the people who don't love you, it's because they see the real you."

"Well...kind of, yes."

"That's not anxiety, that's depression. Ask me how I know."

Dahlia didn't ask him that question, or any other. She felt they had waded into dark territory, darker than she was capable of navigating right now, in this moment, or in any moment at all. And it wasn't because he was wrong, but because she suspected he was right. It wasn't a door she was willing to open even with Gita, even with herself. She certainly wasn't going to open it here, outside, on a mountain, with a relative stranger. And while she wasn't opposed to knowing more about his own story she was afraid of what he would tell her, afraid of what she would see in it that would force her to see herself.

"Are you okay?" she asked instead.

"Oh yeah, I'm fine." Dahlia looked at him. He had said these words nonchalantly, as if it were just a part of his life. "I'd say I'm the opposite. I feel like I've got all this potential, but no one else can see it. And if they did, they'd admire it. And maybe I'd be motivated to use it."

Dahlia was fascinated by this analysis, a sort of inverted version of her own. She sat on it for some time, wondering if there were parts of herself that could relate to this, too.

"My therapist says I'm drawn to emotionally unavailable partners," she said.

"Huh." He considered for a moment. "I think I am, too."

They sat silently with their thoughts.

"I guess all this begs the question," he said then, "of what it is you actually want to do."

Dahlia blinked, staring off into the mountains. Then she laughed.

He turned to her, one corner of his mouth ticked up slyly. "Was that funny?"

"I'm sorry." She shook her head a few times, clearing it. "It wasn't funny, not really. It's just...in all this time, and in all my worrying about it, it's a question I've literally never even asked myself before."

They watched the flowing of the water together, both leaning back on their hands, Dahlia with her legs out before her, Ethan with his legs still crossed.

"I guess I might like to have my own store," she said. "I mean I've never considered it. But the truth is that I really like what I do. And I like living near the store, too. My life is so insular and so predictable, but I like it."

"There's nothing wrong with that."

A soft breeze drifted by them, tussling their hair and kissing their faces.

"What about you?" she asked him. "What would you do, if you could do anything?"

"Oh, I'd write, for sure."

She smiled. "That's great."

"I wouldn't even mind how hard it is, if I could justify the time it took," he went on. "I have a love-hate thing with writing. I think most writers do."

"A cruel mistress."

"For sure." He smiled, then sighed. "But all jobs are hard in their own way, I guess. And at the end of the day, it's the only thing I feel passionate about. It's the only thing that really keeps me going."

Dahlia had the sense that he was speaking quite literally, that there was darkness inside him that he was running from all the time. Maybe they were like each other in this way, though the darkness itself was different. She sympathized with him, and hurt for him. She wanted to reward his honesty and his trust, but didn't want to push him too hard or offend him; she didn't know him well enough to know how much was too much. And she realized in that moment that she was in uncharted waters—she'd never really had a friend with whom she was close enough to try.

She wanted to ask him about this darkness; she felt it might bring a little light to them both. But it was too soon, and she was frightened. She made practical conversation instead.

"It's funny that you write the books, and I sell them," she said. "I couldn't live without my books. Maybe that's why I like marketing so much, it allows me to talk up the books I love. I'm pretty good at the artistic end, and kind of knowing what's going to sell. But I can't imagine writing one."

"Marketing is my nemesis. So I envy you. I just want to write, I don't want to have to worry about selling. Which I guess is half the battle of being a writer. You'd think having a book deal would eliminate the need to market, but unfortunately it's just not the way it works."

Dahlia knew this from working at the store. Many writers ended up taking on the lion's share of marketing themselves. After the initial burst of publication, it was up to them to keep their work in the public eye. It was even more pronounced with small presses. If a writer didn't take this on, they would disappear into the ether, where countless authors had disappeared before. Dahlia wasn't surprised Ethan had not succeeded in marketing. For a writer, marketing required a certain donning of a persona, a certain willingness to pretend. It required forcing yourself into the spotlight, talking yourself up and wearing a smile you maybe didn't feel. She could see how this would be repulsive for someone like Ethan, who preferred blunt honesty and truth, who seemed uncomfortable being the subject of attention.

She said, "What do you think is stopping you?"

"The editing takes up too much time and brain space. It gets in the way. After staring at academic writing all day it's hard for me to get into the zone."

"I can understand that."

They sat in silence for a time.

"My dad thinks it's a weakness," he said. "All of it. Anxiety. Depression. The failure to write. He thinks if I abandoned a good career to write, I should be writing." He paused for a beat. "I don't talk to him about it anymore."

"Do you think," she ventured, nervously, but gently, "that maybe you should talk to somebody else?"

He took a breath. "I don't know. Probably."

"I think you should." She swallowed, surprised by the eagerness with which she'd said this. She hadn't realized until this moment how despite her hesitation, she'd grown to depend on her therapy sessions for clarity. "I've been doing it. And it's helped me, a little." She rubbed her lips together, thinking. "Probably more than I know."

"Maybe I should. Maybe I will."

There was heaviness now, between them, but it wasn't tense or awkward. It was the heaviness of truth, of understanding. It was a soft, comfortable silence. Dahlia let it have its space.

Finally, she said, "I really hope you get to write. I hope it all works out."

"Thanks." He sounded tired. "And thanks for listening. Seriously."

They stood, stretched, and brushed off their clothes.

"Here," he said, pointing to her phone. "I'll get another pic."

She thanked him gratefully and handed him the phone, then stood at the center of the platform and waited for him to be finished. After a minute or two, he gave it back to her, smiling.

"That's a good one," he said.

They headed back down the path, simultaneously with more somberness, and more light. As they navigated the trail downward Dahlia let the thoughts unfold. It was scary, revealing herself like this—acknowledging the darkness within herself. But there was something exciting in it, too. Somehow, she felt less alone. And in a way she wasn't expecting she felt comfort in being that for someone else, too.

She thought about Colin, about what Ethan had revealed about their relationship and about what seemed like Colin's disappointment. She knew it must be a simple misunderstanding. Colin clearly loved his son, and the two had been through such trauma together. Colin had his own darkness; that much was abundantly clear. Maybe Colin couldn't allow himself to imagine his only son's pain. Maybe his own pain prevented him from reaching over the wall, and that if he had someone to help him, like she did, he'd be able to breach that divide.

They emerged from the woods and back into the sunshine, where they climbed into Ethan's car. Ethan pulled out of his spot and onto the highway, his window down and his elbow on the door.

"Hey," he said over the wind, his curls tossing about like wild yellow flames. "Are you feeling adventurous?"

Dahlia hesitated for a moment. She was never feeling adventurous; it wasn't something she was used to or familiar with. She didn't even know what it would feel like if she was.

She looked at him as he drove, his small frame and modest appearance, his casualness and calm. He did not seem like a person who sought danger. And she felt instinctively that he wanted her to enjoy herself.

She faced forward again and grinned. "Sure."

Without a word, he veered off at the next exit, with the sign reading "The Castle."

"What's the Castle?"

"You'll see."

The Castle, whatever it was, was on the other side of the highway, and they drove across an overpass and into another parking lot. The view here was even more grand: they were at the foot of a mountain, which seemed to encase them on three sides, lush with thick forests, a magical wall of green.

There was a lodge-like building at the end of the parking lot. Dahlia noticed something behind it.

"No. Oh, no," she said, her head tilted back as she took in the sight of the wires that ran all the way to the top of the mountain, and the tram cars that were passing each other, one going up, one going down. "We're not going in the lift, are we?"

"I thought we might." Ethan closed the door of his car and stepped beside her. He looked at her. "Do you want to?"

She bit her lip. It was just so, so very high. She couldn't even say if she was afraid of heights because she'd never had an opportunity to find out.

"I don't know." Her heart was racing, her stomach overturning and squeezing in alarm. "I've just never done anything like it before."

"Well, it's up to you."

Dahlia continued staring up the mountain—Mount Lyre, she saw on the sign. She couldn't believe she could be at the top of that mountain in a matter of minutes. Was that really all it took, a few minutes, a tram car, and a friend? Mere seconds ago she wouldn't have even considered it, or seen it as something that was possible. Now all of a sudden she was one word away from doing it, from seeing something she'd never seen before and from coming home a different person than she was before she'd left.

She thought about how she'd wished she could be on a mountaintop, just like the girl in the painting. She watched the tram cars going up and down the mountain. They were all doing this like it was no big deal. Nothing was stopping her from doing it, too.

"Sure," she said, with a smile, pushing her wind-blown hair out of her face. "Sure, yes, let's go do it."

He returned her smile, and they held each other's gaze for a fraction of a second. Then they walked inside the building, where they paid for their tickets and got in line, and waited for the little tram car that would take them to the top of the mountain.

～

THE TRAM CAME SLIDING into the station, and the doors opened. A handful of people stepped out, chatting giddily. Waiting on the platform were Dahlia, Ethan, and a group of three other people. They followed each other into the tram, then waited for the doors to close and for the conductor to welcome them aboard.

The tram began lifting. Dahlia faced the steep mountain before her. Everyone gasped and laughed when the wires tilted abruptly upward, and they were in the air, the lodge already becoming small beneath them.

Dahlia and Ethan were at the back of the tram. Dahlia was transfixed by the view. It was walls and walls of green, cascading in on themselves and revealing dips and turns and mysteries invisible to those on the ground. A lake blanketed the valley, a sparkling puddle from this height.

"Hollow Lake," he said, seemingly reading her mind.

"I thought so," she breathed, entranced.

She felt she was part of a mystical universe, a place she hadn't been meant to see; she felt she was getting a special glimpse into the secrets of the Earth, that the mountain was allowing her to be there, that she was a guest of powerful overlords that hadn't invited her, but hadn't objected.

She moved to the side, equal level to the trees. How many creatures were in these woods, right now? How many little worlds within the worlds? How many dramas were playing out, deep within the darkness? What kind of magic? What kind of life?

She looked at Ethan, who was standing a few feet away. His head was turned to the side so he could watch the view below. His face was unsettling in its contrasts—eyes too large, lips too fine, nose too delicate. She saw again how the architecture of the face itself—high cheekbones, strong jaw, the subtle hollows that caught the shadows—made any softness a misconception. It was, she realized, beautiful, in a way that defied definition.

He noticed her gaze and faced her. Startled, she smiled awkwardly, and looked away. Her stomach squeezed, a strange feeling, likely the effect of the increasing elevation.

They arrived at the top, and waited for the tram to stop before stepping carefully off. They were on a huge wooden platform, with wide views of the mountains beyond. They stood for a moment looking over the railing. Then Ethan turned to her, gesturing with his hand.

"There's an observation tower," he said. "It's only a ten minute walk."

They made their way toward a path through the trees. Dahlia noticed the trees up here were shorter and packed closer together. She looked downward to the forest floor. The ground cover was different, too, patches of moss clinging to crevices and forming low, dense mats of green. Tiny flowers were specks of color against the rocks. Lichen sprawled over stones, and tufts of hardy grasses rose tentatively from beneath. They were scenes of stark beauty, life tenaciously grasping to the edges of the world.

To the right was the forest; to the left, a line of trees, and on the other side, a steep drop off the mountain. Ethan and Dahlia made their way slowly along the path. At one point the line of trees dissipated, and they stood on a stone platform with nothing between them and the mountaintops on the other side of the valley.

"Oh, my God," Dahlia breathed, watching clouds push by the cliff right before her very eyes. "They're really there. The mountains, they're right there."

"It's a pretty incredible view," he agreed.

She was afraid of getting too close to the edge, but she took a few wary steps forward. She felt she was at the top of the world, witnessing the magnificent lives of gods.

She pulled out her phone and clicked on her camera. "Let's get one together."

Ethan stepped beside her and leaned in, and she held her hand out in front of them. They both smiled. She snapped the picture, not looking at it, and moved back to the safety of the forest, relieved.

"I'll send that to you, if you want."

"Great."

They continued on up the path, which wound around the mountaintop, taking them away from the edge and further into the woods. Eventually they came to the observation tower. It was a tall wooden structure, with flights of steps twisting all around the outside.

"The Castle," he said. "We made it. We're here."

She lifted her head toward the top of the structure. They were already higher than she'd ever been in her life. "Do we go up?"

"We came all the way here. Let's do it."

They climbed the first few flights; then, with some kind of unspoken understanding, began racing each other to the top. By the time they arrived they were both huffing and laughing, utterly out of breath.

"A tie," he wheezed, bending over with his hands on his thighs.

"A draw," she said, with a chuckle, doing the same.

They got ahold of themselves and straightened, and walked around the tower. Dahlia couldn't believe what she was looking at. It was a veritable ocean of green, more trees than there were stars in the sky. It was endless, flowing in massive, rolling waves, and all of it teeming with life, with depths unknown and unseen, among the clouds, among the skies.

"I can't even believe how beautiful this is." She looked this way and that, struck by how the colors faded and darkened the further out they went. "I never could imagine anything so beautiful."

"It is a sight, for sure." He was standing at the railing, looking out into the vast beyond. He turned to her with a smile. "I'm glad you like it."

"I love it." She studied him with a somber expression, truly grateful. "Thank you for bringing me here."

"You're welcome." He held out his hand. "The obligatory photo."

He snapped a few photos of her, then handed the phone back.

"Now you have a full record of your day."

She smiled softly as he walked away from her, around the tower. In his absence she paused for a moment to reflect on what was happening. She had done it; she was on a mountaintop. And what was more, it hadn't even been so hard. The realization was far-reaching, and it meant more to her than she could say. She looked forward to going back to her room and looking at the photos, and processing what had happened to her that day, in the quiet solitude that always inspired her deepest thoughts.

After a time they descended the stairs and walked back to the tram to leave. Inside, as they slid down the wires back to the ground, Dahlia felt exhilarated. She'd done something today she'd never done before, something she'd never even expected. She'd taken a chance, and had been rewarded. She felt she'd visited new heights today in more ways than one.

By the time they climbed back into the car it was after five o'clock, and the warm tones of daylight had begun to sink into the cooler shades of dusk. The mountains were black masses in the violet sky. They loomed over the highway like great sleeping giants, their backs knobby and bent as they dreamed their monstrous dreams.

Dahlia closed her eyes against the curves in the road so she could feel the way the mountains moved. She stuck her hand out the window into the cool forest breeze, and wove her fingers through the current, absorbing as much of the mountain as she could before returning to her little village room.

She and Ethan chatted, the mood between them easy and light. He suggested they grab dinner at Moose and Lantern, and the two shared a hearty meal in the dim coziness of the tavern.

When he pulled into the parking lot of the motel Dahlia was almost at a loss for what to say.

"This was a really nice day," she said, hoping to avoid being too effusive. "I really appreciate your offering to do this with me."

"No, it was good to get out. You did me a favor. Got me out of my head a little. You know."

They sat in silence for a moment or two.

"I did some new things today," she told him, smiling sweetly. "Thank you."

"I'm glad," he said, his round eyes kind. "You're welcome."

"Oh, let me send you that photo before I forget."

"Great. Thanks."

He waited a moment while she pulled up the photo of them together, and texted it to him.

"Well." She put her hand on the door handle and made to get out of the car. "Thanks again."

"Hey, you know what we should do," he said then, holding his hand up awkwardly; Dahlia thought his voice sounded a little forced, but she couldn't be sure. "We should check out the rest of the Notch. Like one thing a day. Or something." He shrugged, and his eyebrows rose as he appeared to lose confidence. "I think it would be good for me to get outside more. You know. Get some fresh air, see the sights." He shrugged again. "But only if you want to. Of course."

"Oh...sure," she said, nodding—it was a good idea, and she had nothing else to do here. She'd have to think about what this meant for her time with Colin, and of course it would conflict with her new morning routine, which she'd come to rely on for peace, silence, and quietude. She didn't really like surprises or being put on the spot; the idea of a regular outing was one she'd have to think about, but something was telling her she should take a chance and accept it into her schedule. "Sure, that's a good idea."

"Tomorrow, then?"

"Um." She rubbed her lips together. "Sure."

"'Kay." He smiled again. "I'll text you in the morning. To figure out a time."

"Sounds good." She held her hand up in a wave. "Bye, then."

She stepped out of the car and closed the door, and backed up toward her room. A rush of relief swept through her. Despite the excitement of the day, it had been a long day. Her social battery was close to empty. And she had a lot to think about tonight.

He waited for her to unlock her door and walk inside, and she waved once more as he pulled out of the parking spot and drove off. She closed the door slowly, then watched the headlights fade into the distance down the street.

She flopped onto her bed with her phone and pulled up one of her favorite shows to play in the background as she let the events of the day filter unfettered through her mind. Ethan was so different from Colin, in a lot of ways; there was a somberness to both of them, but it wasn't quite the same. Whereas Colin was perhaps hardened, made wary by experience—Ethan seemed wounded, by a presence he didn't construct himself. He was open with her, unlike his father; in fact she'd gotten from Ethan what she'd originally wanted from Colin, as far as a little background, a glimpse into his life. She wondered if Cindy's death had made Colin firmer with his son, and if this were true, how it was possible that Ethan had picked up his softness and sensitivity regardless.

She was glad to have made a friend in Ethan, who was a calm and relaxed companion. She liked that they could talk to each other, and that he seemed to want to be around her. She hoped they could continue to support each other, and that she could continue to learn about his father, so that she might know better, in the future, how to gently collapse the wall around his heart, so that she might get in, and have the relationship that she wanted.

CHAPTER NINETEEN

$\mathcal{T}$he next day, Monday, Ethan and Dahlia visited "the Stag," which was an overlook off the highway that gave them a view of a deer-shaped natural sculpture in the cliffs in Hanford Notch. Then they drove up to a pedestrian overpass that offered a view of the entirety of the Notch, and stood by the railing admiring the grandeur of the mountains and the sky. They walked to the other side of the overpass and to a trailhead, and spent an hour following the signs to a waterfall, then doubling back to the car to fill the afternoon with as many sights as possible.

They drove a couple of exits further north and stopped in a little town for lunch, then popped into a bakery for donuts before heading back toward home. Dahlia suggested they ask Colin if he wanted to join them for dinner. Ethan called him but received no answer. Dahlia decided to have a light, quiet dinner at the motel after Ethan dropped her off, thanking him profusely for another worthwhile day.

Ethan texted her the next morning.

Are you feeling REALLY adventurous?

347

Dahlia stared at the words for a moment or two, and grinned. As usual, she wasn't feeling adventurous at all, but she also knew she wasn't going to let that stop her. She'd learned that lesson the last time.

She typed,

Shouldn't you be writing?

He wrote back,

The best cure for writer's block is to do something.

He picked her up and drove her into Woodrow, the location of the ski resort she'd heard about from Colin. Open expanse of forest turned into quaint storefronts selling souvenirs, artisans' wares, and athletic equipment, interspersed with cafés and candy shops and bars with mountain decor. Ethan pointed out the wine shop he'd mentioned. They passed a cheese shop Dahlia vowed to come back to another day.

Ethan drove through town until they hit the hotel, then pulled into a parking lot with a sign that said "Goose Wing Mountain Resort."

"We're not going skiing, are we?" she asked him, her stomach dropping with dread.

"Not skiing," he said. "Look there."

Dahlia looked in the direction of his pointed finger. On the other side of the hotel was an outdoor activity center with climbing walls, aerial treetop parks, and—

"A zipline," she breathed, heart hammering. She turned to him. "You're not thinking of the zipline, are you?"

He shrugged. "I was." He parked the car and looked at her. "What do you think?"

"No. Absolutely not."

"You sure?"

She rubbed her lips together nervously.

"Let's get out of the car," he said. "See what's here. We don't have to do it. There's other stuff, too."

Dahlia reluctantly got out of the car and met him on the other side. Goose Wing Mountain was much smaller than Mount Lyre. She noticed a ski lift that went to the mountaintop, and families or couples taking advantage of the view as they were pulled up the slope or back down toward their cars. There was a lodge of some sort on the top of the mountain. A sign at the base said, "Goose Wing Mountaintop Café."

"Hey," said Ethan, nudging her with his elbow and pointing toward the side. "I dare you."

Dahlia looked. It was a large enclosed area with two platforms connected by a walk-across plank, and a soft rubber landing a couple of feet beneath. Leaning against the net were what looked like two oversized barbells made of foam.

"Oh, my God," she said, laughing. "You're not serious."

"Never been more serious in my life. Come on."

She followed him, chuckling, pushing her hair back with embarrassment. Ethan bought a couple of tickets and gave them to the employee at the entrance. Then he picked up a barbell and took the farther platform, and crouched menacingly as he faced her.

Dahlia burst out laughing but picked up her barbell and waited. Behind her, an automated voice began counting.

"Three. Two. One."

A bell sounded, and Dahlia and Ethan stepped tentatively onto the plank. They began swiping at each other with the barbells, wobbling and crying out and doubling over with laughter.

Ethan knocked her barbell with his own, and she lost her balance. She tumbled onto the bouncy rubber beneath them, cursing.

"Beginner's luck," she said, reaching for his outstretched hand.

"Rematch," he said, crouching again as she took her stance.

"Three. Two. One."

The battle began again, this one harder than the one before. The laughing had stopped, replaced by panting. They lasted longer, this time, had quickly learned how to hold steady. Finally Dahlia poked his legs with her barbell, and he fell over, flopping onto the mat.

She reached her hand out to help him up. "I guess we're tied now."

"Two out of three."

They took their places and prepared for the final fight. When the counting had finished, they battled seriously, more able to defend themselves and less likely to make careless moves. Finally he managed to trick her, moving his barbell right and then immediately to the left. He didn't even have to hit her: her quick movement threw off her equilibrium, and she began falling, accepting she had lost.

Out of nowhere he grabbed her upper arm and pulled her steady. She regained her balance, and they met each other's gaze as they stood together on the plank. But he let go too quickly, and they both fell down after all.

"Damn it," he said, with playful seriousness. "I thought we had it."

"You won fair and square anyway."

"It's so much better when everybody wins."

They climbed to the edge and gave up their barbells, thanked the employee and walked away. Dahlia's lungs were full of laughter and of fresh mountain air. Adrenaline was rushing through her veins. The physical exertion had done her good.

"So what do you say to that zipline?" he asked.

She smiled. "Race you there."

They jostled each other as they jogged toward the zipline, laughing and joking. They arrived at the platform, and Dahlia grew silent. The enormity of what she was going to do had hit her, and she was looking around at all the equipment, realizing with dread what she had gotten herself into.

"Um, I don't know," she said warily, watching the person in front of them get buckled in and receive instructions. "I've never done anything like this before."

"I've only done it once or twice. It's pretty easy. Trust me."

Dahlia didn't say anything. He stepped onto the platform, and she followed.

"Hey," he said, taking a step back and patting her shoulder. "We don't have to do it if you don't want to. Seriously."

Dahlia hesitated. It wasn't even really that she was afraid of doing it, so much as she was afraid of looking foolish. She had already gathered that she had to hold her hands a certain way, that she had to lift her feet at a certain time. She very much wanted to see the view and to experience the ride. But the thought of embarrassing herself was too much for her to bear. She imagined herself making a mistake, or getting injured, of how he'd have to tend to her or take care of her, of how she'd be the center of attention, how she'd relive the humiliation for weeks.

"Why don't you go ahead," she said. "Maybe I'll go after you."

Ethan stepped toward the beginning of the zipline and allowed a couple of employees to help him with his clips and positioning. They spoke with him a few seconds, telling him what to do, and Ethan nodded.

"Okay," he told them. "Sure."

He seemed so easygoing, like it was no big deal at all. Dahlia could never be so easygoing. She was already stressing about remembering everything she had to do.

"Whenever you're ready," one of the men told Ethan.

Ethan glanced back at her. "See you on the other side."

He pushed himself off, and Dahlia stepped back to watch him slide down the line. She clapped and cheered as he zipped over the stream and through the trees, and disappeared into the woods.

What must he be seeing, she wondered. *What must the mountain look like, from that angle.*

She let somebody go in front of her and began walking to the bottom of the line. It was quite a distance from one side to the other. They met up with each other a few minutes later, Ethan climbing back up the slope with surprising spring in his step.

"How was it?" she asked him, her face bright with a smile.

"Pretty awesome," he acknowledged, eyebrows raised. "Two thumbs up, would recommend."

Her smile melted into a sly, one-sided grin. She'd taken a chance before, and it was fine. She'd take a chance this time, too.

"Okay," she said, swallowing back a lump in her throat. "I guess I'll give it a try."

They walked back up to the platform, and Dahlia stood in place. She took in everything the employees said to her, making mental notes and nodding even as her heart pattered so quickly she could barely make out their words. Finally they clipped her in place and stood back. It was time.

She looked back at Ethan. He nodded in encouragement.

"You can do it," he said. His round, wide eyes were intent on hers. His face was surprisingly serious, despite the casualness of his stance. "I know you can."

She blinked a few times, and smiled nervously. Then she turned toward the line and looked forward.

She didn't move for a number of seconds. Her feet wouldn't jump; she couldn't make herself do it.

"Need a count?" asked the man standing beside her.

"Yes," she croaked, and cleared her throat. "Thank you."

"One. Two. Th—"

Dahlia pushed off before he said it, and immediately began screaming. She was barreling down the line, nothing between her and the steep drop beneath her, the cascading boulders of the stream and the sharp treetops, reaching toward the sky.

Her stomach was on the floor of the chasm, her heart jumping from her chest. The energy inside her body was exploding, making every nerve of her skin tingle with fire and with alarm.

It was the most exhilarating, most wonderful moment of her life.

She cried out with glee, her smile spread wide. She had never felt smaller, and more part of something grand; from the side of her vision she saw the wall climbers, the fighters with the barbells, who whizzed by in a blur, barely noticing her in the air. Everything was happening as normal, but it hardly mattered now: she was flying, she was suspended in nothing, seeing the magnificence of the landscape in a way she never had before.

The bottom platform came into view; she saw Ethan standing there, arms crossed, watching. She smiled, then faced the platform, where two employees were waiting for her to arrive. She remembered to lift her legs; she slid onto the platform with ease.

"Whew!" she exclaimed, attempting to stand, letting them unclip her and remove her harness. "That was incredible. Thank you, thank you so much."

They wished her good day and prepared for the next rider. Dahlia made toward the stairs, where Ethan was walking up to meet her.

His wide blond curls were wind-tossed, his round eyes bright and sparkling. In his face she saw his true kindness, and she could feel only gratitude and grace.

"Hey," she said, pushing her hair behind her ear as she descended the stairs.

"Hey. What did you think?"

"Amazing. Really amazing."

"I'm glad you did it."

"Me, too."

They stood for a moment while she got her bearings.

"Thank you," she said, sincerely.

He patted her shoulder again. "You're welcome."

They began walking back to the car. Dahlia stopped him.

She gestured toward the ski lift. "Lunch on top of the mountain?"

A lopsided grin emerged on his face. He retraced his steps back toward her, and they made their way to the lift.

THE DAYS ahead followed the same pattern. Dahlia and Ethan would spend the first part of the afternoon together, going on a hike or finding some kind of outdoor activity, finishing with lunch and an understanding they'd do it again. Dahlia was delighted to have this chance to see parts of the area she wouldn't have. It had begun to feel familiar to her; she no longer felt like such a stranger.

She and Ethan never stopped talking. They discussed their jobs, their families, their beliefs, their fears, their impressions. Dahlia felt at ease with him. It wasn't that the pot didn't simmer; it wasn't that the anxiety had dimmed. It was that it was somehow okay with him, acceptable; it was that he assured her that there wasn't something wrong with her, that she wasn't alone in her struggles and that she could help him with his, too.

Saturday they returned from a hike later than usual. She suggested they order dinner to her room. Over spaghetti and wine she told him about Imani, how she felt she'd disappointed her, how she worried she'd lost her respect. She told him about the trip to Los Angeles and how she felt like a failure for her hesitation to do this for her boss. And she admitted that she was hesitant even to tell him this much, that she was not used to talking about her failures and that she worried he'd think less of her, too.

"I think all you can do is accept where you are, right now," he told her. "You're not weak for struggling with something. You're human."

"Yes," she said, worrying with her bottom lip. "I guess that's true."

"You push through hard things every day. So what if this one isn't the thing you can push through right now? Maybe you'll do it, and maybe you won't. Either way, I don't judge you. I get it. I don't want to be judged for my shit, either."

Dahlia smiled gratefully. It was nice not to feel merely tolerated. It was nice to feel fully seen. And in a strange, unfamiliar way, she had begun to understand that it was actually a strength. It meant she was sensitive, that she could see things. It meant she had compassion, that she cared—it meant she had insights that made her a better person.

He told her about how he'd always wanted to be a writer, how he'd sneak his notebooks to school and write when he was supposed to be learning math. He told her about how he'd worked for his father, for a time, through high school, how he'd gone to college despite his father's disapproval.

"He didn't think it was necessary," Ethan said. "He thought I had everything I needed right here."

He told her he'd felt like a failure when he couldn't match his father's enthusiasm, when he'd told him flatly he would never take over his business. He'd felt the sting of his father's disappointment, the sense that he wasn't making his father proud. When he got his book deal he'd felt he'd achieved a dream, and he'd hoped his father would finally appreciate him, that he would see. But it hadn't been long before he'd realized how little it meant, that it didn't make him special, that it didn't mean he was even any good.

"I don't blame you for feeling hurt," she said. "But I really don't think he was disappointed in you. He probably was trying to protect you. He just didn't know how."

"I barely sold any books," he said. "I was always afraid to tell him."

Dahlia understood how hard it was for authors and that talent often had nothing to do with sales.

"I've read a lot of books, Ethan," she said. "A lot. Many more than is normal for a person. And I can tell you right now, none of that matters. If you're a writer in your heart, you're a writer. It's a long game. Don't give up your dream."

He told her he felt like he was treading water, like he couldn't see the path forward.

"I can't tell you how many authors take years to make their mark," she said. "If it wasn't this book, it'll be the next one. And if you've touched one person, you've succeeded. You just can't ever know who you've moved."

They talked well into the night, drinking more than their share of wine. They agreed Ethan couldn't drive home. Ethan set himself up in the armchair; Dahlia offered him the bed, but he insisted. As she fell easily asleep with happy memories of the day in her head it occurred to her hazily that she wasn't at all anxious, that his presence made her feel more safe, not less. The next morning they went for breakfast at the diner, and Ethan dropped her back off. He thanked her for her pep talk and left to try to write. She spent the day reading by the window, staring into the sunshine, thinking of her apartment way back home. She'd been gone now for about three weeks, and she felt neither here nor there. She wondered at the ambiguous feelings inside her, the way she felt simultaneously more lost, and more found. She missed her rooms, and her things; yet she didn't want to be there, either. The pot began simmering as she thought about her nieces; she hadn't been getting enough updates. Were they okay? Did they still know she loved them? Was she selfish for taking this time for herself? Had she abandoned her family, just as she'd abandoned her job? Should she return right now, this very instant? Should she have never even come here at all?

She wondered why nothing could ever be easy for her, or happy. She wondered why she couldn't simply have a pleasant evening with a smart new friend, without inevitably returning to her fears and worries and concerns.

SUNDAY MORNING she texted Colin early, before Ethan had a chance to contact her. She felt she was getting sidetracked and that she was running out of time. As much as she enjoyed Ethan's company, and as grateful as she was that his companionship had offered her the chance to explore the area, she couldn't stay here forever. She had to focus; she had to break through the wall with Colin. She was drawn to him with depth that she couldn't fully understand and took it as a sign that her time with him was not yet over. She wanted to set the foundations for him to speak with her father. Her father was counting on her.

She asked him if he would have any time to see her that day and received a pretty quick apology that he would not. She offered to come by or to meet him for coffee, at whatever time was convenient for him, but he never responded. Dahlia was disappointed. When Ethan texted her to meet for a walk she told him she was tired and that she planned to spend the day inside.

Around dinnertime she decided to get out of her room for some fresh air. The quiet of the day had made her feel reclusive, and she didn't want to drive far. She pulled out of the parking lot and drove past Henninger Roofing, past the highway interchange, and past Colin's development, letting her eyes rest on the entrance for a few moments before once again following the road.

She passed a few solitary structures, as well as a small shopping center. Eventually she came across a restaurant called Alpine Grill. On a whim, she slowed and turned into the parking lot, then walked inside, figuring she'd grab dinner while she was out.

It was informal, but still nicer than Moose and Lantern, with neat rows of tables and intimate lighting, a tea light in the center of each. There was a dark wood bar on the right. Before her was a host stand, where a woman was marking up a floor plan.

The woman looked up. "How many in your party?" she asked with a smile.

"Just one, please."

"Certainly. Follow me."

357

The woman picked up a menu and led Dahlia into the dining room. On her way, Dahlia glanced at the bar, and stopped short.

"Colin?"

He looked up sharply at the sound of his name. So did the woman next to him. They were leaning in toward each other, facing each other, each with a drink in front. Dahlia noticed that Colin was dressed up more than usual, in dark-colored slacks and a crisp oxford shirt. The woman was wearing a short blue dress; her long legs were crossed gracefully, and her blond hair was pulled coyly over one shoulder.

"Dahlia," he said. "Hi."

Dahlia stared at him, unable to move. Then she turned on her heels and stormed away, bursting through the door into the night.

Tears were prickling at her eyes, but she wiped them away. She was running to her car, eager to make a quick getaway, when she heard him calling her name.

"Dahlia," he was yelling. "Dahlia!"

She turned to face him. "What are you doing here?"

His brow turned downward. "What do you mean, what am I doing here? I'm about to have dinner."

"Who are you with?"

"Frankly, I'm not sure that's any of your business."

Dahlia gaped at him in shock. She didn't know what to say.

"You told me you were busy today."

"I am."

"Are you on a date?"

"Not that I owe you an explanation, but yes."

The words hit her like a physical blow. This wasn't the Colin she knew, or thought she knew. He seemed so annoyed, so angry. The edge in his voice, the irritation beneath his words...It was as if they hadn't spent all this time together, as if they didn't have this deep, intimate history over thirty complex years.

"Dahlia." He stepped further toward her; his voice had grown softer. "I'm sorry. I hope you didn't have the wrong impression."

"The wrong impression." She turned the words over in her mouth and in her mind. "What would be the wrong impression?"

"Well, that..." He shifted his weight, searching for words. "I mean I hope you didn't have any expectations."

"Expectations." She was struggling to keep up. In an instant, everything had changed; she was trying to reconcile what she thought she had with him, with what it actually was, which was nothing. "I guess I..." She was so confused; her mind was in a whirl. She hadn't intended to have to say all this right here, and so soon. She hadn't had the chance to do everything she'd wanted, to develop the kind of bond with him that she'd hoped.

She didn't know what to say because she didn't even understand her own feelings. She couldn't bring herself to tell him that she'd memorized him, the way the memory of him had been imprinted into her brain thirty years ago; that she thought about him all the time—that she'd noticed the way he carried himself, that it conveyed confidence and strength he otherwise kept quiet; that she'd noticed the turn of his jaw as he considered his words, the way his mouth turned up a little higher in one corner than the other. She couldn't bring herself to tell him that when she thought of him, her chest grew warm, that her stomach overturned at the thought of seeing him and that she wanted him to feel the same consuming awareness of her. Yes, she'd had expectations. And though she hadn't allowed herself to ponder them too closely, she knew they were full of tenderness, and full of some flavor of desire.

He read it all in the flush in her face and the desperation in her eyes.

He said, "I'm not your partner. And I'm not going to be."

Her mouth opened, but no sound came out. The words had knocked the air from her lungs.

"Dahlia," he said again. His face had now grown sad. She felt pathetic and weak, like a child; she felt herself shrinking under that look. "Again, I'm sorry. But I really don't think I gave you any reason to justify that."

It was all so confusing and so overwhelming. It was moving too quickly, and she felt so many steps behind.

"I drove all this way." Her voice was thick with emotion, heat crawling up her neck as sweat prickled beneath her clothes. "I searched for you. That had to mean something."

"Dahlia, I'm not saying it doesn't mean anything, but come on. This all happened pretty fast. And I'm considerably older than you."

"I thought we could have something real," was all she could think of to say. "I thought you could help me, and that I could help you."

"Help me what?" The anger had returned to his eyes, and he stood up straighter. "I don't need any help."

"But you seemed so lonely. I thought I could—"

"Hey. I don't need saving." He was holding his hands up now, like barriers. Then he coughed into his arm a few times, and pulled a tissue from his pocket.

Dahlia frowned. "I know some home remedies for that," she told him, watching as he sniffled. "I'll share them with you. I think you need something."

"No! You don't know what I need. You don't know me, not really. I'm fine. And I'm not lonely. Well, maybe a little," he added, with a flicker in his eyes that quickly disappeared. "But who isn't? I can take care of myself."

"But I can help you," she repeated, her vision blurred by tears. "I can help you, the way you helped me."

"I didn't want any of this!" Dahlia jumped back at the intensity in his voice. "I didn't ask for it. I didn't need it. I didn't want someone coming up here and adding all this emotion to my life. It makes me uncomfortable, Dahlia, I won't lie."

"Then why did you keep seeing me?"

"I felt sorry for you."

The words blew a hole in her chest and left her lighter than air. Her head spun, and her skin prickled. The familiar sting of shame washed around her, enveloping her in its darkness. She wanted to scramble away where no one would ever see her again.

"Hey, kiddo," he said, stepping toward her still. He held out his hand in conciliation, or apology. "Look, I like you. You're a nice kid. I want you to be okay."

Dahlia rubbed her lips together, steeling her jaw against tears. "But..."

She looked at his face. It wasn't unkind, but it was unrelenting. Dahlia sensed she was running out of time. She took a deep breath and said the words.

"He wanted me to find you. And he's dying."

The sun had fully set; he was a dark form against the cold night sky.

"You're not looking for a partner, you're looking for a father. And I'm not your father, either."

The last of her strength evaporated into the dusk, and she deflated, a crumpled cocoon. She supposed she shouldn't be surprised. She was always messing up like this. She was always embarrassing herself. She added nothing, understood nothing. It wasn't his fault; she shouldn't have expected him to want her, or to love her. She didn't even want or love herself.

"Okay," she whispered. "I understand."

"Look, I'm really sorry. I didn't want to have to say it like this."

"No, it's fine. I understand."

"Goddammit." He ran his fingers through his hair. "I knew this was going to happen."

"It's fine. I'll just...I'll just go back."

"You shouldn't drive while you're upset. I'll wait here with you. Just for a couple of minutes."

"No." She couldn't think of anything worse than being in his presence even a second longer. "No, I'm going. You can go back inside." She swallowed. "I'm sorry for ruining your evening."

She turned and fell into her car in a daze. She flipped on her headlights and drove past him as he stepped aside, and made her way back to the motel, where she climbed directly into bed and lay in the dark, recalling every humiliating mistake she'd ever made, and wondering why she couldn't just be good.

THAT NIGHT DAHLIA dreamed that she was standing on the peak of a mountain, the world stretching indefinitely below her, but instead of clouds she saw shifting water, and the mountaintops around her rose and fell like the waves of an ocean.

She saw her father on the shore, standing firm on dry land; she called out to him, but his face shifted, and it was Colin's, and then he was gone. He kept appearing and reappearing on the distant shore, but he never spoke; she was treading water, but she was exhausted, and as she felt herself sinking she was losing the energy to fight.

Then she saw her own reflection in the water, but it was distorted and unrecognizable, blurred and broken by the rippling surface. She tried to steady herself, so she could see her own face clearly—but whether she fought the current or not, the tide kept pulling her under, and she fell into the depths.

She screamed, but no one saved her. They couldn't even see her anymore. And then she was swallowed whole, sinking into a silence so deep it felt endless, and eternal.

SHE WOKE up gasping for air and confused about where she was. When her eyes cleared and her room became familiar in the weak lights of the parking lot sneaking from behind the curtains she sank back in her bed, exhausted and unsettled. She lay for some time in the darkness with that familiar breathless feeling, resisting the urge to consume the air in desperate gasps and listening to her heartbeat settle and slow.

She was on the verge of something, but she didn't know what it was. Whatever it was, it was just over the horizon, lurking around the corner and waiting for her to arrive. It didn't feel like an answer, and it didn't feel like peace. It felt like a total, complete breakdown, of her mind, of her world, of herself.

CHAPTER TWENTY

than texted her a couple of times Monday, to see how she was feeling and to ask if she wanted to meet up. The first time, she responded with gratitude, telling him she was tired and would stay in for the day. The second time, she ignored him. She couldn't even deal with herself today; she definitely couldn't deal with someone else, especially when that someone else was Colin's son.

She ignored him again on Tuesday when he wanted to know if she was okay, and if he'd done anything to offend her. She spent the day lying in bed, staring at nothing, watching the sun rise and set through her window.

On the third day when her phone buzzed she looked at it with hesitation, and sat up in bed when she saw that it was Colin.

Hey kiddo. Just want to make sure you're okay.

It had taken him three days to check on her, and something about the wording told her he didn't want to have a conversation. He was telling her something, not asking; he was fulfilling an obligation, without venturing too close.

I'm fine, she texted back. *Thanks.*

She put her phone down and thought about it, then picked it up again.

Really. Don't worry about me. But thank you.

She put her phone back down, and closed her eyes, falling into a restless midday sleep.

~

SHE WOKE UP LATE AFTERNOON, and checked her phone. She had a text from Ethan.

Hey, I'm not gonna keep bothering you. I just hope you're okay. If you want to have another adventure (or just hang out) I'm here.

Dahlia's stomach was in knots, as she sensed a difficult conversation was coming. Now that Colin had made his feelings clear she really had no reason to stay any longer. She and Ethan had begun to develop a real friendship, one she valued, and one she'd miss. She knew her company had become valuable to him, too. She didn't want to hurt him, but knew it had to be done. She texted him back that she'd see him, while her motivation was somewhat alive.

He responded right away.

Great! I'd been thinking we could go to Hollow Lake, the one Hanford site we hadn't hit. But it's too late today. Do you want to just come over?

She told him that was fine, and he gave her his address. It would take her about twenty minutes to get there. He said he'd order some food.

Dahlia showered and dressed and started on her way. Ethan lived in Porter's Landing, which was farther south. She drove three exits down the highway and turned off, following the curve onto a smaller local road not unlike the one with her motel. She drove straight for a time, and made a series of turns. She eventually found herself in a residential neighborhood with humble craftsmen houses, and she slowed for pedestrians as she searched for Ethan's address.

It was a simple two story, painted green. Like most of the houses on the street, it was clearly old, but homely and charming. It was in need of a paint job. It had a small front porch, its concrete dull and cracked. It was well maintained, but modest, with low-maintenance landscaping and a cleanly cut yard.

Dahlia parked on the street and glided up the walkway. Either he'd been waiting for her or he'd heard her car door close; either way, he opened the door before she reached it, his face bright and sparkling with kindness. He was wearing his usual jeans and t-shirt, and his wide blond curls gleamed against the dimness inside. He fit perfectly among the scenery, casual and unfettered. Dahlia relaxed somewhat, despite her nervousness.

"Hey," he greeted her, holding the door for her to pass through. "So nice that you came."

"Thanks for inviting me." Dahlia looked around as he closed the door. She was standing in his living room; a small dining room was beyond. The floor was wide hardwood planks, the furniture comfortable and clean and generally in solid-colored fabrics. It was mostly tidy, but there were signs: stacks of papers stuffed into corners, shoes stuck under benches. It was overflowing with books, which filled every space of the built-in bookshelves and were piled on end tables and mantels and in corners of the floor. It had the hectic but comfortable look of a writer, of someone with a frantic, creative mind. It so perfectly suited him. Dahlia couldn't help but smile at the sight of it.

"So what's going on? How have you been?" He was walking toward the dining room, and she followed him. "Can I get you a drink? Wine?"

"Wine would be great," she said. "Thank you." She glanced at the table. It was covered with containers of food. "Wow."

"I know," he said, with a little chuckle, as he poured two glasses of wine. "I went a little overboard. I didn't know what you wanted."

"It smells delicious. Is it Italian?"

"Good guess." He handed her a glass of wine, and smiled. "Cheers."

She smiled back, and sipped, wary of meeting his gaze.

"Well, have a seat," he said, gesturing toward the table. "I would have cooked, but I didn't have time to go shopping."

"No, this is wonderful. Thank you."

Ethan removed the tops from the food and placed some spoons on the table. Dahlia surveyed the spread. She grinned at him wryly.

"Did you order everything on the menu?"

"Pretty much," he said with a little laugh.

"You must have spent a fortune. I'll give you some cash."

"No, no, no. It's on me. But thanks."

As they dug in Dahlia noticed that a few candles were lit in discreet places around the room. The room itself was dimly lit, and the contrast created a soft, intimate feel as the sun finished setting outside the window beyond.

"Do you like to cook?" he asked her, twirling his fork around some pasta.

"I do," she said, sipping her wine. "But it's different, cooking for just one person."

"I hear you."

He subtly drove the conversation, asking her this question and that, picking up on details she'd previously shared and making attempts to expand on deeper levels of his knowledge of her. Dahlia tried to reciprocate. She answered his questions, and asked several of her own, but her mood was dark. She hadn't emerged from the fog of the previous night.

And she knew at some point she was going to have to break some news to Ethan: she was leaving New Hampshire that weekend.

"Hey," he said as they were finishing, laying his napkin on the table and leaning back in his chair. "There's a good ice cream place right down the street. We could walk there. What do you say?"

She opened her mouth to decline, and looked at his face. He'd seemed in a particularly upbeat mood today. As he waited for her answer, his blond eyebrows were raised in expectation, and his lips were upturned pleasantly. That mess of wide blond curls gave him an innocent, boyish look. He really was a nice person, and he'd been such a good friend. After today she'd probably never see him again. She couldn't bring herself to say no.

"Sure," she said, making herself smile. "That sounds great."

She helped him clean up, the two squeezing past each other in Ethan's outdated but cozy kitchen. They tossed the trash out and washed the dishes, and put on their jackets. Ethan grabbed his keys and wallet, and they walked together out the door.

It was nice, walking with him like this, side by side, talking so casually and so easily. She couldn't remember the last time she'd had so many long, easy conversations. They actually had a lot in common, she thought, as he related a story from his college days. They both loved books; they both were introverts. And they both faced inner demons that they didn't quite understand. Somehow, knowing that about each other seemed to make them each less lonely. Dahlia frowned, her hands in her pockets as she walked. She supposed this is what friendship was supposed to be like. She realized it was new to her, that it was something she'd been missing, without even realizing she could have it. It just figured that she'd finally find a friend, and he'd live so far away.

Dahlia insisted on paying for the ice cream, and he reluctantly relented. They walked in the dark, licking their ice cream, and back up the walkway of Ethan's house. In the indigo blanket of night, the house looked almost unbearably charming, so small and safe, with lamps shining out from the windows. Inside, Dahlia saw how truly pleasant it was. The night had made the light inside warm and yellow, and she noticed blankets slung over armchairs, picture frames on shelves. It was snug and agreeable; it was not unlike her own apartment.

"Would you like another glass of wine?" he asked, and his voice was somehow different. He was looking at her with those big wide eyes; but the look in them had changed into something deeper, something more hesitant. He picked up the bottle and raised his eyebrows at her, as if in hopeful invitation. "I know you have to drive home. But you're welcome to stay for a bit, if you want."

"Actually, Ethan," she said, clearing her throat; she had sensed it was time, that before she dove in further she should pull back, for easier escape. "I wanted to let you know something. And I feel kind of sorry saying it."

His face changed again, his brow and lips falling, and he lowered the hand holding the wine. "Oh." He blinked. "What is it?"

"It's just that..." She sighed and firmed herself, rubbing her lips together. "I'm getting ready to leave. To go back home, I mean. To Philadelphia."

He stood watching her in silence; his face had grown steadily more serious. He opened his mouth to say something, and closed it. He placed the wine bottle slowly back on the table and looked at her, his hands in his pockets.

"Oh," he said. "Wow." He appeared to be preparing to say something, but he didn't say it. "It's just...really soon."

"I've been here almost a month." She looked away from him; she couldn't bear the sad look in his eyes. "I have a job, you know? I've been pushing it off and disappointing my boss and abandoning my responsibilities to my family." She shrugged. "Your dad doesn't want me here anyway. It's time for me to go."

"My dad?" The divot between his eyebrows creased. "What does my dad have to do with anything?"

"Well, I mean, I came up here to meet him. That's why I'm here." He couldn't possibly not know this. Despite herself, she grew a little impatient with his lack of understanding. She swallowed and shifted her weight. "I met him, which I guess is all I needed to do."

"I guess." His voice was quiet, and a little airy as he considered. As Dahlia watched him, his face underwent a series of quick and frantic transformations; she felt she could see his mind working, could sense him moving from thought to thought as he processed what she had said. "It's just that..." He was studying her with a furrowed brow and parted lips, as if the words were just inside, and he was urging them forward. "It's that...I'll be honest, Dahlia, I really don't want you to go."

"I know." She looked at him now, her eyes tender with sadness. "I'm so sorry. Really. You've been such a good friend to me, I hate to say goodbye."

A subtle shift in his jaw made his expression more intense.

"I was hoping..." His voice was hoarse, and deeper. "I was hoping maybe...more than a friend."

Dahlia stared at him in silence. Her stomach squeezed and pulled itself into knots. She didn't know how she hadn't seen it. But looking at him now, it seemed so obvious, and she was even more ashamed.

"Ethan, I'm sorry," she said, and the mournfulness in his eyes ripped her up inside. "It just wasn't like that. I've had such a nice time with you, really. You should know that. I can't tell you how much I appreciate the way you've shown me around, and the conversations we've had. You're...you're one of the best people I know."

They looked at each other across space, trying to pick up on signals, to read the unsaid.

"I guess I'm just not interested...in that...with you."

His brow twitched, and his eyes sharpened and narrowed. He seemed to have heard something in her words, something she hadn't intended but hadn't disguised as completely as she'd hoped.

"With *me*," he repeated, and hesitated. His face broke into a grim sort of smile, as if he was making a joke, but one even he didn't think was funny. "I know this is crazy." He held up his hand, almost in apology. His face scrunched a little in confusion. "You don't mean..." He laughed awkwardly. "I mean, you couldn't possibly mean..."

Dahlia's breath was coming quickly, her heart racing in her chest. He closed his eyes for a moment, seeming to gather his strength.

"It's really none of my business," he said then. "But I'm sorry, I have to ask. You don't have feelings for...someone else, do you?"

Dahlia was silent. She knew what he was really asking. She shifted where she stood, looking anywhere but at him.

When she finally looked at him, his eyes were wide with horror. "Are you telling me that...that you have feelings for *my father?*"

Dahlia wasn't ready to get into this with Ethan. She recognized that her affection for Colin was complicated and strange, and had managed to go on by convincing herself the *why* didn't matter. It was something she would come to understand; it was something they could figure out together. She didn't want to face Ethan's dejection, or his anger. She'd just been in the line of fire of Colin's, and it had been more than enough.

She straightened in an attempt to reflect the confidence she did not feel. "I'm not comfortable talking about what's going on between Colin and me."

"What *is* going on? Is something going on?"

"No, nothing's going on." The words were bitter on her tongue, and she was angry with Ethan for making her say them. She shrugged pitifully. "I guess I've just..." How could she explain it to him when she couldn't even define it herself? The longer this lasted, the more she hurt him and the deeper into the hole she fell; the nuance of her emotion was so complex, and suddenly it felt so much easier to surrender to simplicity. "Yes," she told him, her voice shaking as she realized the words' truth. "Yes, I've developed feelings for him."

He blinked a couple of times, staring in disbelief.

"For my dad. For *my dad*."

Dahlia bit her lip and shifted her weight. He stood there watching her, his hands at his sides, as if he were seeing her for the first time, and not liking what he was seeing.

"I'm sorry," he said then, lifting his hands in agreement, or defense. "You're right, you don't have to explain it. You don't owe me anything, you don't."

The air between them was tense. He was holding back, but Dahlia could see the distress in his face. She knew him well enough by now, and besides, it wasn't a face that easily hid emotion.

"You haven't done anything wrong," she said, for lack of anything else to say. She was feeling backed into a corner and unable to think clearly; she wanted to get out of there, to get out of the line of his disappointment and regret. "It's not you, Ethan. I promise."

"You aren't required to like me. I don't have any right to an opinion."

He was reminding her of herself. She always blamed herself, was always apologizing for any discomfort anybody felt.

"Okay." He tapped his fingers absently on the table. "Well..."

She gazed at him sadly. "I'm sorry."

"No, it's okay. Thank you. Thank you for your honesty."

A single tear escaped the corner of her eye, and she wiped it hastily with her finger. If she didn't get out of here, they would sneak up on her, and he'd comfort her, and she'd be stuck.

"You shouldn't be thanking me," she whispered. "All of this is my fault."

"No." He shook his head in protest, and the kindness returned to his face. "I always do this. I go all in with the wrong women. It's kind of my thing." He attempted to smile, but it was short-lived and lined with pain. "I mean I'm not trying to feel sorry for myself," he added quickly. "I'm just saying. Don't worry about it."

There were other things to say, and she didn't want to leave with his contriteness in the air. But her mind was awhirl; she needed time to think. She nodded once, and smiled.

"Okay," she said, and sighed; she considered moving in for a hug, but decided against it. The pain she was causing him made him frightening, even more so in his gentleness. "Thanks again, Ethan. I've had a really nice time with you."

She waved, and stood there, waiting; he waved back, and returned her smile. Then she turned and walked away, out of the house and back down to her car, then drove swiftly off with her eyes wide open, hardly believing the woman making all these messes was her.

DAHLIA COULDN'T FALL ASLEEP that night. She was wondering how it was possible that she'd been so dearly wrong about everything. She spent so much of her life second guessing herself, always worrying about whether she was making the right decision. As it turned out, her worry had been valid. At least when she was passive she had the illusion that she was capable. Having proven herself right was worse than anything she could think of.

She glanced at the clock. It was about two o'clock in the morning. An urge rippled through her, and before she had time to think about it she threw on a jacket and picked up her purse and keys, and went outside to her car.

The stillness was unlike any she'd experienced, and she soaked it into her pores, absorbing its calm and its silence. It was a different world, and alien, one of new sounds and dark corners, one where nocturnal creatures slinked freely in the shadows. The darkness was a presence, and a weight; it seemed to follow her out of the parking lot and down the street, and onto the highway as she raced toward the mountains.

There were no familiar landmarks in such darkness. The road signs she knew were coming, the twists and turns of the road she'd grown to expect, came quickly and without warning, and in the harsh glare of her headlights they appeared stark and sinister, seeming to watch unblinkingly her escape into the woods. The mountains were black-cloaked monsters in the distance, staunch and unmoving, but teeming with mysterious life.

She passed the sign for the Cauldron, and for the Castle and the Stag, and finally for the bridge with the overlook. She veered off the highway and continued on the narrow road to the cliffside, and parked her car in the abandoned parking lot, a single street-lamp casting a pool of vacant light that seemed to present the emptiness to Dahlia personally. She climbed out of the car and shut the door, the sound cutting into the night's silence with startling force that reverberated through the trees. As she walked to the overpass she registered the blackness of the trailheads, gaping holes in the forest with unknown frights waiting just inside. In the daytime, the trailheads offered possibility, scenes surrounded by life and by adventure. In the thick obscurity of night they were entrances into a nightmare, where a single misstep or mishap could leave you lost, pulled deeper inside.

She stepped onto the bridge and kept walking until she was halfway across. She couldn't make out the view; in the darkness it was nothing more than an empty abyss. Her hands on the railing stood between her and the nothingness, and she gripped tighter, her eyes struggling to distinguish something, anything, in the desolation beyond.

She listened for a noise, any noise. But the air was as empty as the darkness. She walked back to her car in a daze, uncertain, for a moment, that she had ever woken up at all. The nightmare was indistinguishable from reality, and a familiar quickening tightened in her chest, making her breath come in shallow, desperate starts.

She drove out of the parking lot and back over the narrow road, and headed in the opposite direction toward the motel.

But the sign for Hollow Lake appeared suddenly in her head-lights, and without thinking she swerved off the highway onto the exit. She hadn't been here before; she and Ethan hadn't made it here yet. At the thought of Ethan she thought of Colin, and the black wave of shame washed over her again. She drove too quickly around the curve in the road, finally arriving at a wide parking lot about fifty feet from the shoreline of the lake.

She parked her car and walked toward the shore. There were several overhead lamps here, and she had a clearer vision of where she was going. To her left was a small bathhouse; to her right was the deep of the forest. Straight in front of her was Hollow Lake, and she stepped right up to the water line, until she felt the lake slip gently under her boots.

She inhaled the damp air. It smelled slightly different here than it did in the forest, something more physical, more complex. The lake was still now, with slight undulations that whispered as it lapped onto the sand. She could feel the iciness through the bottom of her shoes. She bent at the waist and touched the water with her fingers, then dug her fingertips into the sediment below. She rose, wiping the sand onto her jacket. The lake was straddled by two mountains. One of them, she knew, was Mount Lyre, the mountain she'd visited with Ethan. They rose on either side of her, protecting her, closing her in. They were impassable as ever in the darkness, guardians of the lake and of the forests that enveloped them.

She stared out into the lake. She'd taken a risk and left every-thing behind. She'd done so many things she thought she couldn't. But she hadn't found what she'd been looking for. For a while she'd convinced herself that taking action meant she was making progress. It had seemed she was becoming someone new, someone free. But real freedom required reckoning with the depth of her own darkness—the darkness that haunted her no matter how high up the mountain she climbed.

For so long, she had measured her value through other people. Her self-worth was dependent on validation from outside. She guessed she'd hoped that by earning Colin's approval, she'd prove she'd deserved to be saved—that coming up here would redeem her. She'd needed to justify what she'd been given, and she couldn't believe it unless he believed in it first. No matter how many mountains she climbed, it wouldn't be enough until she was secure in herself, without needing the reinforcing echo from a distance.

She berated herself for her weakness. How sad, how pathetic, to need so badly to be seen. She felt this in herself, and hated it, and she was just so, so very tired. Gita had told her that she had so much more resolve. She was aware now, finally, of how true that really was. She was treating the symptom and not the problem. And the problem was an insurmountable mountain of itself.

She'd started all of this for her father—for the promise she'd made, and the guilt she never seemed able to shed. And she'd done it; she'd kept her word. But that didn't erase the hurt she'd caused along the way. Each step forward seemed to leave something damaged in its wake. She made so many wrong calls. She couldn't be trusted not to break what she touched.

These tumbling discoveries seemed to destroy her. They left her feeling raw, foolish, and exposed, like a lost, drowning child. But there was no one to save her, this time—and she was clearly incapable of saving herself.

Dahlia kicked off her boots and stepped into the water in her clothes. It crept around her shins like a voice inviting her further, and she kept going, undaunted, until it had reached the bottom of her thighs. It was licking the hem of her jacket; it was threatening to overtake her waist. Still she kept on going, past all reason, as if she were daring the water to take her this time.

She wanted to feel its pull, and to see what she would do in response.

She lowered her hands and let her fingers become submerged. It was so different from ocean water, so clear and pure and cold. It would feel so good to lose herself in this water, to let it trickle through her hair and slide like silk over her face. The delicateness of its sound was like a song, an ethereal lullaby sung by Sirens over the wind. How peaceful it was here, how tempting was the darkness. There was no shame here, no embarrassment, nothing but the mountains and the trees and the cold. She was a mere speck of life, a spark of nothing, a piece of everything. All her little mistakes were insignificant here, invisible. She closed her eyes and stepped farther, letting the water pull her into its embrace.

Her foot hovered over a drop in the bottom; she stepped backward, awakening from her haze. Her heart was in her gut, her gut on the floor. Fear had jumped into her throat. She pushed herself back toward the shoreline and onto dry land, terrified and shivering in the night.

She ran back to her car, dripping as she went. She wrung out her clothes and fell inside, and peeled out of the parking lot as if pursued by unseen ghosts. Back at the motel she stripped to her underwear and clamored into bed, throwing her wet clothes on the floor. In the morning she thought it was a dream, and lay there, heart pounding with relief, until she spotted her clothes on the floor, still soaking, and her boots, which were covered with sand.

DAHLIA SLEPT through much of Thursday, or lay curled up in her bed, blankets tight, looking at blackness through closed eyelids. It was an appropriate reflection of how she felt, which was nowhere and nothing, someone lost adrift in a world she couldn't see and couldn't understand. She didn't belong here, but she had burned so many bridges back home. Nobody she cared about would think the same of her when she returned; she had disappointed them, even more so than before, and besides, she was different now, and she didn't even know who she was.

On Friday she awoke to the sound of rain hammering on the pavement outside. She managed to pull herself out of bed and sat for a moment, dizzy. Slowly she stood and went to the window, where she pulled aside the curtain and stared at the storm. It was peaceful and quiet, despite the deluge. She turned back to look at her room, the unmade bed, the food containers she had yet to throw away. It was the state of her mind yesterday, but not today. With a strange sense of purpose, she spent a few quick minutes dressing, then put on her jacket and walked outside to her car.

She drove up the highway toward the mountains, making a detour in Woodrow, on a whim, to treat herself to rain boots and a proper waterproof jacket. She walked around one of the tourist shops picking out her things, and she could almost pretend she was one of them, a normal person on a normal vacation, with normal relationships and a normal life back home.

After, she drove to the entrance to the Castle and took the tram up the mountain by herself. The rain had lightened, but it had deterred other visitors, and she was utterly alone as the station grew smaller beneath her, as the majesty of the mountaintops swallowed her in.

At the top, she made her way through the trees and along the ledge, noting once again the miniature foliage, the stunted growth. She went at a steady pace and was breathless by the time she reached the tower, but kept going, stopping only when she had reached the height and was staring at the rainclouds that lay like angels' blankets over the peaks.

She leaned against the railing and watched the clouds glide by. Up here, with miles of heaven around her, everything seemed so simple, and so clear. The thoughts that had hidden in darkness seeped from their hiding spots, and drifted through her mind like the clouds all around her. She allowed them to be free and to show themselves to her, and a picture emerged, strands of truth arranged in a line.

You just need, Gita had told her, *to grow confident enough so your own, true voice shines through.*

Dahlia stood watching the scene before her and inside her, until the clouds parted with the wind. The sun shone brighter, and the mist dissolved, and in the warmth of light Dahlia retraced her steps along the path and down the mountain, back the way she'd come.

ON SATURDAY DAHLIA cleaned up her room. She packed her clothes and arranged her bags, and sat in the armchair reading, working up the nerve to put one last piece in place.

Finally that evening she texted Colin.

Hi Colin. I'm so sorry for what happened. I'm leaving this weekend and was hoping you might be willing to meet with me one last time.

She put her phone down and picked up her book, resigned to accepting whatever he said in reply.

He responded a few minutes later.

Hey Dahlia, why don't you come over tomorrow. I'll be here all day. Just let me know.

Dahlia thanked him and said she'd be over around noon. Then she took a piece of paper and pen from the desk and sat writing and thinking, buoyed by having a clear path forward.

Sunday morning she showered and dressed and waited until shortly before noon, then, a few pages of paper in her purse, she drove the short distance to Colin's. It was a bright, cheerfully warm day. Her heart was hammering in her chest, but she felt lighter with the knowledge that some kind of closure was coming. She didn't want to hurt him anymore; she wanted to clean up her mess. Then she would clean up her mess with her family, and with her job, and do what she could to continue life with the scars.

She rang Colin's doorbell and waited. After a few moments, he appeared, and Dahlia smiled despite her humility and pain.

"Hey, kiddo," he said. He stood back for her to enter. "Come on in."

"Thank you." She took a few tentative steps inside, clinging to her purse and picking at the hem of her shirt. "Thanks so much for letting me come over."

"No problem. Do you want to sit down? Can I get you something?"

"No, thank you, I won't keep you long. I, um." She cleared her throat and, hands shaking, pulled the papers from her purse. "I know this is ridiculous. But I had some things to say and I didn't want to forget."

He didn't say anything, just watched with a straight expression as she smoothed her papers and began.

"It's just notes," she explained, barely recognizing her own voice. "I didn't write a speech or anything."

"That's fine."

She took a deep breath and closed her eyes a moment, then made herself look at him once more.

"First I'd like to apologize," she said. "I had no right to tell you what to do with your time. You barely know me. I barely know you. I'm sorry."

She swallowed; her mouth was dry. She wished she'd let him bring her some water, but she wasn't going to ask him now.

"I came up here to meet you because my father wanted me to. And I've done what I came for. I can give him a name, and a face, and a story."

She could hear her own breathlessness, and was embarrassed to be clearly so nervous and so vulnerable. But it would have to be this way. She was powerless to stop it, and she was fully in it now.

"I don't know what I expected by staying," she said. "Maybe I thought that getting to know you, forming a connection, that it would...fix something in me."

He was watching her silently, the tension visible in his body.

"I thought my feelings for you were romantic." She hadn't intended to tell him this, and she hated herself for doing it—in fact, it was the first time she'd fully acknowledged it even to herself; but as the words turned over in her mouth, a realization was coming to her, and she had to work it through. "But now I don't know. I think I needed something. And I convinced myself it was you."

She couldn't meet his gaze. She folded her papers and replaced them in her purse, and looked at the ground as she spoke.

"I thought this was about him. I mean, it was, at first." Her eyes met his. "But it wasn't."

His stance had relaxed somewhat. He continued waiting, patiently, his brow crinkled a little with attention.

She rubbed her lips together and said the words. "I feel like..." She stopped. She didn't want to burden him with this. With every word she said, she was adding more and more to his discomfort. Her feelings, and her life, were not his responsibility. Why couldn't she even do this, and get it right? Why, even when she tried to fix it, did she make such bad decisions, creating such disaster?

"You feel like what?"

The words were gentle and encouraging. Dahlia mustered her strength, and went on.

"I feel like I'm not supposed to be here. I don't mean *here*. I mean *at all*."

His brow now furrowed, with confusion or concern, she couldn't be totally sure. She kept going.

"It's like I've been spending my whole life making up for it," she said, "like I can never live up to being saved. Like I don't deserve that miracle. Like I've been drowning ever since."

"You don't owe anything just for being alive."

She blinked, surprised. She was silent for a moment, unsure how to respond.

He said, quietly: "That's not a debt you have to repay."

Dahlia continued watching him. Something had revealed itself to her. It peeked out of the back corner of her mind, and she stood still, lest she scare it away.

"I think that..." She rested her fingertips on her temples and closed her eyes. "I think that...that..."

"That what?"

The clouds cleared, and she saw the picture in full. A connection with Colin meant she deserved to be here. She wasn't an accident of fate; she had a right to take up space, to be valued, to be seen.

Her survival had belonged to the man who saved her. Being with him meant she was supposed to survive, that she had some purpose—that fate had led her here.

But it was more than that.

"Dahlia? Kiddo? You okay?"

Dahlia looked at him, eyes wide. Her father was dying; it was something she couldn't control. But this...this was something she could do. It gave her power. She wasn't at the mercy of loss and of fate and of things slipping away. She had agency, she could control it. It meant she wasn't drowning, after all.

"As much as I've tried to deny it..." She inhaled, and closed her eyes. "My father is dying. And I...I don't think...I've fully dealt with it. I think that...maybe I thought that if I found you, if I connected with you...then maybe...then maybe I could put off..."

She couldn't bring herself to say it. She paused for breath, and to calm her racing heartbeat.

He said, "That's a lot to put on someone you barely know."

She hesitated a moment, and opened her eyes. She looked at him then, warily: his expression was soft, and kind.

She swallowed and exhaled. "I know."

Neither said anything for what seemed like minutes.

She said, "You were my savior. You protected me. Just like..."

He frowned and took a step toward her. "Dahlia."

She stared at him with watery eyes. "If I lose you, then..."

He reached out and placed his hand on her shoulder.

A harsh sob escaped her. "I don't know how to lose him."

He embraced her in full, holding her close against his chest. Dahlia wept violently, and loudly, fully submitting to the grief she'd held behind the wall. He stood there straight and firm, his arms around her, his hands pressed tightly to her back. He kissed the top of her head, and shushed her, and rocked her in a soft, swaying rhythm.

Eventually she calmed and took a deep, shaky breath. Her vision was blurred and hazy; his shirt was wet with her tears. She waited a minute to pull back, nestled in the safety and stability of him, the firmness of his support.

"I made another mess," she said, forlornly—and laughed when she saw the mess she'd made on him. She pulled a tissue from her pocket and blew her nose. "Literally and figuratively."

"It's okay." He continued to rub her back. "It happens."

"I guess I was up here for myself, after all. And I made you uncomfortable." A wave of emotion rose up again, and she sniffled. "I'm so selfish."

"Taking care of yourself isn't selfish."

"I feel like anything I do for myself is selfish."

"Well, that's something you need to work on."

They stood there, still embracing, Dahlia's head resting cozily on his chest. She was being lulled by the motion of his rocking. She was suddenly so tired.

"Dahlia."

"Yes?"

"Can I say something?"

She blinked, clearing her vision, and looked at him, then nodded. Finally, they separated. He guided her into a chair.

"Listen," he said, taking the couch beside her. "If you're looking for a father, I don't think it's going to work. I think you have to deal with what you're dealing with. As difficult as that is."

"I know." She blew her nose again and took a slow, calming breath. "And I will. I'm trying." She sighed. "But I'm not really looking for a father. In fact I usually go for the opposite. I tend to be attracted to emotionally unavailable men."

She paused. Neither said anything. They looked at each other in shared understanding—indeed, she'd done it again. They both laughed in unison.

"Seriously, though, Dahlia," he said, leaning forward and folding his hands on his knees. "Whatever it is you're trying to find, it isn't in me. It's in yourself, and no matter how far you drive, you won't find it."

She smiled, and tears sparkled in her eyes. "That's extremely profound."

He chuckled. "Maybe Ethan gets some of his poeticism from me after all."

Dahlia's smile sobered. She took in the sight of him, his salt and pepper hair, the deep lines in his face. "Was she poetic, then?" she asked, with quiet hesitation. "Your wife? Cindy?"

His eyes met hers. Dahlia ached at the intensity of the pain there. For a moment, she regretted asking him this question. But he smiled and relaxed, and took a moment to think, to reminisce.

"You know," he said, rubbing his hands together, and not looking at her, "I don't often talk about her."

"Why not?"

He shrugged. "I don't know. Too painful, I guess."

"That makes sense."

Neither said anything for some time. Dahlia didn't want to be the one to break the silence. It simply wasn't her place to encourage him to talk about Cindy; it wasn't her place to tell him how to grieve.

Then she thought about Ethan, how he'd yearned to hear about his mother. He'd helped her so much. Maybe she could help him, too.

"You don't have to talk about her," she said, her voice quiet with hesitation. "But if you ever wanted to...I'd listen."

Colin looked at her, studying her face carefully. A sea of unsaid words moved between them. Now that he'd witnessed her break-down, they were bonded further in grief. The tears she'd shed, the shattering of her denial, represented the same emotions that had been unseen inside him for almost thirty years. It was a long time to carry something alone. Dahlia's eyes were still red and glassy, her face still stained from crying. She hoped that after seeing her face her own grief, and survive it, that he'd see he didn't have to be alone in his own grief anymore. He'd been afraid of what would happen if he let it into daylight. But maybe he'd seen the cost of silence, that it doesn't help you move forward but rather freezes you in place instead.

He worked his jaw, still watching her. Eventually he made a decision.

"She was a storyteller, for sure," he said, his voice shaking a little, and Dahlia beamed. "She wasn't a writer. But she had a wild imagination. That's why I loved taking her with me on those hikes. It's why I loved her, period."

Dahlia's heart was encased in warmth; she said nothing for a moment, absorbing the heaviness of feeling. "I hope I can find a love that great one day."

He looked at her and smiled. "You will, kiddo. You will."

They talked a while longer about Cindy. Dahlia asked him many questions—what were her hobbies, what was her laugh like, what kind of mother was she.

"Oh, she was the best mother," Colin said, more animated than Dahlia had ever heard him. "She loved that little boy so much. The way she comforted him, held him, sang to him. The stories she made up for him on the spot. It was a sight to see." He stopped a moment, nodded, and wiped the corner of his eye. "Ah. Well. It is what it is."

Over the course of the conversation Dahlia was able to form a clearer picture of this little family, full of love, until they were touched by unspeakable tragedy. It was what she had wanted from the beginning, but somehow, it didn't matter as much now. She was only glad she could be that receptacle for him—it made her feel like she was helping him, a small drop in the ocean of the ways that he'd helped her.

"I hope I'm not overstepping," she said, though she'd grown comfortable by now and sensed that he would not mind what she was about to say. "But I think it's nice that Ethan inherited his mom's creativity. And the fact that he's a writer, it's like he's found a way to channel it."

"Maybe." Colin was leaning forward, his elbows on his knees. He rubbed his hands together in the way he tended to do while he was thinking. "You know, Dahlia...it isn't that I don't want him to be a writer. Look, we are who we are, right? I just always wanted him to have something solid. I didn't want him to struggle. I've got this whole business, ready to go. All the work's been done for him. All he'd have to do is pick up where I left off."

"I think maybe that shows how dedicated he is to his craft. The fact that he's still so determined to write despite how hard it is."

"Mmm." Colin wasn't looking at her; he was staring straight ahead with a straight, serious expression. "I never looked at it that way before. I just kind of figured he didn't want the responsibility."

"I know you worry a lot about him," said Dahlia, kindly; now that he'd opened up to her, she could hear the anxiety and love in his voice, and could easily imagine his struggles to raise a child all alone, in the hopes that he was doing a good job. "Can I say something honestly, though? I don't think it's about responsibility. I've spent some time with Ethan now," she said. "And I think he just won't feel right unless he has an outlet for his thoughts. He's a deep thinker. He's so fortunate that he has the talent to express that in a practical way. A lot of us don't." She smiled sadly. "Myself included. I wish I did."

He took a deep breath; he was studying her carefully. Then he smiled. "Cindy was better at this kind of thing. It's times like this when I miss her the most."

"I know. I'm sorry."

He blinked a couple of times. "Thank you, kiddo. I'll think about what you said."

They chatted about little things for some time longer, until they came to another pause.

"So what's next for you?" he asked her finally.

She lifted her gaze to meet his. "I'm not really sure."

A sad smile touched the corners of his eyes. "I don't have the answer."

She knew he didn't, and it wasn't his fault. He wasn't her savior, not really. He wasn't going to solve all her problems. He was human, and flawed, just like everyone else. She'd put a lot on him emotionally, but he couldn't bear that role. It wasn't fair to expect it. He couldn't save her again.

"I guess I'm going to go back," she said, "and see if I can pick up the pieces." A drop in her stomach made her frown. "I left everyone behind to come find myself. I'll have to make a lot of apologies."

"You shouldn't apologize for finding yourself, kiddo."

They chatted a few more minutes, and then Dahlia stood to leave. He walked her outside to her car, and they faced each other, the tension around them almost palpable.

"Well," she said, her heart cloaked in grief. She'd spent so much of the last year thinking about him, wondering who he was; now that she'd found him, his absence would be a raw and gaping hole. "I really appreciate everything. Not just your saving my life." Tears rose again, and she smiled, wiping her eyes with her sleeve. "I mean for seeing me through this. For your patience."

"Nah, it's nothing." He waved her concern away. Then he frowned. "And I'm sorry, by the way," he said, and swallowed. "About the other night. I was a little harsh with you. Harsher than you deserved."

"Nah, it's nothing." She waved as he had done, and smiled. "Emotions were running high."

He returned her smile, his eyes soft with gratitude. "Thank you," he said. "And I'm glad I could help."

The warmth of their connection overwhelmed her. He looked so casual and healthy, so handsome, and so strong; she let her eyes absorb the sight of him, in case she didn't see him again.

"Thank you for meeting with me. It was very kind of you."

"You bet."

She moved in for a hug, and he accepted, just for a moment. He pulled away and cleared his throat, and watched as she pulled open the door.

"He must be a pretty good dad," he said.

Dahlia froze and turned to him. She smiled as she envisioned her father, his bright smile, his artistic gift. "He is."

"I wish I could have been as good a dad."

Dahlia's eyebrows rose, and her heart ached. "You were. You are. I know you are."

He didn't look so sure. He shrugged and stuck his hands in his pockets, and his foot played with something on the ground. "Well. I know I made mistakes. I hope he knows I love him."

"He does." She paused. "What you told me earlier, about Cindy. About her creativity, her stories." Her heart beat a little faster. "I think Ethan might like to know that."

His eyes turned misty and soft. "I'm sure he would."

Dahlia thought about Colin and Ethan, their little family and the sorrow they had endured. She and Colin weren't so different, she supposed. Maybe they were both touched by loss. And maybe they both had some guilt, some questions about how it was possible to go on.

He called her back one more time.

"Speaking of Ethan," he said.

She looked at him again. The corner of his mouth was upturned, and his eyes were narrowed with mischief.

"I think he likes you." He held up his hand in a wave, and winked at her. "Take care of yourself, kiddo."

He took a few steps backward toward the house, and Dahlia climbed into her car. She took one last look at him as she drove off, watching him saunter off into the distance, away from her, as she had thirty years before.

~

SHE WASN'T ready to go back to the motel. Instead of turning right outside his complex, she turned left, taking the back way into Woodrow, as she had on her first day out with Ethan.

She'd been planning on heading to the overlook so she could visit the peace of the mountains. But as she approached the resort, her eyes fell on the cheese shop. She made a quick right into the shopping center and pulled into a spot, and walked eagerly inside.

It was smaller than it appeared on the outside, and it offered much more than just cheese. There was plenty of cheese, yes, in a refrigerated glass display case and in jars containing dips and spreads, but there were myriad other local products—jams and jellies, knitted socks, art prints, walking sticks, pottery. Dahlia walked around slowly, taking it all in, very much enjoying this taste of local artisanry.

There was a shelf in the corner displaying books by local writers. Dahlia scanned the spines, thinking how funny it would be if Ethan's book were there. Her eyebrows shot upward with surprise when it was. She immediately pulled it off the shelf and held it close to her chest. She was buying the book, without question.

She walked around a while longer, then took her book to the register, where she requested two different selections of cheese wrapped in brown paper. On a whim, she also bought a jar of berry jam, a box of chocolates, and a little salad in a plastic container. She paid for her items and left, and headed without hesitation to the motel. She had a rustic lunch and a new book. Suddenly, she was eager for the quiet seclusion of her room.

Inside, she spread her food on the table and sat at the window. She opened the cover of the hardcover, pleased by the soft crack of a never-before-opened book.

By the time night had fallen she'd read every single story; she sat still, her hands on the back cover, staring into the darkness, her mind adrift in the trees. She wondered what it was about some writers—how they managed to create entire universes, just with the power of their words. It wasn't a new world, not exactly; it was the world she knew, filtered through an enlightened voice. The nuance was not in the picture, but in the tone—not in the events, but in the poetry. It was a previously unseen side of a multi-faceted prism; it was a realization, an uncovering. It was devastating, and devastatingly beautiful.

Dahlia parted the curtain and looked at the star-strewn sky. The world was as strewn with different voices, so small from a distance, each shining with its own bright light. Ethan's voice was quiet, his language sparse, but full of meaning; he didn't use a lot of words, but the words he used were deliberate. Each was like a box wrapped in layers and layers of paper; she'd had to pause in her reading, many times, and ponder the many ways to look at an image he'd painted. Words took on two, three, four meanings— thus he was able to evoke countless images, with the barest of paint on the canvas. She wondered if this was purposeful, or if it was something he did unknowingly. She suspected it was an instinct, a gift—and she sat for quite a long time, in awe, and in admiration for this touch from the divine.

She shed a tear, and on wiping it from her hand she saw her father's green glass bowl. She brushed it with her fingers. How much detail he imparted to his art, a slight bow here, a subtle rise there. Soft streaks of white cut the emerald, like the last breaths of a cloud before dissipating into the sky. You could look at it many times, hold it a variety of directions—it contained layers and secrets and complexities, and you'd never see the same vision twice.

She felt that she was seeing Ethan in a way she'd never seen him before. His words had given her insight into his insecurities and vulnerabilities, his motivations and the things that made him smile. His turns of phrase, the cadence of his lines—they revealed to her the cadence of the person himself, and it was pure, true, and lovely.

She sat for some time, these thoughts swirling vacantly in her mind. At some point, she slept, but she awoke without feeling rested. The night had blended into day the way words blended into sentences, the way white blended into green.

CHAPTER TWENTY-ONE

*H*ollow Lake looked different during the day. In the middle of the night, it had been a black, endless vortex. In the sunlight, under a periwinkle sky, it was benign and inviting, peacefully nestled in a lush green valley, and singing with life.

Dahlia had texted Ethan that morning. She had been vague; in fact, she'd barely said anything at all. She'd sat for the better part of a half hour figuring out how to address what had happened between them, and ultimately had decided to pretend nothing had. She still wasn't sure what it was she wanted to tell him. She still wasn't sure what it was she actually felt.

If he'd been confused or annoyed by her sudden and ambiguous contact, he didn't say so, and he seemed content to go along with her desire to disregard the past. He'd taken her suggestion they visit the lake completely in stride, and had picked her up as normal. They'd chatted with the windows down just as they always had.

Dahlia didn't tell him she'd come here by herself. It was the one thing he hadn't had a chance to show her, and she wanted to let him have it, too. Also, that night had contained demons and shadows that she preferred to deal with on her own.

He had a blanket and some towels, and she'd packed a little basket for lunch. She met him on the driver's side, and they walked toward the shore together, squinting against the sun and against the sparkling of the sand.

"Swim first or eat first?" he asked as they chose a spot along the far side.

She helped him spread the blanket on the ground; it billowed in the wind. "Let's eat first. It'll give us strength to face the coldness of the water."

He helped her unpack the basket, which contained a couple of sandwiches she'd bought that morning, as well as the remainder of the cheese, chocolate, and jam.

"What a feast," he noted, accepting a sandwich she held out for him. "Where did all this come from?"

"I picked up the sandwiches from the diner this morning," she said. She paused. "And the rest I got in Woodrow."

He nodded with interest as he chewed a bite of sandwich. "The cheese shop?"

"That's right."

They ate in silence for a moment or two.

"I also bought your book," she said then, eyeing him carefully. "They had it on a shelf of local authors."

"I knew they had it." He took another bite, slowly; he was looking out onto the lake. Dahlia had the sense he was deliberately avoiding her gaze. His words had been quiet, like he was trying not to ask her any questions.

She grinned. "Yes, I read it."

He swallowed and turned his head to face her. He blinked and smiled politely.

"Oh," he said, taking another bite. He shrugged. "Wow. That's cool."

She waited for him to ask, but she could see he wouldn't, and she didn't want to torture him.

"I finished it all in one sitting."

He took a moment to register what she'd said. His expression remained unchanged, but color had flooded his face. He was trying not to smile, but she could see in his eyes that he was pleased. They were wide and round, as always, but there was a hopeful sparkle in the corners.

She leaned forward and placed her hand over his. "It was incredible, Ethan. I loved it."

His chest rose and fell, and slowly, the corners of his lips lifted upward. He looked so boyish and hopeful, she couldn't help but laugh.

"Really?" He was beginning to believe it. "You're not just saying that?"

"No, I don't lie, especially not about books."

"Wow. I'm so glad. Can I...can I ask you a couple of questions?"

A couple of questions turned into an hour of conversation as she told him which stories were her favorites, what she liked about them, what she took as lessons and how she thought they all connected. The stories were seemingly unrelated, but Dahlia had noticed common threads; she'd found them subtly brilliant, and told him so. The stories were about people and their various relationships with nature, but it was more than that. It was about how people were lost and became found, how they were found and became lost. It was about people who never discovered whether they were lost or found at all. Dahlia loved the metaphors, the way they revealed how people were fundamentally flawed, but beautiful. It made her feel like being in the process was okay. She related to these lessons, and told him she did, though she didn't describe to him quite how much.

"I'm sorry, I feel so ridiculous," he said, after he'd asked another followup question. "You're probably sick of talking about this."

"I'm not, I'm really not." Dahlia shook her head vehemently. "It's my favorite thing to do. It's so rare to have this kind of discussion with someone who loves the same books I do. And you wrote it! It's like a special treat, to get the author's insights."

"Well I can tell you, it's rare for me, too. I mean nobody's even read my book, so I never get to talk about it. It's like I've got all these ideas, all these characters, like they're stuck in a box in my mind. You opened the box. I guess now you're paying the price."

"No, I love it," she said, meaning it. "I love hearing what you have to say."

"You're very patient. Once I get started, it's hard for me to stop."

The air was warm between them, and it seeped into Dahlia's heart. The mood was so light, and so happy. They took a few moments to catch their breath and collect their thoughts.

"Honestly, Ethan," she said. "Your book moved me. I thought about it all night. You're a truly gifted writer." She hesitated, then said, "I wish you believed in yourself more."

He faced her, looking at her very seriously. Then he sighed and turned away.

"Yeah." He was gazing out onto the lake again, playing absent-mindedly with the sand beneath his fingers. "I wish I did, too. But I don't know. It's hard to stay motivated when nothing seems to happen."

"But you can make it happen by putting out another book."

"I guess I'm worried it'll fail, too."

Dahlia sat with this for some time. Somehow his words had disrupted something in her, something she felt deeply.

"I can't tell you not to worry about that. I understand," she said. "But your book isn't a failure. It's beautiful."

They watched the water for a moment or two.

"I don't trust myself to pull it off," he said.

"I understand that, too." She watched him as she spoke. He was listening carefully, she could tell; his brows were lowered with thought. "But I think, maybe, we're our own worst critics. I know you said you don't like for people to see your drafts, and I get it. But if you ever change your mind, you could show me. I wouldn't judge you, not at all. I know it's just a draft. And I know you're good."

He didn't say anything at first. Dahlia thought she sensed his eyes soften, but she was looking at him in profile and couldn't be totally sure.

"I know," he said at last. "I appreciate it. I know you'd be a safe place to land." His chest rose and fell with a breath. "It's just such a damn mess."

"I'll bet it's not as bad as you think."

"I don't want you to think less of me."

"I wouldn't think less of you. I promise."

They sat for a moment in silence, the air tense with unsaid words.

"Well, I'll order *Nowhere* for the store," she said then. "It's the least I can do. I'm good at that stuff. If you want, I'll help you market."

"That's really nice of you. And I'll take the help. Thanks."

He'd been leaning back on his elbows, his legs straight out in front. He sighed again and straightened, now crisscrossing his legs and leaning forward on his knees.

"What do you say?" he asked, turning to her with a sly smile. "Ready to face the cold?"

They rose and stripped to their bathing suits. Dahlia couldn't believe they were doing this. It was only March, and they were in New Hampshire. The mountain breeze was already cool on their skin. She'd ventured into the water that night, but not fully, and she'd been in a thought-heavy daze. In the light of day she knew it would hit her harder. But another part of her was excited about doing something a little adventurous, a little subversive.

They began wading into the water. Ethan shivered and cried out.

"Oof!" he said, rubbing his arms. "Holy crap. If this is revenge for the zip line, I'm not into it."

Dahlia laughed. "Maybe subconsciously."

She kept walking into the water, and he followed, yelping occasionally the more they were submerged. Dahlia kept on laughing. The breeze picked up and whipped around their faces. The lake itself responded, the waves lapping around them in crisp white peaks.

"What the actual hell," he said as a gust of wind blew them back. His wide blond curls were tousled in all directions. It looked like spun gold against the backdrop of the mountains. "It wasn't like this five minutes ago."

"We must have angered the lake gods."

"Oh, yeah?" One corner of his mouth ticked upward. "To hell with the lake gods."

With that, he dove fully in, emerging twenty feet ahead with his hair stuck to his face and neck. Dahlia clapped and cheered. He waved at her with both arms, calling her over.

"Come on," he said, his hands at his mouth. "You can't let the lake gods win."

She braced herself and sat abruptly, soaking herself. Then she swam in his direction, stopping beside him and floating with her arms out at her sides.

She was immersed fully in the water. It had been her fingers here, her toes there, at one point up to her waist. Today she was facing its true depths, for the first time since she'd arrived.

"In all seriousness, this is nice," he said. "Something about cold water."

"Hmm." Dahlia was looking around, in silent awe. She felt like she was inside the mountains. She was nearly eye level with the surface of the lake. She was fully submerged in the scenery; it was filling all of her senses.

They swam around, splashing and playing, their voices carrying over the wind. Dahlia shivered in the water; she closed her eyes, leaned her head back, and let the lake pull at her hair. The frigidity of the water burned away the weight of everything she carried until she was only breath, movement, sensation. The undulations of the lake resonated deep inside her; she felt its rhythm in her bones. There was an inevitable force about it that was comforting. No expectations, no performances—just the lake, the mountains, and the steady pulse of being.

She smiled as she gazed at the sight before her, the way the lake was straddled by the mountains, nestled in deep. On the right she knew was Mount Lyre and the Castle; on the left, Goose Wing Mountain, with its zipline and skyward café. From this vantage point, she appeared to be in the middle. She reflected on what "being in the middle" meant. If mountains were challenges or stages of growth, she was, in fact, in the middle. And the thing about a stage was that it was temporary. On the other side was possibility unknown.

Gita had told her that water could be cleansing. Dahlia felt she understood. A new perspective sometimes revealed an unseen answer. For the very first time, she was beginning to feel ready for whatever it had to say.

Dahlia looked at Ethan as he treaded water beside her. He was facing the mountain, his expression soft, the tension in his shoulders gone. He was not unlike her—always braced, always carrying a weight he wasn't sure how to put down. But here, in this moment, it had lifted. He wasn't second-guessing himself or overthinking. It was a connection she hadn't realized they had—and suddenly, she wasn't just grateful for his presence, but drawn to it.

Her gaze lingered on the curve of his jaw, the way the water beaded on his skin, the way his hair was clinging to his forehead. The warmth in her chest deepened, shifting to something unfamiliar, something demanding her attention. With the quiet pressing in around them awareness settled in, and rested there.

He wasn't just the son of the man she'd been searching for, a passing figure in a passing chapter of her life. He helped her be at peace with herself—he made her feel unguarded, and understood. A new consciousness spread through her, warming her against the water's chill. And she knew that something had changed.

She swallowed, her pulse loud in her ears, and turned away, overwhelmed.

They made their way back to the shore and plodded through the sand toward the blanket. They each took a towel and dried off their hair, and rubbed the lake off their limbs. All the while Dahlia felt strangely disconnected, going through the motions while a frantic crisis unfolded in her mind. The cool air against her wet skin heightened every nerve, and she found herself too aware of Ethan's body next to hers, the way his towel draped loosely over his shoulders, the way his hair looked as its curls sprang back to life. How had she not noticed the quiet strength in his small frame—the broadness of his chest, the defined lines of his shoulders, the effortless grace in the way that he moved?

She tried not to notice, tried not to let her gaze linger, but the effort only made her more nervous. Everything was different now. She didn't know how to talk to him, how to behave, how to pretend the person she was when she'd walked into the water was the same person who'd walked out. She could hear him talking to her, scolded herself to listen—but the necessity of making a quick decision had stolen all the air from her lungs.

"Dahlia?"

She made herself look. He'd slipped back into his t-shirt and stood damp and rumpled on the sand.

He knit his brow with confusion. "You okay?"

The sunlight framed behind him seemed to reveal him to her fully. The refined angelic features in such a sharply structured face gave him a unique, alarming beauty. And those eyes—she'd never seen others like them. Round, wide, and intensely blue, they were the most expressive part of him. There was an openness in them, unmistakable tenderness, and undeniable heaviness of thought. As she looked at him, she had to smile: she doubted, with those eyes, that he could ever truly hide anything.

She blinked a few times, her heart hammering. "Of course."

He watched her dubiously as he slipped into his sandals. "I was just asking if you wanted to take a spin around the trail."

"Oh." She pulled on her shirt and shorts, and stuck her feet in her shoes. "That sounds good. Sure."

They walked side by side around the lake, talking of books and trees and places they'd like to visit. When the sun had peaked and was making its first motions toward the other side of the mountain, they packed up their things and left, tired but exhilarated, and warm with the delights of the day.

They had a quick bite to eat in Woodrow, and took the back way to the motel, past Colin's development, the tavern, the office. Finally Ethan pulled into a spot just before her door. Dahlia sat for a moment, working up the nerve to do what she'd called him to do in the first place.

It had been a spectacular day. The setting sun had turned the sky lapis and lavender, and the air held the crisp tension only the dusk could bring. Dahlia turned to him, relieved somewhat by the cover of early night.

"Ethan," she began, and fortified herself, "I really wanted to apologize to you. You know, for the other day. And also to explain."

"No apology necessary," he said, with an easy smile. "And no explanation, either."

"I know. And I appreciate it." She paused. "But I'd like to, if you don't mind."

He shifted to further face her, and waited.

She rubbed her lips together and inhaled. "What I said...I mean, what I suggested. About your father." She closed eyes, her cheeks flushing. "I can't believe I'm doing this. I'm so embarrassed."

"No, it's okay." From behind closed eyes she felt him pat her hand. "You don't have to be embarrassed with me."

She nodded, then opened her eyes. "I think my feelings were confused. I mean I know they were. I wasn't really..." She couldn't say the words. "I didn't feel..." She sighed, exacerbated with herself. "You know what I mean."

She took a breath. He waited for her to continue.

"I know now that he wasn't the missing piece," she said. "I think I was confused because I'm losing my own father. I was sort of...transplanting feelings onto him. And I didn't understand those feelings, because...I didn't want to. It was like deep down the closer I felt to him, the more I could be in denial. But I can't be in denial anymore. I have to start grieving. But that's not all of it."

He didn't say anything, and she avoided his gaze. She fidgeted with the hem of her shirt and went on.

"I think by coming up here I was trying to prove something. Or trying to escape something, or both. It's like...I've felt so lost, and so confused. I don't even think I realized how much. I was running away from my problems, and trying to find myself here. I haven't found any answers. But I think now I have the clarity to try." She braved a glance at him. "I'd like to thank you for that. You're so kind and patient. You've taught me to be more kind and patient with myself, maybe more than anyone ever has. You've been...really the best friend I've ever had." Tears tingled behind her eyes. "I'm really going to miss you."

He was watching her intently, his eyebrows raised with expectation. At her final words, he smiled sadly.

"I'll miss you, too." He faced the windshield as he thought about what to say. "I'm really glad you told me all this," he said. "And I'm happy for you. I'm glad you've had these realizations. And I'm glad I was able to help you find them."

Dahlia sensed there was more. She tilted her head a little.

"Everything okay?"

"Yeah, it's okay. I mean, no, I don't want you to leave," he said, and laughed nervously. "But I get it." He patted her hand. "All good."

Dahlia was silent. It seemed the conversation was over, but there was lingering tension in the air.

"It's just..."

She looked at him, a wish quivering in her chest. "Yes?"

He sighed, then rubbed his face in his hands. "No, never mind. It's nothing."

"It isn't nothing."

"I don't want to make you uncomfortable."

"I'm sort of beyond being made uncomfortable."

He met her gaze. His brow was creased upward, and his eyes were wide. "I guess I...that I was kind of hoping that in all this, maybe you'd thought a little...about what I'd said. And, I don't know." He shrugged, and Dahlia noticed an almost imperceptible tremor in his voice. "That maybe you'd changed your mind."

Energy was crackling between them; Dahlia could feel it on her skin. He had no way of knowing that she had, in fact, changed her mind, and the unspoken possibility that now existed made her heart thump with anticipation. As soon as she said the words, anything could happen. She sat for a moment in the stillness, savoring the moments before it all changed.

She could see the suspense in his face. His hope and desperation sparked a flame in her, and she with effort restrained a grin.

"Well," she said. "Maybe I have."

His face remained unchanged, but his eyes sharpened and shone. Slowly, his lips curved up just slightly; he was clearly restraining a grin of his own.

Abruptly, his restrained smile fell, and the hope went out of his eyes.

"But you're leaving."

Dahlia was so tired of thinking, and so tired of thinking ahead. She'd spent her whole life anticipating problems. Where had it gotten her? She'd put her life on pause, had tried so hard to head off danger and fear and tragedy; as it turned out, no amount of worrying could protect or alter the future, and no amount of standing still kept the world from moving on without her. Bad things could be just around the corner, or good things—trying to predict them, to head them off at the pass, was only holding her back. She was tired of denying experiences to avoid pain that might not even happen. And she was tired of the exhaustion of this constant, purposeless labor, an exercise in futility.

She offered a playful shrug and a coy little smile. "Then I guess we have nothing to lose."

It was worth it just to witness the realization in his face, the blinking of his eyes and the slight parting of his lips. He straightened and tightened his jaw, as if unsure what he'd just heard.

"Um," she uttered, suddenly nervous, but absolutely determined not to back out now. "Do you want to come inside?"

They unclicked their seatbelts and opened their doors with hopeful disbelief. He stood behind her as she unlocked the door of her room, and they walked inside together, closing the door to the night. As they tumbled together in the darkness, engulfing each other and clinging to each other, Dahlia utterly lost herself, for the first time reveling in the bliss that floating on the waves can bring.

THE NEXT MORNING they lay entwined in each other, her head on his chest and her arm around his waist, his hand on her shoulder and his leg over hers. She was rubbing his arm gently with her fingertips; his own fingers were playing with her hair.

"You smell like the lake," he said, a wide smile on his face. "I like it."

She grinned in return. "I'm not sure that's really a compliment."

"Don't worry about it. I smell like the lake, too."

She leaned her face up to kiss him. He held her jaw in his hand and parted his lips for her, and they lay like this for some time, breathing life into each other like the breeze through the trees.

"You look like an absolute goddess," he said, turning toward her now, and running his finger along her hip. She turned onto her side and faced him. "This long, long red hair."

"No, *your* hair." She took a messy blond curl in her fingers, and twirled it around. "It's like an angel's hair, or a cherub."

"I've been told that before. Not sure how I feel about being compared to a winged child."

"Well, you're certainly no child."

They kissed again, their hands in each other's hair and around their faces. Dahlia slinked her leg through his, and he grabbed her from behind, pulling her close.

They parted with smiles and sighs, and gazed at each other as their cheeks lay on the pillow.

"That photo you sent me, the one of us on top of the mountain," he said. "I've looked at it a thousand times. A million, probably."

A delightful glow stirred inside her, like a tiny sun spilling its light into her blood. Being thought of, desired, truly liked. The object of somebody's affection, and someone pretty great, at that. It was a new and wonderful feeling. She smiled, her happiness astonishing and pure.

He kissed her gently, lingering, his bottom lip brushing hers and eliciting from her throat a soft sigh.

He stroked her cheek with his fingertips. "Why don't you stay a little longer," he said. "I'll try to make it worth your while."

She closed her eyes, warmth swelling in her like waves on the sea. "I'll think about it," she whispered, and pushed him onto his back.

∾

AFTER HE LEFT Dahlia indulged in a solitary evening, using the quiet to consider everything that had happened in the last few days. She still didn't know where she was going; she didn't even really know who she was. She'd made a lot of mistakes. But she'd pushed through, and dealt with them. And there was power in knowing that she had.

Maybe she didn't have to know where she was going. Maybe just being strong enough to keep going was enough.

Was she strong enough? Dahlia didn't know. But she'd taken big steps, albeit clumsy ones. And she'd shown herself that she could survive.

She climbed into bed with a book, ready to read herself to sleep. Three texts came through in quick succession. She picked up her phone: it was Ethan.

Thank you for a special time. Thank you for all you've done for me.

And then,

I'm glad I met you, Dahlia. No matter what happens.

The third was an attachment:

NewBookDraft.doc

PART IV
THE SECOND STORY

CHAPTER TWENTY-TWO

"Hey Dahlia, can you hand me that pot?"

Dahlia put the last of the dishes in the cabinet and reached for the pot on the stove, which she then handed to Tara at the sink. As Tara began scrubbing, Dahlia turned to the leftovers. She scooped food into containers and placed them neatly in the refrigerator. There was enough for her parents to have lunch tomorrow, and dinner. Dahlia was relieved. When she'd cooked for her family that night she'd been hoping it would alleviate a little of her mother's work tomorrow.

Dahlia had been home for two weeks. She'd finally returned after spending another few weeks in Dunbridge, going on adventures with Ethan and falling into a steady new phase of their relationship, one in which they knew each other well enough to anticipate each other's words and needs, and they'd been comfortable enough to take little tasks upon themselves—grabbing an item the other forgot, buying little treats they knew the other would like, slinking into bed to wait while the other brushed their teeth in the bathroom. Dahlia had passed a lot of her time at Ethan's house; their time together had distracted him from his work, and despite his lukewarm feelings about his job he did, he told her reluctantly, still have to do it. They sat on the couch together, he with his laptop and she with a book, or with her own laptop, completing a little work remotely in preparation for her return. Dahlia had had a long conversation with Imani, in which she'd told her everything that had happened to her and assured her she was ready to jump back in.

The motel had served Dahlia well. She had come to enjoy her little room, and even the rather rundown condition of the structure itself. The view had grown familiar, almost as familiar as the skyline outside her apartment. She knew the way the door creaked, the way the carpet looked in the morning light; she knew the sounds of the nocturnal creatures at midnight, and she knew the exact number of minutes it took her to drive to the diner. Despite this, when Ethan had invited her to stay with him for her final week in New Hampshire, Dahlia had accepted. Their week in close quarters had been the most delightful time of her life. It brought in new intimacy, out of necessity had nudged her into being totally, completely herself—and she found that she felt stronger as a result. Besides, there was no way to know someone like living with them. And the more deeply she and Ethan knew each other, the clearer it became that there was something special there.

She and Ethan had seen Colin on occasion, a quick dinner at the tavern or at Colin's or Ethan's home. The mood between Dahlia and Colin was lighter, now that the air between them was cleared. Colin was still Colin, and Dahlia sensed he would always have his guard up, with everyone, even with Ethan. But something about her presence had seemed to mix up the dynamic between father and son. The brightness between her and Ethan seeped into the spaces around them. And Ethan's newfound enthusiasm seemed to bring life to Colin, too.

By the time Dahlia left she and Ethan already had discussed possibilities the future might bring. Dahlia was trying to be reasonable. She had an apartment and a job back home, and a family that needed her. She and Ethan had only been together a few weeks. She knew they had more milestones to pass, more tests to undertake and more challenges to face, before they could think seriously about changes going forward. For now, they would continue their relationship long distance, visiting each other when they could and seeing if they were strong enough to last. Strangely, Dahlia wasn't worried: it was something she knew in her bones. She and Ethan were solitary creatures, getting ready to take a wild leap. It was best that they sit with what was happening, taking it slowly, until the change came naturally, at its time.

Returning home had been a surreal experience. As she drove down the streets she knew by heart she felt a sense of bittersweet nostalgia, as if it were the scene of another life. Stepping into her apartment was like stepping into a dream: it held the same shape, but it had subtly shifted, and she didn't fit in quite the same way anymore. It was reassuring and familiar, but some of the magic was gone. It belonged to an older version of herself, and it no longer felt like hers.

There was comfort in the way the light fell on her furniture, the way the birds gathered on the wires across the street. It was once the only place where she'd felt truly safe. But now, she'd stepped beyond its borders, and she'd experienced something new. The apartment felt smaller now, more confining. Its walls no longer felt protective; they were holding her in, and holding her too tight.

As she'd stood in the doorway for the first time in weeks a quiet ache filled her heart, in addition to relief. She knew in that moment she couldn't go back to the Dahlia she was before. There was sadness in the realization, and fear. But there was also a flicker of excitement, because for the first time, she believed in the future, and believed in herself.

The next day she'd visited her family, who warmly welcomed her. Dahlia gave her nieces gifts she'd picked up over the last couple of weeks—pens and stationery for Evelyn, markers and art supplies for Ginger, and a few toys for Celeste—as well as chocolate for Tara and her mother. For her father, Dahlia had two gifts: a Hanford Notch sweatshirt for his walks outside, and a book.

"*Nowhere to be Found*," he'd said, turning it over in his hands as he sat in the armchair in the living room. "By Ethan Henninger."

"Colin's son is a writer," she'd told him, hoping the flush in her face wasn't as bright as it felt. "His book is really good. He's writing another one now, but in the meantime, I thought you'd enjoy this."

"Huh," he'd said, flipping through it, then regarding her with a look she couldn't identify.

There was nothing else to do but tell them all about Colin. Dahlia gave them a shortened version of events, leaving out the parts about her ambiguous feelings and the confrontations that had occurred. But she showed them pictures she'd taken of her and Colin together, and Colin and Ethan, and had told them all about the man who'd saved her life.

By the end of her story, Edward was in tears. "I can't believe you did this," he said, wiping his eyes with his sleeve. "That you took all this so seriously. When I said it would be nice to meet him, I never thought anyone would. I knew it was an impossible task. And you did it." He looked at her through watery eyes. "Kiddo, you're incredible. A miracle worker."

Dahlia smiled shyly, and blushed. She appreciated her father's sentiments, but as she looked around the room she didn't feel like a miracle worker at all. She'd left him for weeks as she was gallivanting around the mountains of New Hampshire. And in her absence, Tara and her mother had had to pick up all the slack.

"Do you think he'd talk to me?" asked Edward, accepting from Tara a cup of warm tea. "How did you leave things with the family?"

Dahlia had asked Colin this question toward the end of her visit. She smiled at her father. "He said he's happy to talk to you.

He was touched that you wanted me to find him, and he said you can call him any time."

She'd gathered her courage and apologized to her mother and Tara.

"I never thought I'd be gone so long," she said, "or even that I'd leave so quickly in the first place. And I know I didn't stay in touch as much as I should have. It's hard to explain but I think I just needed a reset. It doesn't excuse my behavior. I'm sure you need a reset, too."

"We're just glad you're back," said Tara. "It's okay. We managed."

Her mother's eyes brimmed with tears, and she brought her in for a hug. "Sweetheart, we just wanted to know you were okay. Nobody blames you for needing some time." She rubbed her back; Dahlia closed her eyes, warm in her mother's touch. "I just wish you felt you could talk to us about whatever's been going on."

Dahlia took a chance. "I know," she said shakily. "I should...I mean, we should talk more. You and I. I mean we should make a point of it."

Vera touched her cheek and held her gaze. "I think that's a great idea."

Today Dahlia was visiting after work, where life had fallen back into its swing without a lot of fanfare or hassle. As she took Tara's place at the sink while Tara put the pot away she found herself staring out the window, her thoughts confused and far away.

"Do you want to talk about it?"

Dahlia turned toward Tara, who was taking her seat at the kitchen table with a freshly filled glass of wine. Dahlia sighed and took her own glass, and sat across from her, the simmering in her stomach rising menacingly into her chest.

"Talk about what?"

"I don't know."

Dahlia looked at her sister, her haggard face and unkempt ponytail. "You don't need my burden on top of everything else."

"What do you mean?"

"Come on, Tara. Can we be real, please, for once?" Dahlia could see the surprise in Tara's eyes, and she could hear it in her own voice. She'd never talked to her sister like this before—or anyone, for that matter.

Tara blinked. "Are we not real, usually?"

"I don't know. Are we?"

Tara was silent. Dahlia drummed her fingers on the table and inhaled through trembling parted lips. She looked at her sister frankly.

"No," she said. "We're not." She swallowed. "I don't think I've ever told you how deeply I respect you."

Tara was clearly taken aback. Her shoulders had straightened, and her eyes had widened. "I...I don't know what to say."

"You don't have to say anything. You don't have to do anything. You do everything, all the time, for everyone." Dahlia's eyes brimmed with tears, and she wiped them with a napkin. "You hold everyone together, Tara. You really do. Mom does, too, of course. But it's different with you."

Tara's lips were quivering, her own eyes glassy. She reached for a napkin of her own, and listened, wisps of read hair falling around her face.

"You're so good," said Dahlia. "You've always been. I wish I could be half as good as you."

At these words Tara's brow furrowed. "What are you talking about?"

Dahlia wasn't even sure; she was still struggling to articulate everything she'd been feeling. She didn't want to make this moment about her own insecurities. But they were such an integral part of her, she didn't know how to behave without them.

"I realized that I've always been trying to prove that I was worth saving. It's been hard because...well, you're so strong.

You're so smart, and you've accomplished so much. I..." She shrugged. "I guess I just always wanted...that I worry that I don't know how to be like that."

"Don't be ridiculous."

"I'm not. I'm telling you how I feel. I'm not trying to make you feel bad or to feel sorry for myself, I'm not." She was plagued now by the all too familiar shame; she was botching this explanation, doing the opposite of what she'd really wanted to do. The whole point was to explain her absence, to tell Tara how much she truly loved her. And all she was doing was making it worse.

"Dahlia," said Tara, reaching across the table and placing her hand over her sister's. "You've always been good enough. I feel terrible that you've been carrying this around with you, that maybe I contributed to any of your pain."

"You didn't. It's not your fault. This is exactly what I'm talking about." She thought about Gita, what she'd said about confidence and self-esteem. Dahlia could see that every day would be a work in progress, that overcoming was a journey, not a goal. "I don't expect you to say anything or to have any answers. I guess I just wanted to explain."

"Well," said Tara, sitting back in her seat. "I guess you just don't see everything you do for us. You did all that research for Dad. You went up there and met Colin. You brought us all those presents. And it's not just that." Tara's face turned sorrowful, and kind. "It's just who you are. We love you. You're a kind person. You help in so many little ways, all the time. Look at how you help resolve the girls' problems. Look at how you sense all the little things, the way you pick up the pieces for us all." She smiled now, tearfully. "I wish you saw in yourself all the things we see in you."

"Thank you." Dahlia choked on tears, and cleared her throat. "I'm working on it."

Tara waited a minute for her to compose herself.

"Is there something else?"

415

Dahlia stared at her. She could see in her sister's face that she couldn't withhold her secret.

"Something did happen," she said, fidgeting nervously with her napkin, "with Ethan. Colin's son."

"Oh, really?"

"It wasn't right away, and I wasn't looking for it. But once it happened, it was like..."

Her voice trailed off. She looked at Tara. Tara was watching her with clearly contrived shock.

"Scandalous," she breathed, her hand at her heart and her eyes open wide. "I am stunned, *stunned* that you fell into a whirlwind romance with a handsome writer in the middle of the mountains."

"Tara." Dahlia's face flushed with fire. "It wasn't quite like that."

"What was it like? I want details."

Tara's elbow was on the table, her chin resting in her hand. Her lips were pursed into an expression of expectation. Dahlia laughed, grateful for Tara's levity.

"I'm not giving you...*details,*" she said, turning even more crimson. "But...it was really nice."

"I'll bet. How did it happen? How did you leave it? Come on, spill the beans. I never go anywhere, it's the least you can do."

Dahlia spent half an hour regaling Tara with the story of her and Ethan, telling her how he'd taken her to the mountaintop and ziplining and how she'd read his book in one sitting. When she got to the part about the future, she was vague—she was embarrassed to admit how much she looked forward to it, and she was nervous about the decision that hung there, like a ghost.

"Well," said Tara, now looking genuinely enraptured, "it sounds like an amazing time. He seems nice. I'm happy for you, Dahlia. You deserve it."

"Thank you." Dahlia's eyes watered once more. There was comfort in opening up like this, in inviting someone into her life. She wondered why she'd never done it before, and hoped she'd keep gaining experiences worth sharing. "And thank you for being such a great sister."

"Runs in the family," said Tara, with a wink. She stood, stretched, and patted Dahlia on the back. "Come on," she said. "Let's make some coffee."

Dahlia visited again a few days later. Tara and Vera had gone out; she was alone with Edward in the house. Edward had been feeling somewhat better: the new medication had been yielding slow but definite results, and he'd regained some of his appetite and his energy. He and Dahlia went for a walk around the neighborhood, then returned to the house, where Dahlia helped him into bed.

He was watching her carefully, as he'd been doing since she'd come home. There seemed a curiosity in his eyes, a question waiting to be asked. Dahlia smiled at him as she picked up a glass on the nightstand, preparing to refill it with water before letting him have some rest.

"Tara told me," he said, calling her back, "about how you've been feeling."

Dahlia stopped cold in her tracks. She turned around and looked at him. "What do you mean?"

"She says you've felt a little lost. Like you've been trying to prove your worth."

Dahlia sat down in the chair by the bed, and folded in on herself, crossing her legs and her arms over her lap. "Not really. I mean, yes. Well...a little, I guess."

"Dahlia, kiddo. What's going on?"

Dahlia sighed heavily. "I don't want to put this on you, too."

"I'm your father. I love you. Now tell me what's going on."

She reluctantly told him about the realizations she'd had in Dunbridge, letting her soul flow through her words, guided by the encouragement of her frantically beating heart. As she revealed her darkest self, the fears she'd borne and the doubts she'd suffered, she felt a lightening in her chest. She was finally not alone. But in its place was the new weight of the work she had before her. Speaking these truths to her father, witnessing the warmth in his eyes and recognizing that in those eyes, she was never less than perfect—it reminded her of how far she had to go, of the lies she had to unlearn and the critical voice she had to silence. She was on her way; she'd accepted her worth in her mind. But she knew it would be a while until her heart fully believed it.

"I guess I just felt like I hadn't really done anything with my life," she concluded, and there was something so satisfying in having encapsulated these feelings in words. "It was one reason I felt like I needed to do this for you. Like now I have something to be proud of."

"I'm certainly glad you feel proud. I've always been so proud of you. Who else is going to talk about books with me? Who else is going to bring me my favorites the very first day they're out?"

They talked a while longer. Dahlia studied his face. He was looking bright today, and healthy. And yet her heart was tugging with worry. She didn't know if she could trust this image, or if tomorrow would bring new despair.

"And Ethan," he said finally, eyebrows raised, and Dahlia could tell he'd been waiting for her to bring it up herself. "What's next for the two of you?"

Dahlia rubbed her lips together nervously. "I don't know."

"Well, you can't continue this far apart forever. What are you planning to do?"

"I don't know, Dad." Inexplicably, Dahlia began crying. She pulled a tissue from the nightstand and blew her nose, then dabbed at her eyes. "I'm so sorry. I don't know what's come over me."

Her father was watching her with a smile. "You want to go up there, don't you."

Dahlia couldn't bring herself to look at him. The truth was, she'd thought about it, more than she was willing to admit. It wasn't that she didn't love her town, or that she wanted to be somewhere new. It was that in the mountains, she felt free, and different; it was where she'd found herself, and where she'd shed so much pain. It seemed to welcome her and invite her inside; it had a rough beauty that deeply resonated inside her.

She sniffled and attempted a watery smile. "I'm not leaving."

"I asked what you wanted, not what you were going to do."

Dahlia sighed and slumped her shoulders. It was no use.

"Okay, I'll admit it. I've thought about it." She shook her head and squeezed his hand. "But I'm not leaving you. I can't."

"Why not?"

"I can't leave when you need me."

"I need you to be happy. I need to see you happy."

They looked at each other in heavy silence.

"That's the only thing I need."

He seemed to be controlling tears of his own, and Dahlia knew suddenly that she hadn't told him anything he hadn't already known. He'd seen her fears and her insecurities; he'd seen that she had felt lost. He'd fostered a connection with her, one that only the two of them had—but he'd watched helplessly as she'd turned further and further in on herself, denying herself, and her life.

She let her tears fall without trying to stop them. "But April," she whispered. She was plagued with guilt discussing April this way, when instinct—and newfound self-awareness—told her that April needed help, not criticism. "April left. And now—"

"April's an entirely different person," said her father, his hand on hers, "in an entirely different situation." He smiled. "It's not in any way the same."

Dahlia knew he was right. She couldn't decide if the ache in her heart was a reflection of her intuitive knowledge that this change was coming, or that April was likely in some stage of a similar journey. If there was one thing her time with Colin and Ethan had taught her it was that there was an epic story inside every individual, that it wasn't always visible, and that you never could see what demons they were wrestling. In fact, as she'd learned from Gita, sometimes they couldn't even see it themselves.

"Kiddo," Edward said kindly, with a smile that wrapped around her. "It's time for you to follow your heart. I'm not alone. I have your mom, Tara, Tom, the girls. All the nurses. I'll be okay, I promise. And you always have a place to stay here."

Dahlia kissed him and hugged him, and left him to his rest. When Tara and Vera returned she sat with them for a time, and then headed back to her apartment, which still remained a respite from all the cares of the day.

~

"What does it bring up for you," asked Gita, "to think about your conversation with Tara?"

Dahlia had to center herself in order to answer this question. She took note of the floor beneath her feet, the couch around her body, the color of the walls and curtains, the way the air smelled like Gita's strawberry candle.

She'd already told Gita all about her trip—the beauty of the landscape, the satisfaction of meeting Colin, the delicious tension of a new and promising romance. She'd been honest about her mistakes and her realizations; she'd given her a detailed explanation of her process of learning and growth. She'd discussed with her the conversations with Tara and her father. She'd even described her ambiguous feelings about her beloved apartment.

She was surprised to find herself in tears. She'd been in tears a lot lately. After months of refusing to concede to them, she seemed unable to stop them now. Sometimes they appeared when she was remembering the past. But mostly they were a release of her stress about the future, what it meant for her, for her father, and for her life.

She took a deep, calming breath. "I think maybe it's possible it's the center of everything I'm here for," she said. "All my fears about myself. The lack of control I feel over my own life."

"What are your fears, Dahlia?"

"Well, I just always worry that I'm not doing enough. That I'm never making the right decisions. It's like I have so much anxiety over something happening to the people I love, and I have no control over that. But...I have control over myself. And I just don't seem to do anything with it."

"I think your trip to New Hampshire proves that incorrect, don't you?"

"It's just one thing. Not really."

"But Tara gave you a number of examples. She doesn't seem to agree with you, that you don't do anything at all."

Dahlia knew this was true. But it didn't change the way that she felt.

"It's like my mind knows one thing, and my heart knows another. My mind keeps telling me that none of those things are enough."

Gita was nodding; her face wore a warm smile.

"Listen, Dahlia." She leaned forward, looking Dahlia straight in the eye. "I want you to envision this. There are two boxes, say, a yellow box and a green box." She paused. "Are you imagining?"

Dahlia nodded. "Yes."

"The yellow box is all the things you do right. And the green box is the things you think are wrong." She paused again. "Notice I didn't say the things that *are* wrong."

Dahlia listened in silence as Gita continued her point.

"You're very much focused on what's in the green box. So when something happens that seems to reaffirm it, it just adds to the pile." She held her hand so that it sat in the air horizontally, and raised it higher. "What we need to do is build up your confidence. We need to work on focusing on the yellow box. So that when something comes along in the green box, you've got evidence in the yellow box to the contrary." She held up both hands equally, then placed them in her lap. "It's about building your sense of self-worth, of your own value. So let's start focusing on that."

"Okay." Dahlia agreed this was the root of her problem, and would trust Gita's experience and advice. "Also, Gita, there was one more thing."

Gita's brow rose with patient expectation. "What's that?"

Tears rose in Dahlia again. "What you said a while ago. About medication." She swallowed, and wiped away a tear. "I think maybe I'd like to consider it."

CHAPTER TWENTY-THREE

THREE YEARS LATER

*D*ahlia put the final touches on the display table, straightening a pile and making a last minute change to the order of the stacks. She wondered, not for the first time, if the blue cloth would look better than the white, but once again she came to the conclusion that her first instinct had been correct. The white was prettier, more elegant. It was a much more effective complement for the beautiful books it presented.

She looked around the store. Customers were beginning to gather, browsing the shelves and taking their seats to ensure they had a good view. It was a beautiful spring morning, and a Saturday, which meant the street was hopping with shoppers and families. Dahlia was delighted. There would be a good turnout.

"Penny for your thoughts."

Dahlia turned to find Ethan behind her, making his way to the register to check out a customer.

She smiled at the sight. He was so relaxed, so natural.

"Nothing groundbreaking," she said as he rang up a small selection of books. "I was just thinking that there will be a nice crowd."

"I know I can't wait," said the customer, a regular in the store. "As soon as I'm done here I'm snagging my seat."

"Have you read the book, Anne?"

"Are you kidding? I've read it twice." She pulled a hardcover from her purse and smiled. "I've got my copy to be signed, right here."

Ethan thanked Anne and stepped beside Dahlia in front of the register. He wrapped his hand around her waist and pulled her in, and together they watched the scene before them.

"It's about that time," she said, glancing toward the clock on the wall. "Should we do the thing?"

"Let's do the thing."

They squeezed and excused their way through the throng and took their places behind the podium. As Dahlia smiled at the group before her—from what she could tell, it looked like a healthy mix of regulars and new customers—they understood the event was beginning, and hastily took their seats.

"Good morning," she said cheerily. As the excited din softened into silence she took a moment to appreciate the energy in the room. There was an undefinably striking quality to one's voice when they spoke to a crowd here. Being a small, independent store, it was not built for acoustics. A person's voice sounded more raw here, more real. It was like the difference between a glossy cover and a matte cover. The glossy cover showed off better. But the matte cover was more tactile, more true.

She smiled at the audience and continued. "Thank you all so much for coming out today for this event. I know I speak for both of us when I say that inviting the community into our little home away from home is our favorite part of the job." She gestured back toward Ethan, and there was some polite chuckling from the crowd. "It's even more special to us when we have such a personal connection to the topic of conversation." She gestured toward a sign next to the table. "As you know, a percentage of the proceeds of Ethan's book will be donated to

Children's Harbor of Hope, a charity Ethan and I both believe in. So if you've been considering purchasing a copy, this is the perfect time."

Dahlia said a few more opening words, and then introduced Ethan. Those in the crowd clapped with enthusiasm as he smiled shyly and made his way to the podium. As they passed each other he and Dahlia exchanged a coy, playful look.

"Hello, everyone," said Ethan, raising his hand in a casual wave.

"Hello!" repeated most of the audience.

"Wow." Ethan leaned back a little, pretending to be taken aback, and there was more chuckling from the crowd. He scanned the group before him, and an almost imperceptible grin touched one corner of his lips. "Well, this is either a great turnout or a very elaborate prank."

Everyone laughed. Dahlia watched him with great pleasure. It was his deadpan delivery that made his wit so effective. He'd done these readings before, and she knew he enjoyed them. But he still wasn't used to being the center of attention, and he used his shyness to his advantage. He had a way of speaking close to the mic, but quietly, in a way that displayed his awkwardness in the most charming way possible. It was clear he was being himself, that he was sharing his thoughts as they filtered through his mind.

"So," Ethan said, and cleared his throat, "as some of you may know, I have a new book out, *Everywhere Around Us*. My colleague thought you might like to hear some of it. And by 'my colleague,' I mean Dahlia."

More laughter. Dahlia smiled widely. Ethan gestured toward her with his hand, and there was some light clapping.

"I'm going to read a short story today. Just letting you know in case you wandered in expecting live music, or a puppet show or something." The crowd continued to laugh. He held up his hand and shifted his weight. "Just kidding. But if you really did, please stick around, I think you'll like this. And if not," he said, holding up a crisp copy of *Everywhere Around Us*, "I'm told the book also makes an excellent coaster."

He held the book higher. "So this is my book."

The audience clapped, and he smiled bashfully, clearly restraining himself.

"Thank you very much." He flipped through it and tapped the cover. "Sometimes I can't even believe I wrote this," he said. "A real book. See, it has pages and everything. Very book-like."

Through the chuckling Dahlia sensed admiration and respect. Many of these customers had seen him read before. *Everywhere Around Us* was Ethan's fourth book. The previous three—*Nowhere to be Found*, as well as his second and third books, *On the Mountain* and *Lucid Lake*—were big sellers at The Second Story, the little bookshop he and Dahlia owned and ran together. Everyone knew everyone here in this little town of Porter's Landing. And now that Ethan was a little local celebrity, his dry humor was well known, too.

"In all seriousness," he went on, and his voice took on a more serious tone. "It really means a lot to me that you're here. It lets me do what I love to do, the only thing I want to do. For a long time, I'd resigned myself to the fact that I wouldn't be able to do it, or that I couldn't even justify trying." He turned and gestured toward Dahlia again. "I give all the credit to my amazing partner, in the bookstore and in life. She's the one who pushed me. Sometimes it hurt," he added, rubbing his back, eliciting more laughter. "But without her I wouldn't be here today. So let's give it up for Dahlia."

He clapped, and everyone joined him. Dahlia smiled somberly as they made eye contact. Dahlia's insides softened at the meaning he was sending through his impossibly large eyes, at the unsaid words reflected in the delicate features of his face.

They held each other's gaze for a moment or two. He smiled and winked at her.

"Well then," he said, facing the guests and cracking open the cover. "Might as well get into it."

He threw a glance toward a particular person in the audience. Even in profile Dahlia could sense his wide eyes soften.

Colin had met his gaze and nodded. Father and son shared a moment of connection, and then Ethan began reading.

As he dove into the short story she had read a hundred times Dahlia surveyed the crowd that had gathered and the cozy haven she and Ethan had created together. Some days, she still couldn't believe they'd done it. She still couldn't believe she'd found what she was looking for, that she'd had the strength to make this decision—to make any decision at all.

After she returned home three years ago Dahlia and Ethan had remained close, talking every day, sending little text messages and visiting each other once or twice a month. Ethan had met her family. And then Colin had met them, too.

Edward had been emotional at his and Colin's meeting. He'd shaken his hand and held tight, and embraced him, thanking him for saving his daughter's life so many years before. The two men had fostered a deep and instant connection. Dahlia was surprised by the earnestness with which Colin had welcomed it. Despite their newfound closeness—everyone knew she and Ethan were forever partners, and Dahlia looked to Colin as her father-in-law—she knew Colin was reserved and wary, as a rule. But he seemed eager to be enveloped into this new extended family. Dahlia couldn't have asked for a better conclusion to the story.

Edward was stable but declining. He'd received a host of treatments, which tended to work for a time or give false hope; he'd had some good periods, in which everyone had held their breath, but ultimately he tended to plateau, recovering less fully than before. He was also now largely dependent on a communication device. Dahlia struggled to come to terms with what was happening, and it pained her to be so far away. But he had an incredible support system, as did she. And she visited as often as she could, making it part of her schedule and routine.

Dahlia had had a long talk with her father before making the decision to leave. He'd told her explicitly that he wanted her to make the move to New Hampshire, that he would be okay, that he wouldn't be okay if he thought he was responsible for her sacrificing her happiness and her dream. Dahlia had been frightened, and she'd had to overcome quite a lot of guilt. She'd gone to sleep imagining all the horrible things that could happen to her father, and to the rest of her family—the images had haunted her, leaving her gasping for breath and restless with a racing heart. She'd thought about what it would be like to receive a phone call, and to be seven hours away; she'd spent hours living the worst scenarios in her mind, as if they were actually happening.

But she believed what her father had told her, and she'd decided to take action, to be brave. She remembered what Gita had told her about channeling her anxiety, and she did her best to translate her worry into sensitivity, and to give back to the community or plan a meaningful event at the store. It didn't hurt that she had Ethan's companionship and unconditional love. And after a rough few months of onboarding, her new medication was helping alleviate the worst of her symptoms. Now that her head was above water, she could more effectively use the tools she'd continued to strengthen in therapy.

Tara and her family visited at every opportunity. Dahlia enjoyed taking them on the adventures she'd first embarked on with Ethan. The girls were enamored of the mountains and the lakes. They were especially impressed with the tram up Mount Lyre. Dahlia adored watching them run and swim and carry on. And she delighted in the fast bond Ethan formed with Evelyn.

Evelyn was in awe of the fact that she now had a real author in her family. She spoke to Ethan with reverence, and he took on the role of mentor as she dabbled in a little writing herself. Ethan's kindness and patience with her sweet, creative niece warmed her deeply. She was happy that Evelyn was being encouraged in her aspirations—and that Ethan was able to give that back to her.

After weeks of mustering her courage Dahlia had called her sister April. She was no longer content to simply accept that April had deliberately disappeared. She remembered what Gita had told her years before, that she would always have anxiety, would always be an empath—and that the key was channeling it for good. Looking back, she could see signs that April had been struggling, though with what, she still couldn't be sure. But she'd decided to reach out, to try her best to be the person for April that so many had been for her. April had defenses up, but a slow trust was building. It would be a long road, but it was worth it. Dahlia felt strong when she was channeling her empathy for good. It was, in its way, part of her own journey, too.

Dahlia also had had a long and tearful conversation with Imani, whom she respected with all her heart. Imani had taught her everything she knew, and she'd been so patient when Dahlia had been in crisis. She would miss her deeply. And she felt guilty for leaving her. But like all her loved ones Imani had encouraged her to spread her wings, and to fly.

"I'll never be able to thank you enough," Dahlia had told her as the two embraced on Dahlia's last day. "It's been such an honor to work here. Leaving the store is almost as hard as leaving my family."

"Of course it is, you helped build it." Imani had pulled her tight, then pulled away and rubbed her back affectionately. "It wouldn't have been the same without you. You're one hell of a manager."

"Well," said Dahlia, flushing a little, but smiling. "Except for that one time."

"Except for that one time."

Imani squeezed her shoulder and stepped back, studying her curiously. "Say, Dahlia, now that you're leaving, maybe you can answer a question I've had for a while."

Dahlia's eyes widened, and her stomach flipped. "Sure."

"You were so nervous about going to Los Angeles. You fretted so much over booking the rooms and the flights. But when you decided to go to New Hampshire, it seemed so easy for you to just do it, despite being a much bigger step." Her brow furrowed with thought. "What was the difference?"

It was actually something Dahlia had thought about, and the answer had been surprisingly clear. The simple truth was, Los Angeles was not something she wanted. Working with Gita had shown her that a lot of her anxiety stemmed from a feeling of being out of control. The world had so many expectations, big and small; so much of what a person did was dictated by their family, their circumstances, their job. Dahlia had spent a lifetime dutifully letting life choose for her, and she'd felt more confined than she'd even known. Doing something *she* chose—something subversive, something for herself—had had a novel, alluring appeal.

But she couldn't say all this to Imani. None of it was Imani's fault.

Instead, she'd shrugged and smiled. "I guess it just means it was meant to be."

They parted on good terms and promised it wasn't goodbye, and indeed it wasn't: Dahlia stopped at the store whenever she was in town, and Imani had attended The Second Story's opening. Dahlia had never felt so fortunate to have so many supportive people in her life, people who loved her and who wanted to see her shine.

Now she and Ethan lived together in Ethan's little house, working the bookshop together, complementing each other's strengths. Dahlia still focused on the marketing, for the store and for Ethan's books. And to her great surprise, Ethan flourished when he was face to face with customers. He seemed so easy around them, so free. Dahlia suspected it was what made him such a good writer.

Ethan had quit his editing job, and now whatever time wasn't spent in the store was spent writing. He was already working on his fifth book, and he had a deal with his publisher for two more. Dahlia encouraged him and cheered him on, and it wasn't entirely selfless. As an avid reader, she looked forward to his stories. She was overjoyed that he was doing the only thing he wanted to do. But a finished book was a treat for her. She wanted as many as she could have.

Ethan finished reading, and the audience clapped and sighed. He thanked them humbly and waved, then turned the podium back to Dahlia.

"Thank you so much, Ethan," she said as she clapped with them, watching him step away. "I know I'm biased, but I never get tired of hearing your stories."

The guests rose and filtered into a line for Ethan to sign their books. He sat at a table and chatted them up a little, signing books and taking pictures. Dahlia spotted Colin. The two drifted toward each other, each wearing easy smiles.

"Hey, kiddo," he said, with a quick hug and a pat on the shoulder. "Nice job. He did great."

"He really did. He always does."

They passed a casual half hour while Ethan finished up with his readers. When the crowd had dispersed, he stood and joined them. He and Colin embraced, and Colin clapped him on the back.

"You sound good up there," he told him. "And that story is my favorite."

"Thanks. I know it is."

"I'm real proud of you, son."

"Thanks. I know that, too."

Ethan was called away by a straggling fan, and he turned to sign her book. Colin turned to Dahlia, and crossed his arms, talking to her seriously.

"Hey, kiddo," he said. "I want to thank you for what you've done for Ethan."

Dahlia looked at him with wide eyes. "What do you mean?"

"I know you're the one who pushed him to keep writing. You gave him the confidence to do it. And the store." He looked around and shook his head, impressed. "It's real special, Dahlia. I'm glad for you both."

The tingle of tears pricked her eyes. "That's so nice of you to say. Thank you. I appreciate that."

"I..." he began. He cleared his throat. His eyes had sharpened. He looked uncomfortable but determined. "I'm glad you joined our little family."

Dahlia watched him speechlessly, dabbing at the corner of her eye. "Thank you, Colin." There was so much she wanted to tell him, such complexity in her affection for him. He had saved her in more ways than one. And more importantly, he had opened the door for her to save herself. She could never really impart to him how much he meant to her, and anyway, she didn't think he could handle talking about it. To relieve the tension, she laughed. "I thought you said you didn't need all this extra emotion in your life."

"Well, maybe I was wrong."

Ethan's customer left, and the three talked for a few minutes more. Colin embraced each of them in turn and headed home. Ethan and Dahlia wrapped their arms around each other's backs and looked at their store together, Dahlia with her head leaning on his chest, Ethan kissing her cheek.

"Another one down," he said. "Thanks for putting this together."

"Thank you for writing the book."

They cleaned up the chairs and tables and worked the rest of the day, until the last customer had trickled out and the sun was setting over the mountains. Then they locked up the store and left together, taking their time walking to the car, hand in hand.

"What do you want to do for dinner?" he said. "Should we have another adventure?"

Dahlia breathed in the crisp northern air. She looked ahead toward the mountaintops piercing the lavender sky, and up at the twinkling stars. She thought about all her adventures, how somehow they'd coalesced into a journey that made her hopeful for what was to come. She realized she could never fully know what was around the next corner. She just had to trust that whatever it was, she would use her wisdom and her experiences to help her move herself forward. She had the strength to do it—she'd shown herself, time and time again.

"You know what," she said, comforted by the warmth of his hand, and conscious of the current between them, "let's take a little break from adventures. Let's have a quiet night at home."

"Nothing wrong with that."

They held each other close and made their way home, the mountains dark silhouettes in the distance, great protectors of all the creatures and all the land.

THE END

APRIL GIVES UP THE GHOST

COMING SOON

April Carrow spent years surviving a marriage with an emotionally abusive husband. When she discovers he's been unfaithful—with her closest friend, no less—she walks away with a deep mistrust of others and a longing for the historian career he convinced her to abandon.

With nowhere else to go, she lands in a quiet coastal town in Maine, renting a tiny apartment from her sister's best friend Meredith, far from the cultured city life she once loved. Impossibly competent, suspiciously kind, and radiating a kind of joy April no longer believes in, Meredith has a loving husband, a warm home, and an unshakable belief that the town is touched by magic—sentiments April brushes off as naïve, the fantasies of someone who's never been betrayed.

But the town has a strange way of drawing her in and letting down her defenses. Chance throws a job in the historical society directly in her path, as well as the story of Lavinia—a local legend about a widow who believed her lost-at-sea husband returned as a ghost. As April digs deeper, she begins to wonder if there might be something worth believing in after all—whether in magic, in friendship, or in a budding romance with Asa, the steady, confident man who understands what it means to start over.

Maybe the ghost is real. Maybe it isn't. Maybe magic is just what we choose to believe in. Either way, April is beginning to learn that healing doesn't come from building walls—it comes from allowing yourself to believe and from letting people in.

Sign up for Amanda's newsletter for updates on new books and for a collection of free stories.

www.amandagalebooks.com

THE MEREDITH SERIES

FEATURING DAHLIA'S SISTER TARA

About Book One, *Meredith Out of the Darkness:*

She's created the perfect life. But when it doesn't turn out as planned, can she take what she's learned and find her way in the darkness?

Meredith Beck had it all: the love of her life, a thriving career, and an apartment in the excitement of New York City. Then tragedy strikes, leaving her adrift in a world that's suddenly lost its luster. Optimistic by nature, she desperately attempts to rebuild. But no matter how hard she tries, she just can't muster her former strength.

Then a light appears in the darkness: Nick Kelly, a quiet painter from a small town in Maine. Thoughtful and kind, and utterly without pretension, Nick is unlike anyone Meredith has ever known. She is drawn to his love of nature and is comforted by his purity of heart. Through his eyes, the world seems to hold limitless possibility, and as their romance blossoms, she's delighted to find herself on the road toward a simpler life, with a partner who reminds her of the beauty in every moment.

But it isn't as simple as it seems. As Nick's own demons surface, the life they're building threatens to unravel. Human fallibilities once again complicate best-laid plans. And it becomes clear that before they can embrace the future, they must confront the lingering ghosts of their pasts.

A story of love, loss, and the power of second chances, *Mereditih Out of the Darkness* is first in a slow-burn series of cliffhangers ending with a warm and satisfying happily-ever-after.

ACKNOWLEDGMENTS

Thank you Judy, Gina, Erica, Sandra, and editor Jami Nord. As always, I am beyond grateful for your thoughtful comments and support.